RUTH HAMILTON

The Reading Room

PAN BOOKS

First published 2009 by Pan Books

This edition published 2015 by Pan Books
an imprint of Pan Macmillan
20 New Wharf Road, London N1 9RR
Associated companies throughout the world
www.panmacmillan.com

ISBN 978-1-4472-8766-7

1 3 5 7 9 8 6 4 2

A CIP catalogue record for this book is available from the British Library.

Printed and bound by CPI Group (UK) Ltd, Croydon, CR0 4YY

Visit www.panmacmillan.com to read more about all our books
and to buy them. You will also find features, author interviews and
news of any author events, and you can sign up for e-newsletters
so that you're always first to hear about our new releases.

The Reading Room

RUTH HAMILTON is the bestselling author of numerous novels, including *Lights of Liverpool, Mulligan's Yard, A Liverpool Song, A Mersey Mile* and *Meet Me at the Pier Head*. She has become one of the north-west of England's most popular writers. She was born in Bolton, which is the setting for many of her novels, and has spent most of her life in Lancashire. She now lives in Liverpool.

In loving memory of Laura Latimer, whose surname I borrowed for the main character herein. She comforted my mother when my dad was killed, and was one of the kindest people I have ever known. Until the end of her life, Laura fought to save the church of Sts Peter and Paul, Bolton, which place of worship was so pivotal in many lives, including my own. Sleep well, dear friend.

Also for Zelia Cheffins who died on Christmas Day 2008. She was a much-loved mother, grandmother and great-grandmother. To her granddaughter, Carol Sharpies, I send much affection. Chin up, Carol. Remember her laughter and the pleasures you shared.

One

Many people in the Lancashire village of Eagleton expressed the opinion that Enid Barker had sat at the upstairs window of 5 Fullers Walk since the old mill had been shifted forty years ago. It was further rumoured in jest that she had been pulled down with the mill, and had come back to haunt the newer development. Whatever residents thought of the matter, that grey shape sat, day in and day out, in the same position for hours at a time. Had her son not been so valued by the community, those whose imaginations ran towards the dark side might have likened her to the mummified corpse in *Psycho*, but Dave was a grand man who probably never took a cleaver into the shower in his life, so that particular piece of lunatic folklore died stillborn.

In spite of suggestions to the contrary, old Enid was very much alive. At almost seventy, she was astute, judgemental and extremely well versed in the ways of her fellow man. Because of a condition known as 'melegs', she could not walk very far. The medical reason was diabetic neuropathy, but she couldn't be bothered with words of such a size, so she stuck to 'melegs'. It was melegs that kept her upstairs, melegs that forced her to sit for most of the day, but it was her antipathy to daytime TV, which she could never manage to enjoy, that became the final clincher. Given all these circumstances, the window was the best place to be.

She enjoyed watching that lot scuttering and meandering out there. For a start, there was Valda Turnbull. Valda was wearing a new coat. She was a very fertile woman with five children already, so Enid knew what was coming and she said so. 'Dave?' she shouted. 'Come here a minute.'

He arrived at her side. 'Yes, Mam? Did you want some more toast?'

Enid shook her head. 'Now, you mark my words. Just keep an eye on that Valda. I'll bet you five quid she has another baby in less than nine months. She must be thirty-eight, so you'd think she'd have more sense. Look. New coat.'

'Eh?'

'She gives him sex for clothes. With their Molly, it was a powder blue three-piece. Terry was red high heels and a matching handbag. I think Anna-Louise was a cream-coloured coat, but you get mixed up when there's so many of them.'

Dave shook his head and groaned. Mam was becoming an embarrassment. No, that wasn't true, because she'd been an embarrassment for most of his forty-seven years, but this was interfering in the lives of all the victims who walked below. They knew she talked about them; she had talked about them when she had helped run the Reading Room. Well, at least she no longer had a big audience when delivering her vitriol. 'I got you some talking books from Isis, didn't I? I know your eyes get tired, so all you need to do is listen. You'd get more out of that than sitting here watching life pass you by.

There's some good stuff on that shelf if you'd only try it.'

Enid glared at him. 'This is real,' she snapped. 'Books is all lies.'

He bent his knees, puffing heavily because of the exertion, and squatted beside her. 'They talk about you. They call you the eyes and ears of the world. It's not nice, is it? For them, I mean. Going about their daily business knowing there's somebody staring down at them all the while.'

Enid sniffed. 'At my age, I can do as I like. No need to ask permission off nobody.'

Dave cringed. As a purveyor of many kinds of literature, he longed to uphold decent grammar at all costs. But Mam would not endure correction, so he had to ignore her ill-treatment of the most wonderful language on earth. He stood up and walked away.

At her age she could do as she liked? She had always done as she liked. For a kick-off, he'd no idea who his father was, and he often wondered whether she was any wiser concerning the gap on his birth certificate. How could she criticize anybody after the life she'd led? He still remembered her men friends, noises from the bedroom of their old house, sometimes money left behind the clock. But she was his mam, and he did right by her. 'I'll be going down in a minute,' he told her.

Enid sniffed again. 'Leave me a cup of tea, then go and enjoy yourself.' Her son was a great disappointment to her, and they both knew it. He was a short man, no more than five and a half feet, with a rounding belly and abbreviated legs. Every pair of trousers he bought had to be shortened, while his hair, which had started to thin in his twenties, was allowed to grow long on one side so that he could comb it over. His belts always dug into him, causing the pot to seem bigger than it really was. She was ashamed of him. He looked nothing like her, and she wondered where he had come from. The fact that several candidates for paternity had been on the hustings never troubled her. Enid's memory was selective, and she accepted no blame for anything.

Dave tidied up, picking up the last slice of toast and loading it with marmalade, then taking bites between tasks. Food was his comfort, and he admitted as much to himself on a daily basis. As long as he had a book and something to eat, he was as happy as he could manage. All he had ever really wanted from life was a wife and at least one child of his own. But no one would look at him, not when it came to love and marriage. So he simply carried on with his life, eating, having the odd pint, looking after Mam and running the shop downstairs. He was determined to be of some use to the world, and that was the reason for his Reading Room.

Enid glanced at him. He knew full well that folk hereabouts called his establishment 'the old folk's home', but he didn't seem to care. People gathered in his downstairs back room to drink coffee or tea, eat snacks, and swap newspapers and opinions in a place where they felt safe and welcome. Unlike reading areas in long-deceased branch libraries, Eagleton's Reading Room was somewhere where folk could chat. Conversation was freer these days, Enid supposed, because she was no longer present in her supervisory capacity. She hated not being there; she hated the thought of him spending time with that woman, but what could she do?

Dave's thoughts matched his mother's at that moment. The back room was a happier place without Mam in attendance. Subjects ranging from politics through religion to the condition of someone recovering in hospital were discussed openly now. The atmosphere had improved a lot since Mam had got past wielding the teapot. Having her sniffing behind the sandwich counter had hardly been attractive for customers, so the whole caboodle flourished much better without her.

Dave's helper was a woman who went by the name of Philomena Gallagher. She was a strong Catholic, so she never worked Sundays or Holy Days of Obligation, events which occurred rather too frequently behind the hallowed portals that guarded her complicated and extremely demanding religion. But Philomena made great butties and scones, so her trespasses were eternally forgivable.

'Is she in today?' Enid enquired. 'Or is it the feast day of some daft bugger who chased all the snakes out of Ireland?'

He must not get annoyed with Mam. If he ever did let his temper off the leash, God alone knew what he might do, fired up as he would be by years of anger and resentment. He loved his mam. He kept reminding himself that he loved his mam, because she'd never given him away for adoption even though she hadn't had the easiest of lives. 'No. St Patrick's is in March. She's clear apart from Sunday for a while now.'

'Oh, goody.' Enid didn't like Philomena, because Philomena had taken her place downstairs. Thanks to melegs, Enid had been dumped in the upper storey while everybody praised the newcomer's food. Still, at least the damned woman wouldn't marry Dave, because Dave was Methodist. He was lapsed, but he was a long way from Rome. Anyway, nobody in their right mind would marry

5

Dave. Or so she hoped. Because she had to admit that she'd be in a pickle without him. And that was another cause of annoyance. 'I get fed up here on my own,' she complained.

'I come and make your meals, don't I?' He knew he'd been an accident, but she treated him more like a train wreck.

'I'd be better off in an old people's home.' She knew she was on safe territory with this remark, because the places in which society's vintage members were currently parked cost arms, legs, houses and bank balances. There was no welfare state any more – he couldn't afford to have her put away. 'I'm a millstone round your neck,' she complained.

Dave thought about Coleridge's ancient mariner with his albatross. No. Mam was more like the sword of Damocles, because he never knew when she would drop on him. She owned a barbed tongue, and she used it whenever she pleased. 'Here's your tea.' He placed it on a small table beside her chair.

'Out of sight, out of mind,' she snapped. 'You've no sooner cleared them stairs than you've forgotten me.'

As he walked down to the shop, he wished for the millionth time that he could forget his mother. Other men seemed to manage it well enough, though they usually had a partner with them. She'd trained him. She'd made sure nobody else wanted him – hadn't she all but kicked out every girl he'd brought home during his teenage years? He'd never been Richard Gere, but he'd had hair, at least. His childhood had been difficult, to put it mildly, because she had expected him to bring, fetch, carry, cook, shop and iron. Why couldn't he have been a rebellious teenager? Because none of the gangs had wanted him, that was the undeniable reason.

Downstairs, Dave opened the door to his kingdom. Perhaps it was more like a regency, because Madam upstairs still ruled with the proverbial rod, but how he loved his little shop, even if he was treated by her upstairs as mere minder of the place. It was a lone ranger, as there wasn't another proper bookshop for miles – just chains and supermarkets – and where could a man buy a German–English dictionary these days? Not in Sainsbury's, that was certain. No. They had to use the Internet or come to a proper bookshop. He provided a service. There was somewhere to sit when the weather was cold or rainy; there was a cup of tea served with scones or sandwiches, always with a smile as the side dish. 'Hello,' he said to Philomena. She opened up every day while he gave Mam her breakfast. On holy days and Sundays, Dave did a juggling act, but he didn't mind.

She nodded at him and awarded him his first smile of the day. 'You all right, Mr Barker?'

'Fine and dandy, love.' For a Catholic, she was a nice woman. She'd nearly become a nun, but she'd escaped at the last minute. There weren't many nuns these days, Dave mused. There weren't many priests, either. The chap at St Faith's ran three churches, so some folk had to go to Mass on Saturday evenings just to pass the confession test. Missing Mass was a sin that had to be told through the grille, but dispensation had been awarded by the Vatican due to the shortage of staff on its books. So Sunday sometimes became Saturday, and Philomena's life was complicated.

He walked through to the front of his domain. With

tremendous reluctance, he had become a newsagent. Just to hang on to his precious books, Dave Barker had been forced to allow the premises to be desecrated by the *Sun* and the *News of the World*. It was a pity, but it remained a fact of life – bookshops were dying, and few people seemed to care.

Today was to be another milestone about which Dave was in two minds. He was about to become a mini Internet café. Was he making a rod for his own back? Weren't people already spending enough time glued to the TV or plugged into the ether? 'Go with the flow,' he told himself. He already had a computer – it was essential when it came to ordering stock – but did his Reading Room need that facility for its customers? Would the young start to come in? Probably not, since most seemed to receive at least a laptop as a christening gift.

Ah, well. The world was going mad, so he might as well follow the herd. Being a purist was all very well, but a man needed to earn a living. There was no money in purism, and he needed to allow himself to become contaminated by the twenty-first century. Pragmatism was the order of the day, he had decided.

'Here you are, Dave.'

He took the proffered cup. 'Thanks, Philly,' he said absently. Then he looked at her. She seemed ... different today. Very smart – was that lipstick? Probably not. Perhaps she was going somewhere after work. She left early, because she arrived early to deal with the newspaper deliveries. He supposed she had learned about early in the convent. 'You look very nice today,' he told her.

She blushed. 'Visitor this afternoon,' she said, before fleeing back to her sandwiches and fairy cakes.

Dave stared into his cup. Forty-seven years old, and he still couldn't talk properly to a woman in his age and size bracket. She was shorter than he was, and she wasn't in the best shape. But she had lovely eyes, though he had better stop dreaming, because she was a holy Roman.

Number nine Fullers Walk was Pour Les Dames. Locals had taken the mickey for a while, because Maurice (pronounced Moreese) and Paul (pronounced Pole) presented as a pair of colourful gays with eccentric mannerisms and plenty to say for themselves. The joke had finally died. No longer did anyone ask how poor they were and which of them was Les, and no one had said they were both dames for ages, so they had survived the initial onslaught.

Their logo was an interesting one, as it portrayed the sign used on most women's lavatories, but with a curly mop on its head, a primitive scribble that looked as if it had been perpetrated by a pre-school child. They did good business in a large village surrounded by many rural satellites, and were often up at the crack of dawn preparing for the day's trade, as both were sticklers for hygiene.

Maurice was standing by the window. 'She's got a face like a funeral tea – everything set out in a nice, orderly fashion, but not a desirable event.'

Paul clicked his tongue. 'You're getting as bad as her at number five – Eyes and Ears. Don't let your gob join in, Mo. Before we know it, you'll be sitting upstairs staring at every poor soul that passes by.'

Maurice laughed. 'I don't think so, somehow. But look at her. She's carrying her flowers in now. I can't put my finger on it—'

'You'd better not put your finger anywhere it's no business to be.'

Maurice stamped a foot and dropped a deliberately limp wrist. 'She's bloody gorgeous, man. But her face is kind of dead. There's not one single fault, yet she seems so distant from everything and everybody. A bit like something out of Tussaud's. There's history there – just you mark my words. And history catches up with folk every time.'

Paul came to stand beside his partner. 'Hmm,' he breathed. 'Let's hope our history doesn't catch us, eh? We've all got something to hide, haven't we? But yes, I see what you mean. Lovely head of hair, so why does she bleach it? It's definitely a brunette face, that one. She'd look better with her own colour – it would frame her – so why gild the lily?'

They both laughed, as the woman in question was named Lily.

'Perhaps she's hiding grey?' suggested Maurice.

'Maybe. I don't think so, because I do her roots. If there is any grey, it's not enough to write home about.'

Maurice nodded his head knowingly. 'Exactly. I think she's concealing more than that. I mean, what's she doing round here? That accent's Somerset or Devon, isn't it? Why come up to sunny Lancashire, eh? Imagine living in Devon, all those little fishing villages, the surf pounding on the beach—'

'Hello, sailor,' said Paul in the campest of his range of tones. 'Does seem a funny thing to do, though. Fresh start, do you think?'

'She's running,' Maurice insisted. 'And she's had to run a very long way.' He turned. 'Now, we've Mrs Entwistle for a perm – even though we said we weren't doing perms any more. But if she wants to spend money having her hair assassinated, that's her prerogative.'

'Three blow-dries and two cut and blow-dry,' Paul added. 'Oh, and Sally's coming down later to do some manicures and a bikini wax, so we're booked for the morning, more or less.'

But Maurice was back at the window. 'Paul?'

'What?'

'I swear to God there's been a wedding ring on that finger.'

Paul joined him. 'Your name Hawkeye? How can you see that?'

'Next time she comes in, you have a proper look. I'll bet my Shirley Bassey outfit that she's in hiding. Including the purple boa. She's incognito, Paul.'

'Incognito? Fronting a shop?'

'Yes. Running a shop because that's what she's always done. Going blonde and travelling hundreds of miles because she had to. She's got a business head on her. Blonde, but no bimbo.'

'Your Shirley Bassey, though? Boa as well?'

Maurice nodded. 'Yes.'

'But I can't do Shirley Bassey. We'd get no bookings if I had to do Shirley Bassey. I haven't the waist for it.' At almost thirty, Paul had some difficulty when it came to the imitation of the female shape. Maurice, even though he was a couple of years older, had a smaller middle.

'I know,' said Maurice. 'I always hedge my bets, don't I?'

Paul punched his partner before returning to the task of sorting bottles and jars. As he began to count perm curlers, he heaved a sigh. Some women never learned. A perm in this day and age? Preposterous.

Maurice was still thinking about the woman next door. The unit had been empty for months, then she had arrived with all her bags and moved into the upstairs flat. Within a fortnight, she'd had all the ground floor decked out properly, and the florist business literally bloomed. Lily. It suited her. She was as pale as her natural colouring permitted, looking as if she had stayed inside for a long time.

Inside? Had she been to prison? When she came to get her hair done, she indulged in little or no conversation. Her past was not pure white – of that he felt certain. There was a sadness in her, something that cut very deep, a horrible emptiness. Was she lonely?

'Have you seen that other pair of ceramic straighteners? Another weapon to help kill hair off, I suppose.'

Maurice got on with the job. In time, he would come to know her.

Lily Latimer sat upstairs in the lotus position. Yoga had helped keep her sane, but her sanity tank had started to run low of late, as she had tired herself out with the new venture. She concentrated on her breathing and muttered her own mantra, a saying much used in Lily's life these days. 'Carpe diem.' She had to seize each day and get through it like some alcoholic on a set path punctuated by points and tiny goals. Sad, but true – it was the only way forward.

Lancashire was all right. It was as good a place as any other, and it was far enough away from the situation she wanted to avoid. Although it wasn't a case of want, was it? Absolute necessity was nearer the mark.

The people here were friendly, though the accent had presented her with some difficulty at first. 'Carpe diem.' They spoke slowly, at least. Her landlord was a different matter altogether, as he came from Liverpool. His words were delivered at a speed similar to that of water emerging from her Karcher power washer, an item designed to shift dirt, weeds, moss and any other unwanted matter that might cling to the exterior of a building. But he seemed a jolly soul, and his wife was pleasant enough. 'Carpe diem,' she repeated, a slight smile on her lips.

She was doing well. In the week to come, she had to cover two funerals and one wedding. Weddings were her real forte, as she was a qualified interior designer, but her certificates no longer counted, as they had been issued under another name. A change of identity was all very well, but a person had to ditch the good along with the bad. There could be no half measures, but she would be doing a great deal more than flowers in a few days' time. The wedding would be a triumph, word would spread, and she would be as busy as she had ever been in Taunton. Yet she must not shine too brightly, had to make sure that her work hit none of the national glossies or newspapers, because if it did, all she had achieved would be for nothing. Worse, it would be dangerous.

Lily sighed. She missed home, and she knew that it showed. These lovely people wanted to get to know her, but something in her appearance held them back. She wasn't ugly, wasn't even ordinary-looking, but something in her eyes had died. Killing Leanne and inventing Lily had hurt. Ma and Pa were dead, and she had no brothers or sisters, but she'd known some special folk at home. After a long time away, she had been welcomed back with open arms – there had even been bunting and home-made signs to tell her that she was loved, that she had been missed. How sweet freedom had tasted then. Yet how terrifying freedom could be once its implications became clear. Today was her birthday, and there was no one with whom she might share the joy of having survived for twenty-eight years.

'Carpe diem.' Without a word to anyone, she had upped and left in the middle of the night. Her house and shop were now on the market, and she had brought with her a minimum of furniture, as her exit had needed to be more than simply discreet. She felt terrible about that. Ma's furniture was still there, was to be sold with the building in which it had stood since her grandmother's day. Day. Seize it. 'Carpe diem.'

Thoughts of Gran and Grandpa sent her back more than a quarter of a century. Theirs had probably been among the first organic farms, though they might not have known what that meant. Grandpa had declared himself to be a 'natural farmer', one who disapproved of chemicals and kept their use to the barest minimum.

She remembered shows with huge horses pulling ploughs, competitions to win first place on one draw across a field. The feet on those beasts had been as big as dinner plates, and all the surrounding hair, known as feathers, had been combed to perfection. Until the plough race had started, of course. Prizes. Gran's apple pie from a secret recipe she had taken to her grave; Grandpa's tomato sausages made in his own kitchen – a proper kitchen with huge dressers and a table big enough for Henry VIII and his whole court. The parlour with its display of trophies, teapot always back and forth to the kitchen, scones with clotted cream, home-made strawberry jam, wine produced in a barn ...

This was definitely not yoga. This was long-term memory, mind-pictures of a time when life had been sure and steady. Safety? Did she have to go all the way back to Grandpa's farm to feel a sense of security? Perhaps most people found true warmth only in childhood, when love was unconditional and all decisions came from reliable elders. It was no use wishing she could go back. No one could go back.

The phone rang. Lily stood up and grabbed the instrument from her desk. 'Hello?'

'That you, Leanne? If it is, happy birthday.'

'Hello, my lovely. Thanks for the card. No. I'm Lily. Remember that. If you forget everything else, remember my new name. Though you can call me Lee, I suppose. What's happening?'

'Sorry. We'll be with you in a few days. Are you sure about this?'

'Of course I am. But never forget – I'm Lily. Cassie will have to learn that, too. How are you, Babs?'

'OK. Glad I don't have to change my name. It'll be OK, won't it? If I keep my name? And is there enough room?'

Lily glanced round the flat. 'It's all right. Big sitting cum dining room, kitchen large enough for a breakfast table, and I've given you and the babe the big bedroom. Until I find a house for myself, we'll manage.'

'See you soon, then. I'm more or less packed.' Babs paused. 'I'm a bit scared. It's a very long way, isn't it?'

'Yes, but the natives are friendly. They won't eat you – they trapped a Manchester United fan last week, so they're not hungry. Like snakes, they eat about once a month.'

'Stop it.'

15

Lily said goodbye, then sat on a sofa. How many lives had been altered beyond recognition during recent years? How long was a piece of string? She picked up a pad and wrote *twine*. There'd be plenty of that needed when she did her wedding garlands. Was there enough white satin ribbon? Would the three of them manage living here together? Bridesmaids – what was the colour of their dresses? She had a piece of the material in the desk, so that was OK. The landlord of the shop and flat had been approached, and he was cool about the arrangement, didn't mind Babs and Cassie coming to live with her. The bride was wearing oyster satin . . .

It was a decent enough living space. Lily was fairly sure that the landlord wouldn't object if or when the rent book went over into Babs's name if or when Lily moved out. Babs could front the shop sometimes, and that would leave more time for Lily to do her wreaths and bouquets.

She stood up and paced about. There wasn't a lot of storage for toys – she would buy some colourful plastic boxes. Cassie's dolls' house was probably the largest thing Babs would bring in her little car – that particular toy would have to go into the bedroom. It was big enough, she thought when she opened the door to survey it yet again. The whole flat had been carpeted in tough, natural-coloured sisal, and that should survive most of Cassie's spills. Poor little Cassie, not yet two years old, and having to be dragged away from home just because Leanne, now Lily, had got herself into a bit of bother. Well, more than a bit . . .

It would be silly to leave that fortune in the bank. Grandpa had always said that money should earn its keep by going to work, and he had been wise. How long had he saved for that prize bull? Oh, she couldn't remember. But his money had been put to work, and Grandpa had done well.

Lily's money was . . . different. Some of it was unearned, yet she had paid for it. She supposed it was funny money, though its source had hardly been amusing. There was family money, and she was the last survivor. She would buy a house nearby.

At a front window, she stood and stared at the square FOR SALE sign across the road. It was a large, rather grand building next to the Catholic church, but she dared say that she could afford it. Babs and Cassie would stay here, while she went to dwell in splendid isolation, rattling about in a house big enough for seven or eight people. There was a tree in the front garden that looked at least a couple of hundred years old. The place was too big. Silly.

Was it, though? Investment was never a bad idea. And the house was utterly unlike anything Leanne Chalmers might have dreamed of owning. Leanne liked cottages, beams, cosiness, coal fires and Christmas trees. Lily was more elegant, surely? Perhaps she would go and look at the house tomorrow. Or she might wait until Babs arrived, because Babs usually gave a forthright opinion on any subject about which she was questioned.

She walked to the fireplace and gazed at herself in the mirror. 'Should I have brought them to live here?' she asked the face in the glass. No wonder people did not meet her eyes. 'I look quite dead,' she told the vision before her. The radiance of youth had gone, had been stolen away and left to rot beneath years of torment. Yet it was a good face, well proportioned, the sort of face painters seemed to use. Perfect? No. Without character was nearer the mark. Blonde hair and huge weight-loss were sufficient to disguise Leanne, and she scarcely knew herself.

'I offered them a home because I want Cassie. There, I've said it aloud.' So much for altruism, then. How splendid her behaviour seemed on the surface. She appeared to be rescuing someone whose ordeal had mirrored her own, whose freedom had also been curtailed – but was she really doing that? Was she? Or had this desiccated female decided to cling to a child, someone on whom she could lavish attention in return for love?

There was, she concluded, no way of knowing oneself completely. A person existed in the world and became a reflection, like this one in the glass, because humanity allowed itself to be shaped by feedback, by the reactions of others. 'In the end, we become whatever the rest choose to perceive. We believe each other's lies.'

She must go down and bury her face in freesias. They reminded her of Ma. Today, she needed to remember her mother. She needed to be grateful.

'Chas?' Eve Boswell stood in the doorway of the bedroom she shared with her husband. How far could he get in a flat as compact as this one? 'Where the bloody hell are you?' He kept disappearing. One of these days, he would disappear with half a pair of her size fives planted on his backside. She called again, but he failed to reply. She knew he hadn't gone down to the shop, because a blue light above the door to the stairs was shining brightly, proving that the alarm was still on. With thousands of pounds' worth of alcohol and tobacco on the ground floor, the place needed a good system.

A face appeared above her head, and she clasped a hand to her chest as if terrified. He was going from bad to worse, she decided. What the hell was he doing in the roof space? Another hiding place for dodgy gear? 'You are one soft bugger,' she told him.

'I'm in the loft,' he said unnecessarily. 'Seeing if the pitch is enough to give us a bit of an office and somewhere to put our Derek. He's been getting on my nerves. I heard accountants were boring and quiet, so why can't he stick to Mozart or something of that sort, music fit for an educated man? If I hear one more note of his hippy-hoppy stuff, I'm off back to Anfield.'

Eve tutted. 'I must phone the Kop and tell the team it can rest easy, because Chazzer Boswell's on his way. You'll be able to shout advice from behind the goal mouth again. Now.' She waved the shirt she was carrying. 'How many people have worn this, eh?'

'Only me,' he replied with his usual cheeky grin. 'Why?'

'Butter wouldn't melt,' she said in a stage whisper. 'Did you clean the car with it? Or have you leased it out to the bloody fire brigade?'

'Eh?'

'It's a good shirt, is this. I know because I bought it myself personally with my own money, all on my own, just me, with nobody. It was thirty quid in the sale. Have you no sense?' She tapped a foot. 'Delete the last bit, Chas. I stopped looking for sense in you years back. Liverpool's loss is Lancashire's gain, isn't it?'

He stared at her for a moment, then announced that he mustn't have any sense, because he'd married her, hadn't he? But thinking aloud was never a good idea when Eve stood within earshot. 'You're the best thing that ever happened to me, Eve,' he said by way of apology. 'Except for when LFC won them five cups and Man U got sod all.'

She wouldn't laugh. Every time a bone of contention was dug up, he made her laugh. He'd got her to marry him and to have Derek by making her laugh. There would have been another ten kids by now if she hadn't lost her equipment to cancer, because she'd never stopped bloody laughing at him except for when she'd been in hospital. Private hospital – he'd seen to that, hadn't he? Chas was the best man in the world, and she would kill him in a minute – as long as he didn't make her giggle. 'Get down here,' she ordered. 'Make yourself useful. The washing machine's vomiting again. It's a drip at the moment, but I'm expecting Niagara any time now. They'll be swimming in to buy booze downstairs.'

He smiled again. 'Another thing, love. It's not Lancashire – it's Greater Manchester.'

Eve was ready for that one. She'd had to be ready for ever, because Chas had a quick brain and a quicker mouth. 'You ask this lot round here – them over fifty, anyway – and they'll tell you where to shove Manchester. Now get down here and see to that machine. I'll take the washing down to Mo and Po – they can put it in their machine when they're not doing towels.'

He climbed down the ladder. 'I hope it's not catching,' he said.

'What?'

'Wash my underpants with theirs, and I might come over peculiar.'

She hit him with the shirt. 'They're nice men.'

'Lovely,' he answered, striking a pose. 'Tell you what, though, babe. Their drag act is something else, according

20

to our Derek. Did you know they're going on *Britain's Got Talent*?'

Eve laughed helplessly. 'Oh, God,' she moaned, holding her aching side. 'Can you imagine the look on Simon Cowell's gob when he cops a load of that? He'll have a heart attack.'

'Couldn't happen to a nicer fellow.' He thought for a moment. 'No, I take that back. Cowell speaks his mind. He could become an honorary northerner the way he talks without dressing up. There'll be enough dressing up when Mo and Po walk out with their six-inch heels and eyelashes to match. I can see that panel now – she'll be on the floor laughing herself sick, and Piers Morgan won't know whether to laugh or cry. Face like an open book, that's his problem.' He went off to stem the tide in the kitchen.

Eve made the bed and straightened the room. She'd work on him again later, she promised herself. He was sticking to his guns, because he didn't trust anyone, but she was fighting for a house. They owned the whole row of shops and flats, so he could well afford it. He didn't want anyone else living and working here, because he was always up to something. A few of those somethings had put his brother in Walton jail for three years, yet Chas was still taking chances. It had been just luck and a good following wind that had kept Chas out of prison, and he should start behaving. He was near enough to fifty to have a bit of sense, and she wasn't too many years behind him.

She put on make-up, combed her hair and prepared to go down for her shift in the shop. The first part of the day was usually quiet, and the shop staff operated behind bullet-proof glass, so she was allowed to take her turn. He was so protective of her. As a dyed-in-the-wool operator, Chas liked to think ahead. No bugger was going to burgle him or hurt his family. Set a thief to catch a thief? He went further than that. Chas, well versed in the art of redistributing the wealth of the nation, was also adept when it came to outwitting his fellows. No Scally-Scouser would outwit him. As for the Woollies – they had no chance at all.

Eve shook her head. Just because folk round here talked slowly, he thought they weren't as quick-thinking as the Scallies. But he was wrong. A bad Woolly was hard to spot, but he could do as much damage as a Scouser any day.

Anyway, none of that mattered, because her Chas was going straight from now on. She'd straighten him herself. Even if she had to use an old flat iron to do it.

Philomena Gallagher rushed home to her little stone-built weaver's cottage. It sat on the end of a row next to three of its siblings, all pretty and well kept, all owned by proud people who knew they were sitting on potential gold mines. The rich often bought a pair of such cottages, knocking them together to make a substantial semi-detached house, and the end of a terrace usually attracted a slightly higher price.

She entered an exterior porch, opened her front door and stepped straight into the parlour. Philly's Irish grandmother had christened the room parlour, and Philly carried on in the same vein. A mirror over the cast-iron grate showed a flushed face, so she ran into the kitchen to splash a bit of cold water on her cheeks. She didn't want to appear over-excited, because that was hardly a Christian thing to be.

'Why me?' she asked herself. 'Not much special about me.' Still, she had done nothing wrong, and he had spoken to her pleasantly while announcing his intended visit. A priest coming to the house while nobody was ill? It wouldn't be for money, since Philly had made her pledge and the specified amount went into that little brown envelope each week, rain or shine. But she had better not appear too excited. Nevertheless, a cake stand appeared, both layers covered in her home-made baking.

Her hair was tidy, the house was tidy, the coffee trolley was tidy. Was the garden all right? She rushed to the window and cast an eye over alyssum, lobelia and French marigolds in pretty beds surrounded by pebbles. Yes, the path was clean; yes, the paintwork outside had been wiped only yesterday. The honeysuckle round the door had been given a haircut quite recently, so there was nothing to offend the eye.

Father Walsh. His first name was Michael, but she would never dare use it. There was no respect these days, especially where young priests were concerned. They seemed to neither ask for nor expect it, so it was probably as much their fault as anyone's.

He would be here in a minute. She had better compose herself, or she would be needing a priest for the wrong reason. With her heart in overdrive, she sat and waited for Father Walsh to come. What did he want? Breathe deeply, breathe deeply. All right, then. Just breathe.

A very handsome man presented himself at the counter. He wore faded jeans, and his pale blue short-sleeved shirt was open at the throat. 'Roses, please,' he said.

'Colour?' Lily asked. 'I have red, yellow and cream.'

She didn't look directly at him. Lily didn't trust men who were overly good-looking. She knew all about the confidence they owned, the way they managed to exert power over people they considered to be mere mortals. He was probably just another god with clay feet.

'Cream, I think,' replied Adonis.

She went to select the flowers. 'Some are still in bud,' she said. 'I'll pop in a bit of plant food. Oh, make sure you take the ends off the stems. Some people crush the wood, but I've never found that to be any use. A diagonal cut is enough.'

He handed over a twenty-pound note. Lily used the till, then counted out his change.

'You're doing very well,' he commented. 'Lovely flowers.' He sniffed the roses. 'Are you from Devon?'

'Yes,' she lied.

'Then welcome to the dark satanic mills.' He extended a hand. 'I'm Michael Walsh, parish priest to St Faith's and a couple of other village churches.' He turned and glanced across the road. 'That's my presbytery on the market. I'm such a nomad, I'd do better with a caravan.'

Lily swallowed. She went from fear to astonishment in a split second. It wasn't the first time she'd seen a priest in mufti, but he looked so ... so normal. No. Hardly normal – he was muscular and very well put together. 'Catholic?' she asked.

'Indeed. You?'

She shook her head. Lily wasn't anything any more. From a family of Baptists, she had lost all faith when ... 'No.' When everything had been stamped out of her, when Leanne had begun to die, when the world had gone dark. Lily was a shell, an empty house waiting for furniture, for warmth and safety, for a comfortable chair in which life might just seat itself and begin all over again. 'No,' she repeated. 'I'm not anything, really.' In that house, there should be curtains opened wide to the world. Not yet, though.

Michael Walsh stared at her. There was something wrong, something missing. She had no light in her beautiful blue eyes. A man of astute instinct, Michael lowered his tone. 'Lily, I deal with many people who are not of my faith. One thing you can be sure of in a priest is that he will use his ears, but not his mouth. Like a doctor, I keep secrets – and not just for my immediate family, my parishioners. Should you need to pray, come in and sit. Should you need to talk—'

'I'm fine, thank you.' She still could not meet his eyes. The talking had all been done. One-to-one therapy, group therapy, physiotherapy, baby-steps therapy, hypnotherapy, acupuncture, yoga.

'The offer stands.' He picked up his change and left the shop.

Lily Latimer sank into her chair. 'Hurry up, Babs,' she muttered. She could talk to Babs. Babs was the only one who could begin to understand Lily. Babs had known Leanne. It was suddenly important that the one person who knew everything should be here. Oh, how she wished that she might have stayed at home, that she could still be Leanne Chalmers, possibly the most successful and gifted interior designer in the west country.

But she had to stay away, must make the best of what remained, which was the money. She had inherited some, had earned some, was waiting for some from the sale of the property in Taunton. The rest – her funny money – should also be used. Compensation? How could any amount wind a bandage round her soul, the most damaged of her components? 'Put together enough of it, then make it work for you.' Such a clever man, Grandpa had been.

So. She might well be putting the modern, look-at-me priest out of house and home, because the Catholic church in England could no longer afford to hang on to presbyteries that stood empty for half of the time. Over the phone, she asked the estate agent for details. It needed work. It had over an acre of land with it. It was freehold, and there was an apple orchard in the grounds. She booked an appointment to view.

When the call was over, Lily smiled to herself. She came from scrumpy country, so an orchard would be lovely. He didn't need it any more, did he? And Cassie could stay with her sometimes. The smile broadened, just as it always did when she thought of the child. But she knew it didn't reach her eyes. She remembered the giggling, rosy-cheeked girl she had been. Perhaps, in the orchard across the road, she might find herself again. Perhaps...

Philomena was flustered. He could tell that she was excited and not a little nervous, because her breathing was shallow, while pink cheeks spoke volumes about her steadfast, old-fashioned attitude to the representatives of her religion. This was another woman who needed help and encouragement. But at least a person saw what he was getting in Philomena Gallagher. With the florist, there had been a deadly emptiness, a quality that was sometimes apparent in the terminally ill once they had come to terms with the dictates of destiny.

'Tea or coffee, Father?' she enquired.

'Tea, please. When I'm not in uniform, I'm Michael.'

She didn't like that. Nor did she approve of his

clothes, though she made no comment. 'I'll just . . . er . . .'
She went off into the kitchen.

While Philly just-erred, Michael looked around her neat little house. One of these would be big enough for him, surely? There was a second bedroom if anyone wanted to stay, and he didn't take up a great deal of room. Except for his books, of course. He looked at the alcoves that flanked the fireplace. He could put some in those, others in a bedroom.

She returned and poured tea with a hand that was noticeably unsteady.

'None of these properties up for sale?' he asked.

'I don't think so, Father. If I hear of anyone wanting to sell, shall I let you know?'

'Please.' He took a sip of tea.

'Is that all right for you, Father?'

'Fine, thanks.'

'More milk? Not too strong? Are you sure?'

He told her to sit down and stop worrying, knowing that she would never achieve the latter. Philomena Gallagher might be a woman in her forties, but she still carried within her all the older mores pertaining to the Catholic faith. As an enlightened priest with a broader attitude, he worked hard to understand people like Philomena. They were inestimably valuable, though he wanted to extend their horizons. He was here today to make an effort with this woman's self-confidence. It might all backfire, but it was time to take a risk, time to enliven her if at all possible.

She sat, hands clasped on her knee, looking for all the world like a junior school child waiting to come face to face with the head teacher's wrath.

'Amdram,' he said.

'Pardon, Father?'

'Amateur dramatics. We should use the school hall, bring everyone in, try to liven the place up a bit.'

Philly nodded absently.

'The community needs to come together for projects. There must be some around who'd enjoy being on the stage.'

'But I don't—'

'But you're not one of them. Don't worry about that. All I want is for you to ask Dave Barker if you might use his computer to print some flyers – I'll ask him myself, in fact. Then, if you would organize distribution throughout the parish, we might just get something going. You could perhaps consider being secretary cum treasurer. Keep people in line, so to speak. Your honesty is obvious, and I thought of you straight away.'

Philly nodded again. Why her? Why couldn't he have chosen somebody who didn't mind knocking on doors and giving out leaflets? 'Just Catholics, then?'

He laughed. 'Not on your nelly. We want all kinds of people.' He leaned forward in a conspiratorial manner. 'You see, Philomena, priesthood these days is about community service, and I thought—'

'Isn't community service something criminals do instead of jail?' She felt her cheeks burning; she had interrupted a man of God.

'They don't even have to be Christians. A shepherd looks after all his sheep – he can't choose the prettiest or the woolliest ones, can he? This isn't about religion, it's about giving people something interesting to do.' He paused. 'Will you help me?'

She nodded.

'If it gets too much, I'll find a helper for you.'

28

Philly had her pride. 'It won't get too much, Father. I shall do it. Of course I shall.' She'd make sure it didn't get too much. Even a priest needed showing a thing or two from time to time. Especially a priest who wore the clothes of an errant teenager.

'Settled, then?' he asked.

'Yes,' she replied. She would show him.

He looked at the slight glint of determination that entered her eyes in that moment. He had done his job, and the mouse would roar.

Life sentence. Bloody life for a kid that never even existed. And what will Madam do now with her so-called freedom? She knows I have friends on the outside, knows there's money hidden. But she's no idea about where, has she?

Starting off on 43, stuck on a landing with nonces and perverts. I don't belong here. She put me here – they both did. I've got curtains because we're special up here and none of us expect to see the outside again. Parole board? My name won't be on the list. Still, they're thinking about moving me away from the nonces, said they'll see how it goes. I suppose if I get attacked, I'll be shoved back up here.

They watch me for suicide. As if. Ways and means, Leanne. Just you wait. There's always ways and means...

Two

Somewhere along the line, wires must have been crossed. The man from the estate agency turned a remarkable shade of purple and clapped a phone to his ear as soon as he realized that a mistake had been made. Eve adopted her 'posh' voice, though distorted vowels continued to betray her provenance. 'He'll be having a stroke if he doesn't watch out,' she told her unexpected companion. 'My mam had wallpaper that shade of yuk in the back bedroom. God, look at the colour of him. Is it aubergine?'

Lily stood in the hallway of the presbytery, a clearly agitated Eve Boswell by her side. 'Poor man,' she said.

Eve's jumpiness was soon explained. 'He doesn't know I'm here,' she said. 'My Chas, I mean. I've been trying to make him see sense, only it's like knitting fog. "I want a house," I keep on telling him. But I will get my own way in the end, 'cos I always do. A house makes sense, anyway. See, there's our Derek's music for a start, then there's—'

'So sorry, ladies.' The troubled representative of Miller and Brand clicked his mobile phone into the closed position. 'What can I say? Someone's head will roll, I can promise you that.'

Eve tutted, then discarded her posh voice. 'Ar 'ey,' she said in her best Toxteth accent. 'Don't get some poor devil the sack just on account of me and Lily. We're neighbours, aren't we, love?'

'Indeed,' answered the florist. 'Don't do anything, please. My friend from Som– from Devon should have been here to help me choose a house, and she hasn't arrived, so Eve and I will look together.'

He calmed down a little. 'Nevertheless, this is all highly unprofessional. You are interested separately – am I right?' When both women nodded, he clung to his portfolio and sighed sadly. 'Follow me,' he suggested. Hoping that world war would not break out, he led the way.

But Eve and Lily weren't going to follow anyone. Both women had stood in the hall; both had realized immediately how badly they wanted this house. No matter what the rest of it was like, the solid door with stained-glass panels, and those matching windows at the sides, were enough for them to have fallen head over heels before taking two paces. 'It's lovely,' breathed Eve. 'Needs a bit of work, like. Look at this kitchen for a start.'

Lily was looking at the kitchen. It was wonderful, because it put her in mind of Grandpa's farm. It contained an eclectic mix of items, yet they all seemed to rub along splendidly. Apart from two/sets of built-in floor-to-ceiling cupboards flanking the hearth, nothing but sink and cooker was fixed. Three Welsh dressers displayed a mixture of pottery, while two old meat safes, painted cream, stood side by side just inside the rear door.

'I'd have it Shaker,' pronounced Eve. 'What would you do?'

Lily cast an eye over the old pulley line, admired a scrubbed table big enough for six or eight, glanced at the hearth and at a grate that still needed blackleading. 'I'd change very little,' she answered. 'I like it just the way it is.' She was no lover of brushed stainless steel, was not a paid-up member of the fully-fitted brigade. 'I'd open up the fireplace if it's blocked off – I might even bake bread in the coal-fired oven.' She sighed. 'It's perfect.'

Eve smiled to herself. Lily Latimer's voice had lifted slightly, and there was a faint glimmer in her eye. If this house would fetch her out of the doldrums, then she should have it. Lily's need was far greater than her own. Something on one of the fast-encroaching modern estates would do for the Boswells. There were several nice five-bedroomed detached with double garages and up-to-the-minute streamlined kitchens – there'd be no stained glass, but so what? Lily suited this house, fitted in as if she had always lived here. But Eve would play the game. If she stayed and pretended to be fighting for the property, she might just wake up her listless tenant.

There was a morning room, a study, a formal dining room, a big sitting room and a lean-to that held washer and dryer. Crucifixes and holy pictures made the place grimmer than it needed to be, but the two women were trying to look past the decor. Upstairs, no fewer than five bedrooms and two bathrooms completed the tour. Oh, no – there was another little staircase up into the roof. Lily remembered noticing the odd-shaped dormer.

It was breathtaking. The window was circular. Lily imagined waking up here, with her bedhead against the glass, knew that her white coverlet would be spotted with colours borrowed from leaded lights. There was a small shower room on this top floor, and Lily knew with undeniable certainty that she would fight to the last for this place, that the room in which she currently stood would be her own.

'Lot of money,' said Eve.

'Yes.' Lily scarcely heard the remark. It was worth every penny.

'I'll go home and talk to him,' Eve said. 'Mind, I might as well talk to the fireback for all he cares. But I will be putting in an offer. If he'll listen for once. I'll make him, I will, I will . . .' She left, her grumblings drifting back up the stairs until she was finally out of range.

Lily followed the man down to the first floor. On the landing, he stopped and looked at her. 'Would you like another look round?'

Lily nodded. 'But I can tell you now that I offer full price subject to survey and valuation. Should anything major need doing, I shall lower the offer accordingly.'

'I see. Erm . . .' He shuffled some papers. 'Mortgage?' he asked. 'Do you need help? We are in contact with all the major societies, and we have an adviser to help you find whichever deal is most suitable.'

She shook her head. 'It will be cash,' she said. 'I shall put the wheels in motion right away. Don't worry, I have the Yellow Pages, so I can find my own lawyer and sur-veyor.'

He blinked. It wasn't every day he sold a house of this price for cash. Was she serious, or might she be one of those time-wasters who visited houses for recreational purposes? 'Right,' he mumbled. 'If you would care to come into the office – shall we say Monday?'

'No,' she replied. 'You will need to come to me – I run a business single-handed at present, and can't just up and away whenever I like. To come and view this house, I've had to close my shop.' She handed him a card. 'That's my personal number, and the shop details are below. Thank you.'

He was being dismissed. Yet he had to make the house secure and report back to work. 'I'll ... er ... I'll be downstairs in the room at the front when you have finished. You see, I am required to secure the premises and then I have to go to an appointment—'

The front door slammed. 'Buckets of blood,' cried a male voice. 'I'll get the hang of that door if it kills me.'

Lily and her companion stared down at the top of a head owned by Father Michael Walsh. He was struggling with a pile of books and papers, and was clearly annoyed by his burden. He looked up, saw two people, and dropped everything. 'Sugar,' he said.

Lily felt the corners of her mouth beginning to twitch slightly. He had very untidy hair. 'Good afternoon, Father,' she said.

He opened his mouth, but offered no reply.

The estate agent descended the staircase. 'I'll be on my way, then,' he said, his tone apologetic. He pointed to the mess on the floor. 'I'd help you with that lot, but I'm due to show a house on Bradshaw Brow in twenty minutes.' He left the scene.

'There are rabbits in the garden,' announced Michael.

'Right.' Was he all there? What had rabbits to do with anything?

'And one of them's in trouble. But I had to go and ... There was stuff in the sacristy ... I won't be a minute.' He left scattered items on the floor and ran through to the dining room. '*Watership Down* was never like this,'

34

was his departing remark as he made for the French windows.

Lily followed and watched him as he poked his head into a tangle of exposed roots beneath an old tree. *Watership Down* was a sad film . . . His pose could never have been deemed dignified, as he was on his knees, backside in the air, T-shirt riding high and displaying a great deal of skin. She thought she heard him swear. Well, it might have been 'sugar' again, but she didn't think so. 'Are you all right?' she asked.

'No,' he said. 'The bugger bit me.'

It hadn't been sugar, then.

He pulled the animal out and shoved it in a box. 'Get the cat basket out of the utility place,' he ordered. 'I should have thought. Get it before this nightmare eats its way through the cardboard. Go on! I'm serious. The fellow's a big buck and he hates me.'

She found the requested item and carried it out to the rear garden. The scent of honeysuckle touched her nose as she passed the plastic and metal container over to him.

'No,' he said. 'Open it. Put it on the floor, woman, and open it.'

She did as she was ordered.

There followed a blur of activity which she would never in a million years have been able to describe, but the animal was finally behind bars and the priest was triumphant.

Lily looked at the angry rabbit. 'What's the matter with it?' she asked.

'Big sore on his ear. We'd been getting along famously till now – he even took carrots and stuff from me. Not bad going for a wild rabbit.'

'He's very wild now,' remarked Lily.

'Well – wouldn't you be if your freedom had been curtailed?' He watched the cloud arriving in her eyes, realized that she had seemed almost normal up to this point. He studied his prisoner. 'I am not inflicting you on that poor vet,' he told the furious creature. 'It'll be an antiseptic, then you can take your chances with the rest.' He looked at his visitor. 'We have foxes, too. There's a mum and a dad and some young ones.' He sighed. 'Until just now, I thought of myself as a watered-down Francis of Assisi – he had a way with animals. But I was sadly mistaken.' She was thawing again. 'I'll get the towels.' Suddenly, he ran away.

Lily squatted down. 'Hello, bright eyes burning like fire,' she said. The rabbit immediately became still. 'Why would we need towels?' she asked. 'Are you going in the bath?'

'Here.' Michael thrust a pair of large bath sheets into Lily's hands.

'He's gone off,' Lily told the rabbit when the priest did another of his now familiar disappearing acts.

'Here.' He was back once more. 'Put these on.' It was a pair of thick gardening gloves. 'Strategy. We need to discuss.'

What was this? Lily asked herself. A G8 conference, a meeting of heads of state? 'You first,' she suggested.

'Right, yes.' He rubbed his chin. 'Erm ... I'll get the first aid. Not for us,' he added in a tone that was meant to be reassuring. 'For him. There's a thorn stuck in his ear and he's been trapped in those roots for who knows how long, so no wonder he's in a bad mood. And gentian violet.'

'What?'

'My grandmother swore by it.' He walked away again.

The task proved far from easy. Lily held the struggling animal in two towels, her hands protected by heavy-duty gloves. Michael used tweezers to remove the thorn before soaking the ear in a bright blue dye. 'You can let him go now.'

She released Bright Eyes, watched him lolloping away, was surprised when he stopped, turned and looked at them. 'You'd think he was saying thank you,' she said. 'He looks a bit odd, doesn't he?'

Michael Walsh shook his head. 'A priest's life is often surreal, but this takes the chocolate digestive. We're not even drunk, are we? Pink elephants, purple rabbits – what's the difference?'

'Size,' was her prompt reply.

'He looks cute, though,' Michael said. 'I'm sure the lady rabbits will find him more attractive.' He turned and looked her full in the face. 'So, it is to be you, I take it? Who'll force me out of house and home?'

Lily shrugged. 'You're here only two or three nights a week. Anyway, talk to the bishop and the Pope – it's their fault.' She paused for a couple of seconds. 'Religion's dying, isn't it? They have football now – they can sing in a stadium instead.'

'Very astute,' he remarked drily.

If anyone chose to ask her, Lily would never be able to explain what happened next, why it happened, whether she wished it hadn't. 'You can have a couple of rooms upstairs,' she said. 'For nothing. Just in case there is a God, heaven, hell – all that stuff. You can tell the angels I paid my dues by sheltering a man of the cloth. Who's the bloke with the keys?'

'St Peter.'

'Have a word with him. Tell him I've paid my rent. OK?'

She was a good woman, a hurt woman, a person who had held a terrified creature and helped calm its fears. 'Thank you, Lily,' he said. 'I truly appreciate that. I've a bit of family money, and I was considering buying a cottage, but we'll see. Thanks again. Very good of you.'

Lily didn't know what else to say. She told him that she would keep him advised about the progress of her intended purchase, that she wanted the kitchen left as it was; asked who owned all the furniture. He kept smiling and trying to make eye contact with her, but she couldn't quite manage to look at him. She felt safe, because he was a priest, yet his behaviour was that of a very ordinary – no – a very extraordinary layman. He'd cared about that daft, purple-eared rabbit, had cared enough to expose hands and arms to some angry little teeth. 'There's an orchard?'

'Yes. Way down at the bottom of the garden. Green-house, too. I grow my own tomatoes. You could perhaps propagate some of the rarer lilies?' She was a rare lily, but a damaged one. 'Or orchids? The sort that need a special feed tube in with the rest of the bouquet?'

Lily shook her head. 'Probably not, Father. I won't have the time to spare, not with the business. Mind, I have a friend coming tomorrow. She's bringing her baby daughter, but she'll give me some help, I'm sure. But I like to sell flowers that are slightly more robust.'

'I see.' He looked at his watch. 'I've sinners to deal with,' he told her. 'Confession time.'

'Oh. Right.' She picked up her small clutch bag. 'Good-bye, then.' She walked through the beautiful panelled hall, saw his scattered papers on the floor, picked them up and placed them on a table.

'Thanks.' He stood behind her.

'Oh. Yes. See you soon, then.' Lily stepped out into the sunlight and walked down the path. Feeling like a very silly schoolgirl, she crossed the road, entered her shop and turned the sign to OPEN. He was standing at his gate, staring at her. 'Stupid,' she said aloud. 'Because you know you're safe, you've taken a liking to him.' She shouldn't take likings to new people, because she wasn't allowed to get to know anyone, was she? Thank goodness Babs would be here in about twenty-four hours.

She turned her back on the village road and started to sort out her bedding plants. These could sit outside where passers-by could see them. How quickly the months passed. In a matter of weeks, she would be buying in spring bulbs. Cassie was coming. Cassie could never take the place of the dead, but she did brighten up life. Cassie. She would soon be here.

'Dave?' Enid Barker craned her thin neck and peered into the street below. 'There's two of them been in there this afternoon. Two.' She raised her voice by several decibels. 'Can you hear me? I've seen two going in.'

He dried the last plate and placed it in the cupboard. Could he hear her? She was probably audible as far away as Salford Quays in one direction, John Lennon Airport in the other. 'Here I am,' he said after finishing his chores and walking to her side. 'I have to go back down, because Philly's gone home, and I've left Valda in charge. She's helping out for nothing, so I don't want to take advantage of her good nature.'

'Good nature?' The old woman cackled. 'You'd best watch her, son. Her nature's that generous, she'll have a thriving whorehouse running if you're not careful. She's anybody's for the price of a skirt off Bolton Market.'

He sighed resignedly. As far as he was concerned, Valda's arrangements were private, as were everyone else's. And his mother should be the last on earth to criticize anyone who chose to survive by unorthodox methods. 'Two what been where, Mother?'

She pointed to the presbytery. 'Over yon. I know Eve Boswell's likely Catholic, because most of them Scouse types are, but Lily Wotserface? I don't think she's one of them.'

'Her name's Latimer.'

'Daft name. They went across, then he came home from church with a load of papers and books—'

'Who did?'

'The priest. Oh, I wish you would listen properly. You take all the bone out of a story with all them daft questions.'

He closed his mouth, folded his arms and waited.

'Two women he had inside the house. She's never been to church across there since she came here, that Lily one. As for Mrs Boswell – she's too busy keeping an eye on her old man and his late deliveries.' She nodded. 'Oh, aye, I've seen and heard them in the night. And he keeps stuff in that garage, you know – that's why he has it alarmed.'

Dave maintained his silence.

'Well? Nowt to say for yourself?'

'I don't want to fillet your story, do I? I mustn't take the bones out, you said.'

Enid pursed her lips. 'I sometimes wonder if they gave

me the wrong baby. Somewhere, there might be a tall, slim lad with a sense of style and a bit of humour in him, happen some hair and all. And I got you.'

He'd wished all his life that he'd had a different mother – a mix-up at the hospital might have been a good thing in his case. The computer man was downstairs. The poor chap was surrounded by potential silver surfers who didn't know their pixels from their hard drive. 'I'm going,' was all he had to say.

'You're no fun,' she complained.

'I'll send Valda up with a cup of tea.'

'I don't want her here. She swaps sex for clothes, and she's–'

'Some old women used to sell it for cash,' he snapped before crashing out of the flat. On the landing, he held his breath for a few seconds. God, what was the matter with him? In his hands, he could almost feel her scrawny neck as she breathed her last. He wanted to kill his own mother? Sitting on the top step, Dave Barker considered his options, knew he had just two. He could stay, or he could go. There was the shop, and there was his mother. He loved the shop. As for his mother – well, he loved the shop, and she had the ability to close it. Number three was empty – could he rent just the flat? Would Chas Boswell find a tenant for a lock-up?

Dave rose to his feet. It was an effort, because weight had become an impediment, while his centre of gravity seemed to have planted new roots. Next door was too near. Africa was too near, he supposed, because her tentacles were longer than the Nile. Hatred for one's own single parent was neither usual nor pleasant, but Enid had filled every waking hour he had known. A lousy childhood had drifted into a lousy adulthood, no seams

41

showing, just a natural progression from bad to worse. It was worse because he now understood what she was; as a child, he had simply obeyed the orders of a larger person who had not been averse to slapping his head. He remembered the belt – it had been her father's. She'd used that with relish on the legs of her only child. Then the cupboard in the hallway of their old terraced house, so dark and lonely . . .

Downstairs, he found that the IT man was currently buried beneath a crowd of pensioners.

Valda laughed when she saw the expression on Dave's face. 'He's in there somewhere, love,' she advised him. 'I promise you they haven't eaten him. You're out of snacks till tomorrow, but he's still alive.' She grinned. 'They wouldn't get far with National Health dentures, any road.'

Dave dug his way through the three-deep circle of people. They were looking at soft porn. He smiled to himself, then pushed his way out into slightly fresher air. 'He's all right,' he told Valda.

'See? I told you he was. He asked them what they wanted, and they said dirty pictures. So he did as he was told.'

'I noticed.'

Valda piled up the clean saucers in readiness for the next day. 'How's your mam?' she asked.

Dave sat down at one of his five tables. 'Evil,' he answered.

'Normal, then.' It was not a question.

'Yes.' He drew a hand across his forehead. 'I'd hate to go through life like she does – finding fault after sin after mistake. She can only see the worst, Valda. In all my life, I never heard her say either thank you or sorry.'

'Perhaps she had a hard time and it turned her?'

He nodded. 'Perhaps. But why spend the rest of your life making trouble for everybody else? Is unhappiness something that needs spreading, like margarine?'

'There's folk like that, Dave. It's as if they just can't help theirselves. Take my mother-in-law – oh, I wish you would. You could stick her in with your mother and you'd swear they were twins. She's a right one. Nice to your face, but never turn your back, or you'll end up with a knife in the middle of it.'

Dave stared at Valda. 'You're serious?'

She pursed her lips. 'She's not happy living with us, and she makes my life a misery. Shall I introduce them? Bring her round for tea, cakes and a slanging match? We'd need a referee with a strong stomach, mind.'

He thought about that. Valda was a Catholic, and Mam didn't like them. She didn't like gay people, black people, Muslim people, any kind of people. 'Is your ma-in-law a churchgoer?'

'No. Lapsed. I reckon if she went to confession, it would take her a week to say her penance on the beads. Tell you what, though. We'd be better off with all the bad apples in one barrel, eh? It would make my life easier – and yours. Imagine it. Your life with no Enid, mine with no Mary.'

Dave closed his eyes. 'Bliss,' he breathed.

Valda took her cardigan from a hanger. 'Think about it. I'll think, and all. We're not getting any younger, lad. I've kids to see to, and you've got your shop. Nothing to lose, eh?' She left him to an uncertain fate. The poor IT man was buried under pensioners, and their questions were sealing him in.

'You all right in there?' Dave called.

The man emerged. He was red in the face and decidedly the worse for wear. 'They're keen,' he complained. 'Fortunately, computers are tough these days, but I hope your software survives.' He left his card and dashed off in search of somewhere safer.

'Has he gone?' someone asked.

'Yes,' shouted Dave. 'You had him frightened halfway to death. Now, who has a child or a grandchild who's experienced in computers?'

It seemed that most of them knew someone.

'Send them round,' Dave told them. 'We'll have a rota. Now, you can all go home, because I've things to do.'

He locked the door and looked round his empty shop. This was all he had in the world. Tuesdays and Fridays, he went to the Hen and Chickens for a pint. Tuesdays and Fridays, he got an earful from his mother. It was clear that her selective memory had deleted much of her own past from the hard drive, but it was retrievable – oh, yes. Nothing was ever completely wiped. A word here, a word there, and he could make her life totally unbearable.

The times she had come home the worse for wear; the many occasions on which he had cleaned up vomit because fish and chips didn't always sit well on a bellyful of cider and spirits. Her sex life had been audible and had sometimes involved more than just herself and one other. Did she really believe that he could forget all that? How could she imagine that a child of at least average intellect would not remember at least some of what he had seen and heard?

But. Ah yes, there was *the* word. *But* if he moved out or showed signs of discontent, she could force him to buy her out. 'Maybe I should,' he said under his breath. 'Get a loan, open another kind of shop – or extend into

44

number three – live above number three.' He swallowed hard. There had to be a way. Valda's suggestion might not be as daft as it had first sounded. Two rotten eggs in one carton could be part of the answer.

He stood at the door and looked out onto a beautiful summer evening. Father Walsh was gardening, and a group of children played near the stocks on the green. Stone cottages looked particularly lovely at this time of day, when the sun was nearing its nadir. It was as if Earth's star threw out a last blaze of life before starting to dip towards the west. 'Rose-coloured specs,' he murmured. He knew he couldn't leave Eagleton. After being raised in the back streets of Bolton, he had fallen in love with the countryside. Everything he needed was here – farms, woods, shop, books, plenty to eat.

Sighing, he turned round and prepared to return to the woman upstairs. If he wasn't careful, she would win. He was eating too much, too often. He was eating the wrong stuff. The chances of living long enough to bury her were as slim as he ought to be. She might well outlive him. He wasn't far away from fifty. She was a mere twenty-two years older. 'It's about staying alive. I have to stay alive.' In order to do that, Dave Barker would need to take his future and hang on to it – otherwise, all his efforts would count for nothing.

He needed to diet; he needed to get rid of as much aggravation as possible. Kill her? Lovely dream, but not worth the probable consequences. Eat less, get out. It was time to change.

They were shutting the shop when Philomena Gallagher arrived. 'Sorry, love,' said Maurice. 'I know we say appointment not always necessary, but we're doing a gig

45

tonight. Paul needs so much make-up it takes hours and a builder's trowel. We're going to invest in an industrial paint-sprayer.'

Paul sniggered. 'Take no notice. He's always in a filthy mood when he knows he's got to wear his corsets.'

Philly didn't know where to look. She had never been in Pour Les Dames before, and she knew that the owners of the business were . . . different. It was best not to think about the details of their relationship, but she couldn't help herself. Red in the face, she passed Maurice a leaflet. 'Father Walsh asked me to do this,' she explained. 'There's a group being set up in the school hall. Amateur drama.'

Paul struck a pose. 'Oh, but we're pros, sweetheart. Aren't we, ducky?' He touched Maurice's arm.

Maurice refused to laugh. Paul always went a step too far when in the presence of a bigot. He'd taken a few beatings from homophobes for it, but he still wouldn't help himself. 'Take no notice,' Maurice advised. 'We'll think about it.' He stared at the visitor. 'Who does your hair?' As always, the senior partner in the business put the shop first. This was a potential client. Furthermore, she needed help immediately, and he loved a challenge.

Philly's colour deepened. 'Nobody.' A hand flew up defensively and she placed trembling fingers on her head. 'I do it.'

Maurice nodded. 'We could help you with that,' he said. 'Given a decent style, you'd be quite pretty. It's needing shape, you see. A bit of feathering, a touch of my genius, and you'll feel brand new.'

Philly swallowed. It was a case of give and take, she supposed. But would she be able to bear these men touching her head after they had . . . done whatever they did to each other? 'Right,' she answered lamely.

'Shall we say half two tomorrow? After you've finished at Dave's?'

She nodded.

'We'll put you in the book. Paul?'

'Yes, master?'

'Cut and blow for a start. We'll look at the colour next time.'

'I don't want to be blonde,' she managed after a sizeable pause. What would everybody at church think if she turned up to Mass with platinum hair?

Paul shook his head vigorously. 'Oh, no. Blonde would never suit you, darling. You'll need something a lot more subtle. Low lights with a touch of warm chestnut.' Philly flinched as he touched her hair. 'Good quality stuff, is that,' he announced. 'And plenty of it. Dave'd give a fortune for a sixth of it – wouldn't he, Mo?'

Maurice nodded. 'I dare say. Now, come on, Paul. Get the cement rendering and we'll try to make you look nearly human.'

Philly left the shop at speed.

Maurice turned the sign to CLOSED, then rounded on Paul. 'You could see she was uncomfortable. Years I've tried to drum this into you – button your gob when they don't know you. I can guarantee she'll be telling us her innermost secrets if you behave.'

'Women like a gay hairdresser.'

'Well, of course they do. With a gay, a woman isn't a sex object, is she? She opens up after a while – if you treat her right. Some of them have to be handled with care, that's all. Leave her to me. She's terrified.'

Paul sniffed. 'It's her hair that's bloody terrifying. We should have left her alone.'

Maurice shook his head in despair. 'Look – they talk to us and we keep their secrets. That's why we decided on separate cubicles – remember? We listen and we keep quiet. That's as important as any hair treatment or manicure. We look after the whole person – hair's incidental.'

'What are we? Psychiatrists? Vicars? Hair stylists?'

'All of the above, and don't you forget it. Now, come on. We're due at the Rose and Crown in just under two hours. I've got to wax my arms.'

'Ouch.' Paul grimaced. 'So glad I'm not an ape.'

Maurice looked him up and down. 'Rather an ape than a bitch. So, move it pronto.'

Paul knew there was only one real boss, so he moved it. Pronto.

Philly sat on a stone wall at the edge of the village green. Her face had cooled down, but her heart seemed to have remained in top gear. She should have posted the wretched flyer through the letterbox, then she wouldn't have needed to talk to them, listen to them, think about them. Some children were playing with a long skipping rope. It was good to see them outside. Philly didn't approve of computers, and she wondered why Dave had bothered. Didn't folk spend enough time locked indoors? Some of those screen games were vicious, too. It was a shame; it was a pity that human nature forced people into pushing back boundaries all the time.

Nobody worried about gays any more. Homosexuality was openly accepted – they could even go through a form of marriage if they so desired. It was all wrong. Men and women were meant to get together in order to make children. But the process of child-making had become an amusement, a pastime in which people overindulged. Like drink, it got a hold on them. Like drugs, the habit became hard to break. Now, same-sex couples almost flaunted their status. Gay pride? Well, pride always came before a fall.

A car pulled into the slip road that fronted the five shops. It stopped outside the florist's, and a small woman got out. Lily Latimer received her with open arms before lifting a child from the back seat. Squeals of childish delight fought with the sound of adult laughter while the three greeted each other.

The trio disappeared into the building, and Philly watched as Father Walsh flung down his garden fork and leapt across the road. He pulled boxes and bags out of the car and placed them inside the shop. But he didn't stay, probably decided not to interfere. He walked back to the presbytery, picked up the fork and started working again. But he glanced across the road from time to time. Was he trying to convert the florist?

Looking up, Philly saw the pair of women at the front window of the upstairs flat. The florist was pointing towards the presbytery, while the other woman, child in her arms, nodded and smiled. Was Lily Latimer going to buy the priest's house? Such a shame that it had to go, that Father Walsh was forced to go from pillar to post in order to provide services for the few. And they were a few. Mam and Grandma had talked about the walks, days when Catholics from Bolton and its satellite villages walked through the town to display their faith. The one true faith.

She stood up. The walks didn't happen any more. It was said that they had stopped in the early sixties when the first signs of rot had set in. Little girls in white dresses had been replaced by creatures whose clothes were the same as their mothers', who played with make-up given free with magazines, who wore bikini tops although they had nothing to hide. They were too ... too aware. Innocence was now a luxury enjoyed by very few.

Philly walked into her little cottage and switched the kettle on to boil. Her movements were automatic as she put vegetables to cook in the microwave, grilled her lonely chop and a single sausage, set one place at the kitchen table. She had never expected to receive anything in life, so she had not been disappointed. But she wished with all her heart that Dave Barker had been born Catholic, because he was a nice man and would have been good company. Her single status did not exactly upset her, but the evenings were extremely lonely. She finished her meal and went to make coffee. He was a lovely man. It was a shame.

Excitement died a natural death after an hour or so, as both Babs and the child were exhausted. Cassie fell asleep in the small spare bed in her mother's room, and the two women sat down with a bottle of Crozes Hermitage.

Babs yawned. 'Oh, let me at the wine – get me a bucketful. God, that was a bloody long drive,' she said. 'And Cassie hated the hotel. She was asking for you all the time – I finally got her to call you Auntie Lily.'

'Yes, it's a long way.' Lily slid down into the comfort of an oversized armchair. 'Thanks for coming. It's been a bit stressful on my own.'

'I'll bet. Are the natives civilized?'

Lily grinned. 'Fairly. There's a dreadful old woman

next door, but she stays upstairs. Rumour has it that her son keeps her caged because she bites. On the other side, we have a pair of gay hairdressers and their lodger, Sally Byrne. She does manicures, waxing and so forth. The shop at the far end is run by our landlord – he's from Liverpool, as is his wife. Lovely rough diamonds, they are. They have a son called Derek who's an accountant.'

'And that's it?'

'No, there's a whole village of them. New estates all over the place, smaller villages dotted about – it gets quite lively sometimes. They keep threatening to build a supermarket, but the natives have managed to beat off the developers so far. It's only a matter of time, though.'

Babs stared into the near distance. 'I can't believe what we've done, Lee. Sorry – Lily. To come so far and live among strangers–'

'We had no choice. And if you want to call me Lee, that's OK. I chose Lily because if you slip up, it's near enough to be a nickname. I honestly think we had no alternative. We both need a completely clean slate.'

'Yes. Yes, I think you're right. In fact, I know it. This way, we get a chance to start again, but we can't pretend it never happened, can we? It's not going to come out of the washing machine brilliant white.'

Lily shook her head slowly. 'None of our yesterdays can be bleached away, Babs. You didn't tell anyone you were coming up here?'

'No, of course not. Being an orphan made it a bit easier, I suppose, but it was still an awful wrench.' She nodded in the direction of her bedroom. 'Thank goodness she's young enough for it not to matter. Anyway, I told every-one we were going on holiday to Cornwall, so people saw us leave. It made it a bit less stressful, though I did feel mean – I had lovely neighbours. So Cassie and I are on holiday. We just won't return, that's all. Had to leave the dolls' house. Had to leave everything but clothes.'

Lily stretched her legs in front of her. 'We'll get her a new dolls' house. It's OK here. I promise you, it'll be fine. There's no one who will connect us with what happened, and that's the main thing. We aren't front-page news any more—'

'But we may be when someone reports us missing.'

Lily had thought about that. 'You have to do one thing, Babs. I've already done it.' She sat up again and leaned forward. 'Tell the Bolton police where you are. You have the right to live wherever you like and you have the right to privacy. But yes, folk at home may well report us as having disappeared, though because I have property on the market my absence will be labelled deliberate. You're mother to a young child, so go to the cops and let them know you're both alive. If you choose not to be found, your wish will be respected. After that, it should be plain sailing.'

'Better be.' Babs stood up. 'Is it all right if I go to bed now? I'm absolutely worn out.'

On her own again, Lily watched the priest as he finished his gardening. She wondered briefly about Bright Eyes with his purple ear, hoped he was recovering from the ordeal. Father Walsh had probably brought in the luggage from the car. Or it could have been Dave Barker. Whatever, they were good people and she would settle. So would Babs. As for Cassie, she didn't care as long as she had Mummy and her auntie Leanne, who was now Lily or Lee.

It would never be completely safe, though. Even emigration might have failed to conceal the real truth

52

behind the changes in three lives. Yet it had to be worth the effort, at least. The hardest part was being unable to concentrate sufficiently to read a book, or watch TV, or listen to the radio. The music she had loved had begun to remind her of a time she would never completely forget, and she wanted no prompting. It took a great deal of effort to run the shop, but she was managing that. 'Baby steps and carpe diem,' she whispered.

He was going inside now. If she ever needed to unburden herself, he was the man on whom she might impose. Father Michael Walsh's promise to keep quiet referred not only to Catholics, not only to Christians, but to every soul who chose to confess or disclose. Strangely, it was the rabbit that had convinced her. Any person who would do all that for an animal, who would drag in a near-stranger to help, had to be intrinsically good.

Lily found herself smiling. 'The bugger bit me.' That had been quite funny, especially coming from a man of God. She had always imagined the representatives of Rome to be strict and humourless – he was hardly either of those. With hair as untidy as that, it might be hard for him to be taken seriously. He reminded her of the chap who played Darcy to Jennifer Ehle's Elizabeth. Lily had always thought that the hair of the bloke in that serialization belonged elsewhere, since it made a bloody-minded and self-absorbed man completely childlike on the outside.

He had gone. He had gone, and she felt colder. 'Don't,' she advised herself. 'For God's sake – literally.' That said, she took herself off to bed.

'There's a kiddy next door now,' grumbled Enid Barker. 'There'll be noise – you mark my words.'

Dave placed breakfast on the side table from which she ate. Although she blamed mclcgs for her inability to reach the dining area, the real reason for her chosen position in life was her need to stay by the window. When she required the bathroom, she moved at considerable speed, shooting back to her chair within a minute of finishing her ablutions. She was a fraud – and worse.

'Is there no eggs?' she asked.

'Your cholesterol,' he answered. 'Remember? More in one egg than in a pound of liver? Three a week is your maximum.'

Enid snorted. 'Bloody doctors. What do they know?'

'Enough,' he replied smartly.

She eyed her son. He seemed to be developing a bit of backbone. Pity about his great big belly, then. He was bringing her a visitor, had announced that she needed the company. Valda Turnbull's mother-in-law was coming to tea. They were Catholics, though Mary wasn't sure what she believed in any more. 'I don't want anybody coming here,' Enid said.

'Tough. Because she's coming – end of.'

This was starting to be vaguely interesting. Dave had never answered back, had always allowed her the last word. In recent days, he'd tried coming over all clever, as if he might just be a man after all. 'I'll bolt the door,' she threatened.

'Then we'll break it down. After all, we can't leave an old diabetic who could be in a coma.'

'I'll be shouting. So you'll know I'm awake.'

Dave nodded sagely. 'If your sugar gets too low, you go quiet and confused. If it goes through the roof, you shout and get confused.'

She didn't know the truth of the matter, so she offered

54

no reply. She'd had hypos, but no hypers, and was not in a position to comment. Should she call his bluff, eat a quarter of butterscotch and see what happened? He was winning. Just because she had become an old and dependent woman, he was taking advantage. 'More tea,' she snapped.

He brought the pot and a milk jug. If he'd had any sense at all, he would have remembered the arsenic. 'There you are, Mother dearest.'

Sarcasm now! This game promised to become interesting, because she could close that bloody shop, and he knew it. How far was he prepared to go? 'I'm getting on that phone to Chas Boswell, to ask about Madam next door subletting.'

'The precedent's set,' Dave replied. 'Sally Byrne at the hairdressers' – she has the spare room.'

'Bloody poofs,' she snarled. 'Shouldn't be allowed.'

'True.' He poured in the milk. 'We could put them in the stocks one at a time and throw tomatoes at them. I suppose tinned ones would do. They'd get concussion and brain damage, so that would be all right, eh?'

Enid blinked. He was up to something. The proverbial worm was definitely on the turn, and she would put a stop to it. 'I can get you out of that bloody shop like that.' She clicked her fingers. 'Don't you forget it.'

Dave reined himself in. 'I've got some savings,' he advised her. 'And a clean credit rating.' His heart was working overtime. He really must diet and try to get a bit of exercise. But he failed to stop himself. 'Mam?' He took a deep breath. 'I think it's time I filed for divorce. Do what you like – I'll manage.'

She blinked again, this time very rapidly. 'You couldn't survive without me.'

He folded his arms as if trying to hold back the rising tide of fury. 'I think you'll find the shoe's on a different foot altogether.' He left her with her jaw hanging, slamming the door in his wake.

On the stairs, he sat down, his whole body trembling, head pounding as the blood coursed too quickly through his brain. It would be a stroke, he supposed – or a heart attack. It would amuse her no end if she outlived him. Would she make him buy her out? The business wasn't worth a great deal – it was more scones and goodwill than anything. What would a prospective purchaser see? A shop with below-average turnover, a place that kept two people in reasonable comfort, no more. Savings? He had less than five grand, no big deal at all.

So the shop would change into something else, and that something else would come with the sitting tenant from hell. Dave stood up and crossed his fingers. He prayed that Mam and Mary Turnbull would get on, that he would get out, that the Reading Room would endure. It was time for him to start having some of his own way.

Solitary again, but not rule 43. Wasn't me. I know the bloke who made the knife, but I daren't say a frigging word, or it'll be me with my eye out next time.

Five of us in solitary. It's no big deal, because I like being on my own; few interruptions, time to think and concentrate on what needs doing. Not easy to make stuff happen when you're locked up, but I'm owed a few favours, could get more than a handful of folk sent down if I wanted to.

Food's crap. Sit and think. All the time in the world to work it out. Yes. All the time in the world.

Three

Lily had failed to remember one vital thing about her friend, but she was reminded early on of a particular characteristic that was very much a part of Babs. She talked. She talked on any subject for any length of time, was able to discuss matters about which she had little or no knowledge, and entered conversations even if she needed to interrupt.

She hadn't always been like this. The anxiety had only surfaced after the two women had met, and was probably the result of certain events about which Babs seldom spoke, a series of traumas that had left both of them bruised in more ways than one. Lily had become quiet and withdrawn, while Babs now employed compulsive talking in an effort to distract herself to the point where she might forget some of it. For her, it was therapy, and, if it worked for Babs, Lily would endure it.

In spite of her questions about the population of Eagleton, Babs floated through her early days in the village like a duck on an extremely placid pond. Some feathers might have been ruffled by her head-on approach, but Babs's own plumage remained smooth. It was almost frightening. Like Lily, she had a west country accent; unlike Lily, she was not good at remembering the alibi on which both had supposedly worked, so she often gave Somerset as her place of origin. No one had commented so far, but it might make matters more difficult in the future.

Lily came downstairs, stopped and listened. Babs was talking to a customer. 'No, she hasn't always been quiet. She's been through a lot of—'

'Hello.' Lily bustled in and made herself busy with a bucket of pinks. The customer was Father Walsh, and he was in receipt of the dubious benefit of Babs's wisdom. 'Get Cassie out of the roses, Babs,' Lily begged. 'It's not just a matter of saving the flowers – she could prick herself on a thorn.'

Babs picked up her daughter. 'Right. I'll take you upstairs.' The reluctance in her tone was clear.

Lily eyed the priest when Babs had gone. 'Yes?' she asked.

'I'm begging,' he replied. She looked frightened. 'If you have anything left over on a Saturday – anything that won't last till Monday – could we have it for a special rate for Sunday Masses and Benediction?'

Philomena Gallagher had already made the same request, so Lily repeated her consent. 'Either free or very cheap,' she added.

'Paying your rent again just in case?'

She smiled, but her eyes remained cold. 'How's the rabbit?'

'Pale mauve,' he said. 'And he still lets me feed him.'

Lily picked up a rose from the floor. 'You've met Babs, then.' Cassie had broken the stem.

He nodded. Babs was quite a character. She was pleasant, inquisitive, nervous and damaged. But she was not

58

as traumatized as Lily appeared to be. 'Yes, it was a pleasure to talk to her at last. She's very amusing.'

'Good.' She straightened a pile of wrapping sheets on the counter. 'Anything else? Do you need a kidney, blood transfusion, flowers? No? All right, I have to see to something upstairs.' She left him in the shop.

In the living room, she collared her friend. 'Babs, I wish—'

'I'm sorry, I'm sorry. You know what I'm like. I can't help it.' She shook russet-coloured hair and smiled an apology. 'I like people. In spite of everything that's happened, I still like the beggars. It's how I am, Lee. It's how I've had to become, because . . . you know why.'

Lily sighed heavily. 'We are incognito – well, I am – for a very good reason. And you could ruin it all by letting your tongue wander off on its own without a collar and lead. Babs, I could be in danger.'

'I know.'

'My life and yours could depend on how well we manage up here.'

'I know.'

'Then there's Cassie. I won't draw any nasty pictures, but you know damned well what we could be up against in time. There could be a lot of red in those pictures—'

'I know! I do know!' Babs sat down and burst into tears. 'I shouldn't have come. I should have stayed at home, because I might just say too much and give you away. I'll go back.' She dried her face and lifted a determined chin. 'I'll go back and leave you in peace with a better chance of survival.'

'You can't. You need to be out of the way as well. So does that child. I'm afraid you're stuck here, my lovely.

And when I move across the road, you'll be in this flat with just Cassie. If I can't trust you, I can't move out. And I want to live in that house. Now, dry your eyes again and take this little girl for some fresh air.'

The smaller woman sighed, and there was a slight sob in the breath that escaped her lungs. 'All right,' she said eventually.

'Babs, I don't like upsetting you, because God knows you've had enough misery, but I can't have you running away at the mouth.'

'Collar and lead?'

Lily nodded. 'Straitjacket, if necessary. Now, pull yourself together. That was the shop bell, and I've flowers to sell.'

Back in the shop, she found a tall, attractive man in a short-sleeved shirt that just about contained his muscular body. 'Yes?' she said.

He had come to see Babs. Lily paused and processed his request. Who did Babs know up here? Was he a villager – or perhaps it was someone from one of the estates? Or could it be . . . God, no. Not yet, surely? 'She's busy,' Lily managed eventually. 'Taking her little girl out.' If anyone did come after them, it wouldn't be in daylight or without disguise.

'Are you Lily?'

Fear cut through her like a knife, and she understood all about knives. 'Who wants to know?' Blood pounded in her ears. England was a relatively small country, and news travelled fast. Was this the new face of an old danger? Had she and Babs been cornered already?

'It's all right,' he said. 'I'm Peter Haywood. Sergeant. Greater Manchester Police.'

She relaxed slightly, felt the stiffness leaving her shoulders. It might be an idea to book an Indian head massage on her next visit to Pour Les Dames. 'Ah yes. I'll ... I'll go and get her.' The police were not always trustworthy, yet she had been forced to advise them of her arrival, since friends back home might well be getting her listed as missing. Was he a good cop or a bad cop?

She came back into the shop with Babs and Cassie following in her wake. 'Hello,' Babs said rather loudly. 'To what do we owe the pleasure?'

He passed her a scarf. 'You left this at the station.'

Lily glanced up at the ceiling. She was in the presence of strong chemistry and didn't know where to look. The scarf was silk and had been a gift from her to Babs when they had still lived in Taunton. Babs and the scarf were close companions – virtually inseparable. It had been forgotten on purpose; this visit had been engineered by a clever little woman who had taken a fancy to a tall, handsome stranger at least ten years her senior.

'Shall we go for a walk?' Babs asked the policeman. They left, Cassie toddling between them, Babs winking at Lily. The remarkable fact was that Babs was still on the market. In spite all that had happened, she was organizing a manhunt.

Lily watched them while they sat on a bench at the edge of the green, her mind racing. She wondered whether Babs might change her name via marriage to a man who would protect her and Cassie, but the idea did not sit comfortably in Lily's soul. Cassie was all she had. Babs was the little girl's mother, and Lily had been fighting her feelings for some time, yet the thought of parting with this near-daughter made her ill. Only one good thing had escaped Taunton, and that good thing was playing near the stocks. 'I must distance myself,' she whispered.

There was a wedding to prepare. Philomena Gallagher had promised to sit with Cassie while Lily and Babs took flowers and drapery into Bolton in order to prepare for tomorrow. They had a church and a reception hall to cover, so it promised to be a long evening. Lily folded lengths of satin that would be fashioned in swags suggested by the bride. Given free rein, Lily might have done things differently, but tomorrow belonged to the bride. The bouquet had to be taken away straight after the service, as it was to be professionally dried and framed.

Babs and Cassie were still with the policeman. He would know the whole story, since it had all been broadcast in newspapers and on TV, so he was learning nothing new. Yet Lily's skin crawled each time she thought about people hereabouts learning exactly who she was, who Babs and Cassie were. The sergeant might keep his counsel, might not. Like the purple-eared rabbit, Lily did not want to feel trapped.

She needed more ice. As she came through from the back of the shop, she looked outside again. They were still sitting on the same bench while Cassie played ball with another child. Lily smiled. Cassie couldn't catch yet, couldn't even throw properly. How fortunate the child was. Too young to worry, she simply went from day to day without a care in the world. And that was a blessing indeed.

'She's going to buy the priest's house, and good luck to her. Looks as if she's due a change of fortune. Put these on the shelf.' Eve passed a box of cigars to her husband. 'But I still want to get out of here, Chas. We had our own house in Liverpool, so why can't we have one here? I can't fit a proper Christmas tree upstairs. Last year's looked like an accident that had fallen off the bin wagon. I wouldn't care if we couldn't afford– Take that stupid look off your face and shut your gob – there's a bus coming.'

Chas sighed loudly. 'I like to keep an eye on things,' he said lamely. She'd win. She always won in the end. He was the one who was supposed to be in charge, because he could make her laugh until she changed her mind, but Eve was the home-maker, and she wasn't satisfied with the raw materials on Fullers Walk.

'Then go straight,' she suggested. 'Sell just kosher gear, and tell your special customers to bog off.'

He shook his head. Go straight? He was nearly that already. It was just a few cases here and there, bits and bobs obtained by his brother from a source on the docks. Security was now so paranoid that no one could go out-and-out criminal these days. 'I'm as straight as I can be,' he said.

'But your Robbo or one of the lads could bring stuff to our house, then we could fetch it here in the boot of our car or something.'

Or something. The trouble with women was that they didn't think things through properly. 'The less you know, the better. My eggs here are all in one basket – they need to be.'

Eve's shift was ending. Without another word to her beloved spouse, she walked out of the shop, slamming the door behind her. Chas hated sulking. If she could keep it up for a few days without succumbing to laughter, if she could stick to her decision, she might be in with a chance.

Eve stood at the front window of the flat. The woman who was staying with Lily Latimer was sitting on a bench near the green. She was in the company of an eye-pleasing piece of male furniture, and she was laughing. Babs, she was called. From the same neck of the woods as the florist, she was certainly a great deal livelier than her hostess. The child was pretty, with large eyes and a mass of blonde hair. There seemed to be no husband in the picture, but that was only too common these days.

Both adults were laughing. Lily didn't laugh very often, though. She was beautiful, yet there was something missing in her face, as if pieces of life had been taken out of her. But she'd bucked up in the priest's place, so that was definitely going to be her property. It would be interesting to see if she would come out of her shell after moving from the Walk.

Eve sat down and took from behind a cushion a pile of leaflets sent by estate agents. There were many houses for sale in the area, some old, many new. The old ones were prettier, while the new were more sensible, easier to keep and still under guarantee. There was a lot to be said for a guarantee, but Rose Cottage still sat on top of the pile, because that was where it belonged. Detached and built of thick blocks of stone, it looked as if it had been here for ever – it would probably survive Armageddon.

'I'll have to get inside that one,' Eve told the empty room. 'And there's enough outbuildings for all Chas's palaver.' It looked as if talking him round wasn't going to be easy. But Derek was away on a course, so Eve could play a trump card by sleeping in her son's room. Chas didn't like sleeping alone. Well, if he wanted company, he could always get a bloody cat.

The intercom buzzer sounded, so she picked up the phone. 'Hello?' It had to be Chas – there was no one else around to use the intercom facility.

'You win,' he said.

She wouldn't crow, wouldn't laugh, wouldn't scream with joy. 'You're no fun,' she told him. 'I was going to curl up with Daphne du Maurier in our Derek's room.'

'Is she a dyke?'

'No, she's a writer, soft lad. How much? Because it has to be Rose Cottage. It's just across the road and I like it. You'll like it. Because if you don't like it, I'll kill you.'

'What's the price, Evie?'

'Never mind the price. We're viewing it tomorrow when Derek gets home. And be nice when we get there. We can talk about the price when you've seen it and decided you'd give anything to live there.'

After a pause, he asked, 'How do you know I'd give anything to live there?'

'Because I say so.' She put down the phone and tried not to cheer. Men were easy, she reminded herself. They liked what they were told to like and they'd do almost anything for a quiet life.

The intercom sounded again. 'What?' she pretended to snap.

'Can we have beef and Yorkshires tomorrow?'

'All right.'

'With rhubarb crumble to follow?'

'Yes.'

'Custard?'

'Don't push it, Charles Boswell. I do have my limits,

you know.' She replaced the receiver. Rose Cottage. It was next to St Faith's, while the presbytery sat on the church's other side. Chas would be able to see his beloved shop from the front window. Derek would probably stay here, since it was time he had a pad of his own.

There was a very long rear garden, as long as the one behind the priest's house. The church would be sandwiched between Lily Latimer and the Boswells, as would the graveyard, the size of which was probably the reason for those two long plots behind presbytery and cottage. Eve rubbed her hands in glee. She had always fancied some land. There wasn't even a window box here, but she would make up for that soon enough.

With a cardigan draped across her shoulders, she went downstairs and out through the rear door. There was joy in her step as she crossed the road and looked at the facade of the house she coveted. There were roses everywhere. A very primitive example clung to the masonry outside the front door. Its flowers seemed to have just one layer of petals – was it a dog rose? She would order a book from Dave's shop. In fact, she would order several, because she wanted to grow her own herbs and vegetables as well as flowers.

There would be amateur rose specialists all over the villages. Would she dare keep chickens? Not to eat, of course, because a chicken in the oven needed to be anonymous. But there could be fresh eggs almost every day.

The windows were lovely, sashed and set in sandstone. The rest of the house was in a greyer colour, but it was beyond beautiful – it was absolutely gorgeous. The roof was slate, and probably needed attention. A little water feature sat in the front garden, just stones over which the liquid trickled. Slabs at the edge wore patches of moss, and Eve was glad that no one had cleaned them off. It was an idyll, with a huge plot at the back and civilization at the front in the form of shops and a properly laid main road.

They were still sitting there. The woman named Babs was leaning towards the man. If what Eve had read about body language was correct, she was practically giving herself to him, and who could blame her? He was such a big, handsome fellow, while Babs was a likeable soul. Ah, well. Good luck to the pair of them.

Father Walsh came past. 'Hello, Eve. What are you up to now?'

'I'm up to trying to force Chas into buying this house. I think I may be winning.'

'Oh?'

She nodded. 'He isn't ready to die yet, Father. And I don't want to be confessing to you that I murdered him.'

'Good enough reason.' He wandered off towards the church.

To think she had been afraid of leaving Liverpool. Life here was good, the people were great; even the priest was a nice man. She would never go back. There was still a slight pain in the hole where Liverpool had sat, but she couldn't manage to miss it badly any more. There was something about the villages surrounding Bolton, and that something was probably natural beauty. Movement in the land, soft, gentle slopes in velvety greens, made the area desirable. Patchwork was held together by stitches shaped out of dry stone – it was a wonderful area for picnics. Unlike West Yorkshire, Lancashire was not sudden. It had no steep climbs into the Pennines, just these lifts and falls that looked so peaceful and inviting.

'I am home,' she whispered to her inner self. Had anyone told her twenty years ago that she would be living among Woollies, she would have scoffed. Liverpool had been everything to her, and she owed this new life to Chas's brother. He had been caught; Chas had been lucky. With no record, he had been able to obtain the licence required to sell wines, spirits, beer and tobacco. 'Thanks, Robbo,' she mumbled before going home. 'Thanks for not grassing on my Chas.' Robbo seemed to have done something good after all.

'I can't just go off as and when I please,' Babs told her companion. 'Tonight, we have a babysitter, because Lee – Lily – is doing a wedding, so a woman from the village is minding Cassie.'

'Short for Cassidy?' he asked.

'Cassandra. Lily chose it.'

'Really?'

Babs nodded. 'She did a lot for me, Pete. It could all have turned out a great deal worse than it did, but she stood by me once she was fit. With the way things are now for her, Cassie's as near to a child of her own as she's going to get. Damned shame.'

Pete agreed. 'It was a terrible thing that happened to her. Must take time to get over stuff like that.'

Babs placed a hand on his arm. 'One point. She doesn't like being talked about. It makes her a bit paranoid, and very frightened. Lily trusts very few people. In fact, I am the only people she trusts, so that's just one. Don't try to get her to talk. It's all over, and she wants to leave it in the past. She needs to bury it.'

'That's her privilege,' he said. 'So. When are we going to have our first date? When I met my wife, it took me over six months to ask her out. Six months is a long time at my age, so I'm beating round no bushes.' He was quiet for a moment. 'Since she died, I've concentrated on the kids and the job, but it's time I put on my dancing shoes. What do you say?'

Babs grinned. 'I've got your mobile number. Lily will sit, but let's get this big wedding over with. I promise I will phone you.'

He stood up. 'No rest for the wicked. Back on duty in just over an hour.' He placed a hand on Cassie's head. 'Look after your mam for me, babe.' Then he kissed Babs's hand and walked back to his car.

She sat for a while, her skin tingling because he had touched her. Feeling like a teenager, she separated Cassie from her playmate and walked back across the road into the shop. Lily was placing wreaths for a funeral just inside the door. 'Hi,' said Babs.

Lily looked at her. 'Don't let Cassie near these,' she said. 'They have to be just right – funerals deserve respect.'

Babs scooped up her daughter. 'Are you in a mood?' she asked her friend.

Lily shrugged. 'It's your business, Babs, but don't go jumping into love. Falling is an accident, but jumping is asking for trouble.'

Babs stood very still and tried to hold on to her temper. It got the better of her, though she did not raise her voice. 'Lily, just because you've decided to be a recycled virgin doesn't mean I have to go all straight-lipped and sad. I like him. He likes me. It doesn't mean I'm going to jump, does it? I'm not old enough to give up, not young enough to be completely daft. Please don't look at me like that, because it makes me angry.'

'It's your business. But please, please—'

'Don't talk about you. I promise, Lee. He's a cop, so he knows enough, but he's not interested.'

'Interested in you, though?'

'Yes.'

Lily managed a half-smile. None but the hardest heart could possibly remain angry with Babs. 'Then he isn't a complete fool – he clearly has good taste. And yes, I will mind young Madam while you go out with him, so get up those stairs, put on some don't-matter clothes and wait for Philly Gallagher. What with weddings and funerals – ain't life fun?'

Babs breathed easily again. It was true that for Lily life had to be tackled in bits, or in baby steps, as she put it. No sudden changes for this girl, not yet, anyway. And none of it was Lily's fault, just as none of it was Babs's fault. Lily's head was fully furnished, but her soul remained bruised. Whatever, the Lancashire air seemed to suit her, and Babs would pray for a good outcome.

'No good clothes, babe,' Lily shouted up the stairs. 'And put a mop and bucket in the van, will you? Sewing kit as well – you never know.'

'Well, bugger me.' Enid looked up at her son as he walked in with her lunch. 'Did you see that carry-on outside? Bloody disgrace, I call it.'

He made no reply except to tell her what was on the

plate. 'Bacon, lettuce and tomato sandwich, and one of Philly's fruit tarts.'

Enid glanced at the ceiling. 'So you saw nowt?'

'Nothing worth writing home about, Mother dear.'

The old woman picked up her binoculars. If only she could lip-read, she'd have a much fuller story. 'Five minutes, she's been moved up here from wherever, that Babs one. And there she was, bold as brass, sat on a bench with a man. Hard-faced in my book.'

She never read books. Dave had noticed the couple, and had smiled. Little Babs and her lovely daughter were pleasant additions to Fullers Walk. He hoped they might help bring Lily Latimer out of her shell, because she'd looked very down in the dumps since arriving in the north. 'Were they actually fornicating, Mam?'

Enid blinked. Her son didn't use such words. Her son did as he was told, though he'd stepped just a whisker out of line lately. 'No. But she was throwing herself at him. Acting like a tart if you ask me.'

Dave didn't ask. He poured her tea. She moved to the dining table, groaning with each step, because melegs hurt today. He sat down opposite her, placed his elbows on the table, and rested his chin in his hands. 'You know, Mam, I've had just about enough of you.'

She paused, sandwich suspended in mid-air. Shocked, she could not manage to put her tongue in gear.

But Dave didn't stop. 'When I was a kid, you had man after man in your bed. I heard it all and saw too much for a lad of tender years. Money changed hands. Did my father pay? Did he?'

The sandwich dropped onto the table, spilling tomato seeds and shredded lettuce all over the cloth.

'And you sit here, day in, day out, making nasty remarks about folk who are just going about their business. She's not a whore. She's just a young woman, possibly a widow with a child, and she's looking for friendship – even for love. But there'll be no money left behind a clock for her. Because she's something you'll never be, and that's decent.'

The silence that followed was weighty. Enid clutched at her thin chest, a small groan emerging from thin, pale lips.

'You hit me repeatedly. You used me as a servant and you locked me in a cupboard. These days, I could go and report you to the police, but things were different when I was a kid. You are a nasty piece of work, madam. I don't care what you do – I'm not staying here. You can rot, for all I care.'

Enid closed her eyes. She didn't remember the past in quite the same way. She'd been firm, but ... 'You hate me, don't you?'

'I don't like you. I despise you for what you are, and most of this village feels the same way. You're my mother, and I've tried to look after you, but I've had more than my fill. So.' He picked up the tray on which he had carried up her lunch. 'So, I am moving out.'

Her eyes flew open. 'You've nowhere to go.'

Dave smiled grimly. 'Don't fool yourself, old woman. Everybody round here knows what I have to put up with. There are plenty of spare beds in Eagleton. Someone will take me in, because they understand. They remember how you were downstairs, so they're on my side. You'd better get yourself a new slave, because this one's escaping.'

'Over my dead body,' Enid spat.

'That can be arranged,' he replied before leaving the flat. On the stairs, he paused for thought. What had happened lately to push him so near the edge? Why was he suddenly strong? Or perhaps strength was something he had lost, an element he used to employ during the years when he had tolerated her. Had his skin been worn so thin that his feelings had begun to show? And where was he going to sleep tonight?

Downstairs, three people were arguing over the computer, while a couple sat at one of the far tables doing the *Telegraph* crossword. Philly was brewing a new pot of tea. He beckoned, and she followed him though to the shop.

'You don't look right,' she told him.

'I'm not right.' Dave inhaled deeply. 'I've just told my mother to get lost.'

'Oh.'

'My feelings exactly. I've got to get out of here, Phil. Do you think people would talk if you took in a male lodger?'

She snapped her jaw into the closed position. 'Erm ... Father Walsh might want the spare room when the presbytery's sold.'

He nodded. 'And he's a man. But he won't need you, because Lily's giving him some rooms in the house – that'll save him being disturbed.'

'Oh,' she repeated.

'I won't beg,' he said. 'But I need somewhere. Tonight, if possible.'

Philly organized her thoughts. He was a nice man, but she had never shared a bathroom with a male. It could be embarrassing, because she often spent evenings wearing pyjamas and dressing gown ... 'All right,' she said. 'Just till you find somewhere a bit more permanent.' She pondered for a moment. 'Doesn't she own half of the business?'

Dave nodded. 'Without it, she'd have only a small pension to live on. Anyway, there's a plot on.' He told Philly about Valda's mother-in-law. 'She's coming to see her soon, so they may get on OK and live together.'

'Shall I make you a brew?' she asked.

'Please.' He watched her as she walked away. There was something different about Philomena Gallagher these days – what was it? Ah yes, it was her hair. It had been cut and it shone like silk. He had better behave himself. He needed to be a model lodger.

The business of acquiring the presbytery proved to be fairly plain sailing. There were a few problems, including aged rainwater goods, a chimney that needed stabilizing and a couple of patches of damp. But the house was in good condition for its age, and Lily enjoyed measuring and planning and imagining her future. The garden was the biggest attraction, as it seemed to go on for ever, and she was always finding nooks and tables, sundials, broken benches, and paths that led nowhere in particular.

She was sitting nowhere in particular when she had her next encounter with the priest who would soon become a sitting tenant.

'Who's minding the shop?' he asked.

Lily jumped. 'For goodness' sake, you'll give someone a heart attack creeping about like that. Babs is minding the business, while Cassie's in the Reading Room with Philly Gallagher. She's teaching her to read.'

'Good,' he said, dropping to the ground beside her.

'It's time Philly had a few lessons. I'm fed up with her singing all the wrong words.'

Lily awarded him a glance designed to wither. 'I love this place. It reminds me of that children's story – *The Secret Garden*. Every time I come, I find another surprise.'

'So do I,' he answered ruefully. 'I think I sat on a nettle.'

Another withering glance crossed the small space between them. 'Put some purple stuff on it and call yourself Bugs.' At least there was no wildlife involved this time, no danger of staining her new cream blouse with gentian violet.

She had humour, then. She was different here. It was as if the main road separated one Lily from the other, and she relaxed in the wildness behind the house. Even in repose, a slight smile betrayed a deep contentment. This place would be loved and cared for. 'I'll help you with the garden,' he said.

'Just tidying,' she ordered. 'Don't change a thing. I love the wildness. My grandparents had a farm. Mixed arable and stock – it was great.' She paused. 'My grandpa worked like a dog, saved, speculated, owned bulls other farmers coveted to the point of sinfulness. It's thanks to him that I can take your home from under you, Mr Priest.'

'And did the farm have a wild bit for you?'

'It did.'

At last, the smile was completely real. In that moment, her expression was not pinned in place, was not a garment stuck on to cover nakedness. The woman loved the land, loved nature, loved Babs's child. He'd watched her trying not to interfere, had known that she was fighting her feelings for Cassie. What on earth had happened?

'I had a secret garden,' she told him. 'It was walled, and only Grandpa and I had keys. Oh, that was a magic place. In the summer, I would read in there. No one ever found me. I expect they knew where I was, because no one was allowed to worry. He thought worry was a sin of self-indulgence.'

'He had faith?'

'Meeting house. He was Quaker, but not rigid. There was no standing barefoot on cold kitchen floors for morning prayers in winter.' Again, she smiled. 'My friend Josie told me that her gran's teeth were set in ice on the windowsill, yet they had to stand and pray before break- fast, even on the most vicious of days. No shoes allowed. The fire couldn't be lit until prayers were over. No, my grandfather was brilliant. I would have been named Charity or Sarah had he been a dictator, but he allowed my mother to name me Leanne.' She stopped. 'Lily is my second name.'

'Ah. You have a lot of ells in there. Leanne Lily Latimer.'

'Bloody 'ell,' she answered. Then she giggled.

Michael studied her. The giggle was slightly rusty, as if it needed oil after long neglect. 'You should laugh more often,' he advised. 'You're very pretty when you laugh.'

Something touched Lily's spine. It wasn't real, wasn't visible, yet she felt a cold finger at the small of her back. 'Pretty can be a curse,' she said softly.

'Ready to talk?' he asked.

'No.'

'When you are . . .'

'Yes. If I am ever ready, I'll let you know.'

Philly burst through the bushes, Cassie in her arms. 'Lily,' she cried. Then she noticed the priest. 'Oh. Sorry, Father. I didn't know you'd be here – I thought Lily was measuring.'

'I am,' answered Lily. 'I'm measuring how peaceful the garden is.'

An expression of confusion sat on Philly's face. 'Stay, please,' she begged when Michael stood up. 'He's asked me again.'

Lily turned to her male companion. 'Philly's been babysitting for Babs, so we've come to know each other. Dave Barker's walked out on that cantankerous mother of his, and he's asked to move in with Philly.'

He smiled. 'Is that all? I'd have done the same if you hadn't offered me a few rooms here. What's the matter?' Philly and Lily. Rhyming names, two very different women. 'Philly, for goodness' sake—'

'He's a man,' she cried, cheeks burning. 'And I'm a woman.'

'She's right so far,' Lily said. 'You can't deny any of the above, Father.'

Michael laughed. 'You're worried about what people will think? *Honi soit qui mal y pense.* That means shame on those who think evil of others. Dave Barker is one of the most decent men I know. He's survived a harridan of a mother by all accounts, though it's rather unchristian of me to judge her. There's no harm in him. And you know he loves your cooking.'

Philly's face continued pink. 'I never lived with a man.'

'Your dad?' he asked.

'Don't remember him. He died when I was small. Oh, Lily—'

'Just take one day at a time,' Lily advised. 'That's what I do.' She stood, scooped up the child and went off to demonstrate the wonders of her garden.

'Father?'

'What, Philly?'

'They will talk. And I'm not used to that, not ready for it.'

Michael placed a hand on her head and blessed her. 'Go in the love of Christ and live your life. Take no notice of gossip, I beg you.' He walked back to the house.

Philly sat and pondered. They were right – Dave was a nice man, and he deserved a chance away from his cruel and thoughtless mother. It would be all right. She would make sure that it would be all right.

Maurice was trying not to listen to Paul. As usual, the man was indulging in gossip, and he seemed to be developing a tongue far sharper than Enid Barker's was reputed to be.

'Worms always turn,' Paul announced to his captive audience, a woman from the south end of the village. 'I said to Mo – didn't I, Mo? I said she had it coming. Anyway, he no more than ups and offs and moves in with Philomena Gallagher, the holiest Roman in history.'

Maurice gave no answer to Flapgob – his nickname for Paul. Many gays were total bitches – Mo had met enough of those on the cabaret circuit – but Paul was in a class all his own. 'Do you want a spray of lacquer?' Mo asked his customer. The answer arrived in the affirmative and, as he sprayed, Mo wished the mist could be directed into the face of his partner.

'No backbone, some men,' continued Paul. 'Should have gone years since. No way would I have stayed. These high-and-low lights need doing again if you're going to keep up with them, so shall I book you in?'

Mo knew he would have to do something about Paul very soon. As senior partner, Mo had the final say, but Paul, being a gobby type, always seemed to hack into discussion and get his own way. It would soon be time to terminate Paul's contract. Sally was a dream, but she wasn't a hairdresser, and there was enough work for two stylists. Where would he find a replacement?

At that very moment, Sally dashed in from the back of the shop, thrust a bulky envelope into Mo's hands, then ran out again, a handkerchief pressed to her nose and mouth.

'Excuse me.' Mo went into the store room. He opened the package, dropped its contents, picked up an item from the floor. A grin spread itself across his face as he stared down at the article resting on his palm. With no thought for anything but the matter that was literally in hand, he dashed upstairs, where he found Sally in near-hysterics. 'Calm down,' he begged. 'Come on, you're doing yourself no good. This is wonderful news, so kindly treat it as such, madam.' He placed the positive pregnancy test on the coffee table.

Sally continued to weep. 'But they'll find out. And they'll think we're both horrible people, that you're bisexual or something. You shouldn't have listened to Paul, and I shouldn't have listened to either of you.'

Mo laughed. 'We come clean. You're pregnant, I'm the father – oh, and I happen to be your husband. What's to worry about?'

'The lie we've all lived,' she sobbed. 'Pretending I'm the lodger, while it's really him. Carrying on as if you were gay just to get more customers.'

He sat next to her on the sofa, a hand across her shoulders. It had seemed a fairly good idea at the time. Gay hairdressers did well, and he and Paul were certainly partners on the entertainment front. People had assumed that they were a couple in their private life as well, and no one had bothered to put them right. The fact was that Paul had the small bedroom, while Mo and Sally slept in the larger room. 'I'll sort it out, love,' he said.

'Then there's all my manicuring and waxing – how am I going to manage Indian head massage when my belly's halfway across the road? And he'll have to go.'

She meant Paul, of course. Mo agreed, and not just because of his partner's vicious tongue. Paul was vying for joint ownership. And, worse still, he came on to Mo in front of customers, clearly enjoying himself by displaying affection and a closeness that did not truly exist – or, if it did, that travelled in one direction only.

'He's in love with you,' Sally added.

Mo suspected that she was right. 'Can I leave you for ten minutes?' he asked.

Sally nodded. 'I'm turning the stopwatch on,' she warned.

Mo dashed through the shop like a cat with its tail on fire. Paul, who was up to his ears in Mo's customers as well as his own, failed to stop him.

Mo arrived in Lily's shop. 'Every flower you have,' he

gasped. 'No, I'll have to be sensible. Just loads of flowers. We're pregnant.'

Lily closed her mouth sharply, came round the counter and guided the hairdresser to the customers' bench. 'Breathe,' she ordered.

He breathed. 'Me and Sally,' he said eventually. 'Baby.'

Lily had heard of this sort of thing. It usually involved close friends and an implement whose primary function was to baste roasting meats, but she didn't want to start asking detailed questions. 'Are you all right?' she asked after a few seconds.

He nodded. 'I'm not gay,' he advised her. 'Paul is, I'm not. Sally and I were married last year, and Paul hated it.'

'Does he love you?'

'No idea,' Mo lied. 'He loves himself, and he loves us performing our stage act, so that false closeness was allowed to become part of our other business. For a laugh, and for improved takings, I went along with it, but Sally was always in two minds.' He paused for breath. 'Women having their hair done actually like homosexuals. They don't feel challenged or judged by a gay man, you see. But I've got to tell everybody now. It's not going to be a walk in the park, Lily.'

Lily scratched her head. 'Right.'

'A notice on the window – I'm serious, honestly. A notice saying that Sally and I are married to each other and that we expect a happy event. I don't want her thinking about abortion just for the sake of the business and the drag act.' He stood up. 'Deliver flowers in abundance to my wife immediately. Are you any good at writing?'

'Calligraphy? Yes, I did a course.' It had been in another life and under a different name, but it was the truth. 'Listen. There's no need for a notice pinned to the window, lad. How many customers at present?'

He couldn't remember. His head was full of joy, trepidation and love for little Sally, who was to be a mother. 'A few.'

'More than two?'

'Six. Five, at least. She's upstairs having the screaming ab-dabs in case people start thinking I'm ambidextrous.'

'What?'

'Bisexual.'

Lily stood in front of him and held his hands tightly. 'Maurice, the only people that really matter are children. I have none, and I'm telling you now, I'd give my eye teeth for a baby. Now, you want people to know, right?'

'Yes.'

'Then go back in there and say it. The bush telegraph will spread the news for you. By midnight, there won't be a soul in the five villages who doesn't know. Let the customers do the work for you. Go in. Face him and them. Say it, then get rid of him, because you'll need that little bedroom for a nursery.'

'I'm scared, Lily.'

'Don't be. I'll be there in five minutes with the Chelsea Flower Show in a wheelbarrow. OK?'

He left. Lily stood for a while and wondered whether she had pointed him in the right direction. If the selfish Paul decided to make a scene, it might all backfire and put poor Mo in a very bad light. 'Come on,' she told herself as she started grabbing flowers. 'Colour scheme, plenty of greenery and a big smile.'

Minutes later, in Pour Les Dames, she found half a

dozen silent customers. Paul wasn't silent, though. He was ranting and raving about how he had given up his life for Mo, how he had stood by him, how Mo had cheated on him with Sally.

Lily placed the flowers on the reception desk. 'Shut up,' she shouted. 'Mo isn't gay, and he never was. He married the woman he loves last year, and you found that a bitter pill to swallow, because no one but you should be loved. You've always wanted him, and you can't have him.'

'What do you know?' he screamed. 'Bloody southerner, moving up here and telling us all what's what.'

'But she doesn't,' said a customer whose head was covered in foil wraps. 'If Mo says he's not gay, then he's not. He might be a good hairdresser and a bit camp, but he's a married man with a kiddy on board. So leave them alone.'

Paul was genuinely upset. As long as he'd had a foot in Mo's life, he'd been in with a chance. The intention to turn Maurice had been his *raison d'être* for as long as he could remember. Their drag act was the best on the circuit, while they made a formidable team when it came to hair. 'I'll move out then,' he announced, lower lip trembling. 'But I'm not quitting Pour Les Dames. If he wants rid of me, it's two verbals, then a written warning.' He flounced out of the salon. After a few seconds, he was back. 'Plus, I'm a partner. Let him put that in his pregnancy test and smoke it.' With his nose in the air, he stamped out again.

The babbling began. One woman said she'd been under the dryer since about 1947, while a second worried that her hair would be bleached silver if the wraps didn't come off. Another customer, whose hair had not yet been touched, rushed out of the shop. With any luck, the news would be spreading already, Lily hoped.

Instinct drove Lily the rest of the way. She tore off foils, rinsed hair, began to blow-dry. The woman whose life had been spent under hot air was given a basket into which she might put her rollers. It took an hour, but everyone was very pleased with the results.

'Have you done this before, love?' asked Valda Turnbull.

'Yes,' gasped Lily. 'Let me catch my breath.' She inhaled deeply for a few seconds. 'Babs is a hairdresser. I've helped her when staff let her down on odd occasions. I'm no expert, but I cope.' She smiled when the clients gave her a standing ovation. Then she remembered the flowers. 'Bugger,' she said before gathering them up in her arms. 'I don't think Mo will mind if we don't charge for your hair today. Go and drink the health of these two people and their baby. Use your hair money.' She went upstairs.

Sally was asleep in her husband's arms. Small noises from the other bedroom betrayed the fact that Paul was packing his bags.

'Customers?' asked Mo.

'All gone. I did what I could, and I didn't charge them. Paul left after I said what needed saying. The news is spreading like an oil slick in the English Channel. It'll be OK.'

Mo's eyes were wet. 'Thanks, love.'

She understood why people thought he was gay, because he was a beautiful man. He probably looked fabulous in drag. 'Babs is a hairdresser,' she told him. 'The little I know I was taught by her.'

'Specialty?'

'Babs?'

He nodded. 'Yes. We all have a favourite area – mine's cutting.'

'So's hers, Mo. But I know she loved colouring as well.'

His mind was working overtime. If Babs could get a sitter, she could take Paul's place. Paul would not leave quietly, but he might be disturbed by the sudden arrival of a third hairdresser. Mo would have a word with Babs as soon as possible.

Lily put the flowers in three vases.

'Lovely,' said Mo.

Lily left. The nice thing about her new job was the pleasure people took from receiving a bunch of flowers. There was also the joy she got when delivering. All in all, life was beginning to improve.

I don't know what they expected me to do with the shit they delivered this lunchtime. You never know who's peed or spat in it when it comes to us in isolation.

There were all sorts on my previous landing. Paedophiles, serial killers, a nurse who killed more than he saved. Should be in the nuthouse, something called Munchausen's by proxy. Bollocks. He's just another bad bugger.

Dan came to see me last week. No prison record, though I have enough on him to put him away pronto and for a long time. So now I'm thinking in here and he's thinking out there. Two heads? I know a lot more than two people who'd kill a granny for a few quid...

Four

He would come back. She knew he'd come back, because he had nowhere else to go. Staying with Philomena Gallagher? That would never last – Philly Gallagher was a Roman, all rosary beads, prayer books, choir practice and Holy Days of Obligation. As for the rest of the village – who would want a fat, balding idiot to become part of the household? Enid smiled. He'd be back, red-faced and begging, before the week was out.

He'd taken the rest of his stuff, had used bin bags because Enid hadn't allowed him to borrow the suitcases. After his little tantrum – and even that had been quiet – he had gone about the business of leaving in silent mode, never answering a question, refusing to react whenever she had railed at him. She was all alone now. Except for Mary Turnbull, of course. Valda's mother-in-law came in on a daily basis. She cooked and did basic cleaning; best of all, she liked a good old natter. Without realizing it, Enid was in danger of becoming dependent on another Roman, albeit a lapsed one.

Enid Barker adjusted her reading glasses. The *Daily Mail* wasn't much fun these days, since she was alone in the mornings until Mary arrived, so there was no one with whom she might discuss the contents of the paper.

Philly came up to give her her breakfast, but Enid would have nothing to do with her, and stayed put in her bedroom until she had left. Let the bloody woman interfere in her son's life if she wanted to, but there would be no blessing from this quarter. As for the idea of discussing the situation with Dave's landlady – Enid would sooner eat worms on toast.

She went to sit at the window, taking her usual commanding role in the village. And that was another thing: Philly Gallagher was going around inventing FADS, which was short for St Faith's Amateur Dramatic Society, but with the word 'saint' left out. Dave had joined. Enid tried to picture him as the hero in something Shakespearean, but she failed to manage it. They'd keep him behind the scenes where he could do least damage. If they had any sense, that was. She sniffed. Catholicism and sense didn't belong in the same sentence.

Lily Latimer was still rushing back and forth across the road at least once a day. She'd bought the priest's house, so her common sense wasn't up to the mark. A great rambling place like that for just one person? Daft. Perhaps her friend and the kiddy would move in with her, though it was widely believed that Babs meant to stay in the flat above the florist's shop. Even with three potential occupants, the house would be empty.

Babs had started going out with a man. She'd been half an hour in Lancashire, and she was already on the make. The child was blonde, which fact proved that some people had good luck, as her mother was a redhead and redheads weren't everyone's cup of arsenic. God alone knew who the father was . . .

Enid shifted uncomfortably in the chair. Her own son had called her a whore, and after all she'd done for him.

There'd be no stupid shop without her, no safety net for her well-read but ill-qualified son. He knew she wouldn't sell; he knew she needed the income. He knew other things, too. Yes, she'd had male friends, yes, some of them had been generous with their money, but what had the alternative been? Give him up for adoption and work full time? Enid had been a martyr to that kid, and this was how he repaid her generosity.

It was true that she was unable to name his father, because she had enjoyed the company of several grateful friends at the time of his conception, but she had not been a prostitute. Prostitutes did it every night, sometimes during the days as well. They were dirty and careless, often had teeth missing and were forced to sell themselves cheaply. She had brought her friends home and had never worked the streets.

A whore, indeed. What did he know about it? He was probably still a virgin, with no idea about life. Oh yes, he'd be back. But did she want him back? Could she stand the sight of his face etched so deeply with patience while he dealt with her needs? Did she need the company of a man who was wading through *War and Peace* for the second or third time? He believed himself to be a cut above his own mother, but he certainly wasn't. Had he been half a man, he would have done something about his appearance long before now.

The door flew inward to reveal a breathless Mary Turnbull. 'Enid,' gasped the newcomer.

'What? Get yourself in, woman. Are you ill?'

The grey head shook. 'No, love, I'm all right. But Sally Byrne isn't.'

Enid's ears pricked up. 'Why? What's up with her?

Isn't she the one who does hands, feet and whoops-a-daisies in the hairdressers'?'

'Aye.' Mary was still struggling to regain a degree of composure. She wasn't completely sure about the 'whoops-a-daisies', but she had a vague idea that it might be a euphemism for bikini waxing. 'Pregnant.'

'And?' The pregnancy of an unwed woman was normal in the twenty-first century; had been unremarkable for years.

'The dad is the one they call Mo. Maurice Jones.'

'Eh?'

Mary sat down. 'I've got some yellow fish and eggs for our dinner. Nice bit of haddock with a poached egg—'

'Never mind that. Isn't he queer?'

Mary shrugged her shoulders. 'Hard to tell these days. Some of them swing both ways, some are what they call gay, but they still have babies.'

Enid had read about this kind of carry-on in the newspapers. 'Should be ashamed,' she pronounced.

Mary said nothing. She'd heard something of Enid's past, so she had to be careful not to go too far.

'They use like a syringe thingy, don't they?' Enid went on. 'I suppose they look at photos of naked men, then bingo – here come the kids. They must put it in a cup or something like—'

'Oh, stop it,' said Mary. 'Or I'll never be able to have coffee in that place again when I go to get my hair done. Anyway, there's more to it. Pin your lug'oles back, kid.' She went on to tell the full tale. 'You see,' she concluded, 'with you being sat up here like this, you see it all, but you hear nowt. Time you had another go at being outside, love. I'll help you if you like.'

'I'm all right where I am, ta.' Still, perhaps Mary had a point.

'There's more,' continued Enid's new companion. 'That florist.'

'Oh aye? Her with the pretty face that manages to look like a smacked bum?'

'That's the one. Buying St Faith's presbytery—'

'I knew that.'

Mary smiled knowingly. 'Yes, but I bet you never knew that Father Walsh will be living there and all.'

Enid's jaw dropped. 'With her?'

'Yup. He's got a church house in one of the other villages, but he'll be handy for St Faith's when he needs to be if he sleeps here part of the week. Now.' She looked from side to side as if half expecting to be overheard by some invisible presence. 'I heard Valda talking to our Tom. She said the priest looks at Lily Latimer in a funny way.'

'Funny? What sort of funny?'

'Not funny ha-ha for a kick-off. More like funny isn't-she-gorgeous. And she gives him free altar flowers. And they sit talking in the back garden for hours on end. And he's going very easy on penances. If you go to confession, he'll give you five Hail Marys, not a sign of an Our Father. You could go in and say you'd set fire to the village, but you'd get just the same penance. He's not listening.'

That had been a lot of ands. 'How do you know?'

Mary snorted. 'Not first-hand, that's for sure. I've not been near since 1992, but I know folk who do go. Like my daughter-in-law.'

'What are you thinking?'

The visitor snorted again. 'Pretty young woman,

handsome young man. He might be a priest, but he's still human. They often had live-in housekeepers in the old days, but they were always ancient and ugly. She's not old, is she?'

'She's not, Mary.' There was a lot happening, and binoculars weren't enough. 'Get me that catalogue,' ordered Enid. 'I want a lightweight wheelchair if you're willing to push.'

'Course I will.' Mary fetched the catalogue, then set the kettle to boil for elevenses. 'With a wheelchair, you can sit on the village green and hear all the news. And we can do the shopping together, go down to the next block and buy your meat and veg. If we ever get that supermarket, you'll be able to go inside, up and down the aisles – they have special trolleys for the disabled.'

But Enid wasn't listening. Sally Byrne and Maurice Jones were down below. They were hugging each other. 'Come and look at this, Mary,' she called.

Mary joined her new-found friend. 'Enid?'

'What?'

'Makes no sense, me going home. I can't be doing with Valda, you know. We get on great, thee and me, eh? And there's Dave's empty room. What do you say?'

Enid nodded thoughtfully. With Mary in residence, she'd get her meals on time, wouldn't have to wait for Philly Gallagher, wouldn't be alone. As for Dave – if he wanted to come back, there'd be no room for him. 'If you like,' she replied. 'Move in when you're ready.'

Mary Turnbull relaxed. She would be away from her daughter-in-law, but near enough to see her grandchildren. This place would suit her down to the ground, because the ground floor was the Reading Room, and that was a good place to hear gossip. And Enid and she were like peas in a pod: both interested in what went on in Eagleton.

She opened a box of biscuits. The future certainly looked brighter.

Paul Smith was not in the best of moods. He had loved Maurice Jones for years, and had tried to hide his feelings, but his emotions seemed to have become swamped by absolute fury since Sally's pregnancy had been revealed. Life had changed, and the changes were certainly not for the better.

For a start, there was the business of finding somewhere to live. A guest house in Edgworth was all very well for now, but it wasn't the same as having his own kitchen and bathroom. Yes, he had shared those amenities with two other people, but he had been able to eat what he wanted, when he wanted and where he wanted.

At the house known as Cherrymead, breakfast, lunch, tea and supper were served at certain times and in the dining room. There was some leeway, but not enough for a man who sometimes worked late or started the day early. He had to find a flat, so he decided to have a word with Chas Boswell. Chas was a decent sort who made no judgements about people's lifestyles, and he might have a suggestion for Paul. With fingers crossed, the ex-lodger from 9 Fullers Walk made his way up the stairs into Chas's living area.

'What the hell happened?' Chas asked in his usual direct manner. 'That's a bloody good business you and Mo have.'

Paul sat down. 'Not for much longer – I can't work in that kind of atmosphere. He married her last year, didn't he? But we said nothing, because people had always seen me and Mo as a couple. Sally went along with it, but she made fun of me a lot, and Mo – well, he's always known I loved him. But what do I matter, eh? I'm just one half of a drag act and the gifted half of a salon. What the hell do I have to offer apart from my genius?'

There was a bitchiness in Paul that Eve had noticed when he'd done her hair. He was clearly a bitter man, but Chas remained as impartial as he could. He'd learned long ago about the frailties and faults in human nature, so he wasn't going to start acting differently now. 'Right. What can I do for you, lad? I can see you're not what we might call happy.'

'I was thinking about the empty shop, Chas.'

'And?'

'I could set up my own business.'

Chas sat down in the other armchair. 'Look, Paul. With the best will in the world, I can't have two hair-dressers on one parade – it couldn't possibly work. You'd have number three at daggers drawn with number nine, and you'd all suffer.'

'I wouldn't be a hairdresser.' Paul paused for a moment. 'Actually, I would, but I'd offer a mobile service to folk who want their hair done at home – people who are disabled or have kids and can't get out. A beautician, I'd be, because I can do false nails, hair extensions, facials – all kinds of things. If he thinks he's put a stop to me, he's bloody wrong, Chas. Nice big purple van, I'll have. Red lips on each side, name of the business will be Impressions. I'm not finished, nowhere near. Anyway, there you have it as far as the shop is concerned. It could be either fish and chips or a bakery, and nothing to do with me. Some shopkeepers prefer a lock-up and won't want the flat.'

'Oh. Right.' Chas wondered how Fullers Walk would react to the stench of chip fat, though he was prepared to listen. 'So why is it either or, mate?'

Paul shrugged. 'I've a friend who's a baker, another who wants to set up a chippy. He was brought up dipped in batter – family business. His dad would probably put up money for fittings, so that shouldn't be a problem. Would we be allowed a chip shop here?'

'I don't see why not,' said Chas. 'But I reckon a bakery would do better. Would the cooking be done on the premises? I'd have to get the fire advice people out to check if we're having ovens or deep fryers.'

'No. My friend's dad has a few shops dotted about, and he told Joey he could find another one if he wanted to. As long as it's in a good place, his dad will do the baking at the unit in Bolton and deliver stock to Joey's shop. Joey's OK. He's honest. I might be a partner whether it's chips or cakes. And Mo will just have to buy me out.'

Chas liked Mo. 'So Mo's going to be short of a hairdresser?'

Paul raised his shoulders for a second. 'He told me to get out, and I've got out. He'll not find another like me in a hurry, and that's for sure. I'm not stopping there, Chas. He knows I love him, but I realize now there's definitely no chance for me. I thought ... well, I always hoped he'd come to his senses and pick me over her, but it seems he's not gay after all.'

Chas didn't know what to say, so he stuck to business. 'Look. Let me make this a bit easier for you. You don't have to be a partner in any shop next door. If you can find somebody who wants number three as a lock-up, I can separate the two issues – you rent the flat, and the other person rents the shop. For a kick-off, there's this purple van you're on about. That's not going to come cheap even if you get it second-hand. You'll need some kind of storage system for your hair stuff, manicures, false nails – all that palaver.'

Paul nodded. 'Yes, and I don't use cheap products. But just think – with a wedding, I could do a demo a few weeks earlier, get all the ladies together with a few glasses of wine – one wedding could make a bomb on the grooming front.' He counted on his fingers. 'Bride, her mother, groom's mother, bridesmaids, anyone else who wants to look good . . .' He would show Mo Jones, by God he would.

'Don't get carried away yet,' Chas advised. 'And are you sure you want to punish yourself by living so close to Mo?'

Paul had no intention of punishing himself. His intention was to undercut prices, to leaflet the new estates and to preclude Mo when it came to picking up new business. The bridal idea would be his exclusively, and Mo would come to realize after a while that Paul was the true star of the show.

'What about the drag act?' Chas was asking now.

'He can drag off,' replied Paul tersely. 'He can manage without me.'

'And *Britain's Got Talent*?' Chas knew that Paul wanted to be recognized, wanted that spot on TV. 'You'd be good together.'

'No chance,' Paul snapped, standing up. 'That's all over and done with. I'll get back to you, Chas, when I've

95

spoken to Joey and his dad. The sooner I get out of that guest house the better.'

'You'll need other stuff as well as the van,' the landlord reminded him. 'The flats are all let unfurnished, as you know.'

'Mo will buy me out,' came the answer. 'And he'll be sorry.'

Chas was sitting alone with his thoughts when Eve came in. She studied him for a moment. 'Is this you thinking and brooding? Well, forget it, because we're buying that house even if it's falling down. Don't start coming over all I'm-not-sure.'

Chas looked at her. 'I don't like what's going on, Eve. Paul wants to move next door.'

'Gay Paul? Moving to number three?'

Chas nodded.

'Bloody hell. So the partnership is definitely dissolved, eh? I mean, he must have known he had no chance with Mo. We thought Sally was the lodger in the small bedroom, but they fooled us all. Did he really believe he could turn Mo gay?'

'Love's blind,' said Chas.

'That's what I keep telling myself whenever I look at you,' she said, her eyes laughing. 'But seriously, Paul has to be centre stage. He's always thought he was God's gift to Pour Les Dames and that Mo was there just to make up the numbers. As for poor Sally – how must she have felt with everybody thinking her husband was gay? They say they did it for the sake of the business, but Paul must have twisted Mo's arm.'

'Right up his back,' muttered Chas. 'Oh God, Eve – I told him he could go ahead. What have I done?'

'Not much. Just started a turf war, that's all. Never mind. We'll just buy bullet-proof vests, eh?'

Dave Barker and Philomena Gallagher had more in common than either had expected. They enjoyed reading, crosswords, jigsaw puzzles, gardening and some television programmes. Most of all, both liked to cook and eat. While Philly was not slim, she was by no means obese, yet they studied together determinedly in order to come up with an eating plan that would benefit both without leaving stomachs feeling hollow. The idea arose out of Dave's sudden decision to lose his spare tyre, though Philly was only too pleased to try to lose a few pounds of her own. They raided the Reading Room for books on the subject, discussed likes and dislikes, arrived at compromises and one or two split decisions.

Their routine established itself without any real effort. Both rose early and, since Dave no longer had to look after Enid, they went to the shop together. Breakfast was taken in the Reading Room, then Philly prepared the day's snacks while Dave sorted newspapers. He vacuumed, she dusted. He ordered books, she checked till receipts. Like a well-oiled machine, they ran the business and their home life in perfect harmony. It was as if they had always been together, as each seemed to be aware of the other's unspoken requirements.

Dave was so blissfully happy that he waited for it all to end, because life so far hadn't been like this. If he'd enjoyed school, his mother always spoiled the day for him as soon as he arrived home. If someone called and asked him out to play, she would say he was too busy. He would never be able to count the times when Enid had stopped him reading, when she had torn a book from his hands and thrown it into the fire, when she had screamed at him because reading was for lazy people.

Philly, too, was happy. She had someone to talk to, someone to cook for, someone who liked to cook for her. There was no embarrassment, because they made room for each other. It was almost as if they followed some unwritten timetable regarding the bathroom, as they seldom clashed. The job she had always loved now stretched across the full day, though she sometimes went home for a rest at lunchtime. Despite the fact that she begged him repeatedly to do the same in turn, Dave seldom left the shop. He was happy among books, was keen to order and obtain for customers even the most remote of subjects and titles. Philly admired him greatly, because he was a dedicated man.

The Reading Room continued as busy as ever, though the heat meant that a couple of tables were set outside the shop, and people sat there quite happily with newspapers, books and magazines, most of which had been purchased inside. Dave, always with an eye to business, turned blind when the occasional customer arrived with a book obtained elsewhere. Such items were often exchanged, but Dave maintained his silence. Like Chas Boswell, his knowledge of human nature stretched beyond the breaking of small rules. As long as his business survived, Dave would fail to notice the odd sin or two.

The arrival of the new computer was much appreciated, particularly by the older clientele. Youngsters came to help, and many Eagletonians were suddenly in touch with relatives all over the globe. 'I made the right decision,' Dave whispered to his assistant one sunny afternoon. Screams of glee had spilled out all over the place when an old man had finally contacted a nephew in New Zealand. 'Life gets better, Philly.' Since his mother's exit from the lower floor, Dave's shop had become the chief meeting place for folk of all ages. At last, he felt that his life might just be a success after all. 'Yes, Philly, it gets better.'

'It does,' she replied, though she realized immediately that she had spoken too soon.

When the car hit the dog, Dave was sitting outside while Philly, who was learning how to use Microsoft Word, lingered in the back of the shop until all hell broke loose. She ran out quickly, overturning a stack of newly arrived novels in her haste. Dave had picked up the animal and was beginning to run towards the vet's house across the way. She joined him, noticing that his shirt was soaked in blood, and that the dog's tongue hung out of the side of its mouth. 'I'm coming with you,' she told her employer. Then she looked over her shoulder. 'Look after the shop,' she told no one in particular. One of the dog's hind legs looked crushed. A trickle of blood escaped from between strong white teeth.

It was a long afternoon. Philly and Dave sat together in the vet's waiting room. They scarcely noticed that they were holding hands, as both found themselves near to tears. Dave had always loved dogs, though he had never been allowed to have one. Philly, too, was a lover of animals. The reason for not having a dog of her own was a simple one – she went to work, and dogs liked company. 'It has to live,' she said repeatedly. It wasn't an old dog; wasn't ready to shuffle off just yet.

At last, Tim Mellor came through from the treatment room. 'I had to amputate the left rear leg,' he told them sadly. 'It was too mangled to save. Monitors appear to be saying I've stopped all internal bleeding, but it's still a waiting game. She isn't chipped.'

'What?' asked Dave.

'I have a little machine that tells me whether the dog has a microchip in a shoulder – it's a sign of a caring owner. There isn't a chip. She's about two years old, mostly Labrador, and she's a fighter. I'll have to keep her here for a day or two, but if we don't find the owner I won't get paid. That's a risk a vet has to take from time to time.'

Philly and Dave looked at each other. 'We'll have her,' they said in unison. 'I'll pay,' Dave added.

The vet smiled. 'Do you realize what you'd be taking on? Labs eat anything and everything. They're dedicated thieves and good at their job. On the plus side, a bitch is very faithful, and a Labrador bitch is the best animal on earth. She'll love you unconditionally for her whole life.'

Philly sniffed back a tear. 'And the leg?'

'She'll manage. If arthritis sets in later on, we fit her with wheels. While she's young, she'll hop along quite happily. They accept the loss of a limb and take it in their stride – excuse the pun. Now.' He sat at the desk. 'I have to try to find the owner, since I am legally obliged to do that. But I have to say I hope you don't lose her to someone who didn't care enough to have her chipped.' He smiled. 'If you pay, it'll be five hundred. For anyone else, it's double.' He liked these people, had always liked them. If anyone deserved the love of a Lab, it was Dave from the Reading Room. 'Go home. Any change in her condition, and I'll let you know right away. I promise.'

They returned to the shop. A grizzled old man gave them their takings, apologized for not being able to use the till, and asked about the dog.

'She's fighting and doing well,' Philly told him. 'When she's better, if no one claims her, she'll live at my house. But she's lost a leg.'

The old man tutted. 'It was Derek Boswell who knocked her down – he's gone home in bits. I'll let him know on the way past that she looks as if she might pull through. Nice lad for a Scouser.'

Alone in the shop, Dave and Philly had coffee laced with brandy. 'We can't do anything,' she moaned. 'I wish I could have stayed with her. She needs to know someone wants her alive.'

Dave patted her hand. 'You think Tim Mellor'll leave her? I've known him stop with a pet rat until he was sure he'd won. It'll be all right, love. And we'll have a grand dog. Pity we can't call her Cassidy after Hopalong Cassidy. Babs's daughter's Cassie, so we need another name.'

'Skippy?' suggested Philly.

'The bush kangaroo? Excellent. Let's drink to that.'

Neither realized that love was claiming them, that the accident with the dog had sealed their fate. They were just two good friends drinking coffee together. Weren't they?

Paul made sure that the salon was busy before he came to claim his property. He banged about in the room behind the shop, throwing things into boxes and bags, enjoying every moment of his self-indulgent tantrum.

'Don't worry,' Mo advised Paul's customers. 'I'll see to all of you, and there'll be another stylist here as soon as poss.'

Sally apologized to a woman whose head she was massaging, then took herself off behind the scenes.

'You're behaving like a child,' she told Paul. 'Stop stamping about and try behaving like an adult for a change.'

With a hand on his hip, he stood still and looked her up and down. 'Are you sure you know where he's been?' he asked loudly. 'I think he swings both ways, love. Best get yourself a blood test, make sure you're not HIV positive. Be on the safe side.' The silence from the salon was total.

She crossed the small space between them and swiped him across the face with the flat of her hand. 'He's a dozen times the man you are, you big stupid girl. You're not needed and you won't be missed. Someone is being trained as we speak – well, as we quarrel.'

Mo dashed in. 'You all right?' he asked his wife.

Sally laughed, though the sound was hollow. 'I've taken on bigger women than this one, Mo. He's a mean-spirited, nasty bit of near-human dross.' She addressed the culprit again. 'Get out,' she roared. 'Clear off before I really lose my rag.'

Paul straightened his spine. 'I'll be living at number three,' he said menacingly. 'And plenty of my customers will want their hair done at home, because I have always been the better stylist.' He turned to Mo. 'Without me, you'd be nowhere. I want my investment back.'

Mo reached into the pocket of his white overall and passed a cheque and a sheet of paper to Paul. 'There you are – every penny and with interest. Sign here.'

Paul obeyed silently, then threw the signed document at Mo's feet. 'Traitor,' he hissed.

Mo smiled coldly. 'I've heard on the grapevine that Mr Clegg doesn't want a shop here. Joey's looking over a place in Bromley Cross as an outlet for his bakery. Unless your chip fryer turns up trumps, there's a good chance that Tim Mellor will take the shop unit and the flat. He'll use the upstairs as business premises, because he wants to use his house as a home – number three would suit him down to the ground.'

'And up to the flat,' Sally added. 'Storage, operating rooms, waiting areas – he's very keen. It's a good place for a vet.'

Paul's jaw dropped. He snapped it back into its rightful place, then left the premises by the rear door.

Mo looked at his tearful wife. 'Come on, love. You know you've always said that massage is good for the giver as well as for the receiver.' He led her back into the shop. 'As you were,' he told his silent customers. 'Show's over.'

But the show had moved to the off-licence. 'Is it true?' Paul asked Chas, who was standing behind safety glass.

'Is what true?'

'That Tim Mellor is after number three?'

Chas cleared his throat. 'Well, if it's not going to be your bakery or your chip shop, he'll be having it. I hear Clegg's not interested, so where do you stand on the fish-and-chip front?'

Paul felt his shoulders sagging. 'They don't want it,' he said reluctantly. 'So can I still have the flat while you find someone who needs a lock-up?'

Chas shook his head. 'It's stood empty ever since Greenhalgh's closed down. I'm losing rent, Paul. And I'd rather let it all to one person whether they live in or not. The vet needs all the space. It was only as a favour that I said you could rent the flat if you found someone for downstairs.'

'And I can't open as a hairdresser?'

'No.'

'Since when has Tim Mellor been interested?'

'No idea. You'd have to ask him.'

Nothing loath, Paul crossed the road and knocked on the vet's door. He pleaded for the flat, then for a room in the flat, but was turned down straight away. 'Why?' he asked.

'Because there will be someone living upstairs, and that someone will be caring for sick animals while I reclaim my home. The second bedroom at number three will be for storage. There's no room for you.'

Paul thought about the job. 'I could do it. I'd be there every night to keep an eye on things.'

The vet was not going to be fooled. He didn't like this man, didn't expect him to have feelings for animals or for his fellow humans. 'No,' he replied firmly. 'The person living in will be a qualified veterinary nurse. Sorry.'

Paul found himself standing at the wrong side of a closed door. He was furious and had to force himself not to kick the gate as he stormed out. There was definitely a plot on. Well. There was only one thing to do, and that was to advertise for lodgings. Someone in one of the villages would take him in. The property would have to provide parking for his Impressions van, but there must be someone somewhere who wanted a clean, tidy lodger.

Back at Pour Les Dames, he sneaked in the back way and continued to pack up his belongings. No longer in a position of power, he had lost the urge to make a point through noise. There was a lump in his throat. He had given his all to this shop and his heart to Maurice Jones. There had been a suggestion that the place should be called Alias Smith and Jones, but Mo had insisted on the French rubbish.

Depleted and deflated, he left quietly and packed his property in his old van. It wasn't over. It was never over till the fat lady sang, and from now on Mo would be singing alone. Paul would miss the drag shows, but he had to admit that his partner had been the stronger performer. But Paul had been the mover and shaker, the power behind the act. He had not been appreciated, and that was why he felt so injured.

It wasn't fair. None of it was fair. But he would find a way to get even. If it took him years, he would bloody well show them all.

The dog went home with Philly and Dave, her new would-be owners. No one had responded to advertisements and flyers, so Skippy was theirs by default, though for a while they were concerned in case the neglectful owner turned up and tried to claim her. Derek Boswell came to visit several times. He was terribly upset at first, but he was finally convinced by Dave that there was little he might have done, because Skippy had come from nowhere, and all the witnesses sitting outside the Reading Room had verified that fact.

According to her new family, the dog had really come from heaven. They doted on her, used a towel as a sling to help her walk until all the stitches had been removed, fed her on the best cuts of meat and spoiled her thoroughly. She adapted quickly, and was soon chasing a ball up and down the back garden of Philly's cottage. A natural lunatic, she was even funnier without her fourth leg, and many a happy hour was spent laughing at her antics.

The pair sat with Derek and watched her as she adjusted to life on three legs. 'She's a tripod,' said Dave.

'Though I doubt she'd stay still long enough to be any use as a camera stand. Hey – Derek?'

'What?'

'The vet said Labradors are special. You could put two hundred dogs in a field, and the Labs would find each other. They aren't like most dogs.'

'Canadian wolves,' Derek told them. 'Trained themselves to bring in fishermen's nets, got fed by the fishermen, got tame. They volunteered. Supposed to be sensible, but this one looks daft enough to me.' He stood up. 'I looked Labs up on the Internet after the accident. If I ever have a dog, it'll be one of these. Oh, and thanks. I'd never have lived with myself if you hadn't let me pay the vet.'

'Are you going?' Philly asked.

But Derek lingered, his face colouring as he asked, 'How's that florist getting on?'

Philly frowned slightly. Here was another one who was interested in the newcomer. The vet had asked after her, this young accountant was clearly interested, while the parish priest, sworn to celibacy, came over rather strange whenever Lily Latimer was in view. 'She's all right,' she answered. 'Buying the presbytery – aren't your parents buying the cottage at the other side of the church?'

'Yes. Anyway, thanks again for letting me pay. It makes me feel ... not better, but more satisfied with myself.'

'We know,' said Philly. He was a decent chap who seemed to care about what his car had done to the animal. 'See you later, Derek.'

The gate closed. Like a long-married couple, Philly

and Dave sat until the sun began to sink. 'Am I cooking or are you?' Dave asked.

'Your turn. Spaghetti, I think you said. Use the whole-meal – that's better for us than the usual stuff.' She could scarcely remember life before Dave. He was like a longed-for drink of water that had been presented to her after weeks in the Sahara. 'We'll try to finish that jigsaw later, if you like.'

Dave stopped in his tracks. 'The five-thousand-piecer?'

'Yes. Why?'

'Because there're about eight bits missing. Skippy ate them.' He went indoors to prepare supper.

Philly sat for a while with Skippy, who lay on a blanket next to the chair. In this moment, woman and beast were truly content. 'I can't imagine life without you and your dad,' she said absently. After delivering the words, they seemed to echo in her brain for several seconds until she noticed them. Happiness was not something she had expected or sought, but it was won-derful. She was a Catholic, while he used to be a Meth-odist. Did any of it matter?

The house was finally hers. Lily started painting, carrying swatches of material into various rooms, buying bits and pieces for the kitchen. She felt like a child who had been given free rein with blank paper, because this place was hers and only hers. Onto a blank canvas, she could paint her own life – her own future. Nothing could be done about the past, but her house would be another bandage for wounds that should begin to heal, in part at least.

Because it had been a home for priests, there had not

been a great deal of attention paid to decor and furniture. Everything was basic, adequate and terribly plain, so she decided to go mad with colour. With the same neutral carpet throughout the whole house, she achieved continuity at floor level, then brought into various equations a portfolio she had used years ago, when she had been something else and someone else. Having kept up with trends, Lily knew what was in, what was out, what was for ever.

Babs was delighted to join in. She left Cassie with Philly, Dave and their three-legged friend so that she could come across in the early evenings and splash a bit of paint about. The splashing had to be minimal, though, because although the new carpets were covered in film used by professional decorators, paint was an item that had to be tamed.

'What do you think of the red?' Lily asked. She was standing in the dining room, scarf tied around her hair, a large blob of paint on her right cheek.

'Suits you,' declared Babs, dabbing ineffectually at her friend's red face. 'And I love that huge black flower on the white paper.' This was Lily's true forte. She could probably have thrown a few stones on the floor and still made the place look fabulous. 'Curtains?' Babs asked.

'Muslin floating in the breeze when the French window's open. I'll get thicker ones for the winter. No double glazing, because to destroy these windows would be a capital offence. Reclaimed wood for the table, chairs with full, padded backs, black and white crockery, chandelier low over the table.'

'Sideboard?'

'Will be just that – a board to the side – reclaimed wood again. Just a long table on which to place dishes and so forth. I'll store everything in the kitchen – it's big enough.'

'Will you be giving dinner parties?'

Lily shrugged. 'Perhaps.' She knew only that she was enjoying doing a job she had loved for years, a hobby she could now pursue exclusively behind closed doors. There would be no photographs in magazines, no interviews, no TV people asking her to help with a makeover programme. All her talent must be hidden in here, so she was making the most of it. 'We're losing daylight,' she advised her companion. 'Time to tidy up and go home.' She didn't want to go, but she couldn't stay here yet, because she was waiting for her bed. It was to have a circular wrought-metal headpiece that would emphasize the window against which she planned to place it.

'Hello? Can I come in?'

Babs noticed the slight flush on her friend's unpainted cheek. There was something going on here, because Father Walsh's face was similarly stained when he entered the dining room. 'My goodness,' he said when he saw the paint. 'What are you making here? A bordello?'

'He knows nothing about decor,' said Lily in a deliberately sad tone. 'Such a sheltered life these men of God lead.'

'But red?' he asked.

'This is to be the room for flagellation,' Lily told him. 'We have enough space to cater for the needs of most men.'

She was laughing at him. Inside, where it hid its face, her humour was planning to escape from prison. 'Oh dear,' he responded mournfully. 'Shall I look for lodgings elsewhere?'

Lily wanted to say yes, but she couldn't. If she did answer in the affirmative, he might guess the reason for her reluctance to share a roof with him, albeit on a part-time basis. By ignoring his silly question, she was laying herself open to ... To what? He was a nice man, a good man. He had a cleft in his chin that put her in mind of Kirk Douglas, though the rest of his face was less rugged than the film star's. He still had untidy hair, the sort of hair she wanted to comb— She ordered herself to stop it. This was a priest, and nothing would happen, because nothing could happen. He could comb his own bloody hair if he wanted to look human – he was a grown man, after all.

She stared through the window. Blackbirds were making their nightly arrangements, quarrelling over who slept where and who had let the kids fly away. The scent of honeysuckle tickled her nose, and she experienced a swell of emotion when she looked out at the beginning of dusk. 'Reminds me of my grandfather's house,' she said quietly. 'He had apple trees.'

Michael heard the sadness and decided to lighten the mood. 'First meeting of FADS next week,' he announced. 'You'll do the stage for us, won't you? Lily?'

She turned slowly. 'Why?'

'Your forte,' he answered lamely.

'How do you know I'm not a budding Vanessa Redgrave?'

The priest shrugged. 'Because Redgraves don't bud – they're delivered from the womb with microphones and clapperboards. Do you want to act?'

'I don't know. When I do know, Philly will know.'

Realizing that he had been dismissed, Father Michael Walsh left the room.

'What's up?' Babs asked.

'Don't ask.'

'I have asked. What do you want me to do? Take back my words, put them on toast and have them for supper?'

Lily simply lowered her head and shook it.

'There's stuff happening, isn't there?' Babs whispered. 'He looks like a lovelorn lion – too much hair. And you're acting like a teenager waiting to be asked out for a date. It's chemistry. Like you noticed between me and Pete.'

'It can't be.'

'Cupid doesn't know the difference between priests and mere mortals. Look, you'd better tell him to stay elsewhere when he's in Eagleton.'

'Can't.'

'Can't or won't?'

'I don't know.' That, at least, was the truth.

Outside the church, Michael clutched to his chest the Holy Eucharist, the small circle of unleavened bread that incorporated the sacrifice made by Jesus for all mankind. He was taking it and Unction oils to a dying parishioner, was about to send a blessed soul back to its Maker. He patted a pocket, made sure that he had the purple stole.

She was lovely. He was smitten. This was a very dangerous world.

They found Arthur Moss hanging this morning. Sheet or something round his neck, tongue hanging out like the pendulum on a grandfather clock according to Brian Short. Clock. Time ticking away, but not much I can do about it yet. She disappeared. They both did – three of them if you count the kid.

Arthur's is one way of getting out of this place, I suppose.

Plain pine box, no mourners, one less crim to cater for. The minute they shut the door on you in a place like this, you don't exist any more. They have to feed you, keep you warm and fed and safe, but that's because they're jobsworths. The way they look at me, I know they'd kill me given half a chance.

Ho ho ho. Just watch this space. I'll find them, by Christ I will.

Five

Babs, Pete and Cassie were having a day out on the town. He was on a week's leave, and they had decided to make the most of it. The pair seemed a perfect match, but Babs, the more seriously wounded of the two, had been persuaded by Lily to take her time. 'He's a widower, yes,' Lily had said. 'And he's been through a tragic loss that resulted in his having to rear kids all by himself. Not easy. But your history is nastier. Be careful, hon. Like I said before – don't jump. It's better to walk in or out with your eyes wide open and your ears pinned back.' Lily talked a lot of sense, and that fact was sometimes annoying.

Babs was about to hand over her child to the tender mercies of Valda Turnbull. Valda had five of her own, and three of them were at school. She was a registered child-minder and an excellent mother. Little Cassie, an only child, was going to learn to interact with her peers, because Babs was returning to work with Maurice Jones. Maurice had trained under Herbert of Liverpool, a character, a hard taskmaster and a stickler for detail. Babs had much to learn, and she had decided to enjoy these last few days as a full-time mother.

A little fair had been set up on the Town Hall square:

rides for children, Punch and Judy, some jugglers and a few clowns on stilts. An old-fashioned barrel organ made a splendid noise, while a monkey in a bright red suit tumbled happily on top of the instrument. The place was bustling with people who had taken a rest from shopping in order to watch the fun and games. Babs, a people-watcher, was more interested in the crowd than in the entertainment. It was good to see so many people laughing and enjoying the sunny day.

Cassie had a wonderful time, but she began to tire after a couple of hours of enthusiastic cavorting and was fast asleep in her pushchair by four o'clock. The two adults ate sandwiches and drank tea from a flask. Sitting across from the civic buildings, Babs commented on their undeniable beauty. 'I think I love Bolton,' she remarked.

'People imagine dark satanic mills when referring to northern towns,' Pete told her. 'But Le Mans Crescent was built by factory workers during the cotton famine ages ago. It reminds me of Bath.'

Babs nodded her agreement. Bolton had been both a shock and a surprise, the former because the accent was so different from her own, and the latter because the area was extraordinarily beautiful. 'I like the moors as well,' she said. 'It's all a lot prettier than I expected. Of course, I had to get used to the way the natives talk – so did Lily. I suppose you find our accent odd.'

'Reminds me of the servant in that film – *Ladies in Lavender*. That was set in your neck of the woods.'

She remembered it well. 'Judi Dench was in it. Lily likes it – she has the DVD. Young lad nearly drowned, and he turned out to be a whiz on the violin. I cried buckets because Dame Judi played an old woman who had never been loved by a man. Sad. In her heart, she was eighteen.'

'Like you.'

She dug him in the ribs. 'I'll let you know when I'm old, my lover. I'll send you a telegram.'

Pete knew that 'my lover' didn't mean anything, yet the phrase struck his heart with a soft, warm pain. Babs and Lily might not have survived all that had befallen them in recent years. Twin monuments to the strength and power of womankind, they had relocated, had made lives for themselves and were battling memories and fears that were known only to the unfortunate few. Unfortunate? He shook his head. Terrified might have been nearer the mark.

'Why shake your head?' she asked.

'Thinking,' he replied. 'About you and Lily and Cassie.'

Babs pondered for a moment. 'Cassie knew nothing. In time, I expect she will be told. As for Lily – well, there's a lot more to her than meets the eye at present. I never in all my life met such anger, strength, kindness – she's not always been quiet. Not that I knew her, of course. Until . . .'

'Until Clive Chalmers.'

Babs nodded. 'That's the pig, yes. Though Lily loved her grandad's pigs, so I apologize to the pig world. He brought us together, you might say. She'd go mad if she knew I was talking about her. She still feels trapped, you know. She's started to peep through the bars of her prison, but she has a fair way to go yet.'

The policeman cleared his throat of a mixture of emotions. 'I'm a copper, love. I know most of it already.

The details are yours and hers. But.' He wiped his eyes to remove what might have been perspiration, might have been a couple of tears. 'But you're great women, both of you.'

Babs lowered her head. 'If I'm great, it's because some of her must have rubbed off on me. I've never been what you might call a bad person, but she altered me. I was having a rare old time – hairdresser during the week, mad as a hatter at weekends. Expecting Cassie stopped me drinking right off, I can tell you that for nothing. Then I met Lily. She was cross with me at first, and then–'

'Then it happened.'

She sniffed. 'Yes. I happened and he happened. The rest of it was all over the newspapers, wasn't it? When she was away, I prayed for her day and night. Not in church – I'm not the churchified kind. But anything I did, like someone's hair or a bit of cleaning, I sort of offered up as what the Catholics call penance. The harder I worked, the better were her chances of coming home. Daft.'

'She came home, though.'

Babs laughed. 'She would have come home anyway, Pete. Her survival was nothing to do with the way I handled a difficult customer or scrubbed a floor. I can't explain.' She stopped for a few seconds. 'Some people have a kind of light in them, a burning centre that doesn't always show. Like the middle of the earth – white heat. Nowadays, it's sometimes there in her eyes, like when she's doing up that rambling place she bought. I think the light is the child we all used to be. Growing up completely isn't a good idea. The Lily-child is on its way back. At least, I hope it is.'

Pete placed an arm across the back of the bench and

rested his hand on her shoulder. '"Go forever children, hand in hand." Wilfred Owen, I think. You're right. Never grow up.'

Then he kissed her lightly on the lips, not caring where he was, not worrying about the world and his wife's witnessing a police sergeant loving a woman on the Town Hall square. 'You should write poetry,' he told her.

'I already do,' she answered.

He was not surprised. Nothing she did would surprise him. For the first time in well over a decade, Sergeant Peter Haywood was in love.

'That Babs one is going to retrain as a hairdresser.' Mary Turnbull placed her shopping on the table. 'And yon chap she's hanging around with is a Sergeant Haywood with the police. Widower, or so I heard. Anyway, he seems to like Babs well enough and it looks as though she likes him.'

'Hmph.' Enid peered through her binoculars. 'Lily Latimer's looking set to move across the road any minute. She'll be rattling about like a pea on a drum, because it's big enough for a family of six or more.' She placed the binoculars on a table and looked at her new flatmate. 'Did you see him?'

Enid nodded. 'Downstairs with her and that three-legged dog. It's getting well behaved, I have to say that. It begs for food, like, and it mithers the old folk a bit. But ... er ...'

'But-er what?'

'They keep smiling at one another. I've noticed that a fair few times. Always smiling.'

'Him and the dog?'

'No. Him and her.'

Enid delivered another of her famous snorts. 'Who'd look at him? Can you imagine Dave with a woman?'

Mary shrugged. Dave was a bit overweight, but he wasn't ugly, and he was a lovely man. 'They've always got on,' she ventured tentatively. 'He's not a bad bloke, Enid.'

'Nor should he be. I raised him, didn't I? But he's chapel, and chapel doesn't mix with Roman. Anyway, she's no bloody oil painting either. She's not what you'd call a beauty, Philly Gallagher. Her mam was plain, and her grandma, too.'

Mary decided to shut up. Compared to Enid, Mary judged herself to be a gentle soul, though everyone knew she was capable of giving as good as she got. She'd never met anyone quite like Enid Barker. Enid seemed to hate just about every soul in the village, and her own son looked to be top of her list. 'Will I make a brew?' she asked.

'Aye. And I'll have a couple of arrowroot biscuits – they aren't too bad on my sugar. I'm bad with melegs today, have to be careful what I eat. Bloody diabetes. Type one, I am – had it nearly all my life.'

While Mary made tea, she wondered whether Enid had ever used the words please, thank you or sorry. Mary wasn't renowned for politeness, especially when it came to her opinion of her daughter-in-law, but she'd never been as nasty as Enid seemed to be. Had she done the right thing by deciding to move in here? Reluctantly, she had to believe that she had, because the grand-children were too many, too noisy and too near her bedroom in her son's house. But Enid was a big pill to swallow. She moaned all the time, and never had a good word for anybody.

They sat drinking tea. 'When's the drama kicking off?' Enid asked. 'This stupid society they're supposed to be starting.'

'In a couple of days, I think. Why?'

'You should go.'

'Me?' cried Mary. 'What the bloody hell could I do in drama? Can you see me as Lady Macbeth or the back end of a pantomime horse? I'm well past all that.'

Enid nodded. 'They want people as can sew and make costumes. Then some poor bugger has to sit at the side with the book in case they forget their lines. There's all kinds of jobs. You could keep an eye out for me. You'd hear all the latest in that school hall.'

Mary sighed. The sooner that wheelchair turned up, the better. Though Mary would have to push the damned thing, she supposed. Weren't there chairs with motors? With one of those, Enid Barker might be able to do her own spying. 'I'll go, then. But if I don't like it, I'll not go again. I don't like shoving myself in where I'm not needed.'

Something in Mary's tone told Enid to shut up, so she shut up. People were not as easily manipulated as they used to be. They didn't listen to sense any more, were no longer open to ideas or suggestions. Used to her placid son, the old woman was not pleased about having to moderate her demands. This was her flat, and Mary Turnbull should be doing as she was asked, but there was no point in over-labouring the drama society thing.

The main problem for Enid was that things just weren't the same any more. She needed her son, though she would never admit that to herself. It had been more fun with him around, because he was vulnerable. On the outside, he was a strong, stocky man, but she had been able to get to him. Even when he made no reply or pretended not to hear her, she could tell by his stance, by the back of his neck or the curl of a hand, that she was affecting him. Mary was different. She was a woman and she was stronger. More than anything, Enid wanted Dave back. He would come back. Wouldn't he?

'That cuppa all right for you, love?' Mary asked.

'Lovely.' Her flatmate would go to the initial meeting. For now, that would have to be enough. 'I wish that wheelchair would hurry up.'

Mary nodded. 'I was just thinking the same thing myself. And I wondered about them motorised ones – you'd have to keep it downstairs, but you could get anywhere you wanted with one of those.'

'We'll see,' snapped Enid. 'Now that my own son's abandoned me, I suppose I'm going to need all the help I can get.'

Mary sipped her tea. The only thing that amazed her was the fact that Dave had stayed for so long. Would she stay? Could she tolerate the drip, drip, drip of something caustic on a daily basis? Time would tell, she supposed. Meanwhile, when her tea was finished, she would go downstairs in search of more pleasant company.

Dave's clothes were hanging quite loosely. At last, he was losing weight, because Skippy needed to be walked. In spite of the loss of a limb, the young bitch loved her daily exercise. She also liked the shop and all the people who visited it, especially those who slipped her a bit of sandwich or scone on the sly. She was hard to resist when it came to looking hungry, but Tim Mellor had stressed that she must not put on weight. 'You'll be on a diet soon,' Dave advised his pet. Then he told Philly, 'I'll have to be going for some new things soon, though I don't want to spend a lot, because I'm not halfway there yet.'

She smiled to herself. She, too, was losing weight, and it was amazing, since neither of them seemed to be suffering any great pangs of hunger. 'Bolton Market,' she told him. 'Couple of shirts, a pair of trousers – you'll get by until you've lost the rest. You don't need to go mad, and I may be able to alter some of the stuff you already have.'

He chuckled. 'We're doing great, aren't we, Philly?'

'We are. Come on – Skippy wants her evening walk. We'll take her behind the church, because it looks like it's thinking about raining, so we don't want to go up into the hills.' Exercise was vital, because the young Lab ate like a horse and would soon be the size of one if care wasn't taken.

Moving as one person, they swapped slippers for shoes, put on lightweight, waterproof jackets, called the dog. She stood in front of them, tongue extended and quivering as she panted her excitement. Philly fastened lead to collar, stood straight and found herself looking into Dave Barker's eyes.

'You all right?' he asked. Her face was flushed, while frown lines between her eyes told him that something or other was afoot.

'Yes.' Of course she was all right. Or was something showing in her face – did she look guilty? She hadn't done anything, not really. Like Dave, she needed new clothes; unlike Dave, she had allowed herself to be persuaded in the direction of fashion, but he hadn't seen any of the catalogue things. And she could send them back to the company if she changed her mind. Some of the items were ... not exactly racy, but a far cry from anything she had ever bought in her whole life. She was forty-three. She was still blushing. 'Come on,' she said. 'Before it starts to rain.' Busying herself with the excited animal, she opened the door and stepped out.

They crossed the village green, each aware that the eyes of Enid Barker were boring into them. If looks could kill, Dave thought, he and his companion would be pools of grease on the path. 'She never leaves that window,' he said. 'Sitting there taking the mickey out of everybody – and that's on a good day. Mostly, she moans and curses us all. I've wondered all my life what the hell it is she gets out of hurting people – mostly me.'

'Take no notice of her,' ordered Philly. 'We're doing nothing wrong.'

Behind the presbytery, they heard banter passing from Father Walsh to Lily Latimer and back again. They were clearing part of the garden, and he was obviously the labourer, while she was acting foreman.

'If you lop any more off, it'll be a bush, not a tree,' cried the female voice. 'I'd like to see you making chips – I bet there's more peel than potato when you're let loose with a knife.'

'Rubbish,' he called. 'And if a job's worth doing–' This reply was cut short.

'You're going to fall if you don't stop playing the fool,' Lily shouted. 'Just be careful, because my insurance doesn't cover mad clergymen.'

'I am not playing the fool – I am a fool. Or I wouldn't be up here trying to be the Texas chainsaw massacre-ist.

This isn't easy, you know. The ground is very uneven just here.'

'Just don't saw the bough your ladder's leaning on,' was Lily's answer. 'You're getting more like a Buster Keaton film by the minute. Forget the Texas thing, you're definitely Keystone Cops.' A door slammed.

'Well,' muttered Dave. 'They seem to be getting on like a house afire.'

Philly was of the same opinion, though she found nothing to say on the subject. If her parish priest had decided to stray, it was none of her business, and he would have to deal with his soul via his own confessor. He and Lily Latimer would have been well suited had he not taken Holy Orders.

Skippy had spotted a rabbit and was hopping along behind the frightened animal. Philly called her name, and the dog came back immediately. Skippy was well fed, and therefore obedient.

The rain began very suddenly, pouring from a leaden sky, huge drops at first, then a steady stream that soaked them both right through to the skin. 'Waterproof?' scoffed Dave. 'Ridiculous. I'm fair witchered.'

Philly smiled. The old Lancashire word probably came from 'wet-shod', and it was certainly appropriate on this occasion. She re-fastened lead to collar, then began to run past the back of the presbytery, the graveyard and the end of Rose Cottage's garden.

When they reached home, Dave panting slightly from unusual exertion, each started to laugh at the other. Philly's hair, which had been newly coiffed and coloured at Pour Les Dames, dripped all over her face like lengths of dark, soggy string. Dave took off his jacket, opened the front door and wrung the item out in the fashion of an old washerwoman from days long gone. 'There's rain and there's rain,' he commented. 'But this rain is filled with bad intentions. God's emptying His watering can. Why does it always have to be Lancashire?'

Philly went off to dry the dog and set the kettle to boil, while Dave climbed the stairs and changed into pyjamas and dressing gown. There was no point in wearing proper clothes, as he had no plans to set foot outside on a night as determinedly bad as this one had decided to become.

When Philly had taken her turn upstairs and Dave had poured the tea, they sat in armchairs near the fireplace. Philly turned on a little halogen heater that she used in summertime when the weather turned inclement – it was not worth lighting a real fire, as she explained to her lodger.

Dave drank his tea. 'You know, Philly, this is the first time in my life that I've been happy.'

'Me too.'

The following few minutes were spent trying to avoid each other's eyes. Neither was used to announcing feelings; neither was used to having anyone who cared about those feelings. Dave washed dishes in the kitchen while Philly talked to the dog. She wanted Dave to stay for ever, and she wanted him to be more than just a lodger. That was a frightening realization. She stood up and hung wet clothes on a maiden near the heater.

He came in. 'Philly?'

'What?'

Dave sat down in his chair. It was his chair. Right from the start, each had known where to place him or herself in relation to the other. It was as if they had been together for twenty years or more. 'I don't know how to put it,' he began. He was afraid that she would throw him out, because the words he needed to use might well offend her Catholic sensitivities beyond endurance.

'Just say it,' she said. 'No matter what, just say it.'

So he did. It all tumbled out of him in a disorganized, stupid mess, possessing neither rhyme nor reason, no framework, no boundaries, no finesse. And she was fighting a smile. He couldn't be a Catholic, but they might marry mixed, and any child would be reared within her faith. He wasn't a good-looking chap, but he loved her. She might be too old to have children, anyway, and that would be all right, too. They got on well and they both loved the shop and they both loved Skippy. He'd never thought of himself as fit for marriage, and his mother hadn't helped. 'I'm certainly no Heathcliff,' he finished.

Philly nodded and tried hard not to look pleased. As well read as he was, she denounced in moments three of the greatest heroes in English literature. 'Heathcliff was a sociopath,' she said, 'and Rochester a fool. Why try to marry an innocent governess when you've a killer wife locked in the roof? As for Darcy – well, he was socially inept, ill-mannered to the point of boorishness and, if Colin Firth was anything to go by, needed a damned good wash, a haircut and a shave.'

'Right,' said Dave.

Philly stood up. 'I'm going to bed now,' she said. 'And I'll think about all this. I don't want to spoil our friendship by saying yes or no just yet. At my age, marriage is a big step.'

He understood, and he said so.

Philly ran upstairs like an eighteen-year-old. She lay on her bed and stared at the ceiling. Dave was a lovely man, one of the best people she had ever met. He was kind, generous, thoughtful and intelligent. She was happy working in his shop, was even happier sharing her home with him and Skippy. He'd looked so worried when he'd said all that – could she leave him lying awake all night and wondering what she would say, what she would do?

At just before midnight, she slipped out of bed, walked past the bathroom door and let herself into Dave's bedroom. Even in the darkness, she knew he was awake, because his breathing quickened as soon as she went in.

'Philly?' he whispered.

'Who else lives here? It would have to be me or the dog, you daft thing.'

Neither would ever be able to account for what followed. She was standing, then she was sitting, then she was in the bed beside him. There was no question about it – Philomena Gallagher was not her usual self on this occasion. She was alive, abandoned, liberated. And she cried. The weeping happened not afterwards, but during, because she realized what she had been missing for the past two decades. Sex was beautiful; sex with a man who was loved and loving was something that defied description.

They lay together in the single bed. 'I've got cramp,' announced Dave, 'but it was worth it. You've gone quiet.'

She had been extremely noisy. Fortunately, the walls were of thick stone, the woman next door was as deaf as a post, and Philly's house was an end of terrace. 'It's a sin,' she said.

'We're all born of sin, Philly.'

'Yes, so we are. And we need a bigger bed.' She kissed him on the forehead and went back to her own room.

The next morning, Dave woke with a smile on his face. He looked into Philly's bedroom, but she was not there, so he went to find her downstairs. She wasn't there, either. Skippy, too, had disappeared, so Dave assumed that Philly was doing the first of the dog's walks. He made tea, went back up to get showered and dressed, came down again to an empty house.

It was time to get to the Reading Room, because the newspapers would need sorting. He and Philly breakfasted there almost every day. On Sundays and some holy days, Dave would be alone, but this was neither Sunday nor a holy day, because she would have informed him had she needed to attend church to celebrate the life of some long-dead saint.

An uneasiness crept over him, chilling his body right through to the bone. She was ashamed, and could not look him in the eye. Desperation had driven her to have one sexual encounter in her life, and he had happened to be there when she'd needed a man – any man. The mirror told the truth. Dave Barker was not handsome. Not desirable. Where was she?

At the shop, he sorted papers and set them out on stands. Breakfast was out of the question, since his stomach seemed to have moved north and was threatening to heave. What had he done? Why hadn't he kept his bloody mouth shut, just as he had when sharing space with his mother? He couldn't go back there, wouldn't go back to the flat above the shop.

Why hadn't he been satisfied with what he'd already had at Philly's house? There had been no quarrel, no holding on to the rising tide of temper, no dread of going home. Where was she? And why hadn't she left a note? Perhaps he should have searched her bedroom to see if she had taken any clothes, but no, Philly would never leave a house that had been in her family for three generations.

The door opened, and there she was, complete with a smile and a happy dog. 'Did you get my note?' she asked.

'What note?'

'You see?' she cried. 'It's as if you're already family. I expect you to know that we always leave messages next to the clock.' She kissed him on the cheek. 'I'd better get moving. Sandwiches don't make themselves.' She went through to the Reading Room, dog and employer hot on her heels.

'Where were you?' Dave asked.

'Oh ... yes ... sorry. I had to wait for Father Walsh. There's a funeral this morning, so I knew he'd be here. Before that, I went for a walk to clear my head. Anyway, the short story is that he knows.'

Dave's spine was suddenly rigid.

'It's a sin,' she advised him. 'Though Father Walsh said – what did he say? It's not that big a deal – something like that. He'll sort it all out and marry us. After that, it won't be a sin. Oh, and I told him I was a bit old for having babies, but that any children would be raised Catholic.'

Dave dropped into a chair. 'Do you tell these priests everything? Like what you had for breakfast and what you watch on TV?'

'No.' Philly studied the man she loved. 'There's more to it, Dave. There's a lot more. You know how some folk have to go and see psychiatrists because they're not well?'

He nodded. 'Came close enough myself when I lived with . . .' He pointed to the ceiling.

'Sometimes, when I go into the confessional box, I haven't a lot to say. You can go through the Commandments and decide that your problems are on a different list. Little sins like wishing you had a baby or a partner or even a friend. A bit like jealousy, but not that strong. And he listens. You get a blessing and come out feeling a stone lighter.'

'So it's therapy?'

'Definitely. I didn't go into the box this morning. I told him face to face. And I could tell he was pleased for me. He went on a bit about sex not being the worst thing unless it was rape. Then he wished us happiness and told me you're one of the best men he's met in his life.'

'So we're all right?'

'Better than that, because he approves.'

Dave nodded. 'And if he hadn't?'

Philly shrugged. 'Never mind if. Open that door, because Bert and Sam will be here for breakfast and a newspaper in about two minutes. Oh – one thing, Dave Barker.'

'What's that?'

'No more shenanigans till we're married.'

'All right.' With a big fat grin on his face, Dave went to invite the day to enter his shop. Philly was very Victorian. Dave, who had studied the enigmatic queen, knew that her composed exterior had hidden a multitude of passions. No more shenanigans, indeed. Philly was the one who'd come to him in the night. In that moment, he was the happiest man on earth. For the first time ever, someone valued him.

Lily, who had received all monies from the sale of her home and the business premises in Somerset, paid off the bridging loan and took possession of the deeds to her latest acquisition. She owned the huge house, and that meant something. The pile of bricks and mortar was testament to a past that had not been wasted; it stood proud and tall in memory of Leanne Chalmers, the most successful interior designer in three or four west country counties. In part, it belonged to her grandfather, who had left a small fortune for Lily in his will. He would have approved, she thought. He would have loved that wild garden with its meanders, sundial and orchard, and the broken-down summerhouse. 'Make money work for you, Leanne.'

Leanne was not dead. It was she who dictated to Lily what must be done, she who colour-coded and themed the rooms, who chose drapes, cushions, rugs, and bartered for fireplaces reclaimed from purveyors of architectural antiques. Was this Lily's happiness? Or were she and her previous self merely papering over cracks with materials that cost an arm and both legs? 'Oh, Leanne,' she breathed on the evening of the first FADS meeting. 'Name this house for me, will you? Come on, you know you can do it.'

The name Chalmers could never come into it – didn't deserve to be used. Latimer had been her grandmother's maiden name, and she was tempted to use it as the replacement for St Faith's Presbytery, but the need not to be discovered dictated that Latimer was rendered unsuitable. She had deemed it safe to have as an adopted name for herself, but she didn't want it chipped into stone near the front door. 'You're silly,' she told herself sharply. 'You have it as a surname, but you don't want to advertise? Per-lease!'

Who knew her grandmother's maiden name, anyway? Probably no one, yet she must leave no trail, no solid evidence on which people might work in order to find her. The church was St Faith's. St Faith had been a martyr in the fifth century, or even earlier, and her death had been nasty – grilled over an open fire, then beheaded. Oh, joy. She wasn't going to use that. 'Faith, hope and charity,' Lily said aloud. 'And the greatest of these is charity.' That wouldn't do, either, or she might have every tramp in the district begging for food at the door. Charity House? No.

Hope seemed just about right. Hope House. Where there was life, there was hope, and that was another little riddle solved. 'Thanks, Leanne,' she breathed. It was almost seven o'clock. Tonight, after the meeting in the church hall, Lily would be sleeping for the first time in Hope House. The room with the circular window was ready. Excitement did battle with trepidation, and Lily forced the former to win. She would not be afraid. Fear had belonged to Leanne, who was doing a good job on the house, since her soul lived on in Lily Latimer. But this was Lily's house, and she would claim it right away.

In her best jeans and a T-shirt, she made her way for the first time to the St Faith's school hall. Unlike the church, this was partly modern, with cheap, almost pre-fabricated classrooms fastened on to the original building. Inside, every centimetre of wall was covered in posters and the work of children, bright colours clashing joyfully on walls panelled in plasterboard. It felt happy and busy, exactly as a primary school should.

The first person she met was Michael Walsh, and this time he was not attached to the supposedly less dangerous end of a motorized tree-trimmer. He wore a dark shirt, black trousers and no dog collar. His hair looked as if it had taken a walk on the wild side, so there was no improvement in that area.

'We're starting off with a pantomime,' he advised her. 'For January. That gives us plenty of time to write it, learn it and get dressed up for it. Though one of us is dressed up already.' He led her into the hall.

Maurice Jones, having heard that it was to be pantomime, had arrived to claim his place as dame. He staggered about on red high-heeled shoes wearing a terrible dress with false boobs clearly straining towards freedom, while his face was a multi-coloured mess. Topped by an incredible red wig and some huge hooped earrings in scarlet plastic, he looked marvellous.

His wife touched Lily's arm. 'I couldn't stop him,' she whispered. 'Look at the state of him – ever the exhibitionist.'

'Nor should you stop him,' said the priest. 'He's got it, so he should blooming well flaunt it. Unfortunately, there is no dame in *Cinderella*, but he can be one of the ugly sisters.'

When Mike Walsh had left them, Sally sat down with Lily at the back of the hall. 'He's nothing like a priest, is he? I thought they were dead serious miserable creatures.'

Lily shook her head. 'Not this one. But if you ever get a garden and he offers to help, say no. He tramples. He cuts shrubs back at the wrong time of year, and he rescues things like foxes and rabbits. I let him loose and am beginning to regret it.'

'He's nice, though,' remarked Sally.

'Yes, he's very nice.'

The very nice man was clearing his throat and welcoming all to FADS. The pantomime was to be *Cinderella*, and he would write it. Philomena Gallagher was in charge of meetings and money, Lily Latimer would do sets and props, others would be acting, making refreshments, selling tickets, keeping order in the hall – this was a school, so they had to leave it as they found it. Costumes needed to be sewn and fitted, strong men would be required for scene-shifting, and he would produce and direct. Next time, someone else could have the hard job of keeping everyone up to scratch.

'He's doing a lot,' said Sally quietly.

'He does,' answered Lily. 'And he's lumbered me with sets, even though I never quite agreed.'

'Is there dissent in the ranks at the back?' he called.

Sally shook her head, but Lily stood up. 'Thanks for volunteering me without my permission,' she said loudly.

'No problem,' came the reply. 'Always happy to help. You'll make a very fine job of it, Lily.'

She sat down again. There had been quite a good response to Philly's leaflets, and Lily recognized only about half of the faces. She poked Sally's arm. 'Isn't that Valda's mother? Over there, near the front.'

'It is. She's staying with Enid Barker, isn't she?'

Lily nodded. 'And God help her.'

Philly was there with Dave and the Boswells, and Babs had dragged Pete along. He was holding Cassie, who would be late to bed tonight. 'They look cosy,' Sally commented. 'Philly and Dave, I mean. Do you think there's something going on?'

'No idea.' Tim Mellor was present, as was Derek Boswell. Both had begun to buy rather a lot of flowers. Lily, whose radar was powerful, awarded no more than a glance to Dave and his landlady, because she was suddenly aware that the two men were not looking at her. The vet's eyes were temporarily fixed on the priest, while Derek's gaze was wandering about like a dog released from its lead. She could have done without this. All she needed now were complications in the form of interested males.

'She'll go mad.' Sally was whispering now.

'What? Who?'

'Mrs Barker. She can't stand Philly, because she's a devout Catholic and she can cook. Mrs Barker's cakes were designed to break teeth, and she knows we were all glad when she retired to the first floor.'

Lily looked at Philomena Gallagher and her lodger. 'You may be right,' she said. 'And if we can see it, so can Mrs Turnbull.'

'I like Dave and Philly,' said Sally. 'They're looking like a couple already. It'll be handbags at dawn.'

Michael Walsh brought the inaugural meeting to a close. 'I've nearly finished writing,' he informed the room. 'We'll meet again next week for casting. Come even if you don't want an audition, because we need a lot of help.'

Maurice stood up in his finery. 'Mike?'

'Yes, my love?'

The hairdresser waited until the ensuing laughter died. 'I'm not ugly,' he said in a very effeminate voice.

'People would die for looks like mine. Is it all right if I read for Cinderella?'

'Do what you like,' replied the man in charge. 'But save yourself for me, ducky. I'll meet you later behind the bike sheds. Any other business?'

Had anyone in the room still considered the parish priest to be a dry stick, they would have altered their opinion immediately. He was just a bloke with tatty hair, and he wanted to do something for the community.

Maurice hadn't finished. 'Free haircut for you, young man. It's time we tidied you up. You look like a string mop parked the wrong way up.'

The any other business part of the meeting went completely downhill after that. Lily, anxious to get out as quickly as possible, slipped through the door and into the corridor. But men have notoriously long legs, and the vet caught up with her almost immediately. 'Fancy a drink?' he asked, his tone engineered to be casual.

'No thanks, Tim. I've stuff to do at home.'

'So you've finally made the move?'

'Yes.'

'I'm moving,' he said. 'Business, not house. I'll have a nurse on stand-by in case we get something serious in, but number three will be largely work premises.'

'Right. Good luck with that.'

'Thank you.'

After bidding him good night, Lily walked home. On the long path that led to the front door, she found herself almost running. She was supposed to have stopped doing that. Her vow to have nothing whatsoever to do with men still stood. Neither Leanne nor Lily needed courtship, but there was no need to run. 'This is a safe place,' she said as she entered the house.

Inside, she leaned against the door. The building was so big, so silent. Had she done the right thing? Time would tell, she supposed – and she could sell it on if necessary. There was someone at the other side of the door. Its thickness meant that she heard nothing, yet some sixth sense warned her that she was not alone. Was Michael Walsh thinking of sleeping here tonight? Would she feel safer if he did?

The someone tapped quietly on the knocker.

'Who is it?'

'Derek. Derek Boswell. Wondered if you might come for a drink or two.'

Lily sagged against the wall. 'Not tonight, Derek.'

'Oh. OK, then. Another time, perhaps?'

She made no reply. In the kitchen, she sat at a white deal table that looked as if it had been there since the house was built. Something was missing. She closed her eyes and took herself back to the farm. Carbolic. The table had always been scrubbed with that harsh soap. Another scent she recalled was new bread in an oven. She remembered blue-rimmed enamel bowls left near the fireplace while their contents proved; the sight of her mother kneading, breaking dough and shaping loaves. Plaits, oven-bottom bread, cobs, pound loaves still hot from baking, butter dripping after it was spread.

So safe, she had been in those days. Nothing could touch any of the family, or so she had believed. Innocence. People dying, no more bread, kitchen table no longer as clean as it had always been. Cows sent to market, fields left fallow, living with an aunt, going to college, growing up, meeting him.

Her eyes flew open. How had she failed to see what was hidden behind the sparkling eyes and handsome face? Suddenly, she was weeping. It wasn't an ordinary weep, wasn't just a few tears and a bit of sniffing; this was a full-blown event, loud, painful and draining. Nothing had changed since yesterday. There had been no new trauma, no earth-shattering event that had altered irrevocably the course of her life. One of the doctors had warned her about flashbacks, but she hadn't been thinking about the night when it had all gone—

'Lily?'

She almost jumped out of her skin. 'Father—'

'Mike. When I'm not in uniform, I'm Mike. Makes me feel human.' She had been breaking her heart, and she didn't need a witness. 'Do you want the keys back? You can kick me out and change the locks – I won't be offended. I'm intruding.'

The shock made her stop in her tracks. 'No. I said you could stay, and you can. I'm just … just remembering.' She dabbed at her face.

'Can I help?'

'Of course not. You weren't there. How can you help me remember?'

'Perhaps forgetting would be better.' He sat opposite her. 'Talk to me. Did I upset you by lumbering you with the stage dressing?'

'No. Well, yes, but that isn't anything to do with … with anything.'

'Right. Where do we stand on the cuppa front? Do I bring in my own, do I pay you, or do you drink strange herbal stuff?'

'Tetley's,' she answered. 'Just get on with it.'

While he pottered about, Lily repaired to a ground-floor bathroom in order to compose herself. The poor man was only trying to help, but he couldn't. No one could. There was just Babs. Babs would probably be spending the night in bed with Pete, because Cassie now had her own room. Lucky Babs. She had found a man who seemed solid and strong, someone who would take care of her and her little girl. Would they take Cassie away?

She splashed water on her face. Her distance from Cassie was greater than ever, because it had to be. Cassie could never be her daughter. She stared into the mirror and scarcely knew herself. The weight she had shed had not returned, and the round-cheeked Leanne was unrecognizable. There had been no need for plastic surgery, because she looked completely different. After all this time, she should have grown used to the blonde hair, but she felt she never would. She missed herself, mourned the woman she had been before ... before Clive Chalmers. Even thinking the name made her want to vomit.

'Tea,' Mike shouted.

Lily re-entered the kitchen. 'Sorry about that,' she said, her voice still shaky. 'I don't know what came over me.'

'Yes, you do. You know perfectly well, and I'm sorry to have invaded your space. Goodness knows you paid enough for this house. If you like, I will go and make other arrangements, but you must unburden yourself to someone, so why not me?'

'I don't have the answer.'

He poured tea and handed her a mug. 'Now that was Father O'Hara's very own drinking vessel. I nearly put it into the grave with him, because he went ape if anyone else used it. But he's dead, so enjoy.'

Lily stared into the mug. 'I suppose he must be dead if you buried him.'

He nodded sadly. 'Yes, but I was sorely tempted on many an occasion to have the burial before the death. He was into his eighties, deaf as a post, and I think he went to the same charm school as Adolf Hitler. I was a young priest and scared to the bones of him. Then I realized that he was actually stupid, and stupidity must be forgiven. He couldn't have been academically unsound, as a priest has to learn some difficult stuff, but he—'

'Like joined-up writing? Did you learn that?'

'Yes.'

'And pantomime?'

'All right, all right. Stopped you crying, anyway, didn't I? But he'd no common sense. He needed the simplest things doing for him, and his personal hygiene was questionable—'

'And this is his cup?'

'It's been washed.'

Lily got up from the table and brought her own mug. Mike filled it for her. 'Better now?'

'It comes and goes.' She didn't want to look at him, wished he would go into another room. 'It will be some time before I can talk sensibly. But I'll tell you now that it was serious enough for me to change my name, give up a promising career, consider cosmetic surgery and come up here.'

'And Babs?'

'Part of the same package. You don't ask her about me, either. Understood?'

'Yes. Now, I'll take myself off and think very seriously about the threat made tonight. Maurice Jones is a decent enough chap, but he should leave my hair out of things.'

'Out of your eyes would be a start.'

She was calmer. He knew that he could leave her now. Michael Walsh was a man of the world. Priesthood had not diminished him; on the contrary, it had served him well, because he now knew more about human nature than most psychiatrists ever managed to learn. His inner core was attracted to the sad female at the table. It wasn't the first time he had felt physical desire, though he had seldom experienced anything deeper. But now he was on the brink of something or other that could alter his life for ever. Falling in love? No. It wouldn't happen.

Lily washed the cups and left them to dry. She walked out into her massive garden and sat on a flagged patio just outside the dining room and kitchen. A security light turned itself on as she settled herself on a broken-down chair at a decaying table. She looked at the wilderness that was freehold and hers. It was a big undertaking, and she needed a better gardener than the one upstairs. Her heart skipped a beat when she reminded herself of his kindness, his gentle, forgiving nature, his acceptance and understanding. It was a pity that many religious figures seemed not to learn from those who toiled at the coalface of life.

The magic happened then, while she sat and surveyed her extensive domain. Unafraid of the light, they stepped out of shadow and stood staring at her – the father, the mother and the two cubs. When she rose from her seat, they did not move; when she returned with meat on a plate, they were still waiting. She placed the food at the edge of the paving stones, then went inside.

In darkness, Lily Latimer stood at her kitchen window and watched the foxes. Babies scuffled and took what the parents gave them. Never before had Lily been so close to a fox. Grandpa had shot them, because they killed chickens. She could not do that, no matter what. Nevertheless, she would keep no hens. Tears flowed again, but she was smiling through them. The fox family walked away, one of the parents stopping to look over a shoulder, as if saying thanks.

Life went on. No matter what, day became night, dawn broke the dark, evening brought longer shadows. 'Accept, just like the foxes do,' she said softly. One day, she would talk to him. One day, she would need his help.

Six

Enid Barker sat in her usual bird's eye position, turning to look over her shoulder only when her flatmate walked in. 'I missed them coming out of the meeting,' she moaned. 'The school's at a funny angle, anyway, but I had to go to the bathroom, and even with the walker melegs were all over the ... What's up with you, Mary? Have you swallowed a gobstopper or something?'

Mary sank into the armchair nearest the door. She couldn't just say nothing at all, because somebody else would say something when Enid decided to become well enough to sit listening on the stairs, and it had to be dealt with sooner rather than later. So she let it all pour out in a steady stream, her voice flattened to the point where no emotion showed. When she had finished, she closed her eyes and leaned back in her seat. It was like waiting for the wrath of God to descend upon her, and she wished that she had never gone to the flaming meeting of FADS. This business was nothing to do with her, and she regretted her change of address yet again. She'd seen Tommy and Valda, and they'd talked about building a small granny flat at the back of their house ... Enid had turned a funny colour, and her mouth was hanging wide open.

It hung open for quite a while. 'Mary?' she cried when her lips finally met each other again. 'What the bloody hell are you telling me? Hand in hand? Dave walked back to her house holding hands? With that blinking Gallagher woman of all people? And everybody watching? The whole bloody village finding out before me?'

When Mary looked properly at her companion, she noticed a further change in the colour of Enid's skin. It had turned an interesting tone bordering on pale puce, if such a shade existed. 'I could be wrong,' she said sheepishly. 'It's possible, you know.' But she knew that other villagers had commented on the new closeness between Dave and Philomena. 'Enid, I don't think I should be responsible for telling you—'

'No. You're not wrong, Mary. You weren't wrong about Valda not being good enough for your lad, and you've stuck to your guns right from the off. Give you your due, love, you're like me. You're a woman of very strong instinct. There's something going on all right.'

Mary didn't want to think of herself as being like Enid. Enid Barker might well have a degree in nasty – even a doctorate – because she did nothing but find fault with everything and everybody. 'Calm down, Enid,' she pleaded. 'No sense in making yourself ill over it, is there?' It was time to make peace with Valda, because the alternative might be to end up like this crazy harridan. She had to get out of here. Whatever the cost to her pride, Mary needed to go home to her own little room or to the extension currently under discussion. Noisy grandchildren? Stupid daughter-in-law? They were infinitely preferable to this way of so-called life.

But Enid was past the point of no return. 'Hand in hand? I'll give him hand in hand when I get hold of him.

He's had it drummed into him since he was a lad. No Roman Catholics. So what does he do? He starts walking out with a saint who's not dead yet. It must be like courting one of them daft holy pictures they carry round in their prayer books.' She shivered. 'This has got to be put a stop to. I can't let it happen, Mary. Everything in me screams that I have to do something straight away before he goes too far. Hand in bloody hand?'

Mary nodded.

'She's RC.'

Here came the bigotry again. Enid Barker seemed to enjoy repeating herself, as if she chose to underline in red ink every opinion she expressed. Mary needed to scream, wanted to tell her companion to shut up about the Catholic thing, but she dared not. 'I know.' She sighed. 'But it's the twenty-first century and folk don't seem to—'

'Too old for kids, she is. All they'll have for family is that bloody daft dog, and that's only three-quarters furnished in the leg department, never mind daft as a brush in its head.'

Mary knew that Enid was completely legless at the moment, because she had tried to stand seconds earlier and had failed miserably. She was probably in some sort of shock, yet Mary Turnbull could not quite manage to worry about her hostess. 'Shop's being run by Valda and two of the old blokes tomorrow. I heard Sam Hardcastle telling Bert Thompson that Dave and Philly are going out somewhere, probably to town.' She wondered whether they might be going to buy a ring, but she dared not air that possibility, or Enid Barker might literally have a fit.

Enid's heart, pushed along by a great surge of adrenalin, was well into overdrive. 'Get that bloody wheelchair sorted – I saw it being delivered, so I expect it's in the store room at the back of the Reading Room – and help me down them bloody stairs. Well? What are you waiting for? The three-fifteen to Manchester?'

'You're going nowhere,' replied Mary with as much determination as she could muster. 'I saw you trying to stand before you got really worked up. I'm no spring chicken, Enid. I can't get you down below while your legs aren't working. We'd both break our necks. Sorry.'

Enid managed not to scream. 'How can I stop them, then? But I'm having a stairlift put in, and I'll see if I can afford a motorized scooter or some such item. Then I won't need help from you or anybody else. But I can't get them things by tomorrow, can I? Fetch me that phone. If I can't get there in person, I can speak my mind, at least.'

Mary experienced a sudden desire to be elsewhere – preferably in the southern hemisphere. If Enid phoned Dave and Philly, they would know that she had gone back to the flat and started tittle-tattling to his mother. 'Why don't you wait till you feel a bit calmer?' she suggested.

'Because I'm not going to feel any calmer. If I let this go till morning, they'll be at Preston's of Bolton and she'll be wearing a diamond set in platinum. Philomena Gallagher's out for what she can get. I mean, look at him. Fat as a pig, does no exercise – when I'm out of the way and he drops dead, she'll get the business.'

'But it's half past nine, Enid. A bit late for a phone call—'

'Thank you, speaking clock. If I'd wanted the time, I'd have looked at my watch. Get me the phone.'

Mary brought the instrument, handed it to Enid, then walked into her own bedroom. She didn't want to hear any more, but she heard it anyway. She had a strong suspicion that Manchester might have heard it. She turned on her television, and managed not to listen to the ranting from the next room.

Philly answered the phone.

'Is my son there?'

'Yes. Just a moment, please, Mrs Barker.'

He came to the phone. 'Mother?'

'You're carrying on with that fat Catholic, are you? Going to marry somebody whose life runs according to the Roman calendar, all holy water and plaster statues, who can rob a bank on Monday and get forgiven by a priest by Friday?'

'That's right.'

Enid gritted her teeth before wading in again. 'Then you can buy me out.'

'Whatever you wish, Mother.'

Taken aback, Enid was silent for a couple of seconds. Her pension was pennies. The bit of income that floated into her bank from the shop once a month was the only bright spot in her life. A diabetic needed good food. An old woman needed good food. As she listed herself in both categories, she was twice as needful as most people. 'Are you marrying her?'

'Yes.'

'Why? Is she pregnant?'

'No.'

'What have I told you all your life, eh? We don't mix with Romans. They're not right in the head if they think a bit of bread turns into flesh. Whispering confessions to a bloke who carries on like he's big enough to talk to

146

God at a different level from the rest of us, carrying pictures of saints in their handbags—'

'I promise not to carry saints in my handbag, Mother. The rest of it is none of your business. Philly's a Catholic, and that's an end to it.'

'It should be the end. And where are you going tomorrow?'

'Why? Do you want to come along for the ride?'

'No, I bloody don't.'

'Birmingham,' he said.

'Birmingham? Why?'

'Jewellery quarter. Anything else? Are we playing twenty questions?'

'You can't marry her,' she screamed.

'Better that than coming back to you, Mother. Better to get married than carry on like you used to, selling yourself for a few quid shoved behind the clock on the mantelpiece. I'm grown up now. You can't whip me, can't lock me under the stairs, can't frighten me any more. You've done your worst. It's my turn now, and I am doing my best for myself and for Philly.'

'How dare you?'

'Because I am talking to an ex-whore who doesn't even know who my father was. Because Philly is a good, God-fearing woman who wants to marry the ugly son you bore. And I dare because you have pulled to bits every decent body in this village and the residents of at least another five. So bugger off. I can't be bothered with you, Mother.'

She heard the phone as he threw it into its base. Her fingers shook when she dropped her own handset. From a pocket, she took a glucose lozenge and placed it on her tongue. The shock had pushed her towards a hypo.

Dave had a lot to answer for. Then, as if presenting the last straw, Mary Turnbull emerged from her bedroom and stood near the stairway door, a suitcase in her hand. 'What . . . ? Where are you . . . ?' For once in her life, Enid ran out of words.

'I've had too much of this,' Mary announced. 'I can't do it any more, Enid. God knows I'm bad enough, but you're in a class of your own. Even my telly couldn't drown out your screaming just now. I can't be your yeswoman. Things aren't right here, so I'm going. I'll send for the bigger stuff in a day or two.'

'Who'll look after me?'

Mary lowered her chin for a second. After counting to three, she raised her head and looked Enid Barker straight in the eye. 'The devil will mind you. He's your best mate, anyway. For now, I'm off to throw myself on the mercy of your lovely son and the nice woman he's been lucky enough to find. My grandchildren will be asleep, and I don't want to disturb them, so I'll crawl back to Valda tomorrow. Because I've learned something while living here, love. I'm not as bad as I thought I was, and I am prepared to apologize. You'll never do that.' She left the flat, closing the door softly.

Enid gulped, almost choking on fizzing glucose. There was nobody here. For the first time ever, she was completely alone. She could phone Dave again, she supposed, but he'd know in a few minutes that Mary had left her, so there was no point. Who would see to her now? Who would make a cuppa when melegs got worse, sit with her when she needed company, help her when she wanted a shower? Where could she apply for help? The Catholics had it sorted, of course. There were so many of them hereabouts that Father Walsh had made a rota for the elderly and disabled, and he didn't stick just to Catholics. But Enid would die before she'd beg at his door.

Reaching out for her walker, she managed to stand. Fear made her weak. The knowledge that no one would come if she fell terrified her, but she was determined. She could walk and she would walk. Given a stairlift and a scooter with a motor, she could do anything she liked. Couldn't she?

Philly, who had clearly been crying, opened the door. Dave had shot upstairs after the call from his mother, and Philly was giving him a chance to recover. 'Hello, Mrs Turnbull,' she said. 'Come in. You look upset.'

Mary entered the cottage. 'I am upset, love, and so are you. But can I borrow your sofa for the night? Only I don't want to wake my grandchildren, you see. I don't know what sort of reception I'll get from Valda, and if there's a row when I turn up—'

'She'll be all right. Valda's a good woman. You're both good women, Mary, but you're going to have to make space for each other. And I don't mean separate living rooms – I mean inside, in your heads. If you do that, she'll be fine with you.'

'Better than what I've been living with, and that's for sure.'

Philly went into the kitchen to make Lancashire's universal cure, a cup of tea. She popped her head through the doorway and asked whether Mary would care for a biscuit. 'No thanks,' was the reply. 'I couldn't stomach anything after what's gone on. Sorry I told her. But it's all round the village anyway—'

'Don't worry. It'll be all right.'

Mary sniffed, dried her eyes and wiped her nose. 'Will Enid be all right, though? Her legs are terrible today.'

'That's our problem now. I know what she's like and I know what she thinks of me. What's had me in tears is finding out about how she's treated her son. She gave him a terrible life, and she intends to carry on doing just that. But I'll sort her out, don't you worry.'

'You?' Mary failed to keep the shock from her face. Philly was a gentle soul, far too kind to survive more than a couple of rounds with Enid Barker.

Philly nodded, and a watery smile appeared on her lips. 'I'm stronger now.' She didn't know why she was suddenly confident, though she nursed a suspicion that her new status owed something to the fact that she now considered herself a complete woman. 'We won't be here tomorrow.'

'I know.'

'So I'm going to fetch Valda now.' Philly raised her hand. 'She won't be in bed yet. The meeting finished only just over half an hour ago. Don't try to stop me, because I've made up my mind.' She left an open-mouthed Mary with a cup of tea and no company except for Skippy, who was begging for food again.

Until Dave came down. When she saw her master, the dog laid herself across the hearth rug. There were no biscuits anyway, so she might as well pretend to be obedient.

'Where's Philly gone?' Dave asked.

'For Valda.'

'That's the ticket. I'll get myself some cocoa.' He went into the kitchen.

Before he returned with his drink, Philly and Valda

arrived. The latter approached her mother-in-law without any hesitation. 'You're coming home,' she said. 'I know we haven't always got along, but we're going to – and that's a threat, madam. Your son loves you and wants to look after you. When we've finished the extension, you'll share our kitchen, but you'll have your own bedsit and bathroom. You'll be able to bring friends home to your own part of the house, and the kids won't come into your bit unless you say so.'

Mary burst into tears. She didn't deserve it. She'd been a bad mother, too possessive, and she'd been horrible to Valda. These statements emerged crippled by tears.

'Oh, shut up,' Valda said. 'You're coming back with me, and that's an end to it. If you start being difficult, we'll lock you in the shed with a crossword and a pot of tea. Every mother thinks no woman is good enough for her son. God alone knows what I'll be like when my kids start bringing folk home. I'll be on to Babs Cookson's policeman to ask if any of them have criminal records. Just get back to our house and stop whingeing.'

'What now?' Philly asked when she and Dave were alone.

Dave raised his shoulders and spread out his hands. 'I don't know. I've never known what to do about a mother who switched from prostitute to saint as soon as her looks went. Not a Catholic saint, mind. She'd have to be a Methodist one.'

'Are there any? I think most saints are Catholic, created by a pope.'

Dave was suddenly deep in thought. 'The problem is, we have an ageing diabetic who needs help. Everybody's sick to the back teeth with her, but the fact remains that I'm her son. As she has alienated just about everyone within a ten-mile radius, who's going to want to help her?'

Philly swallowed hard. 'I'll do it. You'll do it. We'll do it together.'

'But what—'

'Never mind that what-ing and iffing. It has to be done. Since ... since you and I got together, I've changed. I can do the water-off-a-duck's-back thing. She'll not frighten me. Now, if she's ill while we're at the shop, she can ring a bell – get an electric one fitted. If we're at home, it's only a couple of minutes away, and she has a phone.'

Relief made him smile. 'Thanks, Philly.'

'You're welcome. Now, off to bed with you. I've never been to Birmingham before. What shall I wear?'

'Clothes?'

'Ha-ha.'

'All right. Clogs and shawl, then they'll know where we come from ...'

Eve Boswell was in her element. Rose Cottage was theirs, though the mortgage was considerable – and she was going to have a party before moving in. She had invited so many people that caterers were involved, and there would be no furniture to speak of until after the celebration. She'd no intention of filling the house with nice stuff just for people to abuse it while drunk.

'Where will they all sit?' Chas asked.

'A sensible question for once,' Eve said. 'They can bring deckchairs, garden seats, tea chests, bean bags – three-piece suites – I don't care. They're not messing it up with booze and food after I've decorated and furnished. And it's a massive garden. If the weather holds, I might let you loose with a bit of charcoal and a packet of sausages. Tomato sauce, too, if you behave.'

'Gee, thanks,' was the enthusiastic reply. Chas wasn't keen on the garden. He called it the Devil's Jungle, and had been overheard on many occasions stating his determination that he wasn't going out there alone, as there might be tigers and other large beasts secreted within its depths. Whenever gardening was mentioned, he said he wanted a guide, a gun, a compass and a tent.

As far as the inside of the house was concerned, Chas quite liked the oak beams, though he expressed a desire to skim over the rough plasterwork. He survived the ensuing barrage from his wife, who accused him of planning quite deliberately to be obtuse, ignorant and downright daft, though he knew she could tell from his face that he understood the value of Rose Cottage's original features. 'Can we have some proper glass in the windows? The world out there's distorted,' was another cause for argument, so he stopped teasing her, because Eve had a swarm of bees in her bonnet when it came to history and conservation.

'That glass was hand-made in a sweatshop hundreds of years ago, probably by children.'

'No,' he contradicted her. 'The kids were all up chimneys, weren't they?' However, if he heard her yelling once more, 'It's seventeenth century, you soft lad,' he might well get a headache, so he tried not to mention draughts, bumpy walls, uneven floors and doors that didn't quite fill the gaps for which they had been constructed.

The party was to be a double celebration, because the engagement of Philomena Gallagher and Dave Barker was to be announced. Dave's mother had been invited.

She had neither accepted nor declined, but no one expected her to turn up. 'She'd put the best of us off our vols-au-vent, anyway,' said Derek.

Derek, who had taken a liking to Rose Cottage, had changed his mind about remaining in the flat over the shop, to the consternation of his father, as Chas had wanted Derek to keep an eye on things at number one. Now he would have to make do with Paul Smith, the hairdresser who had gone mobile in a big purple van. Nobody seemed to like Paul, but beggars couldn't be choosers. Chas was desperate, as was Paul, so that was an end of the matter. The importation of illicit goods for special customers might well have to cease.

The trees nearest the house were decked out in fairy lights of many colours. As the weather held, food was spread on trestle tables on a paved area outside the dining room. Philly, who had been a great help, fussed about with various covers in an effort to keep insects away. She overused her left hand, smiling when the half-carat diamond reflected light from the decorated trees.

Dave arrived by her side. 'Well?' she asked.

'Spitting bile, as usual. Going on about Valda swapping sex for clothes. And that's coming from somebody who bartered with her body until I was about ten years old. She's got this wonderfully selective memory. Her life started the day she put on a dowdy coat and walked down to the Methodist chapel. Everything before that never happened. I think she's had her hard drive surgically removed.'

Philly shook her head. 'She's not coming.' It was not a question.

'No. And when I explained to her that Tommy and Valda had always wanted a big family, and that he buys her an outfit once her pregnancy's confirmed, she shut down. She didn't shut up, though. Wanted the price of your ring and to know had we bought anything else. When I told her about the matching wedding ring, she went a funny colour. But at least poor Valda got a rest for a while.'

Philly stopped messing about with food for a few minutes. 'I think you should stay away for a week or so. Let me deal with her.'

Dave stared blankly at his fiancée for a few seconds. 'She'll eat you alive. You know how rotten she was with you when you took up her elevenses. Philly, you're too nice for her.'

She smiled. 'Am I? Watch this space, David. Just you wait. She's seventy, and I'm a stripling of only forty-three. Anyway, I'm different now.'

It was his turn to grin. 'I wonder why?'

People began to arrive in serious numbers, many in possession of fold-away chairs, large cushions, stools and, of course, the obligatory bottle. As most of the booze had been bought from Chas's shop, he decided to enjoy himself after all. Although he wasn't exactly built to specification for al fresco parties, he threw himself into the event quite literally, and was dragged out of a small pond by villagers who were finding the occasion every bit as hilarious as they had expected. Scousers were guaranteed to be amusing, and Chas was certainly up to standard.

He stood there dripping. When the laughter faded, Eve approached him with a small paper napkin. 'Dry yourself,' she ordered as she handed him the flimsy item. 'And don't forget behind your ears, you big wet nelly.'

'What's a wet nelly?' Valda asked.

'Him,' replied Eve. 'It's also yesterday's cake gone stale. It sits in the shop window, only drenched in syrup to jazz it up a bit. You serve it with custard.' She cast a disdainful eye over her beloved husband. 'Yes. Looks a lot like that,' she said before stepping away to see to her guests.

Chas walked home to change his clothes. He squelched across the road and almost collided with Babs Cookson and her policeman boyfriend. 'Oh. Hiya,' he managed. 'I fell in the pond.'

'We'd never have guessed, would we, Pete?'

'I'd have to look at the evidence and get forensics on to it.'

Chas was allergic to policemen, so he walked on. Babs shouted, 'Is Lily there yet?'

'No.'

Pete and Babs stopped at the gate to Rose Cottage. 'I'm going to have a look at her,' Babs announced. 'Sorry, but I need to know if she's OK.'

'What if she's not ready? What if she doesn't want to be in a crowd? Babs, think of what she's been through. People take different lengths of time to recover.'

'Wait there. I know what I'm doing.' The determined little woman marched off past the church to Lily's house. At the front door, she paused and waited for a while. There were voices coming from within, and she didn't know whether to listen or make a hasty retreat. The voices became clearer. 'You can't hide in here.' It was the priest.

'Mike, leave me alone. I'll come along when I'm ready.'

There followed a long pause during which Babs pinned her ear against the letter box.

156

'You have to talk to me.' The man's voice rose in pitch. 'Whatever has happened to you, unburden yourself and leave it all in the past where it belongs. Allow this village to keep you safe. It's that kind of place – we'll help you.'

The door was not locked. Babs walked into the house, stood with hands on hips in front of Father Walsh, and gave him both barrels. 'Listen, you,' she said, her colour heightening. 'I don't care who you are – priest, rabbi, vicar or some lunatic sitting in a nappy on top of a hill until he dies. Leave her alone. You've no idea what she's been through, no knowledge of what she suffered. Pete's a cop, and he knows enough to leave it be. If she wants to come to the party, she'll come. It's nothing to do with you, so bugger off.'

He opened his mouth to speak, thought better of it, and buggered off as ordered.

Lily sank into a chair. 'Babs, you shouldn't have done that.'

'Why? Have you not had enough browbeating from a bloke who thought he knew better than the rest? Just tell him to sod off, Lee. Pick up speed when you're ready. Stay in, or go out when you want to, not when someone pushes you.'

'It's just—'

'It's just in case somebody who saw you on TV recognizes you. You don't do crowds. If you don't do crowds, stay where you are. And there's the vet and Derek sniffing after you, so make up your own mind. Don't be listening to him just because he sometimes wears his shirt collar back to front.'

Lily shook her head. At the ripe old age of twenty-seven, Babs sometimes managed to sound like somebody's grandmother. She was wise and silly at the same time, was a good friend in spite of the inauspicious way in which the two of them had met. 'He's a nice man, Babs. He means well.'

Babs threw herself onto a stool. 'They're all after you, missus – even the priest. There's that Derek – far too young–'

'Four years,' said Lily. 'I'm twenty-eight, he's twenty-four–'

'A middle-aged vet, that man who delivers flowers, the milkman, the postman, even the priest.' She shook her head in mock-despair. 'Look, stay here if you want to. I'll get back to Pete.' She waited for a few beats of time to pass. 'I'll stop here with you if you want, my lover.'

Lily bowed her head and sighed. 'I'm tired, Babs. I've been tired ever since it happened, and I'm sick of trying to grow eyes in the back of my head.' She groaned softly. 'They've moved him to Walton jail in Liverpool.'

'Where Charlie Bronson threw all the tiles off the roof?'

'I don't know. Probably.' Lily stood up. 'Only forty-odd miles away. Sometimes, I think I can hear him breathing in the next room. His asthma often gave him away.'

'And the cops know you're here?'

Lily nodded.

'But they still . . . Where's the sense? Look what you've given up, from a job that paid a fortune to your beautiful hair. When will they learn? I'll talk to Pete about this. Something's got to be done.'

'No.' There was vehemence in Lily's tone. 'Look, I trust Pete and I know you do, but who will he talk to? Leave it, Babs. Promise me you'll do nothing. Pete can't change this – he can only make it worse by inadvertently talking to a bent cop or probation officer. Silence is best.'

Babs ran a hand through a tangle of dark auburn curls. After all their efforts to leave the past behind, it was following them. Would they have to move again?

Lily answered the unspoken question. 'No more running. We stay, and we keep quiet. All right?'

Babs nodded. 'It's Cassie I worry about.'

'Me too.'

'Are you coming to this party or not? He's not even drunk yet, but Chas Boswell's already managed to baptize himself in that ornamental pond. Lily, if you're scared, I understand. But you run a shop. People come and go in there all week, and there's easily as much danger of you getting recognized while you're behind the counter as there is at a party. A party's just all the customers coming at the same time and refusing to form an orderly queue.'

'He'll be there.'

'Who?'

'Mike. He won't let me call him Father. I can't look at him. It's as if I owe him a confession, a list of sins. He looks straight through me.'

Babs tutted her impatience. 'He's a man, babe. You are still one extraordinarily good-looking woman. Remember that chap from the telly? He was going to leave his job, his wife, his kids and his brain behind just to sit at your feet. And now that the light's started to come back in your eyes, you're giving out signals without knowing it. Pete reckons you should be in Hollywood.'

Lily shook her head. 'If I went to California, he'd find me, or get someone else to do it for him.'

'We're not talking about Father Wotsisname or Pete now?'

'Of course not. Babs, Clive's got money hidden at his mother's house. He's got friends on the outside. The planet ain't big enough.'

Babs sat for a while, then excused herself to go off and find Pete. Her babysitter, a young girl from a nearby estate, had to be home by midnight, so Babs would need to leave the celebrations relatively early. And Pete didn't deserve to be left standing for too long.

Lily stared into an empty grate. Although she was enjoying doing the work on Hope House, she could never be completely happy while Clive Chalmers lived. Everything had been spoilt or killed by him, the man in whom she had placed all trust. Forty miles away, he would be on a landing or a wing with men who, like him, had attacked the most vulnerable members of society. His companions, with whom he might never mix, would be paedophiles, child-killers and rapists. If he was still on 43, that was. Should he be moved to an ordinary wing, he'd be meeting all kinds of people who—No. She mustn't think about him employing someone to make matters worse. Lily sighed. Wormwood Scrubs had seemed far enough away, but it hadn't been. Mars might have been OK, but only just.

Why had they moved him, though? And why up here? His mother, who had been completely shocked and incredulous when he had been arrested, would have difficulty travelling to see him, and that was a shame, because she was a nice woman. Perhaps that was the reason; perhaps the authorities were moving him to a place where he would have few contacts.

But she knew him. There was an evil streak in him,

broad as a motorway, complicated as Spaghetti Junction, and he would find her. It would be by proxy, because it would have to be, but there was no real hiding place.

It was nine o'clock. She checked her make-up to be sure that her mascara hadn't taken a trip down her cheeks, dragged a comb through her blonde, carefully streaked hair, and walked down the hall. In spite of all she was going through, she smiled when she remembered Maurice Jones and the advice he had given. 'Don't be all blonde, sweetheart. Let's throw in some low-lights. After all, we need to be convincing, don't we?'

What had he meant by that, she wondered as she locked her front door. It didn't matter, because Maurice was a gentleman, which was more than could be said for his ex-partner. Paul was doing his best to pull the rug from under the feet of Mo and Sally by undercutting them, by trying to blacken Mo's name, by working twelve hours a day. Lily knew how it felt when the ground became unsteady, when a person to whom one had been close suddenly turned into a monster.

She reached Rose Cottage, took a deep breath, then walked round to the back of the house. It was chaos. Chas was playing the mouth organ very badly, while Derek, who had probably been commandeered against his better judgement, accompanied his father on the spoons. Eve, having taken rather a large amount of Chardonnay, could not find the right notes on her accordion. The resulting noise had sent most of the party fleeing to the far end of the garden. Only the stalwarts and the tone deaf had the guts to remain and face this poor excuse for music.

Derek's eyes were immediately on Lily. He put down his spoons, which were, unfortunately, the least offensive of all the murdered instruments, and made a beeline for her. Eve ceased playing for a few blessed seconds and nudged her husband. 'He's setting his cap at her,' she whispered.

Chas stopped blowing into his mouth organ. He shook it, muttered something about the bugger being full of spit and beer, then continued the torture. It was arrested abruptly when his wife's words finally registered after negotiating a route to his brain past Stella Artois and red wine. 'Well, he won't get her. Nobody will. She's built a wall the size of Hadrian's around herself.' He started to play again, after shaking more moisture out of his harmonica.

Eve watched her son. The enthusiasm had gone out of her playing, while Chas, whose mouth organ was still delivering all the wrong notes in the wrong order, also gave up. 'Where is everybody?' he asked.

'In the jungle,' his wife replied. 'They made a dash when you started the assassination of "Amazing Grace".'

'I never played "Amazing Grace",' he said, his tone reflecting deep injury. 'It was "Knees Up Mother Brown".' Chas armed himself with a yard brush and another can of ale before venturing forth to rescue friends and neighbours from wild animals, killer insects and dangerous snakes.

Ghostly figures began to emerge from the depths of Rose Cottage's not inconsiderable acreage. Lily saw Valda and Tommy, Philly and Dave, Maurice with Sally, Babs and Pete. There were many others whose names she didn't know, but the main problem was Derek, who had taken up a nonchalant position against a wall. One look at Lily's face had told him to stay away. Tim Mellor was approaching her, but he was easily fifty, so he didn't count in Derek's inexperienced book.

'How are you?' asked the notoriously cheerful vet.

'Fine,' she answered. 'I shan't stay long, though. I'm not a great drinker.'

'Me neither.' He took a long draught of beer, covered a belch with a polite hand. 'We should get to know each other better,' he continued. 'You must come for dinner one night. Mind, I'm not the best of cooks, so it would be takeaway. There's been nothing decent cooked in my kitchen since the wife ran off with the rep for a company which manufactured diet food for dogs. She's on the Isle of Wight now. I suppose someone has to live there.'

For a non-drinker, he was terribly drunk. Lily excused herself and went to talk to Babs and Pete.

Just on the edge of her vision, Mike Walsh stood, drink in one hand, Skippy's lead in the other. He had probably taken charge of the dog so that Dave and Philly could cut their engagement cake. There were speeches, followed by applause, then ABBA blared out all over the garden. It was clear that Skippy was not an ABBA fan, because she bolted just as 'Waterloo' began, the priest hanging on to the lead for dear life. Lily smiled. The dog had lost a leg, but she could shift, while many people here were more legless than Skippy would ever be.

Mike regained his composure and handed Skippy back to her grateful owners. He approached Lily, a hand beating his breast. 'Mea maxima culpa,' he said.

'Can't you get ointment for that?' Lily asked.

He made a remark about people who didn't know Latin, so she reeled off a list of plants with names that were inches long.

163

'Touché,' he said before wandering off.

Lily sat alone for a while, just watching other people having fun. This was how ridiculous the inebriated seemed to the sober, then. Chas was standing on a chair. For some reason best known to himself, he was reading out the American Declaration of Independence. His wife, the lovely Eve, had decided to show everyone her curtain swatches, some of which had ended up in the pond. Dave and Philly were sober, as were Babs, Pete, Valda, Tommy and Sally, but the rest of the company were in a state of sore disrepair.

Tim Mellor had attached himself to a piece of eye-candy from the other end of the village, while Maurice was making a collection of garden gnomes, strays left behind by a previous owner. He was lining them up under the dining-room window, and he seemed to have plans for them. 'He's going to drown them in Fullers Brook,' a voice said. 'There will be a suitable service conducted by himself in a frock.'

It was Derek. If he asked her to go out for dinner again, she would have to make herself clear. It was no, had always been no, would always be no. He must have seen the expression in her eyes, because he staggered off without further comment or request.

Lily decided that she was a miserable cow, and went to put that right. Eve, having eaten enough to soak up the wine, was one of the least tired and emotional revellers present. She greeted Lily with enthusiasm. 'Good to see you, Lily. Glad you decided to come.'

Lily smiled. 'If you'd like to stop by my house one evening, I have a portfolio that belonged to a friend of mine. She was in interior design, and she had a way of making the truly modern work without spoiling the history of a house. It's all Belfast sinks and brushed steel, but it works given the right colours and textures.'

Eve was delighted. 'Oh, ta, love,' she gushed. 'Here, have a prawn vol-au-vent. I'd say I made them myself, but it would be a lie. Yes, I'd be glad to look at your porto – what was it?'

'Portfolio.'

'Like an artist has when he goes to college?'

'Yes.' Lily pulled Eve to one side. 'You won't be offended if I go home, will you? It's a headache.'

'You go, sweetheart. I'll see you tomorrow, if that's all right.'

Lily took herself off. She couldn't drink more than a couple of glasses of wine, because she had seen first-hand what happened when people over-imbibed. Sober, Clive had been evil; drunk, he had always become the devil incarnate. Alcohol changed people, and seldom for the better.

At home once more, she wondered whether she was now doomed to be a mere spectator, an outsider like Mrs Barker who sat all day at a window and watched a life in which she no longer took an active part. She had been reduced to this by marrying too young, by marrying the wrong man. He would have been wrong for just about anyone.

In the dining room, she stood in darkness, because the outside security light was on, and she knew it was announcing the presence of her little fox family. They had begun to allow her into their lives, because domestic food was palatable and they were becoming unnaturally tame. Was that a good thing? Had they managed to make a friend of the one animal that had always been their greatest enemy?

Out of the shadows, a human figure stepped, and Lily's heart began to crash about until it seemed to threaten her ribs. But it wasn't a stranger. It was Mike. He sat down carefully at the edge of the paved area and reached out a hand, and one of the adult foxes came and took food from him. It was unutterably touching. Here, in a dark garden, a man trusted by timorous beasts seemed to portray all that Lily had lost. He was no threat. He removed nothing, gave everything, was full of love for all around him.

Lily's heart slowed to its normal pace, and she retreated from the window to sit on a dining chair. She could still see him, could tell that he was talking to the creatures. The babies, growing older and more sensible, skittered about less enthusiastically now that wisdom was colouring their behaviour. But they didn't run away. Nothing and no one ran away from him. Except Lily Latimer, of course.

He came into the house, and she was drawn to join him. At the kitchen sink, he washed his hands, turned, saw her standing there. 'Lily?'

'They're so tame now.'

He nodded. 'And you are in charge when I'm not here. On the one hand, we have upset the balance of nature, but on the other we are privileged beyond measure.'

'They'll be inside the house soon,' she said.

'Perhaps. But keep them away from your Chippendales.'

'Imitation Chippendales. I'm not that wealthy.'

He hung up the towel. 'What now, party girl? Scrabble, dominoes, Monopoly?'

'I hate Monopoly.'

'Cards?'

166

'No. I think bed is the best place for me.'

He lowered his head for a few seconds. 'Lily, this isn't the first time.'

'What? First time for what?'

'I've fallen in love before. Never did anything about it, but it's more frightening this time.'

She didn't ask why, because she already knew.

'This ... feeling is travelling in more than one direction. Isn't it? That's why I have the courage to speak to you. Emotion as strong as this couldn't exist in a cul-de-sac, could it?'

With anyone else in the world, Lily would have shrugged it off. She might have called the man foolish, stupid, deluded, would probably have advised him to go away and play with the other infants in the school yard. But with Michael Walsh, there had to be absolute truth at all times and at whatever cost. She whispered, 'No,' then sat at the table. 'But nothing will be done this time, either, Mike. Not just because of your position in the world, but because I'm not suitable. Too damaged.'

'I need to find somewhere else to stay.'

'No. We're adults and we are in control.'

He sat opposite her. 'I'm glad you feel like that. But sometimes, if I wake in the night, I am sorely tempted to climb that second flight of stairs. Just to look at you, just to hold you ... but we both know it wouldn't stop there. I should have more sense at my age – I'll be forty in a couple of years – but I'm like a teenager whose hormones are just kicking in.'

In spite of herself, she smiled at him. Then, with a more serious expression on her face, she gave him a part of her past. 'There is a possibility that I may not be able to ...' Oh, God, how could she put this? 'There was physical hurt, you see. I was very badly injured, in and out of hospital for eight months, in a coma for the first couple of weeks. I had some extremely fancy embroidery done on my . . . abdomen. None of the blood in my body was my own. They started me on O neg, did the tests, gave me the right group. I owe a lot to the hospital, everything to blood donors. I should have died.' There was no need to tell him that she had wanted to die at the start, when she had woken from the long sleep.

'God,' he breathed.

'No, it wasn't God – it was a surgeon named Myers. He put me together again. I was luckier than Humpty-Dumpty, you see.'

He reached across the table and took her hand. 'I'm sorry you went through all that, Lily, but I'm so glad that you survived it. I don't care what you can or can't do – this is more than sexual. That's why it's different.' It was powerful and dangerous. It was true that he had been attracted to women in the past, but this was the first time he had been afraid. Beyond the fear loomed excitement, adventure and the loss of his job. But she shone more brightly than anyone he had ever known, and he would sacrifice anything at all to be with her. He squeezed her hand. 'Your face was dead when you arrived here. Now, you're coming to life.'

Her hand tingled as if hit by a bolt of lightning. She didn't believe in any of it, had never set much store by the concept of chemical love, as she termed this kind of attraction. The idea of love at first sight was similarly alien to her mind. Yet the fact remained that she was shaking inwardly, that she wanted to dash round the table and hold him in her arms. But Lily was an adult. 'It will be all right,' she said, her voice slightly unsteady.

'How can it be all right?'

She looked straight into his eyes. 'It can be all right because it isn't hell. I've been there, so almost everything is easy after that.'

'Who did it?'

'A man.'

'Lily—'

'Go to bed,' she told him. 'Go and sleep in the room that was always yours, and I shall go to my room. I'm not ready for any great changes, and I don't know whether I shall ever be ready. You are a priest, and I don't need to tell you what that means. You're a good man, and these villages round here need you. Not just for church, but for—'

'Pantomime, last rites, rotas for loving thy neighbour. Most of all, for pantomime.'

'For the community, yes. It's not just the Catholics, you see. Apart from Mrs Barker, who hates almost everyone, this whole area values and loves you. Can you imagine how they would feel if you gave up all that for me, abandoned them for me? Or for any woman, come to that. We have to act our age and just carry on carrying on.'

'And without carrying on in the other sense of the word.' He held on to her hand as if it were a lifebelt. 'Who are you, Lily? Who sent you here?'

She shrugged. 'I came all by myself. Stuck a pin in the upper part of the map, and here I am.'

'Like a piece of magic.'

'No, Mike. Like a wounded animal that daren't trust its own kind. I may be ten years younger than you, yet I am half a century older, because what happened to me made me old.'

'Was Babs part of it?'

She nodded.

'But she wasn't injured.'

'Her heart was broken, but her physical hurt healed. And she has Cassie. Cassie is the only good thing to have emerged from the whole sordid mess.' She freed her hand and stood up. 'If you are truly tortured in my house, find another place. But I like having you here. You're the closest I've come to trust. Apart from Babs. She and I have needed to believe in each other. Good night, Mike.'

It was lonely upstairs. Even the circular window didn't cheer her. Nor did the crisp sheets, the mirrored French furniture, the beautiful curtains. He was suffering, and she hated that. She was used to pain, physical and mental, but he had never asked to be dragged into this, whatever 'this' was.

On the floor below, Mike undressed, showered, said his prayers. He was a priest. Priests could overcome just about anything, because God was on their side. He groaned. Sexual attraction he might have dismissed as a feeble effort by Satan to get him on board. After all, hadn't Christ Himself been tempted by the devil?

Neither slept well that night. Each was tormented by the knowledge that comfort and understanding were just a few steps away. Each was wise enough not to take those steps.

The trouble with screws is that the government pays peanuts and gets monkeys. Give a monkey a nut to chew on, and he'll follow you home.

Some following has to be done. We follow the money. Her house is sold and her shop, too, has changed hands.

Those places were sold by Leanne Chalmers. Even if she has changed her name, there are people in banks and solicitors' offices who are open to suggestion. So. We need to know the area to which the money was sent, the bank into which it has been paid, the name under which it is making interest.

Walton's OK. It's not the Ritz, but the locals are amusing. Bright, too. Scallies, as Liverpool calls its fallen ones, are not without brains. That quick-fire humour conceals nothing, and it shows intelligence behind such wit.

I know a man who'll pay a man who'll pay another man. Leanne, I'm on my way, babe.

Seven

'Right. You can eat it or leave it, Mrs Barker. I'm not going to stand here worrying like Dave used to. If you don't eat, the insulin you've injected will be too much for you, and you'll get confused, fall over and may go into a hypoglycaemic coma. That'll be you in hospital for several days at least.'

Enid's hands closed into fists. Here was another one who'd swallowed a bloody dictionary. Between them, Dave and his fiancée knew English inside out, and they used it as weaponry. If only she had her health and strength, she'd send this one back downstairs at a faster than normal rate. There again, if she had her health and strength, she wouldn't need to be in the same room as Philomena Gallagher, because she'd be fending for herself. Determined not to talk to this madam, Enid allowed only a small grunt to punctuate the ensuing silence.

'Well? Shall I get the doctor to come? Shall I tell him you're sulking and making yourself ill by refusing food? Because he'll put his foot behind you, mark my words. Acting like a child, refusing food—'

Enid picked up a fork, stabbed half an egg and transferred it to her mouth. Who the bloody hell did Philomena Gallagher think she was talking to?

'Good decision,' said Philly before rushing back downstairs. She was in a state worse than Russia, and she had to deal with a certain matter immediately.

It was a computer day. Bert and Sam, a pair of recidivists who couldn't go a day without the Reading Room, were fighting over a woman they'd both met online. Bert, who walked with the aid of a stick, was a few years older than Sam. 'I'll be bloody dead in a few months,' he cried. 'You can have her when I'm gone and buried. The way your arthritis is thriving, I'll leave you my stick and all.'

Sam snorted his disgust. 'What is this? Pass the parcel? Leave a girlfriend in your will? She likes me, not you.'

'Children, children,' Philly shouted. 'Stop the fighting, will you? I've trouble enough upstairs without you two kicking off. Skippy, who gave you that scone?' She looked round the Reading Room. 'Stop feeding the dog,' she ordered. 'In case you haven't noticed, she's one leg missing and we have to keep her thin.'

'Don't get your corsets in a twist,' said Sam. 'You've gone all . . . what's the word, Bert?'

'Religious?'

'No, is it heck. You've gone all . . . wotsit since you got engaged, Philly.'

She gave him the word. 'Bolshie,' she snapped. 'I've gone difficult.' She smiled, then reminded herself that she shouldn't be smiling. Because there was a question that needed to be answered right away.

Nevertheless, she was proud of herself. For years, she'd never said boo to a goose, but now she could tackle a gaggle or a skein, because she had Dave to back her up. Feeling powerful, she clicked the computer off line. 'Now,' she said, a finger wagging at the two old men. 'Stop courting and fighting in here, because we've no licence for entertainment.'

Bert made a rude sign, while Sam stuck out his tongue.

Philly, referring to the latter protrusion, expressed the opinion that its owner should leave the object to medical science, as it owned more coats than most women's winter wardrobes.

'Clever,' said Sam.

Philly picked up her handbag and went through to the washroom. She locked the door, sat on the lid of the lavatory and tried to get her mind in order. It shouldn't have happened. It couldn't have happened. Knowing her luck, it probably had happened. She followed instructions to the letter, stood, and stared in the mirror while waiting for her fate to be decided.

Several minutes later, she shot through the shop like a deer with a dozen stalkers on its heels. Where had he gone? She dashed back into the shop. 'Where did Dave go?' she asked.

'Memory's buggered,' was Sam's delivered opinion.

'Market – for trousers,' said Bert. 'He's going to slide down the bath plughole if you keep starving him.'

Philly blinked, then backed away. 'You're in charge,' she told the two elderly men as she moved. 'Bert – books and papers. Sam – Reading Room teas, coffees and whatevers.'

'We want bloody paying this time,' yelled one of them as she disappeared altogether.

Philly stood on Fullers Walk wondering what she was supposed to do next. She couldn't do next, because Dave was supposed to be next. He was the father, so she should talk to him first. She felt sick. Feeling sick was probably part and parcel of the situation in which she found herself. Unable to keep still, she marched up and down outside the florist's and the salon. 'Stop it,' she said under her breath. 'He'll be here in a minute.'

'Philly?'

She turned to find Lily Latimer behind her. 'Oh. Hello.' Their names rhymed. Was this an omen? 'Can we go inside?' she asked. 'Only I'm not myself today.'

They entered the flower shop and Lily shut the door, turning the sign to CLOSED. 'What's the matter?' she asked.

Philly pointed to the ceiling. 'I told Dave I'd see to her, because she whips the rug from under his feet every time he visits. So I decided to stop her. She hurts him. She's been hurting him since the day he was born.'

Lily nodded encouragingly. 'You've done a lot for him. He's even had a proper haircut, hasn't he? No more plastering down the long bits to cover the baldness. And he's a lot thinner.'

'Yes.' Philly looked round the shop. 'Has Babs started next door?'

'Maurice has begun to re-educate her. Cassie's with Valda.' Lily paused. 'What is it?' There was definitely more than the old hag behind all this. 'Are you ill? Is Dave ill?'

Philly shook her head. 'No, no, we're fine. I want Dave, but he's gone into Bolton again to get trousers from the market. He'll have three different sizes now. All he needed was a bit of love and encouragement.'

Lily stared hard at her visitor. 'You have to tell him first?'

Philly nodded.

'A baby?'

Philly stayed very still.

'You haven't told me. You haven't said anything, my lovely.' Lily ordered herself to fight the jealousy. It was normal, but it was ugly. It was probably impossible for Lily to ever go full term, but she must not resent this lovely woman who had to fight her own guilt. The Catholic Church thrived on guilt, nurtured it, drummed rules into the heads of infants, some of whom then grew up with a distorted view of life. If the worst thing a woman ever did was to get pregnant before wearing a wedding ring, that was a small crime. In fact, it wasn't a crime at all, and Lily said so.

'But we have to get married.'

'You are getting married.'

Philly began to pace about the shop. 'It has to be quick. Father Walsh is arranging it, because we're a mixed couple, but it has to be now.'

'This minute?'

'Almost. Only I can't speak to my priest before telling Dave, can I?

Lily supposed not. 'Stop marching, Philly. You'll be wearing out the floor if you carry on like this.'

'Sorry.'

'And don't panic. If you are carrying a child, you don't want to make yourself ill.' Why were men never where they should be when you needed them most? Did they follow a different clock, or a calendar women hadn't heard of yet? 'When did he go?'

'Don't know. Can't remember.'

'When did you buy the test kit? I'm assuming you've done a test?'

Philly nodded. 'Nine o'clock, when the chemist opened.' She coloured. 'I told a lie, said it was for some young girl.'

176

'And Dave had already left for town?'

'Yes.'

'So you do know. You know he left before nine. Sit down.'

Philly sat while Lily opened the door and stood waiting. Feeling as if she carried someone's proxy vote, Lily lingered in the doorway,

coming inside only to serve three customers who arrived at roughly ten-minute intervals. 'His van's coming now. Look. I'll go upstairs and you get him in here. Go through to the back. If I get a customer, let me know. You can't tell him in his own shop – it's full of computer loonies. Do it here among the flowers.'

So, after announcing that he was now the proud owner of two more pairs of trousers, Dave Barker was standing alongside buckets of summer blooms when he learned that he was to be a father. He blinked stupidly as if waking from a long sleep, then wept a few tears of happiness. 'We'd better track your Father Walsh down,' he said when he regained some composure. 'I've never been happier, Phil. Thank you so much for loving me.'

Lily sat at the top of the stairs, skirt held tightly to her ankles, head bowed onto her knees. She was empty. There was a part of her that was so empty that sometimes she wanted to die. Not now, not at this moment. She was happy for Philly and Dave, because they were wonderful people who deserved to be fulfilled. Nevertheless, Lily's pain was almost physical.

But she was an adult and she would cope. She would sell flowers, make wreaths for the dead and bouquets for the hopeful. She would sleep in a house where a beautiful man sometimes stayed, and she would be sensible, as

177

would he. The wheel of life turned daily, and she had to carry on.

'Feather it.' Maurice Jones stood back and cast a critical eye on the workmanship of his new trainee. 'What did they use in Devonshire?' he asked. 'A flaming plough-share?' He stepped forward and demonstrated again, explaining to the model that the styling was free, that she was a guinea pig, that she would be all right once he had put Babs's small mistake to rights.

'I think I'll give up,' Babs moaned.

'No, you won't. You've got promise.'

Babs laughed. 'Well, God help any bad hairdresser who comes your way. I've not had any praise from you at all, and I was very well thought of down south.'

He grinned at her. 'You think I'm difficult? The bloke who trained me's a tartar, but he gets results.'

'Was Paul better than me?' she asked.

'Of course he was, because I trained him all over again, didn't I? Also, what you're doing isn't necessarily wrong – it's just not what we do at Pour Les Dames. Right. Come here, madam, and do this bit. Round the ear – shape it back. Now, we want a couple of tendrils feathered down – that's right. See? You're not as daft as you look.'

'I couldn't be.'

Sally drifted in. She was having what she described as a sleepy pregnancy, because she could scarcely keep her eyes open for more than an hour at a time. 'I'll go and heat my wax,' she told her husband. 'And I'd love a cuppa, if anyone's offering.'

Babs went to brew the tea while Maurice finished off the model. Up to now, Babs had been allowed to wash and put finishing touches to hair, but Maurice's style of cutting was a whole new world for her, and she was enjoying learning in spite of the exchanges of words and the heavily applied advice.

Sally returned from her little space next to the store room. 'Mo?'

'What, love?'

'I've no wax, the trolley's been taken apart, the clients' couch is slashed to shreds, and everything's in a right mess.'

Maurice paused and laid down his implements. 'What?'

'Somebody's broken in and ruined everything. There's acrylic nails everywhere, nail polish poured all over the place, towels soaked in God knows what. I can't do manicures, pedicures or waxing. All I can do is Indian head massage on your clients in here.'

Maurice stormed into the back of the shop. Babs looked at Sally. 'Who do you think did it?' she asked.

'Paul, of course.'

Babs went to finish off the tea-making. Paul was a nightmare. Keen to wipe his ex-partner off the face of the earth, he had set up Impressions and had over-booked himself, failing to account for travelling time between appointments, and ignoring the fact that some clients needed more attention than others. Paul Smith was an extremely angry and aggressive man. If he had done this, he needed dealing with, and pronto.

Maurice looked grim when he returned. 'Stay out of there, love,' he told his wife. 'It's a crime scene. Let's get the police.'

Babs's head was suddenly filled with a scenario that might damage Maurice and Sally. 'Just a minute,' she said before drawing the two into the rear end of the shop, well away from today's guinea pig. 'He can make things worse,' she advised. 'From what I've heard, he was head over heels with you, Mo.'

Maurice shook his head. 'If you want to meet a real bitch, choose a jealous and furious gay. If he'd loved me, he wouldn't have done all this to Sally. This isn't love.'

'No,' Babs agreed, 'it isn't love – it's territory. Mo, if this goes to court, he can call you a stinking good-for-nothing bisexual man who hurt him. They won't know the truth. Why did you let it come to this? Why did you allow the world to think of you and him as partners in the closer sense?'

Mo hung his head. 'We were already well known as a drag act. Some on the circuit knew we weren't a couple, and those who came on to me were aware that I was straight. I just drifted into it, Babs. Psychology. A woman likes a hairdresser she can talk to. Women talk to gays rather than to other women or straight men.'

'Sally?'

Sally answered Babs. 'I hated it. We were man and wife upstairs, but Mo was a caricature down here. Everyone thought I was the lodger, and yes, I was unhappy about all of it. Now that I'm pregnant, Paul is as mad as a frog in a box.'

'Then don't let him tear you to pieces in court. I'll deal with it. Well, Pete will.'

Mo stared at his new recruit for several seconds. 'Thanks, Babs,' he said.

Babs was only too pleased to help. 'I can't promise anything,' she said. 'But I'll do my very best.' She wished she could do the same for Lily. But the threat to Lily's well-being was not visible, was more than a slashed

couch and some spilt polish. If Chalmers ever got to her
... She shivered.

'Are you cold?' Sally asked.

'No,' she replied. 'Something just stepped on my
grave.'

Eve Boswell and her husband were in their forties, yet
they seemed to have retained a youthful and open
attitude to life. Eve, especially, was a lively soul, and
every time she visited Lily in Hope House she arrived
overflowing with ideas, material swatches, paint charts
and photographs of furniture. These offerings were often
a mixed bag, so Lily guided her through the portfolio,
explained about direction of light, where to place the
first length of wallpaper, how to best enhance crudely
plastered walls and bare stonework.

'There's only one room for wallpaper,' Eve explained
'Some soft sod skimmed over the original walls, like my
husband suggested.'

'Chas? He didn't.'

'He was joking. He knew it would be a capital
offence.'

'Ah.' Lily opened one of her files. 'Look at this one.
Same shades from front to back, lighter colour in the same
group on curtains and cushions, darker for the carpet,
take the carpet through to the rest and you have continuity without boredom.'

'Let me have a study of this lot, then.'

While Eve did her studying, Lily set the kettle to boil.
She was grateful to this Liverpudlian woman, because she
had not expected to make close friends at this end of the
country. But Eve was amazing and amusing. She carried
her own mental portfolio filled with pictures of her youth

in Liverpool, word sketches that she drew in her own inimitable manner.

Her husband, she had explained, was in women's underwear. Lily smiled as she remembered how confused she had been – wasn't he in wines and spirits? But Eve had returned a ready answer. Chas's brother and Chas had been a pair of knickers, though the K had been dropped from the front of the garment. Nickers were thieves, so the point became clear eventually.

There had been generations of nickers in the Boswell family, and one of the more famous had been hanged for accidentally killing a chap during a theft from the docks. The Boswells spoke of their deceased ancestor with pride, because he had paid the ultimate price for his chosen vocation. Chas and his brother had been luckier, though Robbo had been caught robbing – there sat another pun that was not allowed to pass unnoticed – while Chas was a lucky bugger and had avoided a criminal record by the skin of his teeth. Had he been caught, he would never have obtained the licence to sell alcohol and tobacco. 'He's going to have to let his special customers down,' Eve said now. For some reason she could never explain completely, she trusted Lily Latimer. Lily knew all about bother – it was written on her face.

'Special customers?' Lily passed a mug to her visitor.

'Boswell business,' replied Eve. 'They still manage to release the odd case of spirits from prison in a bonded warehouse, and Chas sells the stuff round the back of the shop – from the garage. There's ciggies as well. That'll have to stop now, because Paul Smith's moving in.'

'Oh.' Lily didn't like Paul, but she said nothing.

'My Chas is a good man, Lily. You can be a villain and still be a good man.'

'I know.' Lily also knew a villain who was so bad that he was not allowed to mix with normal, decent criminals. At least, she hoped he was still segregated … 'Have a look at this second folder, Eve. Notice how magnolia doesn't need to be a cop-out.'

Eve stared steadily at her hostess and guru. She knew an awful lot about interior design, so why was she in flowers? The new file, which depicted the interior of a country cottage, rang a muffled bell in the deepest recesses of Eve's mind. She experienced a déjà vu moment, but everyone had those. 'Lily?'

'Yes?'

'Do you mind if I ask you what you did before you came here?' There were secrets. Most people had one or two of those, but Lily's careful guardianship of her past was not typical. There was something big there, the sort of event that left emotional scars.

Lily tried not to look afraid. 'This and that. Some party planning, wedding flowers and so forth.' Her heart raced. This should not be happening. She was a fool to think she could use Leanne's portfolio and get away with it.

'And Babs?'

'Was a hairdresser.' Well, that was the truth.

'Ah.' Eve leafed through the pile. She had seen the photographed house before, but she couldn't quite place her finger on where. Then it crashed into her mind like a jackknifed articulated vehicle on the East Lancs. 'Leanne?' she said quietly.

Lily staggered back a couple of paces. She swallowed painfully and looked through the window.

'Leanne Chalmers? Dark hair, dirty laugh, the interior version of Wotserface Dimmock that did gardens with her bouncy boobs?'

Lily remained silent.

'Not that Leanne Chalmers had bouncy boobs, but she was every man's idea of feisty high-class crumpet.' Eve paused for a few beats of time. 'I'm right, aren't I? You're Leanne Chalmers off *Makeover Madness*. Your catchphrase was we do the impossible, miracles only if pressed. You're so thin, so changed . . .'

Lily nodded. Eve Boswell was an all right person; Eve Boswell would not let her down.

Eve covered her face with her hands. 'Shit, shit, shit,' she whispered. 'They put it about that you'd moved abroad, but that was because of . . . Oh, Lily. Oh, my God. And here am I sitting and saying that criminals aren't all bad. I am so sorry, queen.' She was. 'You're smaller, blonde . . .'

'It's all right.' Lily sat at the table.

Eve was weeping openly. 'Who knows?'

'Just you. Babs does, of course. No one else. Oh – Pete has access to details. Mike can tell there's something major wrong with me, but he hasn't placed me yet. He probably never watched the programme. Don't cry, Eve.'

Eve saw the headlines, read them all over again. Jill Dando, God love her, had died. But this wonderful, vibrant, cheeky and opinionated woman had survived. Hadn't she? Had she? It had been so horrible when it was printed. Seeing something written down was some-how far worse than hearing it. Lily was a shadow now. 'You don't look right with blonde hair,' was all Eve could manage.

'It had to be done, Eve. He has friends – well, he knows a lot of criminals who aren't doing time.'

Eve could see Leanne strutting about, ripping off

wallpaper, consigning a householder's belongings to a skip on the path. 'Where is he?'

'Walton. Just been moved from the Scrubs.'

Eve jumped up and began to pace about. It was like Philly all over again, back and forth, stop and think, back and forth like a quickened pendulum.

'Keep still,' said Lily. 'And dry your eyes. I don't want tears all over my bits and pieces, thanks.'

Eve sat down. 'I know people in Walton. Chas even knows a couple of the screws who've been good to their Robbo in the past—'

'Don't waste your breath. He might well be segregated.'

The little Liverpool woman placed a hand on Lily's arm. 'The segregated can be dealt with – remember the Yorkshire Ripper lost an eye? What you went through, babe, was just beyond anything normal. He should be bloody well shot. I'm supposed to be a good Catholic, but I'd kill him as soon as look at him. Christ, I'm angry.'

Lily nodded. 'As was I. I'm still angry, I suppose. For a while, the anger turned inward, because I should have got away before the situation became so horrible. The depression was awful.'

'Must have been, love. Look, I won't say a word.'

Lily smiled. 'You can tell Chas, because I know this is too big a thing to keep inside. You're so close to him, and I'd rather he knew what's affecting your mood. I know it must hurt, because we've become good friends.'

'We have,' said Eve emphatically.

'But don't tell Derek. It's not a matter of trust, it's that I can't stand to be pitied. Pity is painful to receive.'

Eve lost interest in interior decor. She pushed away the files and drank her cooling tea. 'Lily?'

'What?'

'You frightened?'

'Yes.'

'There's ways,' Eve said. 'Say the word, and I'll do my best to get him dealt with. You wouldn't be afraid if he got killed.'

Lily nodded thoughtfully. 'The difference between me and Chalmers is that I can't commit murder. I couldn't help anyone else do it, either. Leave it, Eve. Tell Chas the same. And if your parish priest asks about me, say nothing.'

'He's taken a shine to you, hasn't he?' Eve noticed a slight flush on Lily's cheeks after the words had been delivered.

'He's a friend, Eve.'

Eve, having been raised in a city full of life, bustle, gossip and interesting characters, was astute when it came to instinct. Father Walsh had a way of looking at Lily that gave him away. Sometimes, he didn't look at her. Those were the occasions on which he thoroughly betrayed himself, because he could not bear to expose his true feelings. So. Eve cleared her throat. So it looked as if Madam here had gone from frying pan to fire. No, he wasn't a fire, he was just a bloke in a dog collar. But was Lily moving from one impossible situation into another? 'Lily?'

'What?'

'Have you told him nothing?'

'Who?'

'Our parish priest, that's who. I'm a good judge of

character, love. You have to be when you live among vagabonds like my Chas's lot. And there's something.'

Lily shrugged. 'Eve, no way.'

'What do you mean by no way? Did you never see that programme about the Irish priest who had a kid by his housekeeper?'

'No.'

'The priest's dead, the housekeeper's dead, and the kid's out in the cold, because nobody wants him. His dad was forever on *The Late Show* about contraception and should priests marry – he was famous. He was there when the Pope arrived in Ireland, there when somebody wanted him to sing. And all the time, this bloke the Irish worshipped was having his leg over. They do have relationships.'

'Not in my house.'

Something in Lily's tone made her visitor quiet. There was still an air of authority about her, a small remnant left behind by the woman who had chased decorators across the television screen, who had put together impossible marriages of colour and made them work, who had changed the nation's ideas on home decor. 'Hey, Lily?'

'Yes?'

'Do you remember the chap who reckoned to know everything about ergonomic furniture?'

Lily smiled. 'God, yes – that pompous prat.'

'And you told him his 1950s retro chair was good for hitting him on the head with?'

'And he walked off the set?' Lily giggled. 'You meet some fools in that game, Eve. I mean, I'm all for retro stuff – we should mark every development in architecture and furniture by keeping or imitating great examples. But I wasn't having a lump of red plastic in a room filled with French pieces.'

Eve was laughing. 'And you said about bringing the garden into the house, so they played a trick on you.'

'Oh, yes. Ten rolls of turf carpeting a conservatory – that was funny.'

'You miss it. You miss the tricks they played most of all.' It wasn't a question.

'I do.'

Eve gazed at her new-found friend. 'You'd still have all that if it wasn't for him.'

'I'd have a lot more,' Lily said. 'I'd have everything.'

Eve burst into tears again. She was determined to go to the central library and read the newspapers on microfiche. The framework was still in her mind, but she'd forgotten some of the details and she needed to know. To ask Lily to fill in the blanks would be cruel, so– 'What are they for?' She fixed her eyes on two items Lily had just placed on the table in front of her.

Lily sat down. 'If you're going all watery, you can peel my onions.'

Sometimes, thought Eve, Leanne Chalmers came back. She peeled the onions.

Sergeant Peter Haywood sat in his car outside the flower shop. Lily was tidying up in preparation for closing, while Babs and Cassie had gone upstairs to the flat. Peter had seen the mess at the back of Pour Les Dames and was waiting now for the alleged perpetrator to come home in his purple van. Babs's boss didn't want to go to court. His wife was pregnant, and he was worried about how far Paul Smith was prepared to go in his search for revenge.

Pete sucked on a Polo mint. He didn't like being involved at this level, as he believed that matters should be dealt with in a proper fashion – forensics, statements, court – but he would do just about anything for Babs. She was a character. She pulled no punches, was humorous, affectionate and devoted to her daughter, so Pete was about to break his own mould, and that worried the policeman in him.

The beautician arrived eventually. His purple van swung left behind the row of shops, presumably to be stored in the alarmed garage at the rear of the off-licence. Pete waited for five minutes, then locked up his car and went to ring the bell at the back of number one. The garage was closed, so Paul Smith was probably inside the flat.

The door to the private stairs was flung open, and Paul presented himself. He carried a rolling pin, and was clearly ready to do battle with the man whose premises he had burgled the night before. 'Oh.' The weapon was suddenly hidden behind his back. 'Aren't you . . . ?'

'I'm Sergeant Peter Haywood, Greater Manchester Police.'

Paul tried and failed to produce a convincing smile. 'No uniform?'

'Not today. I thought you'd rather I did this in mufti. We need to talk. May I come in?'

Paul led the way up to the flat. He was still living out of boxes and bags, and he was forced to move a few items so that his visitor could sit. 'Well?'

Pete cleared his throat. 'There was a break-in at the

hairdresser's,' he said. 'Someone destroyed everything Sally Jones needs to do her job. They know it was your way of punishing Mo.'

Paul gulped audibly. 'They know wrong, then, because it wasn't me. You've no right to go about maligning—'

'Who were you expecting just now?' Pete asked. 'You seemed to be looking for trouble with your rolling pin – what was all that about? I can't see any pastry hanging about waiting to be rolled. Were you expecting Maurice Jones to come round and give you a good hiding for upsetting his pregnant wife? He won't descend to that level, mate. So. Come on – I'm waiting. Why answer the door with a rolling pin in your hand?'

'Well – I just thought—'

'You just thought you'd arm yourself for the fun of it? Now, listen to me. I'm doing you a favour by volunteering to come here. My colleagues have been to the shop,' he lied, 'and they found prints. Forensic evidence seldom lies.'

'I was in and out of there every day for months on end—'

'Fresh prints. Where the window was forced.'

Paul scoffed. 'Rubbish, because I was wear...' His voice died.

'Wearing gloves?'

'No. I wasn't there. I didn't do it.'

The large policeman leaned back in his chair. 'If this comes to court, you'd be better pleading guilty. If you say not guilty and are found guilty, it could mean a custodial sentence.'

'And?'

'And what Maurice wants is reassurance that you

won't do anything like this again. If you give me that reassurance, there is a possibility that charges may not be brought.'

Paul Smith was fed up to the back teeth. Even when Maurice had married that girl, Paul had still clung to the hope that the man would appreciate that Paul loved him more than any woman possibly could. Then, when Mo had stood by Sally, Paul's fairy tale had fallen apart at the seams.

Happy ending? The van had cost an arm and a leg, beauty equipment wasn't cheap these days, and the circumstances in which he worked were often far from ideal. Doing a set of acrylic nails took an hour, and he dared not charge more than twenty-five quid. Then there was the petrol—

'Well?' Pete was losing patience.

'All right.'

A corner of Pete's mind felt sorry for the lad. He was clearly gay, was jealous of Sally and Mo, and was out on his ear. He would probably have loved to be in the pantomime, too. 'Why don't you go to the next FADS meeting? Mo isn't the type to bear a grudge, and that daft priest is having to play the other ugly sister. You and Mo could do your drag act. Between the two of you, you might well turn that panto into something the village would never forget.'

Paul shrugged. He and Mo could have done 'Big Spender'. And 'Diamonds are a Girl's Best Friend'. They'd have stolen the show between them.

'Swallow your pride, lad. Pride's worth nowt a pound. You'll meet somebody soon enough. And Babs can only do part time at Pour Les Dames. You could do the other part and still have your own customers for Impressions.'

Paul eyed his supposed adversary. 'I'm not crawling.'

'No. But I can get Mo to come and visit you.'

'After . . . after what's happened?'

Pete shrugged. 'What do you have to lose apart from stubborn pride, Paul? The job you're doing isn't easy.'

'No.' The beautician pictured himself at some old lady's kitchen sink, the only rinsing implement available a Pyrex jug, the only certainty to hand the knowledge that he was already half an hour late for his next client. 'I work in difficult conditions.' The word impossible would have been nearer the mark.

Pete thought for a moment. 'How do you feel about elderly folk?'

The younger man smiled. 'They make me laugh and I enjoy helping them feel good. And I enjoy their stories and their memories. But it's difficult. They tend not to have the right facilities.'

'It would be different under contract to an old people's home with a proper room for hairdressing.'

'It would.'

'Leave it with me. I have a relative involved in caring for the aged. And I'm going to send Mo to see you.' The policeman smiled. 'I know what it's like to be thwarted in love, mate. We all feel pain, gay or hetero.'

'Thanks.'

'Listen. It's one thing being a gay hairdresser – imagine what a homosexual cop has to face. Even in this age of protected minorities and positive discrimination, comments are made. Cheer up and stop hurting folk. At the end of the line, it's yourself that gets damaged.'

When Pete had left, Paul stood at the window and looked out. Dave and Philly were running across the road again. They'd been knocking at Lily Latimer's door for a while. He wondered where the fire was, before going to grill a few fish fingers and warm a can of beans.

He shouldn't have done it. Mo would never love him. Even if the marriage broke down, Mo would be looking for female company. 'The bloody wedding nearly killed me,' he told the grill pan. 'Best man? I was a spare part.' To Maurice, he would never be more than another well-trained hair stylist, a partner on stage, a bloke who could dance in five-inch heels and a strappy frock. The dream had never been more than that, just a fantasy, one-sided and doomed to die.

The fish fingers were overdone, while the baked beans were cool. In number seven, he, Sally and Mo had shared the cooking. Yes, there had been some strange meals, but there had been company and laughter and fun. And the greatest of those had been fun. 'Right,' he told the mess on his plate. 'Canal Street, here I come.'

Lily brought them into the house. They had been back and forth all day like a pair of ping-pong balls involved in a bizarre doubles match, twin spheres under pressure, their consciences acting as the bats that drove them over the net with a frequency that had become monotonous. 'Sit,' she ordered.

They sat on a sofa, clutching each other's hand. 'Are you sure he's in Eagleton tonight, Lily?' Dave asked. 'Only she's getting herself in a right state here. I mean, I don't know what he can do to hurry things up, because we're a mixed marriage and there are things—'

'Protocols,' interposed Philly. 'But I have to tell him.'

'She has to tell him,' said Dave.

Lily had prepared a few nibbles, because she knew the couple would be back. She set these offerings and a pot of coffee on a low table in front of the sofa. 'Help your-selves. Nobody refuses coffee out of my Susie Cooper original pot. I save this for special people.'

'All matching,' remarked Philly. 'And a different col-our inside each cup. Where is he?' The question was added seamlessly to the previous remark.

'Funeral in Edgworth,' replied Lily. 'Huge Irish family. The relatives have invaded, so it'll probably go on until quite late. But you can wait.' God forbid that she should be the one to send them home to a sleepless and worried night. 'I don't mind – honestly. But I want to say that you're lucky. Some people try for years and never have a child.'

'Just the once for us.' Dave's cheeks were stained with embarrassment. 'But we have to get married, Lily. And it has to be in the Catholic church, otherwise it doesn't count.'

'Doesn't count,' Philly echoed.

Lily covered a smile and left the room. They were already behaving like a long-married couple, one repeat-ing what the other said, each aware of the other's ways, both open, simple in the best sense of the word, and very honest. Where was he? She'd waited until the ser-vice would have been over then phoned him on his mobile, had left a message that the business in hand was not urgent, though it was important.

She was learning that Mike was not just a priest. He was a man who liked people, who loved a good laugh, who was at his best in company. If what she had heard about Irish wakes was true, the event he was attending might well go on until about Thursday. Or did they have the wake before the burial? Wasn't there something about having the deceased present in an open coffin?

Lily shivered. The idea of a corpse being guest of honour was hardly palatable.

She used her phone again. He was sorry that he could not take her call at the moment, but if she left a message, he would contact her at the earliest opportunity. 'Mike,' she snapped. 'This is becoming ridiculous. I've two people here waiting for you. If this carries on much longer, I'll get on my broomstick and fly round till I find you.'

Lily sat in an armchair and thought about Eve. Scousers were supposed to be alert, and Eve had gone a long way towards proving the legend. It was inevitable that she must pass on to Chas all she had learned about Lily, because they shared everything, and Eve's new knowledge was too burdensome to be kept inside. Lily kept it hidden, and therein lurked the danger. Perhaps she should speak to Dr Clarke about getting some more help. She was managing in the physical sense, but her nerves were beginning to fray slightly.

They were whispering in the next room. Lily closed her eyes and pictured them clinging together for dear life. It must be wonderful to have someone dependable like Dave. He wasn't the best-looking man in the world, but he cared. He would work hard for his wife and child; he would even make sure that his terrible mother would be safe and fed.

Where was Mike? She felt like the proverbial wife waiting behind the door on a Saturday night, poker in hand, list of questions printed in upper case on the front of her mind. Where have you been? Are you drunk again? Who is she? Why are you never here when I need you?

Giving up smoking had seemed a good idea at the time, but Lily found herself longing for just one drag on a Superking – low tar, of course. For how much longer could a two-o'clock funeral last? Why wouldn't he answer his phone? He seldom obeyed orders, was still at odds with the hierarchy about contraception, hadn't even had his hair cut. He was probably considered to be something of a maverick, but she was glad about the hair. It was the tatty head that made him human, she had decided.

She closed her eyes and tried to relax. Mr Darcy, with his square chin, fierce eyes and proud expression, had been completely let down by his hair. How could Elizabeth Bennet have taken seriously the supposed coldness of a man whose hair had been that of an unruly child? Mike had Firth hair. No matter what he did with it, the stuff went its own way, and to hell with whatever the world thought. With short hair, Colin Firth wasn't as pretty. With short hair, Mike would look too . . . ordinary.

It would soon be ten o'clock. She had an early start tomorrow: flowers to be received at seven, shop to be spick and span by nine, another wedding to organize, contracts to fulfil for shops in Bolton. A grand place called the Last Drop wanted quotes for guest bedrooms, public areas and restaurants that needed fresh blooms arranged and delivered on a regular basis. Even as a florist, she was becoming famous locally.

Five minutes to ten. Were they building a mausoleum? Had guests been merry enough to fall into the grave with the coffin? Worse still, had Mike been involved in an accident? She shifted in the chair. The thought of him lying in a hospital bed was horrible. The idea of life without him was a killer. Life with him? If she stole a priest from a number of parishes, would she ever be forgiven? He wanted her. She wanted him. For the moment, she needed him to act normally, switch on his bloody phone and re-join the human race. It was OK to cut oneself off from the world during a Requiem, but the service had to have been over hours ago. Even allowing time for burial and ham sandwiches, he should have been back by six at the latest.

A car coughed. She recognized the congested breathing of Mike's geriatric Volvo. Relief flooded her veins, but it was contaminated by impatience and anger. He should not have put her through this. She now understood the moaning and groaning of so many neglected pub widows.

The door opened, and she was there in a flash. 'Where the bloody hell have you been? Where's your phone?'

He steadied himself against a wall. 'Hospital,' he managed. 'Heart attack. Don't start on me, Lily – I've had more than enough today.' Today? He felt as if he had been gone for two or three weeks.

'Oh, God. Are you all right? Why have they let you out after a heart attack? Shouldn't you be plugged into the mains with about fifteen wires?'

'Eh?'

'Heart attack?'

'Not me, woman. The dead man's mother. She keeled over in the cemetery and I followed the ambulance to town. Phones had to be switched off, and I forgot to turn mine on again. I managed to get the necessary from St Pat's, so I did Extreme Unction. She lived only four hours, bless her.'

'I'm sorry.'

'Not as sorry as I am. She was good fun, a down-to-earth Dubliner, full of Irish jokes and a laugh that would curdle skimmed milk. I liked her, and she died holding my hand. Burying her only son was simply the last straw for her.' He shook his head wearily. 'Some days are just plain nasty.'

'Sorry,' Lily repeated. 'But Philly and Dave have been coming and going all day. She's in a terrible state, and he's worried about her being in a terrible state. You'd better go through – they're in the second sitting room. I'll make myself scarce.' She went upstairs in order to be out of their way. She knew what was going to be said, but they still required a semblance of privacy.

He walked into the room and saw Philly's face. 'Before you start,' he said, 'I'm pinching a drop of whisky. Just don't ask me about today, Philly.'

They waited until he had furnished himself with the required medication.

'We only did it that once,' Philly began, hands twisting in her lap.

'Just once,' said Dave.

Mike grinned. 'And you've made a baby? That's the greatest news I've had in a while. Leave it to me. I'll talk to the bish and we'll get it over and done with before you can say wedding cake.'

'How did you guess?' Dave asked.

The priest continued to smile. 'What else might it have been? Just look at the state of you, Philomena Gallagher, soon to be Barker. Anyone would think you'd bogged off to Wales and emptied the Royal Mint. There's a new life inside you, a precious child—'

'He'll be Catholic,' said Dave.

'He'll be fine,' pronounced Mike. 'So stop looking as if you're responsible for the state of Iraq. To be perfectly honest, I wouldn't care if he or she was Jewish or Muslim.'

Philly frowned. He was certainly unlike any other priest she had met, was a thousand miles apart from the clerics who had populated her childhood. What would Mam have thought if she had heard him saying it was all right to be Muslim or Jewish? And he was one for the ladies – she knew that well enough. He was kinder to women, and he listened to them very attentively. She thought about Lily, who was more beautiful than many film stars – they lived together here for some of the time . . .

Mike was going on about the rules, mentioning consanguinity, affinity and spiritual relationship as barriers to marriage. 'That's it, then,' he finished with the air of one dismissing an audience. 'Please, let me sleep. Today was a month long.'

They left. Mike finished his whisky, poured another, prayed for the lovely Mrs Maguire who had departed this life on the day of her precious son's funeral. Her levity had been the cloak she had worn to disguise her grief, but the grief had killed her. How many people died because they had simply given up, because their reason for continued existence had been eradicated? Mrs Maguire had been fiercely alive. It was she who used to drag the family across the Irish Sea every time Liverpool FC played some special match, she who had organized the funeral, the wake, the flowers. No one had attended the wake, because they had all been at the hospital praying that she would live.

'Mike?'

She was behind him. She was behind every thought,

every step, every waking moment. Perhaps it was time to run, to start again at the other end of the country – just as she had. Was she an emissary from Satan, a messenger sent to tempt him? Never. 'What?'

'Sorry I was angry with you.'

He drained his glass. 'No matter. I should have checked my messages, but the whole thing became a bit fraught.'

'It would. Will she be shipped home, or will she be buried with her son?'

'Dublin, I imagine. She was a beautiful woman. A widow. Five daughters, one son. She'll go home, I think. The majority vote will carry her back.'

Lily came to stand next to him. The feelings she was experiencing in the presence of this man were supposed to be dead. They had died on the end of a far-reaching knife, words that had cut, fear that had turned her into a near-murderer. While she had fought for life in an intensive care unit, her lawyers had also borne arms, and charges against her had been dismissed. But this was her real sin. Her brain knew full well that there was no future with Father Michael Walsh, but her heart would not be quiet.

'Difficult?' he asked.

'Yes.' How did he manage to know what she thought and how she felt? What had he said? Something about feelings as strong as these moving in two directions? This was not a one-way street – it was a ring road, round and round the edge, don't turn left or right, do not pass Go, do not collect . . .

'I'm falling in love with you, Lily Latimer. It isn't your fault.'

'Is it yours?'

He shrugged. 'I should know better. When I see the bishop about Philly and Dave, I should talk to him about this, too. What normally happens in such situations is that the priest gets transferred. I ought to move on to a different place.'

'I want you to stay.' Feeling desperate, yet brave, she slipped her hand into his. 'Never in my life have I felt like this, Mike. Like you, I know it's wrong.'

'Wrong?' He laughed mirthlessly. 'It's normal. We were created to create. And beyond the merely physical, I have this urge to protect and guard you, while—'

'While I want to touch your hair. Don't cut it. Don't you dare.'

This time, his laughter was real. 'No, I should get it cropped. If you can't love me with short hair, the problem is solved.'

It would never be solved. By some strange quirk of fate, the newly created Lily had travelled from the outskirts of Taunton – well, from the centre of Taunton if she counted her business premises – to a largeish village in the north-west of England. Here lived a man for whom she was forbidden fruit, and she had become his Eve. Was this meant to happen? Could she have been sent to release him and to free herself of past nightmares? 'What are we going to do?' she asked.

'You know perfectly well. Unless you really are too injured for such activity.'

Lily swallowed her fear. 'I don't know. But I was left in a mess. I have healed, but—'

'But you may still have pain?'

She nodded. 'I don't care.' She wasn't a reckless woman, not any more. Since the incident ... since the series of incidents that had ended in near-death, she had become protective of herself. But she wanted this man Did she want him because she shouldn't have him? Was the old Leanne still alive and kicking, still wanting to cock a snook at the world and his wife? 'I'm not afraid of you,' she said.

'Nor should you be.'

The first kiss lasted for several minutes. Each was completely lost in desire for the other; it was so right that Lily concluded it had to be wrong. But her heart won the battle, just as she had expected. The whole thing was inevitable. Neither could make a decision about the future until after the event. So, when the kiss ended, she allowed herself to be led to the stairs.

In her room at the top of the house and on a three-quarter bed, Mike and Lily became lovers. There was no pain for her. Sometime in the future she might well find herself wishing that there had been some discomfort – it might help when options were discussed. But, for the present, she was deliriously happy. Lying in the arms of her man, she was too content to worry about the future. He was a priest, yet that no longer mattered.

Remembered reading Charlie Bronson's Good Prison Guide. *He was quite kind to Walton, as he had done thousands of pounds' worth of damage to the roof, and he had a whale of a time. People can say what they like about Charlie, but he definitely has a sense of humour.*

He was right about the Scousers. They are humorous almost to the point of being completely mad. I like them. They don't suffer fools.

Am off 43, keeping my head down, just making chit-chat and listening to jokes. Bloke called Lofty came to see me. He's under five feet tall, and very useful when it comes to burglary, because he knows alarms. Dan and I have got a solicitor's clerk in our back pockets, and Leanne's money is being traced. I bet a pound to a penny she changed her name.

See, the trouble with this country is that nobody gets paid enough. Bent screws are ten a penny, because their take-home pay is peanuts. Within a couple of weeks, you can get a screw interested in earning a few bob. Drugs, info, booze – whatever – you can get it all in here. All you need is cash – that would have been a better title for the Beatles' song.

Same with solicitors' clerks. All he has to do is find his boss's password and I'll be on to Leanne. Well, somebody will. Just a matter of time. Have to be patient. Am making boxes out of matchsticks. The excitement is killing me.

Eight

There was no embarrassment.

Lily woke the next morning to find her lover standing by the bed, a breakfast tray in his hands, a yellow rose stolen from her garden clamped between his teeth. With a flourish, he produced a tea towel, and when she had raised herself into a sitting position, he spread this rather less than clean item across her legs and placed the tray on top of it. The rose was handed to her with all due ceremony, then he sat down and poured tea. 'Breakfast, madam. No orange juice, so no Buck's Fizz.' He stood back and bowed. 'Should Modom require anything further, room service will provide anything within reason. Except, of course, we do not have the aforementioned Buck's Fizz.'

'Pity. But thank you all the same.' She was strangely hungry. Having expected to find the morning after extremely difficult, she discovered herself to be completely at ease with him. Had this been casual sex and no more? She found herself hoping not. Last night had not been his first experience with a woman; he was adventurous, uninhibited, gentle, yet powerful. 'Have you eaten?' she asked.

'Music is the food of love, so I listened to Lonnie Donegan.'

'Who?'

'"My Old Man's a Dustman".' He sang a few bars for her, then mopped up spilt tea. 'It's a very romantic piece, and you should not be laughing – it betrays a lack of soul,' he said. 'If your spirit can't share the moment with me, don't spit tea, I beg you. Would you have preferred "Does Your Chewing Gum Lose its Flavour on the Bedpost Overnight?"? It lacks a certain romanticism–'

'Stop it, or I'll choke. You're killing me, Mike.'

He stretched out beside her. The instinct that had drawn him to Lily in the first place was in no way diminished. He needed to make her happy; he wanted to make her laugh. There was, he knew, a lively woman buried deep under layers imposed by life, and he longed for her to tell him her secret fears. But he now knew that he must not push for disclosure, because she would tell him when she chose. He yawned loudly. 'The good thing about you is that a man could never get truly bored. There's always an alternative, you see.'

'Really?'

He nodded solemnly. 'When sex loses its appeal – as if it ever would – there's always noughts and crosses.'

'What?'

'The scars. If you had a small tattoo to lengthen one side, you have the grid on your belly. Bags me being the X, though. I'm always X.'

He displayed none of the misplaced respect syndrome that might have inhibited any other man. The scars were a part of her, so he embraced them and tried to find a silly use for them. Mike Walsh was almost unbearably lovable. He took hold of life, bit down hard and got on with it. He was doing the same with her toast. 'Get your own,' she advised him. 'I'm starving.'

'Now, that's a compliment,' he said, rising from the bed. 'I am going shortly to do my job.' He stared through the beautiful, multicoloured window. 'Don't be afraid,' he whispered. 'Whatever happens, I'll be here for you – or somewhere for you. The somewhere I have to be today is with the Bishop of Salford. The wedding – Dave and Philly – plus a couple more diocesan matters, like how the hell can I run three churches single-handedly. Everyone expects miracles these days.'

'Oh, yes. The wedding. She was frightened to death, poor Philly.'

'I wonder if they'll have a three-legged Labrador bridesmaid?' he mused aloud. 'There's a possibility that I may mention another small matter to the bishop. Because I don't want an affair with you, Lily. I want more. He'll have to be told. Dishonesty is not an option.'

She touched his arm. 'Mike, don't do anything in a hurry. We may burn out, then you will have gone to a lot of trouble for nothing. Please wait.'

'No. I've waited long enough, and I didn't even know I was waiting. It has to be done, with or without you. Not something that can be taken lightly, I grant you, but the Church and I parted company somewhere between Spaghetti Junction and contraception. I have given absolution to several Catholic women whose pregnancies have been terminated for a plethora of reasons. I can't condone abortion, but I uphold their right to make that terrible, often life-shattering decision. However, I have gone where no good priest should tread – off the map drawn by Rome. Until we get a pope under the age of seventy, priests like me will always be at odds with our bosses.'

Lily didn't know what to say to him. He loved people,

enjoyed his work, was at ease with himself and with God. 'They used to marry, didn't they? Priests, I mean. I think they should, then they'd have a better idea of their parishioners' lives.'

He nodded. 'True enough, they were married. Then some medieval anal retentive, who was probably impotent, decreed that celibacy was the flavour of his particular month. It stuck. We're now running out of clergy, the seminaries are empty, and no pope has budged. I can live with what I have done, as can my God. But the bish will have to be told. Many priests go to him only when their women become pregnant. They keep quiet for as long as possible and hope they'll get away with it.'

'What happens when there's a pregnancy?' Lily asked.

He sighed heavily. 'You won't like the answer. Suffice to say that bishops, too, are human. Churches need to be staffed, so priests are encouraged to remain on board whatever the human cost.'

'And their babies?'

'Sometimes adopted. Often, the woman is left to her own devices. Husbands rear children who aren't their own. When a woman is abandoned to her fate, she frequently makes a certain decision. In the eyes of the Church, the sin is hers and hers alone.' He turned from the window and smiled down on her. 'The hands of the hierarchy remain clean wherever possible. The women are allowed to pay the price on their behalf.'

'And your paedophiles?'

'Don't make me angry, Lily. Oh, not with you – I didn't mean angry with you. They hide behind their cassocks for as long as possible. When the stories break, they run to senior clergy and weep, blame the drink, blame a terrible childhood. Historically, they've got away with it. Some months away on retreat within a monastery, then back to work in a different place. But it's also back to square one, because there is no cure. Recently, though, successful prosecution has begun. I think America and Ireland led the way. So we'll lose more clergy again.'

'Thank God,' she breathed.

Mike smiled sadly. 'We're not perfect, you see. Life is full of mistakes, and my church is a part of life.' He kissed her forehead, then went off to begin another of his flawed days. 'See you later for noughts and crosses,' he called up the stairwell.

Lily knew that the flower man would have left her order in the back yard – he had a key. She also accepted that the shop would open a few minutes late today, and she could not manage to worry about it. She felt lighter this morning, steadier and healthier, almost optimistic.

Before stepping into the shower, she paused for a few seconds, because she didn't want to wash his scent from her skin. That, she informed herself, was the reaction of an animal. Mike didn't wear perfume. The aroma he had left was warm and embracing, but she had to be clean. 'At least I won't need an abortion,' she said aloud as she stepped into the cubicle. The words of her surgeon were engraved on her soul – 'It is unlikely that you will carry a child to full term. Pregnancy might even threaten your life. However, you are not going to find conception easy.' Fair enough. She began to weep. It wasn't fair at all, was it? Cassie. She was doing so well in her effort to avoid the child – Auntie Lee was probably guilty of neglect.

The tears dried. Lily could not continue unhappy today, because the night had been wonderful. She could love again in the physical sense. Even if that was all she had learned, it had been worth it. But, like him, she wanted more. Life with him was what she longed for. He would not be able to live without work. But Mike was one of the bright sparks who had used his brain before embarking on years in a seminary. He was a fully qualified psychologist, so, if he did quit the church, he would soon find employment. But could he be happy without his flock?

She applied make-up to a face that looked different this time, as if a cloud had moved away from the sun to allow light through. People would notice; Babs would certainly comment. Babs would be in Pour Les Dames now, because Mo was going to see Po. If those two daft creatures could mend a few bridges, Mike's winter pantomime promised to be brilliant.

'You're still you,' she told her reflection. 'You're still Leanne Chalmers, whichever wrapping paper you use.' A legally changed name could never alter the past. The husband she had divorced continued to exist in a crowded jail just a few miles away. All that separated them was the East Lancashire Road – or a couple of motorways – and while he lived, Lily's life was in danger. But she had to forget about all that, had to move onward like a good Christian soldier. Well, perhaps not, because this Christian soldier had bedded a priest, so she was rather less than good.

She walked out of the house and across the road. Mike might also become a target if the relationship endured. Clive's jealousy had driven him and her wild, because it was so angry and uncontrollable. Scissors, curtain material, knife, blood. Lily shivered. When she relived the event, it moved in slow motion across her mind, his face twisted by hatred, her heart pounding with fear. In truth, that final attack had probably been over in seconds. She had to pay for a lifetime; he would probably be free in under ten years. Nevertheless, Lily achieved a smile. Noughts and crosses, indeed. Where was the respect in that suggestion?

For Clive, Leanne had been perfection. A brunette with cornflower blue eyes, good posture, remarkable figure – he was in his element. Until she became successful. Until other members of the human race had the ability to watch her chasing decorators and carpet-fitters on TV, until she had become so popular that anyone who was anyone used her to furnish their home. He hated her spreads in the glossies, couldn't bear her to talk to any other man about any subject whatsoever.

Mike was completely different from Clive. He had stopped asking questions, was not afraid of her supposed beauty, made fun of imperfections he had discovered in intimate moments. He loved her, and not just because she was attractive. Her abdomen was a mess, yet he had embraced those criss-cross scars as an integral part of the woman he happened to love. Did the fact that he would need to change his job matter? Many people altered direction, moving to the other side of the world, giving up a career for children – why should he be different? Because his was a vocation rather than a job? Because he needed to remain at the helm in order to push for reform within the faith?

There was a part of Mike that would be forever priest, she supposed. But first and foremost, he was a man. He was the man she wanted and needed. Yet the decision must be his alone, since he was the one who was disobeying mortals who considered themselves to be in authority over him.

She rescued her stock from a very hot back yard. The sun was beating fiercely, and the flowers needed to cool. Her phone buzzed in the pocket of the tabard she wore for dirty work. The message made her smile again. *Remember I am X. U R O. Have bought indelible pen, forget tattoo. X.*

Maurice Jones perched on the edge of a sofa and leaned against a black bag filled with his ex-partner's clothes. The position was not exactly comfortable. 'Aren't you going to unpack?' he asked. 'The place looks like a bomb hit it.'

Paul explained that he would sort himself out eventually. He was busy; he had a lot of work.

'I know you're working hard,' Mo replied. 'But there's not enough time in a day to do all that travelling. Keep your best clients, then work part time for me. We'll forget what happened. Your old dears in particular miss you. They ask for you all the time, and can't get you through Impressions, because you're always fully booked. And the little girls miss you, too.'

'I'm over-booked.' Paul Smith was thoroughly ashamed of himself. He was bitchy, and he knew it. Jealousy was a terrible burden, and he had to get rid of it. 'Pete the Plod's trying to get me an old people's home. I'm sorry, Mo. Poor Sal. But I always loved you, and because you act more camp than I do, I really believed that you'd turn to me in the end.'

'It ain't gonna happen, mate. We should never have lived the lie in the first place.' Mo glanced at his watch.

'Look, I'll have to go, because Lily's coming in for colouring, and I'm not used to her hair yet.'

'Right.' Paul dabbed at a tear. 'On your way back, pop into her place and tell her if she'll wait till tomorrow, I'll do her. If she needs it done today, I have her file here.' He pointed to a box on the coffee table. 'Her colour charts are on top, list of treatments below. She needs a lot of conditioner, because I use some fierce stuff. But try to hold her off until tomorrow, because I can do her then.'

'In the shop?'

Paul nodded. 'Yes, I'll go half and half. Half Impressions, half the real thing. Sort out the hours with Babs – that little girl needs her mam.'

Maurice stared at the floor. The other sad thing about Paul was that he loved kiddies. With children and oldies, the man was in his element. Paul would have made a great dad. 'Thanks, Paul,' he said. 'So Mo and Po ride again, eh? Two bundles of trouble in one small shop.' He paused. 'I know you've been an angry bitch, but I also know you're not all bad. We've not seen the best of you yet, mate. Come home, and we'll soon be those two bundles of mischief and magic again.'

'Three, shortly to be four,' Paul answered. 'Well, five if we count Babs. I reckon she could start a war in a phone booth. Now, get gone while I sort out my schedule. Some of us have to work.'

Skippy had a job. There had been no forms to fill in, no interview and no trial period, as she had created her own area of expertise and was definitely the best dog for the post. There was no travelling involved, lunch was provided by her employer, and no tools were required.

Skippy had appointed herself receptionist, welcoming committee and keeper of order in number three, Fullers Walk. Perhaps she remembered that Tim Mellor had saved her life; perhaps she had become fed up with newspapers, books and old men fighting over computer dating. For whatever reason, Skippy turned up for work on the day the newly located practice began to function.

Mornings were open surgeries, and the waiting room was often congested. With a professionalism seldom displayed among humans, Skippy disposed of all negative feelings. Dogs, cats, rabbits, birds and rodents were all treated with respect, though she continued to chase anything that moved when she was taken out for exercise by Philly or Dave.

Everyone was amazed. She woofed a quiet welcome to all who arrived, led people to their chairs, and always knew whose turn it was to go into the treatment area. She hopped about on her three remaining legs, led the next victim to the business end of the shop, and was in receipt of many pats and cuddles of praise.

The veterinary nurse was astounded. She had seen many dogs in her lifetime, but she had never met an animal with so much sense. The first few days were peppered by her exclamations. 'She's done it again – are you sure you're the next to go in?' and 'Who trained her to do this?'

Skippy lapped up the praise. She was a different dog, a special dog, and she made sure that everyone knew it.

Philly and Dave were nonplussed at first. Didn't she want to live with them any longer? Had she chosen the vet over them? But she came back to the Reading Room after lunch each day, and made no effort to attend evening surgeries. They decided that Skippy, like Babs, wanted to work part time and, once they were sure that she was in no danger, accepted that she was simply a mornings-only workaholic. The dog made no attempt to enter the vet's premises on Sundays, even if an emergency arose. Skippy, they concluded, was a people-pleaser, and they were bursting with pride.

They were also on pins as they waited for Father Walsh to call them. The baby, according to a book Philly had borrowed from the shop, was now the size of a very small pea. She wanted to protect that tiny person from the disgrace of illegitimacy, and her nerves were fraying. When Dave's mobile finally rang, Philly almost jumped out of her skin. She dragged her man out into the back yard. 'Answer it now,' she begged. 'Come on, come on!'

After a few yeses and a couple of thank yous, Dave smiled at her. 'Two weeks,' he said as he turned off the phone. 'He'll do us in two weeks.'

The baby might be the size of a mature marrowfat by then. Philly's hands were twisting. 'Not enough time to get ready,' she gasped. Yet they must be ready, because the baby needed them to be ready. 'Wedding clothes, a party for our friends—'

'Stop.' Dave stepped forward and grabbed her anxious hands. 'No party. Get a smart suit and two witnesses – in that order.' He inhaled deeply. 'We have to tell her upstairs.' Both raised their eyes to an upper window. 'She'll hit the roof. Knowing her, she'll just bounce off and land in a bed of roses. She's always right, you see, always falls on her feet. Well, she would if it weren't for melegs.'

Philly's mouth set itself in a firm line. 'We do it together,' she said. 'You're not going up there on your

214

own, but I can't do it by myself, either. She's your mother—'

'I don't need reminding about that—'

'She's your mother, so you tell her, but with me there. She's more wary of me, because I'm a woman.' Philly entered the shop and asked a couple of old stalwarts to keep an eye on the place. 'No fighting,' was her parting shot.

'What?' Dave's eyebrows moved north. 'Right now? Do we have to do it this minute?'

'No time like the present,' replied Philly. 'But your mother won't like the present we're taking with us.'

When they entered the flat, Enid Barker was in her usual place. 'That Lily one seems right pleased with herself today,' she said. 'I heard her singing in the yard before while she tiptoed through her tulips or whatever she's selling these days.'

Well, at least Madam was speaking.

The old woman turned and saw them standing hand in hand. 'Oh, both of you,' she exclaimed. 'Whatever have I done to deserve a full state visit? Will I get my best cups and spoons out? Is my hair good enough for royalty?'

Sarcasm. On a good day, Enid Barker used that instead of head-on abuse. Was this a good day, then? Dave opened his mouth, but the words emerged from Philly. 'We're getting married in two weeks,' she said. 'Not quite sure of the date yet, but Father Walsh has had permission from the Bishop of Salford. He phoned just now and told Dave.'

Enid blanched. 'Are you in the club?' she yelled.

'I'm pregnant, yes.' Philly surprised herself. Even a few weeks ago, she could not have stood there and made that statement. The strength Dave had given her was beyond measure; he, too, had gained in confidence, and it showed in several ways, including the new haircut and a flatter belly.

'And what's that to do with the bloody bishop? My son needs no bishop to tell him what he can do and when. We're Methodists. We don't run round breaking rules just because we can get forgiven by some jumped-up Irish priest with—'

'He's not Irish,' Dave said. 'He's of Irish descent.'

'A quick descent to hell is what you'll get, David Barker. What have I told you all your life? Keep away from bloody Catholics.'

Dave stood his ground. 'Mixed marriage,' he said, 'and Philly needs permission to marry me. I have to promise that the child will be reared Catholic.'

Enid inhaled sharply. 'You're a disgrace,' she told her son.

He had taken enough. He approached the woman who had birthed him. 'My child will have a father on his birth certificate. He'll know who his father is. That's where he'll have the advantage over me, Mother. Why can't you be pleased? For once in your life, why can't you be normal? Even pretending to be normal would do for now.'

She turned her back on both visitors. 'I won't be at your wedding,' she snapped.

'Good.' Dave returned to Philly's side. 'Because you wouldn't be welcome. We don't need any miserable old women to come and spoil our special day. Anyway, we've told you what you need to know. If you want anything, ring the bell. Philly will be up later with some food.'

Outside on the stairs, Dave remembered how often he had shaken when standing on this very spot, how much she had upset him, how great a job she had done of undermining him. 'My kid will have a proper mother,' he said softly. And he wasn't shaking any more.

It took a few days for Eve to take on board all she had learned about Lily Latimer. Several times, she found herself on the brink of talking to Chas, but the fact that she alone was in possession of the details made her cautious. Chas was not a gossip, but his mouth sometimes ran away with him, coasting along like a car out of gear on a slope. Unless his wife happened to be around to apply the handbrake, he sometimes sped along like a ship in full sail. Yet she needed to tell someone, since the burden was a heavy one, and it was affecting her performance in the shop and at home.

The cottage was coming along, because Lily, true to her word, had helped greatly with searches for pieces rescued by builders and sold through architectural reclamation yards. But Eve was not at ease, would never be comfortable until she had talked to Chas. No matter how pleasing the ring-turned legs on her table, she couldn't enjoy anything until she had offloaded some of the worry.

On an evening in August, the pair sat in their rear living room. Derek was minding the shop, and Eve was glad that her son was out of the house. 'The fewer people who hear this, the better,' she told her husband. They hadn't switched on lights, because this was the loveliest time of day. Through open windows, the scent of stock and honeysuckle drifted on a summer breeze. Blackbirds fussed, while a lone nightingale began a prelude from the uppermost branches of one of the trees.

Eve simply said it all, allowing it to pour from her lips in one solid section, no tears, no emotion at all. It was like a work of fiction, so vicious had the crime been. She could have wept over a story in a book, yet what she was saying now was too bad for tears, because it was real. When she had finished, she leaned back in her rocking chair, closed her eyes and waited for him to react. But he remained silent. 'Chas?' She raised her eyelids and looked at his outline against the frugal light of dusk. 'Chas?'

'What?'

'Did you hear what I just told you?'

'I did.'

'And?'

'And bloody what? What do you expect me to say? Slime like that – I'm not wasting energy on him. Anybody who treats a woman so badly wants hanging. I'm going.'

'Where?'

'To clear that flaming mess outside is where.'

She heard him, felt his fury as he stamped about and banged into his workbench. He stumbled round in the little brick-built lean-to, clattering tools in an ancient slopstone, cursing after tripping over something metallic. He was in a temper. This didn't happen often, but when it did he needed a clear deck to manage his anger, and she should leave him to it. Dared she do that? His red-hot temper was one thing, but this white heat advertised a fury that matched for temperature the magma vomiting from a volcano. It was just too hot, and it was burning him on the inside. In such a state, he would hurt only one person, and that was himself.

Then he walked down into the Devil's Jungle, and began slashing and cutting at anything and everything in his path. It was almost dark, and he would injure himself if he didn't slow down. She shouldn't have told him. His dad used to hit his mam, and stories like this one probably picked scabs off wounds that would never heal completely. 'I shouldn't have said anything,' she announced to a watercolour next to the fireplace. Poor Chas. Poor Lily . . . 'I need to be stronger and keep things to myself.'

'Get back, you bastard,' Chas was shouting now.

Eve ran out. He had reached a tangled mass of brambles and bindweed, and he was in a very dark mood. 'Chas? Stop it. Stop it now, or I'm going to fetch our Derek. What the bloody hell do you think you're doing at this time of night? Them thorny bushes will have your eyes out – show a bit of sense, lad. You'll have the village coming round here en masse any minute. Give it up, Chas. This is something you do during the day.'

He stopped, but was still breathing heavily. 'Where's Capability Brown when you need him?' he asked, before bursting into tears.

Eve held the weeping man in her arms. 'Shush,' she whispered. 'Can you hear him? Our nightingale. He's done his overture, and he's coming over all Mozart.'

They clung together and listened to Nature's court musician while he poured out his soul to a darkening sky. 'How many in Toxteth have heard a nightingale so close? Or in Berkeley Square, for that matter?' she asked. 'We're lucky, babe. Just try to calm down a bit. I know it's a terrible story, and perhaps I should have kept my gob shut—'

'I'm your husband, damn it.'

'And you're upset.'

He nodded, then wiped his nose on the sleeve of his shirt. 'There's something else, love. Our Robbo's been framed. Some job at the back end of Bootle. He never done it. The one time he's absolutely innocent, and it looks like he'll get a stretch, because some guard got a bang on the head.'

'Are you sure he didn't do it?'

Chas nodded fiercely. 'But he bought some of the stuff off them that did do it, so he's banged up. Magistrate Monday for referral to Crown. No way will he sidestep this one, Eve. I'll have to go over and see him. It's not fair.'

'I know, love.'

'See, we've never damaged people, have we? We might have pinched a few bobs' worth of booze and stuff off the bleeders who pretend to run the country, but our Rob would never hurt a fly. He's like me, isn't he?'

Eve offered no reply.

'It's all wrong,' Chas continued. 'Take that lovely girl – Lily. She had a smashing job and a good life and look what happened. He's in jail. In jail? I'd have him drawn and bloody quartered in the middle of London. He's gone and ruined her life. Now, he should never come out of prison, but I bet you anything you like he'll be free in a few years. Things like that shouldn't be allowed to walk about, but our Rob? He could get a three stretch for something he never done in the first place.'

'Yes, it's wrong. But come in, Chas. No point putting yourself in hospital. This garden wants somebody with the proper stuff to have a go. You know – big machines that rip everything out and turn the ground over. Then we grow spuds.'

'Eh?'

'Spuds. First year is potatoes. They help the soil.'

'Have you been reading books again?'

She nodded.

'I'm going to get drunk,' he announced, leaving her to tidy away his tools. 'If anybody wants me, I'll be in the pub,' he called through the window.

Eve picked up all the bits and pieces, carried them into the little workshop and stood for a while looking round the lean-to, one of many additions made to the cottage since the original build. It had a low sink called a slopstone, and she pictured women long dead who had stood at sinks like this one, rubbing and scrubbing till their hands were red raw and stung by carbolic. This must have been a very small wash house. It would have held just one slave at a time, she guessed. Life was so easy now. Except for people like Lily.

The cottage was taking shape. Lily had told her to go incongruous and enjoy it, so Eve had looked up the word and taken her friend's advice. Among dressers that took up whole walls and next to doors made from vertical planks, Eve had placed her washing machine, dishwasher, dryer and cooker. But she had hung on to the black grate with its open fire, drop-down hob and swinging kettle-hook because it was beautiful. The old oven, too, remained. One day in winter, Eve would make bread in it. She would do it because the oven deserved to be used, and because bread made in these primitive appliances was supposed to taste better than any other.

She hoped he wouldn't get too drunk. She hoped his

mouth wouldn't run away with him, because the last thing Lily needed was sympathetic attention from her neighbours. In fact, Eve would go and join him, in case he needed someone to stop his gob before it got away from him. She combed her hair, grabbed a cardigan and stepped out into the cool evening air.

Halfway to the Reaper and Scythe, which was her husband's favourite hostelry, Eve stopped for a moment. An unusually short man was standing outside Pour Les Dames. He dropped a cigarette end and ground it to death with a foot. Slowly, he melted away into the darkness up the side of Fullers Walk. Was he waiting for Chas? Did he have something questionable to sell? Was it Lofty? Lofty, who had gained his nickname because he was about three inches short of five feet, was a Liverpudlian who would do just about anything for money. No. Lofty would have gone to the shop, and Derek would have sent him on to Rose Cottage.

Eve stood still for a few moments before pulling herself together. She was a woman on a mission, and she had to keep Chas quiet, so men with cheap booze for the shop were low on her agenda. The main thing was to get to the pub as quickly as possible.

All thoughts of the undersized man were deleted from her mind when she walked into the bar. Chas was doing his darts show, so he was all right. Blindfolded, he scored double top twice. Bending down and throwing the dart between his legs, he managed a near bull's eye. He wouldn't talk tonight, because humour was his own therapy and he was using it well.

She sat with Babs and Pete, trying hard not to feel like a gooseberry. But she wasn't uncomfortable for long, because these two lovely people were not a closed shop. 'Hey,' whispered Babs.

'What?' Eve grinned at the copper-headed southerner.

'Lily's up to something.'

'Is she?'

'Take no notice,' said Pete. 'There's nothing wrong with Lily – she's just that bit happier, that's all.'

Babs dug him in the ribs. 'Listen, Plod. I know that girl better than anyone round here, and I'm telling you, she's changed.'

'Into what?' Eve asked. 'A pumpkin?'

Babs blew a raspberry. 'Shut up, ye of little faith. If she's happy, something's happened. I know stuff you two don't know.'

Eve knew enough, but she kept her counsel. 'It's time she cheered up,' she said. Chas was still in his element. With his sleeves rolled up and his forehead furrowed, he concentrated on acting the clown. As long as he didn't actually kill anyone with a dart, he would be OK. 'I'm going,' she said. 'And, if I were you, I'd have an ambulance on stand-by, because he gets dafter by the minute when he's showing off.'

Outside, Eve breathed in the scents of the countryside. She remembered wanting to remain in Liverpool, remembered feeling that she would never be at home anywhere else. She was still congratulating herself when she entered her newly acquired home. Rose Cottage reminded her of a patchwork quilt, since so many extra bits had been added over the years since it was built. But it all fitted; it was all good.

She was staring at the bellows on the kitchen hearth when a tremendous pain arrived in the back of her head.

Staggering, she fell awkwardly onto her rocking chair and turned slightly. This time, she saw the weapon as it descended. This time, she slipped gratefully into unconsciousness.

Eve didn't hear the small noises made by men rifling their way through the house in search of treasures; nor did she hear the criminals leaving. She simply lay there in a beautiful house on a perfect summer evening. The nightingale did not wake her, nor did the owl. Her sleep was too deep to be disturbed.

Skippy was fooling around again. Good as gold when helping to run the vet's surgeries, she remained a puppy when out on her walks. After almost getting stuck down a rabbit hole, she was now tethered to her master and on her way home to the cottage. But she wasn't exactly behaving herself.

Dave and Philly had taken her down to a place known as the Dell, a steep dip in the land behind church and graveyard. She had paddled about in the brook, had chased a frog, and was now dripping her way homeward. Dave hung on to the lead. 'She's powerful. With an extra leg, she could have pulled a dray from here to Manchester. Something in the Dell upset her – did you see her messing about and whining near the water?'

'I did. She's never done that before. Be a good dog,' Philly chided. But the animal seemed to be distracted.

When they reached Eagleton's main street, the bitch began to whimper again. 'She gets like that if I try to stop her going into the vet's place in a morning,' said Dave. 'Are we giving her too much of her own way? They're like kids, you know. They can be spoilt.'

'She's not herself.' Philly stopped walking and spoke to Skippy. 'What's the matter?'

The dog whined.

'Is she in pain?' Philly wondered. 'Shall we go and knock at Mr Mellor's door?' She bent down and patted Skippy's head. 'Come on – let's go and get your dinner. You've got chicken and lamb's liver...'

The word 'dinner' might have been designed for this greedy Labrador, but on this occasion it had no effect on her. The whining grew louder, dropped in timbre and became a near-growl. She wasn't going home. She had no immediate interest in food. She knew where she wanted to go.

Dave removed the lead. Since her accident, Skippy had needed next to no constraint, since she had learned the hard way that vehicles were bigger and faster than she was. Released, she dashed through the gate of Rose Cottage, her owners hot on her heels.

Dave slowed down and grabbed his fiancée's arm. 'Remember, you've a passenger on board, love. Slow down a bit.' He looked round, and the dog had disappeared. The front door was open, and an old armoire had toppled across the opening. Skippy had clearly run underneath this angled furniture, but Dave had to set it upright again before entering the house. 'Chas?' he called. 'You there, Eve?' But the place remained silent until Skippy howled. This time, she sounded like a wolf baying at the sky. 'Stay where you are, Philly,' Dave called.

He entered the hell that had been Eve's kitchen, where Skippy sat beside the still form of Eve. Although there was little light, Dave saw blood seeping from the woman's head into a folk-weave rug in front of an upturned rocking chair. He dropped to the floor and felt for a pulse. 'Phil?' he cried. 'Ambulance and police. Do it now. Don't come in here.'

He listened and waited until she had made the call. 'Go to the shop and get Chas,' he ordered. 'Right away, love.' When her footfalls were no longer within earshot, Dave continued to search for signs of life. A faint, thready pulse faltered in a wrist. Eve's breathing was shallow, so he turned her into the recovery position, thanking God for the Red Cross and the course he had done with them. She gurgled, and more blood came from her mouth. 'Dead men don't bleed,' he whispered. 'Stay with me, Eve. It's Dave from the Reading Room. Philly's gone for Chas.' The blood in her throat might have choked her had she remained on her back, but that hadn't been the greatest of her problems. Her skull had been battered at the back and on the left temple. 'Eve, you're going to be all right. Stay with us, lass. Don't you dare leave me, don't you dare.'

Derek entered the room at a run. 'What's wrong?' was his first question. Then he saw his mother. Shocked, he slid down the wall and sat on the floor. 'Oh, my God,' he repeated continuously. Then, thickly, he uttered, 'Get Dad – try the Reaper and Scythe.'

Dave called out to Philly and sent her on a second errand as soon as she entered the hallway.

By the time Chas arrived from the pub, the siren of an approaching ambulance was growing louder. Chas crouched beside his wife while Dave went to switch on the lights. There was a great deal of blood. Her head was no longer the right shape, but the bleeding had slowed.

'Who?' asked Chas, his voice thickened by fear and grief.

226

'No idea.' Dave placed a hand on Chas's shoulder. 'Looks like a burglary gone wrong. The door wasn't closed, there was furniture tipped over – the dog came in, I followed, and found . . .' He waved a hand in Eve's direction. 'The parameds are here now, Chas,' he said, gently pulling him away. 'Let them get to her. Come on, we're only in the way. They have to take her to hospital and get her sorted.'

From the hallway, Chas, Derek and Dave listened to commands about fluids, bags, stats, ventilation, defibrillation. It was a while before Eve was stable enough to be moved. She was carried out on a stretcher, a spinal board beneath her, a collar round her neck. Only then did the dog return to her master. 'Good girl,' whispered Dave. 'Whatever happens, Skip, you did your job.'

Philly was in the front garden when Eve was placed in the ambulance. She expected Chas to accompany his wife, but the vehicle screamed away at speed before he was given the option. Eve wasn't dead, Philly kept reminding herself. Had she been dead, the paramedics would have driven at a slower pace. She ventured into the house.

Dave shook his head and placed a finger to his lips. On the floor beside him, propped up by the walls, sat the husband and son of Eve Boswell. Not a sound was uttered by either of them. It was eerie. Neither was reacting, and Dave realized that they were in deep shock. 'We can't go in the kitchen,' he told his wife. 'It's a crime scene and we've already contaminated it. Open the shop and make sweet tea for these two.' He gave her a bunch of keys.

The village had arrived outside in the street. It seemed that someone from every house in the immediate vicinity had put in an appearance, while both pubs had spilled out customers in various stages of bonhomie that died immediately when they realized what had happened. Some tried to talk to Philly, but she pushed her way through, because she was focused on her mission. Sugar for shock, she kept telling herself. She glanced upward, saw Dave's mother at the window as usual. But the old woman was standing, so perhaps she had seen something?

While waiting for the water to boil, Philly went upstairs. 'Mrs Barker?'

'Three of them,' came the reply. 'The cops are there now – send them up here, will you? And make me a hot drink. Please.'

Philly paused for a split second. Please? But there was no time to lose. She dashed out, took tea across the road, told a policeman that Mrs Barker had something to say, then returned to her side.

'What happened to Eve Boswell?' asked Enid.

'Somebody beat her halfway to death, Mrs Barker. She's gone in the ambulance. The house looks as if it's been burgled, and Eve's been hit about the head. Dave's with Chas and Derek – neither of them can move for shock.'

Enid shook her head. 'One of the men was less than five feet tall, I swear. The other two were normal size, dark clothes all three of them. I think the little fellow hid behind a bush in the front garden while the other two followed her in. But I can't be sure where the small chap went – I can only say what I saw and what I think went on. They waited for her. For a burglary, they'd have gone in while the place was empty. It's her they were after, I'm sure.'

228

Philly sat down. She felt sick, and she wanted Dave, but she couldn't leave his mother on her own at a time like this.

'Philly?'

'What?'

Enid bowed her head. 'Stuff like this makes you think. I'll never alter, but this has shook me to the bones. I'm sorry. I'll tell Dave I'm sorry, too. Life's too bloody short, isn't it?'

Philly burst into tears. Eve's almost lifeless body had been the bridge across which Enid had walked to make her first attempt at peace. Was Mrs B intending to join the human race?

'Don't start skriking. We've enough on without all that. Go. Go on – get out and send me a policeman. And tell Dave to get that man and his son to the hospital. She'll need them there when she wakes up.' Enid shook her head. 'If she wakes up, God help her.'

Philly felt as if she had been running up the steepest bit of Everest. She found Dave, Derek and Chas in the hall of Rose Cottage, but the Boswells were mobile now, and clearly preparing to leave. 'I've told the police to talk to your mam,' she whispered to her husband. 'She saw a lot. And she apologized to me.'

Dave grunted, his eyes fixed on Chas.

'Come on, Dad,' begged Derek. 'The taxi's waiting.'

Chas allowed himself to be led out of the house. He looked like an improbable cross between a child and a very old man. Skippy remained on guard at the door. She wasn't sure about these police people, but her master and mistress seemed to trust them, so they deserved the benefit of the doubt.

After their interviews, Philly and Dave repaired to his

mother's flat. She made no comment about her canine visitor, but she spoke very clearly to her son. 'She'll have told you what I said, eh?'

Dave nodded.

'Well, same goes for you. I likely won't improve, but I'm saying sorry anyway. Give that dog a drink, it looks parched. And there's some bits of ham in the fridge – keep her going till she gets home.'

Dave stared at the floor while Philly fed the dog. He owned too gentle and reasonable a nature to react badly to his mother's words, but had she no concept of the harm she had done for forty-seven years? Was it all over and forgiven because she had finally climbed down from her high horse?

'I know what you're thinking,' Enid said. 'And I can't say I blame you. What can I do or say, Dave?'

'Nothing.'

'Exactly. Just wait till the police come, then leave me. I'll remember better on my own.' She looked at the dog. 'She's all right for one with a leg missing, isn't she?'

Philly almost smiled. 'She came up from the Dell and went straight to Eve's house – we couldn't do a thing with her till she got to Eve.'

Enid nodded. 'That's because whoever was in Rose Cottage tonight must have got away across the brook. You were probably only about two minutes away from them on your walk. They didn't come out through the front door. Your dog will have picked up the scent of something bad down in the Dell. They definitely went the back way.'

'That's true,' said Dave. 'They shoved a cupboard across the front door. There could be evidence in or near the water.' He walked across the room and threw open a window. 'Officer? My mother says she thinks they escaped the back way. If they went through that garden, they'll be scratched and nettle-stung. I dare say they climbed over into the graveyard. You'd better come soon and talk to her.'

'They could be covered in poor Eve's blood as well,' said Philly.

'Well, they've got police dogs out there now.' Dave closed the window. 'They should have borrowed Skippy.'

Enid sighed. 'I've never liked Scousers. But it doesn't do to feel like that just because somebody talks different. Happen I've learned my lesson.'

Dave let a detective into the flat. 'My mother's seen a fair bit tonight,' he explained, 'but we'll leave you to it. You've a better chance of getting details if she's got no distractions.' He led his fiancée out and down the stairs.

In the shop, they sat with their dog and stared across the road at Rose Cottage. 'Eve never did anybody any harm, I'm sure,' said Dave. 'So why her? Why did they have to pick on her? Mam's sure it wasn't a burglary. Stands to sense they would have robbed the house while it was empty instead of waiting for somebody to come home.'

'Chas knows some funny folk, Dave. His brother's been in and out of prison since his teens. But Eve? She's a lovely woman. I'm sure she'd never break the law.'

Dave held her hand. 'Stay calm, love.'

She sniffed away a tear. 'Can I sleep in your bed tonight? Just for comfort and company?'

'Course you can, Phil.'

They took their precious dog and walked home. They

would never forget tonight; Dave, in particular, would carry with him the picture of Eve Boswell's injuries. He needed Philly as much as she needed him.

Like I said, nobody gets paid enough in this bloody country. It's going to the dogs, and I'm probably best off in here. All kinds of asylum-seekers and Europeans coming in, undercutting our working men, bringing British folk to their knees.

Anyway, the solicitor's clerk, who remains anonymous, traced the money through his employer's records. She's a florist in a place called Eagleton, pronounced Eggleton. All her mail goes to the shop, but she doesn't live there. Seems she bought a house across the road. Calling herself Lily Latimer, bloody daft name.

Taunton and Liverpool are in cahoots. Money's come from Taunton, but the workers up here will be paid. She has it coming. Right from the start, wherever she went, men's eyes lit up and followed her every move. What did she do? She went on TV so that more of them could ogle her. Makeover Madness? *Lunacy, more like. Even pregnancy didn't stop her. If anything, she was more beautiful when carrying the kid, though I never fancied her then, did I?*

It'll be soon. I suppose they'll have someone keeping watch while it happens. Can't be done in the shop, has to be in the house. Seems she's doing well enough with her buttercups and daisies. There'll be men after her, but that won't last, because she'll be either dead or disfigured – I hope she'll be dead. When I know she's not out there showing herself off, I'll be OK.

And all I have to do is lie here and wait…

Nine

Mike's idea of a romantic evening was, at best, hilarious. Lily was beginning to grow used to his sense of adventure, so she was hardly surprised when she found herself in the Canal Street district of Manchester. Here, the gay community lived its life to the full, and Mike was clearly no stranger to the area, since he was on first-name terms with many of the people who sought entertainment in the bars and clubs. 'They need spiritual guidance just like everyone else,' he told Lily. 'And there's still a lot of prejudice. Apart from all of which, they cook the best food in England, so that's as good a reason as any to come here. I do enjoy a well-presented meal.'

They finished their tour in a restaurant cum nightclub named Sisters. Their dinner was superb and they were served by cross-dressers. All waitresses were men; all waiters were women; and, on the whole, they were a handsome crowd. A band played, and several people were making use of the dance floor.

'We're here for a reason,' Mike announced as they ate a delicious crème caramel. 'Mo and Po are performing tonight, and I wanted you to see how good they are. I asked them what they were doing, and it's quite a mixture. You should know that your hairdressers are a great deal more than simple crimpers. They are stars in the making. As long as Paul hangs on to sense and doesn't collapse into one of those black holes. He does love Maurice, you know. It's sad when love is one-sided, but there's nothing can be done. I always thought they were daft for not telling the truth in the first place.'

'Right.'

'The real reason we're here is because I have decided to go very PC with the panto. It's time certain social problems were addressed. No more of the same old same-old. It's time for the revolution.'

'Oh, yes? Shall I make a banner?'

He smiled benignly and, for a moment or two, looked rather like a priest. 'Why Cinderella?' he asked. 'Every damned fool seems to worry about her with her rags and her sweeping brush and her hard life. What kind of a role model is she for today's women? The concept of a human female accepting such treatment is positively Victorian. We must move on.'

'I thought her poverty and ill-treatment were the point of the story. Virtue reaps its own reward and all that jazz.'

He drained his glass and ordered another double orange juice on the rocks. As he was driving, he could not drink wine, but he still liked to display the air of a man living dangerously. He was living dangerously. She was lovely, she was his, and she was definitely forbidden fruit. 'Cinderella's got the looks, kid,' he said. 'And we all know that a pretty woman has a head start in life. Why the hell did suffragettes bother throwing themselves under horses, chaining themselves to railings and getting force-fed in jail if Cinders is going to carry on unliberated in the hearth every winter? What about her two unfortunate stepsisters? Has no one ever given a thought to their situation?'

'They're ugly,' said Lily.

'Exactly. Ugly and in the bin just because of unfortunate faces. Now, why should they suffer because they look like the back of a crashed bus? Just picture this. Buttons is a surgeon. OK? All in white, even has to sing through a mask.'

'I'm trying to imagine that. It's not easy.'

He motored on. 'So Salmonella and Pneumonia are as ugly as mortal sin: warts, bottle-bottom spectacles, manky hair, big feet and fat bellies. They're so hideous that no man will ever give them a second glance – or a first, for that matter. People have dropped dead of heart attacks after looking at these two.'

'And they're played by Mo and Po? They're working together again, so I guess they'll play together.'

'Yup.'

Lily leaned forward, as the place was becoming noisy. 'They're beautiful men, Maurice and Paul. You'll never make them ugly.'

'We can soon change that. I'll duff them up behind the bike sheds – I was a terrible bully at school, so I know how to break a man's nose. And we'll have a make-up box, of course.'

Lily laughed. He was in his element.

'The Fairy Godmother is on their side, because she's a Communist and all for the underdog. And believe me, they are definitely dogs. So the uglies get the tickets to the ball – plus a special offer of reduced-rate facelifts as long as they buy four hundred boxes of cornflakes. Oh, and there's liposuction available at sale prices via the *Daily Mail*. Fairy Godmother's also Mafia, therefore she can be bribed, so all that wand-waving will serve to iron out any residual wrinkles after the fat has been hoovered off. You see? I cover every eventuality. Buttons does the plastic surgery, then Salmonella and Pneumonia cop off with a couple of princes and—'

'Where's Cinderella?' she asked through laughter. Could a Communist be a member of the Mafia? Weren't Mafia folk Catholics? But Lily kept these questions to herself, because Mike was in full flood.

'Cinders is a theatre nurse. We all know how much surgeons make, so Buttons will do for her. See? It all dovetails together wonderfully. This fairy tale has been waiting to be written.'

Lily thought about it. 'Buttons?' she asked.

'What about him?'

'I hope he used stitches and staples instead—'

'Instead of buttons? I am ahead of you, girl. When the ugly sisters first appear, they'll be ghastly. We'll need vomit buckets for the first few rows of audience. Then two pretty girls in similar clothes will come out of the wings and meet their bridegrooms once the swellings have died down. Damage from surgery, I mean. A much better story, isn't it?'

Lily wasn't sure. But it didn't matter what she said – he would go ahead anyway. Loving him was so easy. He had the imagination of a child and the brains of a professor, so he was a rare creature. On the brink of leaving a career for which he had endured years of training, his main aim in life seemed to be to replace himself, thereby saving the bishop a job. He had a friend returning from Africa, and he would suggest him to the bishop as a suitable candidate to take over the parishes. Mike wasn't giving up; he was moving on.

'I'm not an ugly sister any more,' was his next line. 'Not a priest, not an ugly sister – there's no place for me.'

'You should carry on being a priest.'

'With a mistress?'

'Possibly.'

It wasn't just her. He needed to get out anyway before he exploded, before he lost his patience and took issue with the bishop, the cardinal, even the Pope. If the Church didn't grow up, it would die in its cradle. Two thousand years was a relatively short lifespan, and there would be no chance of resuscitation once the grass roots had stopped providing oxygen. Places of worship were emptying; people congregated instead at football and concerts, raising their voices to heaven in praise of a team or a pop group. If Catholicism was not prepared to get real, it would cease to exist.

'You've gone quiet,' Lily complained.

'Enjoy. It happens very rarely.'

She studied him. He was an amazing man with excellent looks and a way with people – any people. His charm could probably get him just about anywhere, yet he seemed to have chosen a florist from a small shop in a large village. 'Mike?'

'What?'

'Don't give up the priesthood for me, will you?'

'No. You're just one face on the dice, Lily. There are at least five others, all stamped with a reason for me to quit. Stop worrying. You're not guilty, whatever the outcome.'

A fanfare ripped through the air and the MC, a very butch girl in top hat and tails, announced Maurice et Paul. The latter was dressed as a very handsome woman.

His costume was Spanish and red all the way from patent shoes right up to the scarlet mantilla and comb. A recording of traditional Spanish music was played, and Paul danced as well as any female performer of flamenco. He played the castanets, executed brilliantly the steps made famous by gypsies of Andalucia, and took away the corporate breath of a very large audience.

Maurice emerged with his cape. It was red on one side, gold on the other. Like Paul, he was a true professional, and his body was the perfect vessel from which to pour the passion expressed in a matador's cloak. 'Nice bum,' whispered Lily to Mike.

'It'll be a good pantomime,' was the quiet reply. 'What a pity he'll be wearing a skirt. With a backside like that, he'd certainly please the ladies.'

The set ended with a standing ovation, and the pair of triumphant performers left the stage to prepare for their next piece. In the meantime, a small jazz band filled the gap, and Mike ordered coffee. 'There's true talent in those two,' he pronounced. 'They don't need me. They don't need anyone, because they could fill the school hall ten times over. But I'll write the script.'

'You'd better. No one else would think of something so original. What's the title?'

'*Never Mind Cinderella, What About the Rest?*' he suggested.

'Bad title. Too wordy.'

'Then you choose one. I didn't realize I was going to marry my chief critic.'

Several beats of time passed before Lily absorbed what he had just said. Her hand shook when she picked up the coffee cup. It had been like this last time. Clive had made all the decisions, and she had found herself engaged, then married. This man was nothing like Clive, yet the speed at which he travelled still managed to frighten her. Did she want to re-marry? Did she need to? It occurred to her that she might feel safer in an alliance with a priest, as there could never be a marriage while he remained in his post.

'Lily?'

She looked at him. 'I may not want to be married,' she said.

'Then we shall live in glorious sin. Over the brush, they call it in these parts.' He knew he shouldn't have said anything, but it wasn't the type of statement that could be changed easily into an amusing aside. He wondered whether she understood that she had been a final decider, certainly not a catalyst or a vehicle to transport him out of the clergy. 'Lily, it doesn't matter what we do afterwards.' He paused. 'That's not true, because I'd like to marry you. But I was going to quit anyway. Although I've received absolution from my father confessors, the way I treat my parishioners is not in line with many of the edicts emerging from Rome. I am not forgivable.'

'You are,' she replied. 'And that's the problem – my problem. But you must realize that I have fallen head over heels in the past and the relationship didn't work out. In fact, it was damaging. I've known you just a few weeks—'

'A couple of months.'

'All right, a couple of months. And you're wonderful. You make me laugh, you're clever and handsome and very beguiling. It all terrifies me. Speed frightens me, Mike.'

'Then I'll slow down.'

A smile played on her lips. Slow down? He had several speeds, and the lowest was overdrive, while the fastest broke the sound barrier. Mike didn't know how to go slowly, except in a car. Strangely, his quickness was one of the main factors that contributed to his charm. He had not allowed adulthood to contaminate the inner child, had never permitted sense to interfere with his goals. Yet he remained one of the cleverest people she had met in her life. And oh, how tempted she was!

'Sorry,' he said.

'It's OK. As long as you don't take me for granted, Mike. Remember, I've been through . . . hell.'

'How can I remember what you won't tell me?'

'I'll tell you when I'm ready.'

The MC was back.

This time, Mo and Po had a bash at the overdone piece 'I Will Survive'. But this was survival with a difference, because it ended with a punch-up that involved flying wigs and torn dresses out of which false breasts fell to litter the small stage. The MC rang a bell, the contestants retired to their corners, seconds appeared, gum shields were inserted, and boxing gloves entered the fray. As did towels when both were counted out. At the end, Mo and Po were carried off on a pair of stretchers, lifeless hands trailing on the boards.

Lily found herself weeping with laughter. She stood with the rest of the audience to salute a performance in which timing had been perfect, singing excellent until punches had landed, and costumes glorious. It was no wonder that they were going up for *Britain's Got Talent*. They had the special magic born of true individuality.

'Shall we go?' Mike asked.

'All right.' She was feeling tired. This was her first real night out since she had recovered, and the exhaustion she experienced was almost total. Something called ME had been mentioned after a blood test, but she had ignored it. No way was her working life going to finish when she was not yet thirty. In Lily's opinion, sixty was rather young for retirement.

He drove slowly, and that was another point in his favour. And he didn't return to Eagleton right away, because he wanted to show Lily more of the beauty that belonged to Lancashire. They went up hills and down dales, past remote farms and tiny hamlets, while the route became steeper. 'This is the way to the Pennines,' he said. 'The backbone of England. It's stunning on this side, but we must go to Yorkshire at some stage, because West Yorkshire is nothing short of magnificent.' Even in near-darkness, the landscape was amazing.

After another drive, they landed at the foot of Rivington Pike, where Mike delivered a lecture on history. This was not the Sermon on the Mount, he explained; this was the sermon before the mount was climbed. The pike, he told her, was twelve hundred feet above sea level, and on a clear day, landmarks for miles around were visible. 'You can see the Isle of Man, Blackpool Tower, the hills of Wales and the Cumbrian fells. You could see Ashurst Beacon, which was lit as a warning during wars, but they've moved it now to the Last Drop Village.'

'I do the flowers for that place.'

'Good for you. They use only the best.'

'Of course. What was Rivington Pike for?' she asked.

He told her about hunting parties using the tower, about roaring fires and mulled wine. 'But it's no longer enjoyed. All boarded up, no windows, no way in. Sad. Everything of note has to be protected from the very people who are supposed to appreciate it.'

'They're too busy collecting ASBOs to take an interest in an eighteenth-century folly,' said Lily. 'Do you mind if I ask to go home? It's been my first night out since . . . since my last night out.'

'Which was a long time ago?'

She nodded. 'A couple of years. But I've enjoyed myself. Thanks for Manchester and thanks for this lovely countryside.'

'Thank God, not me,' he answered. 'He made this lot. Mind you,' the car came to life, 'I'm not sure He made Manchester. No, we mustn't blame Him for that . . .' Before taking off the handbrake, he stroked her cheek. 'Keep me on the list, Lily.'

'List? What list?'

'Of potential suitors.'

'I'll think about it,' she promised.

Skippy wouldn't settle. They tried her downstairs, upstairs, on the landing, even at the foot of their bed. 'She wouldn't fit in with us, anyway,' moaned Philly. 'This is only a three-quarter bed, and you take up two-thirds of it.'

'Is that a complaint?'

'Yes.'

'Then do it in triplicate and send it to management.'

'Who's management?'

'The dog is,' he replied wearily. He sat up. 'It's no good, I'll have to take her out again. I can't sleep, anyway. I keep seeing that poor woman every time I close my eyes.'

Philly agreed. She hadn't seen Eve in the kitchen, but the memory of her almost lifeless body on the stretcher was enough. Poor Dave had been witness to everything. 'We may as well give up and get dressed,' she said.

'You're pregnant,' he protested. 'You can't be running about half the night.'

'Pregnant, but not ill,' she reminded him. 'And I'm stopping nowhere on my own while there's somebody out there attacking folk.'

'You heard my mam, Philly. What she saw more or less proves that Eve was targeted. They'll be miles away by this time – it's coming up eleven o'clock. Stay where you are.'

'No. I won't,' she replied. 'I feel safer with you and Skippy. That's a compliment, in case you hadn't noticed. Till we get over this – if we ever get over it – we stick together.'

'Yes, Sarge.' Dave performed a comical salute.

Once outside, the dog dragged Dave along until she was almost choking. She displayed no interest in Rose Cottage, preferring to struggle onward past Fullers Walk until she reached the end of the block. She stopped suddenly, and Dave managed, only just, not to fall over her. 'She's got good brakes,' he said. 'Nearly had me on the floor then.'

Philly took a torch from her pocket and shone it on the tarmac that led to the rear of the shops and all the garages. 'Dave?'

'What?'

'I can't be sure, but I think it's these two cigarette ends.' She shone the light on Skippy's spine. 'See? She's got her hackles up.'

Dave agreed. Skippy was doing a fair imitation of a

243

Rhodesian ridgeback. 'Don't touch anything, Phil. The cops are still across the road – I'll fetch somebody.'

A nervous Philly waited with Skippy until Dave returned with a policeman. The dog was growling again. It was clear that she had no affection for the person whose scent she had pursued so avidly. The officer stopped and pulled on a pair of purple surgical gloves, picked up the cigarette butts and placed them in a small transparent bag. 'Is this the famous three-legged dog that led us to the crime scene?' he asked.

'Yes,' Dave answered proudly. 'She was a stray, but we took her in after she lost her leg. Anyway, we were walking her behind the church and she set off whining. She was very fretful near the brook, yet she wanted to turn back. There was nothing else for it – she had to go to Rose Cottage, and you know the rest. She wouldn't sleep. The way she's carrying on, there may be a chance that one of the criminals smoked those cigarettes. Before you go, can we ask how Mrs Boswell is?'

'Not sure,' said the policeman. 'Last I heard, they were trying to stabilize her to make her fit for surgery. You may get good news in the morning, please God. Tell you what, though. We've a vanload of dogs out there, but we'd make room for this one. If it turns out that these fag ends are connected to the crime, yon dog will be declared a genius.'

'She is a genius.' Philly's voice trembled with pride mixed with many other emotions. If Eve Boswell lived, it would be because of Skippy; if the poor woman died, Skippy had done her best. 'Come on, Dave. Let's get Madam home.'

*

'She's still not in.' Babs glanced over her shoulder at Pete, who was lying on a sofa and trying to recover some energy. 'She never goes out. If she did go out, she'd tell me where she was going and what she was doing.'

Pete groaned. He'd had a hard time tonight, and he genuinely needed rest. 'Come away from the window, love. She'll not get home any faster if you stand there worrying. Put the kettle on.'

Babs felt like screaming. If she drank one more cup of tea or coffee, she would drown. And there had definitely been a change in Lily of late. It had been quite sudden, too, and joy connected to the house she had bought was not wholly responsible for it. There was a new lightness in her step, and her skin, which had become dull in recent months, had started to glow again. 'I can't stand this,' Babs moaned. 'The hospital tells me nothing about Eve, Lily's gone missing–'

'And I'm tired after helping out across the road. You'll be ill next if you carry on like this, lady.'

But Babs remained where she was. When the news had reached the pub, she and Pete had spilled out with the rest. After Eve had been taken away in the ambulance, Babs had gone straight to Lily's house. But Lily had been nowhere and was still nowhere. Well, she was probably somewhere, but she wasn't at the somewhere she was supposed to be. 'She'd never, ever go out without telling me,' she insisted.

'You'll drive yourself mad,' Pete said. 'You're getting your knickers in a twist over nothing – Lily's a grown woman. She doesn't need to sign a late book or ask permission – she's not on probation. If you like, I can get her an ASBO and she'll be on curfew with a fancy tag bracelet round her ankle.'

Babs tutted. 'The minute she comes home, I'm going over there. You stay here in case Cassie wakes. I have to be the one to tell Lily what's happened. She'd grown quite close to Eve. In fact, I'm ashamed to say I was a bit jealous, which isn't fair, because I've got you and Lily's got no one.'

'Glad to hear I'm better than nobody,' he said.

Babs stamped a foot. 'Stop twisting my words, Plod. You know what I mean, and you know I really care about you, so shut up. Where would she go on her own, though?'

'How do you know she's on her own? She might be talking about flowers with a bride-to-be, or perhaps she's gone to see a film or a play.' He closed his eyes and tried to rest. It had been a dreadful couple of hours, and the police dogs were still out there in the hollow behind the church. They would have to give up soon, because officers might be needed elsewhere, there was no light, and little could be done until forensics had tackled the bits of evidence that had been recovered.

'Pete?'

'What?'

'Come here. Come on – hurry up – she's back. And look who's with her! Blood and Carter's Little Liver Pills, I don't believe it.'

Pete joined Babs at the window. 'So what? They share a house from time to time, so why shouldn't they go out for a meal or something?'

'It's the or something I'm wondering about. I mean, he's a priest, and—'

'Hey – are you in training to become the next biggest

Lancashire gossip? You'll be overtaking Mrs Wotserface soon.'

'Mrs Barker. And I'm a south-westerner, thanks. Pete?'

'Yes?'

'He's holding her hand. See? He's pushed her into the house and he's running past the church to Rose Cottage—'

'Or you could become the new commentator for the Grand National. Give over, Babs. You're getting on my nerves now.'

Exasperated, she abandoned him to his own devices and ran downstairs. Poor Lily. She'd probably had a nice night out, albeit with a Catholic priest, and she was returning to this. It was plain to anyone arriving that something serious had happened, because Rose Cottage was cordoned off by the familiar blue and white police tape. And the priest had gone and left her on her own in that massive place . . .

Babs knocked at the door, and it was opened immediately.

'What's going on?' Lily asked.

Babs led her friend through to the kitchen and sat her down. 'Now, don't panic. We don't want you back on the don't-jump-off-the-roof pills, do we? Eve's been attacked. She's unconscious in hospital, her husband and son are with her, and the cops are still at the cottage.'

Lily's face blanched. 'Who did it?'

Babs shook her head. 'No bloody idea, my lovely. One minute we were in the pub, Chas was doing tricks with darts, and Eve was sitting with me and Pete. She went home. Then Philly came in, Chas disappeared like a magician's rabbit, someone shouted about an attack, and we all came to see what was going on. Next thing was the ambulance, then the police, then everyone was interviewed.'

Lily began to rock back and forth.

'Don't start that, Lee. You'll have me seasick.'

'Is she going to live?'

Babs raised her shoulders. 'They won't say anything at the hospital, except they told me the doctors were with her. I don't like to keep telephoning, because those nurses are busy enough without me making things worse. The short story is we'd be better waiting till morning.'

Lily remembered those very words. 'Wait till morning,' the nurses had said repeatedly. Friends had come, friends had gone and, many times, she had wanted to shout, 'I'm here – look.' But she hadn't been able to. Nurses had told people to try again tomorrow, that there was always the chance that she would wake at any minute. She hoped that Eve wasn't in that condition. Hearing the voices of those around her, needing to talk, wanting to answer questions, trying to prise open her eyelids – it had been so hard. Eventually, Lily had woken properly, but the nightmare had been true. It had all happened; it hadn't been just a bad dream.

'Lily?'

'What?'

'You don't think . . . ?'

'Think what?'

'Never mind,' said Babs. 'Forget it.'

'I won't forget any of it, Babs. She's in a condition similar to mine, right?'

'No. She got bashed on the head.'

'So she's unconscious. The method isn't important –

248

the result remains the same. I was out of it for a couple of weeks.'

Time ticked by while Babs allowed the possibilities to enter her mind. She didn't want to ask the question, yet she knew she must. 'Him?' was all she said.

Lily bowed her head and thought. 'Yes. Definitely. I'd bet my life it's him.'

'From prison?'

'Yes. He's in the ideal place for it, because the old lags will know people on the outside, and this isn't far from Liverpool.'

Babs pondered for a while. 'But your name's changed. Where you live's changed. All letters and stuff are addressed to Lily Latimer—'

'At the shop. The shop is still my address. No mail comes here. Haven't even had my driving licence altered. It's changed to Lily Latimer, but the address is number seven Fullers Walk. How he found me I don't know and may never know. But Eve has dark hair like mine used to be, and I've lost an awful lot of weight. To someone with a description of Leanne Chalmers, Eve would be the nearer match. I know she's older, but she's dark-haired and about my height.'

'So someone's found you for him? But presumably they've seen you in the shop and know you're blonde. So why would they attack someone else? They must have looked at the village. Don't they case the joint first?'

Lily shrugged. 'I don't know how he worked it out. Perhaps he paid off solicitors — I've no idea. The shop's too busy, anyway, so they'd want to do it away from Fullers Walk. And the blonde in the shop could be Lily's assistant. Clive knew I had money from my family as well as from my own job before I became Lily. And there was the compensation fund – I'm wealthy, Babs. I could afford an assistant.'

'Yes.'

They sat in silence for a few moments, then Lily shot from her seat in one swift move. She ran to the dining room, only to return seconds later with a cardboard box. 'You see?' she said, her tone desperate. 'It's my fault – I should have changed it.'

Babs said nothing.

'Look!' Lily opened the package and took out a wooden sign. 'Hope House,' she cried. 'Outside, this is still St Faith's presbytery. Right. Listen to me. Say nasty people came to find me after he'd traced my new location by some means. And say they saw me in the shop, but I'm blonde.'

'OK.'

'Leanne Chalmers is brunette. So the woman in the flower shop would be Leanne's assistant.'

'All right.'

'So if a man – or a woman, for that matter – wanted to know where I lived, anyone in the village might have said I'd bought the house across the road next to the church.'

'Still with you so far, Lee.'

'In the past, Rose Cottage would have suited me better than this place. I don't know how much the attackers know about me, but I always had a cottage in Somerset, didn't I?'

'You did.'

'So, these unknown criminals cross the road and check out the houses near the church. This one has St Faith's Presbytery on the sign. It's a priest's home. No one would look twice at it if they were looking for a woman. Rose Cottage still has FOR SALE outside, but with SOLD plastered across the middle of the board. Which house would you choose? Eve dyes her hair dark brown to hide her grey—'

'And they got her by mistake.'

'Yes.'

'Oh, my God.'

It had nothing to do with God, Lily told herself inwardly. Poor Eve had been attacked by servants of Satan himself, and they had gone for the wrong target. They might come back; they might carry on picking off women until they got the right one. 'It's my fault,' she whispered. 'If I hadn't come here, Eve would still be staining that beautiful staircase in her cottage.'

'Stop it, because—'

'And I never saw a happier marriage. Even when she's telling him off for being daft, you can see how much they love each other. If she dies, he'll die inside. Just perfect together, those two.'

'You can't blame yourself.'

'Can't I? Oh, I know I've done nothing – but neither has poor Eve. Babs, if I'd stayed away, none of this would have happened.'

'And if wishes were horses, beggars would ride.'

'My gran used to say that.'

'And mine.' Babs busied herself with tea-making, because she felt she had to do something that appeared sensible. It had been her experience in life so far that doing ordinary things meant staying inwardly sane and outwardly calm, and she had to be both. Lily was terrified all over again; someone had to give the impression of level-headedness. She set a tray with cups, saucers, milk jug and sugar bowl. Lee wasn't a sweet-tooth, but she was in shock.

Lily stared unseeing at the tray when it arrived on the table. 'He's put a curse on me, Babs.' A thought struck. 'And what if he comes after you and little Cassie? He sees you as part of his downfall, and we know he doesn't care about children.'

Babs swallowed hard. 'I'll get Pete to stay with us.'

'Twenty-four seven? He does have a job.'

Babs gulped again. 'What are we going to do, Lily?'

'We're going to run.'

'What? I've got Pete and a job. I've got Cassie settled with Valda and her kids. I like it here.'

Lily nodded. 'So do I. I like it very much. But after what's happened here tonight, I don't trust anyone – not even the police. We're two hundred miles from Somerset, yet we've been found. Think about Cassie and only Cassie. Babs, we know he'd kill anyone.'

'Tell the cops that he's organized this from jail. Tell them he needs sending to Siberia or somewhere.'

'Proof?' Lily asked.

Babs poured the tea. 'You're having sugar, because you need it. We both do.' She sat down. 'You're right, it's down to proof. They'll need to catch the people who did this and make them talk. And what are they going to do to him? Give him a longer sentence? He'll still be there. He'll still be able to pay people to come after us. And, at the end of the day, it could have been a simple burglary.'

'It wasn't. Lord, I hate sweet tea. You think there's no hiding place? So do I, but we can play for time. Babs, we're going. I'll sell up here, then—'

'No. If we go away, it's just for a short break, to give them time to find the attackers and get them to confess.

252

We can't let him dictate our lives from now on. We belong here. You have to learn to compromise.' She lowered her eyelids and glanced through the lashes at her friend. 'Lily?'

'What?'

Babs paused and took a sip from her cup. 'What's going on with Mike?'

Lily stared stonily across the table. 'Shut up and drink your tea. Now, nothing will happen tonight. The offenders are on the run, and this village is too hot for them. Send Pete home. If he's asleep, get rid of him as early as you can in the morning. Order a taxi to pick you up behind the shop, not at the front. I'll be outside the village on the top road – near the telephone kiosk. Transfer your luggage from the taxi to my car, and we'll bugger off for a few days. Or weeks. I'll be there from about seven o'clock.'

'If you insist.'

'Bring Cassie's child seat and clothing. We'll buy her some toys when we get there.'

'When we get where?'

Lily sighed. 'To the end of whichever bloody road. I don't know.'

The front door opened. 'It's Mike,' said Babs.

'Yes. Go now. Not a word to Pete.'

'What about the shop?' Babs whispered, standing up.

'Closed till further notice. Can't be helped.'

Mike entered the room. 'Lily? Babs? Are you all right?'

Neither replied.

'I'll stay tonight,' he said. 'Though I'm expected in Harwood tomorrow morning. This is a terrible business, isn't it?'

Babs, who was standing uneasily in the line of Lily's penetrating stare, made her farewell and left the house.

Mike sat in the chair she had vacated. 'Eve's still alive,' he said. 'They're trying to stabilize her for surgery, something to do with bloods and gases – I don't understand medical jargon.'

Lily sighed. 'I do. I've been there. I've been in Eve's position and I know she could die on the table if they took her in now. They have to get her body as balanced as possible before taking a proper look at the wounds. She's already in shock, and the trauma of surgery might kill her. They'll be working damned hard to save her.'

He looked steadily at Lily's face and decided once again that he must ask no more questions about her own past crises. All he wanted was to comfort her, but she wasn't here any more. The woman who had laughed herself silly just a few hours ago, who had enjoyed his tour of the countryside outside Bolton, had disappeared. In her place sat an animal as terrified as the rescued rabbit had been after its long containment under the tree. If anything, she looked worse than she had in the first few weeks after arriving in the north. 'Go to Harwood now,' she told him. 'I need to be by myself.'

Mike leaned back in the chair. 'Aren't you afraid?'

'It's already happened, hasn't it? They aren't likely to come back tonight, because they'll be too busy putting as much space as possible between themselves and this village.'

'You don't need me?'

Lily paused before speaking. 'In the last couple of years, I've made sure I don't need anyone. And I like my own space.' She did need him, but she didn't want him to get involved with the dreadful truth – not yet, not until she had decided what to do in the long term.

'Plenty of space for you here, then. This house was built to contain more than one priest – and their house-keeper – so you'll have plenty of room to rattle around.' She wasn't telling him anything. Instinct and experience informed him that what had occurred tonight in Eagle-ton impinged on her in some way. It was a great pity, because she had been making progress in leaps and bounds. 'Eve and you have become friends,' he said.

'Yes. I like Eve. Chas is a good man, too.

'I'm praying for them, Lily.'

'Oh, good. Everything will be all right, then. I'm sure God will listen to one of his ministers who's been break-ing every rule in the book.'

'Sarcasm doesn't suit you.'

'Sorry, Mike. But nor does the knowledge that some-one I care about is in hospital with her head bashed in. Mike, will you please leave? I have to be alone tonight.'

'Will you visit Eve tomorrow if she's better?' he asked.

'Not sure. Now, I am exhausted. Please go. Go now.'

He rose from his chair, opened his mouth to speak, thought better of it and went upstairs to collect some of his things. When he came down, he stood for a few seconds in the hall, but the whole place was silent and dark. Whilst every instinct prompted him to stay, he realized that he had to go. This was her house, and she didn't want him here at present.

In the kitchen, Lily sat in complete silence. The happy evening seemed to have taken place months ago, per-haps in some parallel universe she might never visit again. But he had gone, at least. She couldn't have packed with him there, would have been incapable of accepting comfort or love. After what had happened to Eve, she didn't want anyone coming close, because she was perilously near to tears.

The front door opened – he must have left it on the latch. 'Lily?'

'Who is it?'

'Paul.' He ran in. 'What the hell's been happening while we were in Manchester? Thrilled to bits to see you and Mike in the audience at Sisters, but– What's the matter, love? Oh, bugger, I didn't mean to upset you.'

'It should have been me,' she said, her defences suddenly flattened. Emotion came crashing in. Oh God, poor Eve. Lily had held herself together in the company of Mike, but she was too tired, too bone-weary, to keep up the act. 'Eve might die, and it should have happened to someone else . . .'

'What should?'

'They got Eve.' In a voice that was on the brink of cracking, Lily gave an account of what had befallen her friend. 'That's all I know,' she said. 'Because I wasn't here, either. They were looking for me, those murderers.'

'What makes you believe that?'

She sniffed back a disobedient tear. 'There was a load of folk in the pub. Chas was messing about, and Eve was sitting at the table with Babs and Pete. She went home, and the attack happened then. Not a burglary, you see. Burglars like an empty house. They were looking for me, Paul.'

'Never!'

'I'm sure of it. Babs and I are going away for a while tomorrow. We're on a hit list. Oh, I know it sounds a bit

Chicago, but it's true – all connected with stuff that happened before we came up here. No one knows about this – except for Babs, of course.' And Eve ... 'We have to keep Cassie safe, Paul.' These were the words she ought to have said to the man she loved.

'God, yes, that lovely little girl. I'll tell Mo that Babs's absence couldn't be avoided. I'll say she's sorry to let him down. I'll have to do more hours.'

In spite of everything, Lily found herself almost smiling, because Paul had failed to remove all his make-up. 'You look like a doll in a shop window,' she said. 'Thanks, Paul. I don't know why I've allowed you to come near to the truth, but ... oh, you look ridiculous, man.'

'We were good, though – weren't we?'

'Brilliant.'

He sat and held both her hands. 'Look, keep in touch with me and only me. I'll give you a card with my mobile number. I'll try to take full notice of what's happening round here, and—'

'Thanks, Paul—'

'And it should be in the newspapers, so you'll get the bigger picture wherever you go. You know what? I'm so glad that you told me some of it. Makes me feel a bit special. How do you know you can trust me? Is it the gay thing?'

She shrugged. 'Not entirely sure, but it could be. Because you treat us like people, you see. It's easier for a woman with a gay man, because she doesn't have to dress up and pretend to be anything she isn't. But the other thing is that you're a family sort of person, Paul. Like a brother? Oh, I'm not sure why I'm sure, but I trust you.' Why hadn't she been able to tell Mike? Paul was a long way from perfect, yet her instinct was to lean on him.

257

'I'll leave you to do what needs doing,' Paul said. He kissed her on the cheek and left the house.

Mike loved her, and the truth would hurt and anger him. Telling Eve all of it and Paul some of it had been easy, because she had no plans that included either of them. But she could imagine Mike's reaction, and she wasn't ready for it, not yet. She was going to miss him. Apart from her family, she had never missed anyone as badly as she was going to miss Mike. He was so ... unusual, so gentle and understanding, funny, different, uninhibited. 'I love him,' she told a very old mirror.

It was time to start packing. In the hall, she noticed that the answering machine showed a green light, so she clicked to hear her messages. There was just one, but it was enough to prove that she was doing the right thing. A clerk from the Taunton solicitor's office had disappeared. He had broken every confidentiality rule in the book, and it was not her bank's fault. The clerk had managed to crack a cipher and had contacted a junior executive at her branch in Bolton, whom he had persuaded to 'confirm' her name and business address. He had probably sold the details to someone connected with her ex-husband. 'I thought I should let you know, because there could be something sinister behind all this. I'm sorry, Miss Latimer,' said the disembodied lawyerly voice. 'The manager of your bank is mortified, but the damage has been done.'

So. There it was. Clive was at the back of everything again, and was controlling her life just as he had since the day of her wedding. She picked up her mobile phone and sent a text to Babs. *Solicitor proved me right. Should have been me, not Eve. It's Clive. See you in the morning.*

In her special room with the beautiful circular window, Lily packed a suitcase. She couldn't take much, because she needed to leave space in the boot for Babs's stuff. And Cassie's. She looked down at the pair of sensible shoes she was taking with her. Cassie. 'If anything happens to her, I'll find a way of killing him myself,' she announced to the suddenly lifeless room. Street lighting illuminated the coloured glass, but it needed sun to make it truly effective. She didn't want to go. Mike's reaction to her disappearance would give him away – the whole village could guess the truth.

At a table, she penned a note to him.

My darling Mike,

Please try not to be too upset by my sudden disappearance. Babs and Cassie will be with me, and there is a very good reason for running away. Don't look for us. I shall find you when I feel strong enough to come back.

Please know that I am falling in love with you and I want to see you again as soon as possible. Suffice to say that I now have proof that Eve was mistaken for me. I am taking the only action that seems possible at the moment. Cassie is in danger, too.

I didn't mean the nasty things I said tonight. Sometimes, we hurt so badly that we turn on those we love. Please carry on praying for Eve and for Chas. Talk to God about yourself, too. He loves you. So do I.

Lily x

She re-read it several times, then lay on her bed. She had always believed that she could never love again, but he had wandered into her life with a rabbit and some foxes ... The foxes. She jumped up and added a PS that advised Mike to watch out for her pets, as they were becoming too tame. They liked Pedigree Chum, though she didn't know whether it was good for them, and the babies loved eggs.

Sleep proved elusive. She tossed and turned, finally dropping into a restless doze after three in the morning. Clive was in the dream again. There was the knife, and she saw those black-handled scissors, blood soaking through the material in her lap. Twenty pounds a metre, she remembered. Good value, heavy fabric with years of wear in it. She stood, he staggered, she screamed and the neighbour came.

Lily's eyes opened. It was dark, almost as dark as those weeks had been. Coming out of the coma had been frightening ... She switched on a lamp. It was a quarter past three. The dream that had lasted for ever had, in reality, spanned just a few minutes. Would she be fit to drive? More to the point, would Eve Boswell ever be well again?

By seven o'clock, Lily was sitting in her vehicle near the telephone kiosk on Ashford Road. There was very little traffic, as the road led only to a few farms, so she was reasonably sure that no one would spot her. Time crawled. Babs and Cassie arrived at ten minutes to eight. 'Sorry,' said Babs. 'Pete stayed the night and didn't leave till gone seven.'

The taxi driver transferred luggage and child seat from his cab to Lily's estate car. Lily paid him, and he drove off. 'We're doing the right thing,' she advised Babs. 'The solicitor said his clerk had disappeared because he knew he had been found out. He provided the information for Clive. Whoever hit Eve thought she was me.'

Babs fastened Cassie into her seat, then placed herself next to the driver. 'Where are we going?'

'Not far today. I've had too little sleep.'

'Blackpool?' suggested Babs.

'It'll be busy.'

'Exactly. We'll be just three more tourists looking for a good time on the Golden Mile.'

Blackpool wasn't too far. Lily switched on her satnav and turned the vehicle round. 'We're going for a holiday, Cassie. We'll get you a bucket and spade, then you can bury Mummy up to her neck in Blackpool sand.'

'Thanks, Lee,' said Babs. 'I always knew you were on my side.'

Got the signal that it's all going ahead. The golden makeover girl will be finished, and I can sit out my sentence at Her Majesty's pleasure, no stress, ignore the useless screws, get what I need out of the others.

Sit back and wait now. Lofty'll let me know as soon as he can. Patience is a virtue I'm trying to develop, because I've a long sentence. All kinds of fights in here, but I try to stay out of that sort of stuff. Reformed character. Never lose my temper any more, don't get into arguments, become a model prisoner.

Models. We make a lot of those in here with matchsticks. You can buy matchsticks, but they don't strike, because they're made just for us. Some soft swine are making the Titanic *and* Concorde *– just as well they're serving life, otherwise they'd never finish.*

I read a lot. She used to read a lot, thought she was a

cut above. It's not a bad life if you keep your head down, though the food is gross. When we get salad, it sometimes walks off the plate. Prison cats can't keep the rat population down. If they could, we'd have a few loose screws, ha-ha.

Yes, I'm keeping my head down. I wonder how Leanne's getting on? I hope they do her slowly. I hope she realizes I'm at the back of it . . .

Ten

While Lily and Babs were making their escape from Eagleton, Chas, Derek and Mike remained prisoners in the hospital. Mike, who had arrived shortly after midnight, telephoned Monsignor Davies and arranged for another priest to attend a recently bereaved family in Harwood. There was no chance that he would leave the Boswell clan in their current state. Chas, who was speechless for the most part, was the more worrisome of the pair. Derek, once the initial shock had begun to evaporate, was agitated but talkative; Chas, however, seemed to be existing in a state of trauma far too deep to be reached.

'I'm worried about my dad,' Derek said.

'So am I. Has he said anything at all?'

Derek took the priest into the next corridor. 'Something about Lofty. Lofty's under five feet tall and he comes from Liverpool – Dad knows him. But then he said it wasn't Lofty, it was his twin – there's about an inch difference in their heights if I remember rightly. Mam and Dad used to joke about Lofty and Titch when we lived in Liverpool. They're Scallies. Lofty would have recognized Dad if he was near enough, but whoever it was just walked away. I don't think Dad's ever met Titch. He'd know him by sight, but—'

'What's a Scally?'

'Scouser gone bad. The twins get used a lot, because they can fit through small windows when there's a robbery. I don't know what Dad was on about. I asked him when and where he'd seen Lofty's twin, and he just said the man had walked away. Then he started that terrible staring into thin air again. I might as well not have been there. He's sitting and waiting, but I'm not sure he knows what he's waiting for. It's as if he's gone missing, but his body's still warm and with us.' Derek swallowed hard. 'He won't manage if she ... He can't manage without Mam.'

'Let's pray for the best, Derek.'

They returned and sat with Chas, who had refused all sustenance since arriving at the hospital. Cups of tea had been left to cool, a ham sandwich was curling on a paper plate, while the man for whom these items had been purchased sat with his head bowed.

Mike tried again. 'You should eat and drink, Chas. You'll be no use to anyone if you don't make an effort.'

Chas raised his head. 'I think it was Titch,' he said clearly. 'Not Lofty. They couldn't use Lofty as a look-out, because he's as blind as a bat when it comes to distance. I thought he hadn't seen me properly with his eyes being buggered, but I'm sure now it wasn't him. Lofty can read the phone book without specs, but he'd mix up a double-decker with an elephant unless they were parked under his nose. I was close enough to be recognized, though. It was Titch, deffo.'

'Deffo' was Liverpool-speak for definitely, Mike guessed. He glanced at Derek. All this time, Chas had been concentrating, it seemed. 'Titch?' he asked.

'Twins. Titch is shorter than Lofty. I know Lofty. He's

visited me in Eagleton, but I've never seen his brother round there. Till I was on my way to the pub. I nearly shouted out to him, then I saw the ciggy. Lofty doesn't smoke. Titch is a chain smoker. I realize now he was keeping watch for whoever did this to Eve. Never gave it a second thought at the time.'

'So it was deliberate?'

'Oh, yes. But I think they got the wrong house.'

'Why?'

'I just know it. Eve . . .' Chas gulped hard. 'Eve told me there's somebody nearby in a lot of bother. She spilled it all out before I went to the pub.' He swallowed again. 'I was messing about with the arrows when she came, doing my blindfold tricks, the upside-down darts, arsing around as bloody usual. Never even spoke to my old woman. She went. Next time I saw her, she was . . . a mess.'

Mike asked Chas for the identity of the person in 'bother', but Chas closed down as suddenly as he had come to life just minutes earlier. 'Derek?'

'What, Father?'

'What's he on about?'

Derek had no idea. 'First thing I knew, Philly Gallagher came running into the shop and told me to get home quick. She didn't give me any details, because she hadn't seen Mam. I don't know what happened, but I do know my dad. He's working something out, and when he does work it out, God help whoever clobbered my mam. I thought he'd gone into shock, but he's thinking hard. Nobody gets away with hurting my mother.'

A door opened and a tall figure entered the corridor: Mr Hislop, Eve's surgeon. 'How's the husband doing?' he asked Mike.

'Strangely lucid, then back to square one. He's concentrating his energy on working out what happened and why – still not completely with us.'

Chas stood up. 'I can talk for myself, thanks. What's going on with my wife?'

'Sit down, Mr Boswell.' The surgeon dragged a chair into position and sat opposite his patient's husband. 'We've done the scan. Strange to say, but the person who hit your wife did her a favour. As long as there's no damage we've missed, that is, and we're ever hopeful in my job. What's your first name?'

'Chas.'

'I'm Richard, but that's a heavy name to carry – Richard the Third and all that – so I'm Rick to my friends. The bleeding has stopped, and we have managed to release blood that had collected in her skull. She's had transfusions, so we've topped up her tank. There's a growth, Chas. Knowing Eve's history – now that we've read her notes – we looked for malignancy, but the path lab's initial findings point to a benign tumour.'

'In her head?'

'Yes. We've exposed the bugger right down to its roots. Benign it may be, but it could have grown to a size that might have precluded surgical intervention. It could have affected her life in many ways, so we've stopped it in its tracks.' He smiled reassuringly. 'There'll be a steel plate in her head. That is one tough little lady, Chas. She'll need a wig when she gets home.'

A lone tear tracked its way down Chas's right cheek. 'She will come home, then?'

'Let's take one step at a time, shall we? I have to go and do my work on Eve, but I'm pretty confident about the operation. There's no denying the brain is something we still don't fully understand, but she shows every sign of coming out in one piece. You cross your fingers, and get your priest to pray. She'll be in intensive care for a while, but she's steady for now.' He patted Chas's shoulder, and left the scene.

Chas seemed to have come back to life. 'I'm going outside,' he said. 'I want to use my mobile. This means war, Derek. I'll get the bastard who did this if it takes me what's left of my days.'

Mike shook his head. 'Revenge isn't worth the price you pay, Chas.'

'Oh yes? I'll play the game with my rules, thanks, Father. And the less you know about that, the better. Go home. Me and our Derek can manage now. Thanks for coming.' Chas picked up the stale sandwich and bit into it. After ordering his son to find him something more palatable, he went outside.

Mike sighed heavily. 'Law of the jungle?'

'Law of the Dingle,' replied Derek. 'That's where he was born – the Dingle in Liverpool. Keep out of it, please. My dad's a tank with no brakes now, so don't be thinking you can stand in his way and stop him, because he'll run you down as soon as look at you. It's a matter of honour. Read your Old Testament – the Israelites knew a lot about justice. Our faith concentrates on the New Testament. But remember, the Commandments were given to Moses, and the Red Sea was parted for him and it drowned his enemies. Plagues and all sorts came down on Egypt – it was bloody rough.'

'I suppose it was.'

Derek half smiled. 'I did RE at A level. Seems daft for

an accountant, but it was interesting. If we had Moses and Solomon and a couple more of that lot back, there'd be no ASBOs.'

'No, but there'd be a lot of brutally punished people, Derek.'

'Exactly. So look on my dad as a junior Moses. And again, stay out of it. You'll be safer that way.' Derek went in search of food for his father.

Mike stretched his legs. He walked up and down the corridor for several minutes before deciding to take Derek's advice. He had learned over the years that people made up their own minds when it came to the serious areas of life, and little difference could be made by intervention when a man was in a blind rage. Perhaps Chas would cool down after a few days. And perhaps he wouldn't. Whatever, Mike needed a shower and a change of clothing, so he set off towards Eagleton, his mind still reeling about the Lofty and Titch twins. He'd lost track and forgotten who was who ... 'I hope Lily's all right,' he said aloud. 'And Eve, too, of course, God keep her.'

He drove like a bat out of hell all the way back to the old presbytery. She wasn't there. The panic hit him immediately – he couldn't lose her, wouldn't lose her, panicked at the idea that the criminals had got to her while he'd been at the hospital. He went into her bedroom, interpreted piles of clothing and a rejected suitcase as evidence of recent packing, even went so far as to peep inside her two wardrobes. The summer one was almost empty. So Lily was definitely the person in trouble; she had run, because the crime committed against Eve had really been meant for her. A powerful dart of fear pierced his chest; he had to find her, had to protect her from whatever was out there. Where was she? Like something from a Disney cartoon, he ran stupidly from room to room, knowing that she wasn't there, yet managing to hope that she might be.

He found the note, read it, re-read it, ran across to the flower shop. CLOSED UNTIL FURTHER NOTICE was the message on the door. No one answered when he rang the bell connected to Babs's flat. Would Pete know? How could he find Pete? Entering Pour Les Dames, he asked Mo whether Babs was supposed to be in today.

'Yes, she is, but Paul's filling in for her. Paul?' yelled Mo.

Mo's partner entered, face rather flushed. In his left hand was clasped a big lie in the form of a mobile phone. He had just received a message from Lily, who had used a new SIM card. He alone had her phone number. 'Babs has gone away with Lily,' he said lamely. 'No idea what it's about, but I suspect it's some sort of family trouble in the south. Or a friend in difficulty,' he added, his voice rising slightly in pitch. 'Babs told me because I have to fill in for her.' He busied himself at a washbasin, his cheeks darkening even further.

Mike was used to lies, could spot them from a great distance. Paul knew more than he was saying, but he had probably given his word to Lily and her friend. 'Thanks,' he said before leaving the salon. If necessary, he would work on Paul later, though he suspected that Paul just might be a person who didn't break promises. In which case, he was a better man than most, and should be forgiven for recent behaviour.

Outside, he stood helplessly on the Walk and won-dered what the hell to do next. Then he remembered the eyes and ears of the world. She hated Catholics, but Mrs

Barker missed next to nothing. The Reading Room was open, and Mike stepped inside. Dave had begun organizing daily newspapers and some magazines. He stopped when he saw Mike. 'You're the early bird today,' he said. 'We didn't get much sleep, either. How's Eve?'

Philly, abandoning her scones and sandwiches, ran through from the back room, Skippy hot on her heels. 'How's Eve?' she echoed.

'She's being operated on now,' Mike said. 'And it looks hopeful, although we have to wait for her to regain consciousness. The surgeon is very optimistic, but it's still a waiting game for the rest of us.'

'God love her,' breathed Philly. 'I'm praying, Father. I'm even offering up my work as prayer.'

Mike smiled at the good woman. 'But have you any idea where Lily is? Or Babs?' he asked, his tone deliberately light.

Dave offered no explanation.

Philly sat down. She was full of tears, but she managed, just about, to stem the tide. Journalists were coming to ask about their clever dog, and she didn't know what to say because she was too upset. 'They're calling Skippy a heroine, and I'm proud, but I can't stop thinking about Eve and Chas,' she said. 'Father, are you sure she's going to be all right? I mean, when I saw her on that stretcher, mask on, bloody bandages, big collar round her neck – well – I wondered if she'd ever be Eve again.'

Mike told her again what the surgeon had said, and decided that Philly was in no fit state to hear any more about the disappearance from the village of two further women. 'May I go up and see your mother?' he asked Dave.

'Have you got your hard hat?' Dave asked. 'No, I'd better re-phrase that, because she's decided to start being nice. I'm warning you, Father, because it may come as a shock to your constitution. She's mending her ways. Now, I don't think she'll mend them all at once – nobody has a long enough darning needle for that job. But you may not need a gun or an anti-stab vest. Good luck with her, anyway.'

Mike ascended the stairs and knocked.

'Come in,' called a disembodied voice.

The priest entered Enid Barker's personal arena. Prepared to find himself in the modern equivalent of a lions' den, he was surprised when her only comment was, 'Oh, it's you.'

'It is indeed, Mrs Barker. How are you?'

She sighed audibly. 'Get in if you're coming in – I can't be doing with hoverers. How am I? Different. Angry. Tired. That Liverpool woman never did anybody any harm as far as I can work out. Makes you think, doesn't it? I've not slept. Well, I might have dozed off a time or two, but I've kept my eyes and binoculars pinned to this bloody window nearly all night. They've not been back, them bad beggars.'

'They won't come again, Mrs B. The place is too dangerous for them. Shall I make a brew?'

'Aye, go on, lad.'

This was progress indeed. He had gone from 'that holy Roman' to 'lad' in a matter of minutes, so she must be on the mend. It was strange how the worst for some people brought out the best in others. Until this moment, few would have believed that Mrs Barker had a better side, but he could see it now. He brought her a cup of

271

tea. 'You should sleep,' he said. 'A full night awake's bad for the constitution – I should know. Get your head down.'

'I can't yet, but I'm sure I will soon. I just need to know she's all right. I phoned the hospital, said I was her auntie, and they told me she was in theatre. How's her husband taking this?'

Mike couldn't tell the truth, dared not say that Chas was bent on vengeance. 'Eating at last, walking about a bit. I'd say furious and afraid.'

Enid nodded. 'See, till it lands on your own doorstep, you don't think, do you? Any road, your landlady's gone. She was up before seven and planting luggage in the back of her car. Later on, her friend took the little girl in a taxi from the back – I saw them through my other window. It looked as if they didn't want to be seen leaving together. Babs had luggage, too. None of them's come back.'

'I know,' he said carefully. 'I don't suppose you've any idea where they've gone?'

'Not a clue, son. Fetch me a digestive, will you? No sleep means my diabetes is up the pole.'

He handed her the packet of biscuits and his card. 'Any time you need me, Mrs B.'

'Thanks. Go on now, off with you. I'll have to catch a few minutes' sleep before I start seeing things. They'll be parking me in the funny farm if I have one of my hypos.'

Taking this as his dismissal, he walked to the door.

'Hang on a minute,' she ordered. 'That Lily one likes you, doesn't she?'

He nodded.

'And you like her?'

Again, Mike simply bowed his head.

'Well, bloody good luck to you. Time priests got flaming well wed and found out how the rest of folk suffer.'

'Priests can't marry yet,' he told her.

'Oh, aye? What will you do?'

'The priesthood is not imprisonment, Enid. May I call you Enid?'

'It's my name.'

'I'm Mike.' He left the flat. Should he have denied 'liking' Lily? Should he have insisted that there was nothing going on? No. That might have seemed like protesting too much.

Enid watched him as he walked across the road. It was as if his shoulders had become heavy, because he looked shorter. He was a good-looking bloke. That Lily was a pretty woman if she'd just liven herself up a bit. They'd look good together, that pair, and they'd probably have handsome kids. She wondered for a moment what her grandchild might look like, because neither Dave nor Philly was much to look at. Ah, well. It couldn't be helped, she supposed. She had to try to like Philly, must make an attempt at peace with her son. It wasn't easy, because her nature was angry.

So. She had a secret. And it was time she learned to keep such information to herself, because folk expected her to talk behind their backs. The priest and the florist – it sounded like some Victorian never-darken-my-door-again kind of story.

Enid closed her eyes and slept fitfully. In her dream, everything was her fault. She woke in a lather, sweat running into her eyes. Dave was right. She had been a bad mother and there could never be an excuse for it.

Old dogs and new tricks? 'I can only do my best,' she told herself before dropping off again. This time, there was no dream.

While Derek went off to buy essentials for his mother, Chas stayed at her bedside. Apart from breaks to eat and visit the lavatory, he did not move. Nurses in the unit were impressed by him, as he talked almost constantly, reminding his sick wife of how they had met, their wedding day, holidays, getting the shop, moving to Rose Cottage. Almost every tale he told was funny. 'And I'm not staying there without you,' he told her. 'So you'd best buck up, because it's your bloody choice, not mine. The state of that flaming garden for a kick-off – OK, I haven't found a tiger yet, but the missing link's living in a hole near the privets. Says he wants a telly, a washing machine and a fridge. Oh, and double pay on Sundays.'

Members of staff were fascinated, many lingering for a minute or two after completing necessary tasks, since this man was a born teller of stories.

'Remember when your red high heel got stuck down the grid? And the lads pulled the whole thing up, and you had to carry the grating home so that your dad could get your shoe out? Hey? You were well pissed that night, babe. I mean, standing there screaming at the Liver Birds because the shoes had cost a tenner? I think that was when I knew I'd marry you. If you'd have me, like. I'm glad you did, girl.'

Rick Hislop, Eve's surgeon, was checking something on Eve's chart. He smiled encouragingly at Chas. 'That's good,' he said. 'Sometimes, patients can hear you. I've known them come out of coma and talk about what was happening around them before they woke. Carry on with the good work, Chas.'

Chas was worn out. His shop was shut, but he managed not to care a fig about that, because his wife was shut, too. There were machines bleeping and drawing lines on a screen; there were tubes and plasters and all kinds of things stuck to her. In fact, the more he looked at her, the more she looked like a re-sized aerial photo of a plate of spaghetti. Or, if he concentrated on her head, an Egyptian mummy. 'Eve?'

There wasn't even a flicker.

'Eve? If you don't talk to me soon, I'm going to cut up your Barclaycard. And your chequebook.'

Nothing.

'And your American Express. It's time we cleared out some of your mess, too, kid. You keep saying things'll come back in fashion – when? After the next Preston Guild?'

Was he mistaken, or had that left eyelid flickered?

He took hold of her hand carefully, keen to avoid interfering with her wiring. 'I'll sing to you,' he threatened. 'I'll sing till all these intensive care buggers wake up and run away. Would you like "You'll Never Walk Alone"?'

The eyelid definitely twitched.

'Or I could have a go at "Bright Eyes". Remember? *Watership Down*?'

Both eyelids moved.

Chas pressed the buzzer, and a nurse appeared. 'She flickered,' he said. 'Left eyelid, then both. If I sing, she'll do it again, I'm sure. My singing's so good, it makes all the dogs for miles around howl. She's going to be all right, isn't she?'

The nurse looked at the readings, then shone a torch in Eve's eyes.

'She won't like that,' said Chas.

'Pupils equal and reacting,' said the young woman.

'Eh?'

'She may well wake up soon. Now, you come with me.' She almost had to drag him into the office. After pushing him into a chair, she delivered her lecture. 'Don't be afraid if she appears to have forgotten things when you get her to wake. Her brain's been shaken up, so it may take a while for her to get her memory back.'

'You don't know my Eve.'

She sighed. 'All I'm asking is that you be patient with her. I know you love her – we can all see that. But she might not respond properly for a while, and we don't want you getting downhearted.'

He nodded, then leaned forward. 'Listen, love. She was made in Liverpool. She's a twenty-four-carat piece of Scouse, my wife. She's coming to because I threatened to cut up her credit cards and get rid of all the clothes she's collected over the years. As for shoes – Imelda Marcos has nothing on my wife. She once went out and bought eight pairs. Eight pairs in one shop.' He shook his head. 'If she'd just wake up, I'd buy her every bloody pair of shoes and boots in Bolton. Mind, I'd get no thanks, because she'd still want something different, even if I'd bought the whole lot.'

The nurse couldn't help laughing. 'All right. Go back and keep talking.'

'I've only just started,' he replied. 'Wait till I tell her I'm selling her house.'

'She'll have a stroke!' she said.

'As if.'

'Just be careful. You might frighten her.'

'No, I won't. She'll get out of that bed and tear a strip off all of us.' He gulped. 'God willing.'

'Mr Boswell?'

'Yes, love?'

'You're doing a grand job.'

'Ta.' He rushed back to his wife.

When Derek arrived with toiletries and nightdresses, he found his father fast asleep in an armchair while his mother, who was supposed to be the comatose one, was wide awake and glaring at Chas. 'Thank God,' Derek breathed. 'Mam, we've been so worried about you.' He blinked away a few tears.

His mother fixed him with a steely stare. 'Where've you been?'

'Buying things. We can't get back in the house yet, because it's a crime scene. So I got you some nighties and stuff. I hope they're the right size.' He unwrapped one of his purchases. His mother was alive, and he no longer cared about his shopping being wrong or right. 'There's this blue one, and there's a—'

'Where did you go for that article?' asked the head injury in the bed. 'Rent-a-Tent?'

'It is a bit on the large side,' admitted Derek. 'The woman said it was medium, but she was about the size of the *Titanic*. I suppose it's all relative.'

Eve decided to give her attention to her snoring husband. 'Typical. I wake up and he drops off. He's going to destroy my credit cards and sell the house. I had to come round to stop him.' She winced. 'I've got a terrible headache.'

Chas woke. A huge smile crept across his face, while his eyes filled with saline. 'Hello, love.' He grabbed her hand. 'Oh, God, oh, God—'

'Oh, shut up,' ordered the patient. 'And leave my bloody credit cards alone.'

Chas wiped away a tear and pressed the buzzer.

The cheeky young nurse appeared. 'Mrs Boswell. Hiya. I'm Sarah. Good to see you looking so well.'

'Well?' She looked at Chas. 'She calls this well? Have you seen the state of me? Tell her I'm in pain. I want three aspirin and a boiled egg.'

Sarah folded her arms and tapped a foot. 'Right,' she said. 'Shall I send the wine waiter and the à la carte?'

'I don't want a cart, or a horse, for that matter. Just a four-minute egg and some soldiers. Grenadiers will do. I like their hats.'

Chas laughed through the tears. 'See? What did I tell you? Twenty-four-carat Liverpool, my wife.' He gazed steadily at Eve. She was the most beautiful thing on God's earth. 'They found something in your head.'

'Oh, good. If it had been you, they'd have come across a few bits of fluff and a sea breeze.'

'But Eve—'

'I heard them. Benign growth, frontal lobe, lucky woman. If I hadn't been walloped, I'd have been in trouble.'

'You can have a drink of water,' Sarah said.

'Gee, thanks, babe. Can I have drugs? My head's like a busy soup kitchen just before payday. And perfume. I want my perfume.'

Sarah threw up her hands in mock despair and went off to ask Mr Hislop whether Eve's hunger might be appeased.

'I'm not wearing that,' Eve told her son. 'Go and ask for your money back, then get yourself to our house. Tell those police buggers I want my stuff. I'm not lying here without my perfume and my own knickers.'

'And the mail,' Chas added. 'I'm expecting something by courier, so bring all the letters.'

Derek kissed his mother and left.

Eve opened her mouth to say something, but Chas had pursued his son. 'Derek?'

'Hiya, Dad. Now, stop crying. Come on, she'll be all right.'

But a sudden surge of emotion drove the father to hug his son. Chas hung on to the boy as if life depended on this moment, and held him uncomfortably close. 'Derek,' he managed when the sobs subsided. 'I don't mean to use you as a bring-me, fetch-me, carry-me, but I need that letter. There's a VO in it.'

'Eh?'

'A visiting order.'

Derek processed the information. 'But Uncle Rob's not in jail yet.'

'That's right.' Chas swallowed a stream of sad and angry words. He would not break down completely, because he was the man of the family, and he had better remember that. 'Derek, I just want to say I'm proud of you, lad. I know I rag the arse off you, but it's only in fun.'

'I know.'

'And I wanted you to have brothers and sisters – we both did. You must have been lonely.' Chas told himself to shut up, but he couldn't.

'You what? Lonely? With Mam and you? It's been more like a bloody three-ring circus ever since I was born. No worries, Dad. I know she lost her womb and it can't be helped – I'm fine.'

'Get me that VO, son. And make them hand over your mam's stuff – nighties, knickers, perfume – you know the score.'

Derek paused for a moment. 'Why the VO, Dad? What the hell are you going to do with one of those things?'

'Don't ask, lad. It's better if you don't know. Just remember we love you.'

The younger man turned to leave, then came back to face his father again. He knew Chas very well, realized there was something grossly amiss. 'Dad, they saved her life in a way.'

Chas nodded. 'They didn't set out to do that, though, did they? The fact that your mam has a thick skull is just a piece of luck. And they haven't finished. Oh, they may not go for my Evie again, but they've not done. The buggers'll be back, lad.'

'Dad, this isn't nicking a few boxes of Scotch or betting on a horse. You can't do anything here without risk. This is the big lads, the ones who play to win.'

Chas straightened his spine. 'Ah, well. I played to win when I put my last five grand on an accumulator and won enough to get us where we are today. And where my family's concerned I'm in the big boys' class too, Derek, and I'm not just the milk monitor. I know people. I know people who know people. This is going to be nipped in the bud before somebody else gets hurt.' He glanced up and down the corridor. 'They weren't after Eve, son. Your mam was a mistake, and yes, I know the mistake saved her a lot of bother with that thing in her head. But they're out to get somebody else we know. They didn't do any of this out of Christian charity. Now, bugger off out of it and do as you're told.'

'But Dad—'

'Now, Derek. My mind's made up. It was made up last night when I saw the state of her. Nobody does that to one of mine. And nobody does it to a good friend of one of mine, either. See you later.' He walked back into intensive care.

'You'll have to get me out of here,' complained the love of Chas's life. Some of her wiring had been disconnected, and she looked well, if rather pale.

'That's right, girl. I'll put you somewhere private.'

'No. I didn't mean that. If I'm forced to stay in jail, an ordinary ward'll do for me. Looking at these poor people around me does nobody any good, God love the poor souls. I need somewhere among the living. But I'm not going private.'

Eve was another who refused to be shifted once her decision had been made. He smiled at her and hoped she couldn't see that he'd been weeping again. 'There's two cops in reception,' he told her. 'They've been hovering like a pair of bluebottles over a pile of shite ever since you were brought in. I suppose they'll be wanting to talk to you.'

'Are they good-looking?'

He shrugged. 'I wouldn't know.'

'Well, I want something to eat first, then a good wash, get my hair done and then ... Ah. I've been shaved, haven't I?' She touched her heavily bandaged head. 'Bugger. And I've spent a fortune on that colour, too. Lovely, my hair was.'

'Yes, but you're still lovely, babe.'

'Right. Get me a wig catalogue. I can have a different colour every day of the week.'

Chas groaned. It was going to be like the shoes all over again, but at the other end. Seven wigs? One for each day of the week? 'You can have anything you like, Eve. Now, shall we put these coppers out of their misery?'

'All right, then.'

Out in the corridors once more, Chas found himself leaping about and punching the air like a kid at his first football match. He hadn't wanted to go overboard in front of his wife, because she'd just had brain surgery, but he certainly needed to let off steam. And, he decided when he caught a whiff of body odour, he could do with a shower as well.

The constables followed him back to the intensive care unit. They were given five minutes, and they learned nothing except that Eve saw a large item dropping through the air just before she was hit the second time.

When they had finished, Chas followed them out into the corridor. 'Any idea who it was?' he asked as casually as he could manage.

'Three people are being interviewed, Mr Boswell. We're hoping they'll be charged sometime soon, but we have to be sure. There's lab work going on. DNA's brilliant, but it doesn't work overnight. Though we're quietly confident that the men in question should be of some help with inquiries. One's squealing like a stuck pig already.'

Chas breathed an audible sigh of relief. He didn't

want to ask any questions, because he had plans, and it was best to keep quiet.

'Mr Boswell?'

'Yes?'

'Two women have disappeared from Eagleton overnight. One's left a new job and taken her young daughter, while the other seems to have abandoned a nice little business. Any ideas? It seems strange that they should go so soon after your wife's attack. And we're told that Miss Latimer and your wife are good friends.'

Chas knew why they'd gone. Poor Lily was on the run, and she'd taken her hairdresser friend with her. 'No idea,' he replied, fingers crossed childishly behind his back. 'But your seniors might know – something to do with Miss Latimer needing to get away from the south. Is it all right if I get back to Eve now? Only she's not been awake long.'

They gave their permission, said they would talk to Eve again as soon as she was better, then walked away.

Chas sat on a chair in the corridor for a few minutes. So much had been packed into the past few hours. Eve had told him about Lily before the attack, he had lost his rag and gone to the pub, Eve had followed. 'I should have stopped messing about. I should have gone home with her,' he whispered into space. But they might have hit him too; they might have killed him, and what would have happened to Eve then?

A stop should be put to all this before it went any further. Chas had been an opportunist, though he had never set out to do any real harm. Luck had got him where he was today, but a man sometimes had to create his own good fortune. Eve was everything to him, and he had to ensure her safety. Somewhere out there, either on the loose or in a police cell, lay the answer. The men who had hurt Eve were the tools of someone else's trade, and that someone was probably in jail. Chas knew folk. He knew those who kept company with the big boys. He was well respected, because he had helped many an old lag to survive in a cold, cruel world.

This situation could arise again. Next time, Eve might be visiting her new friend in intensive care or at some funeral parlour. No wonder Lily had fled; no wonder the poor woman had been scared halfway to death when she had first arrived in the village. For Eve's sake, Lily Latimer had to be safe. Eve had taken a shine to the woman, and that friendship needed to be nurtured.

When he got back to the unit, Eve had fallen asleep again. Visitors were kept to a minimum in intensive care, so he crept out and asked Sarah to tell Eve that he'd gone home for a shower. Surely the cops would have finished by this time? 'Shall I bring you a corned beef butty when I come back?' he asked the nurse.

She grinned. 'I'll be off duty soon,' she said. 'And I can't stand corned beef.'

Chas could. For the first time, he felt really hungry, and his mouth watered at the thought of two big doorsteps of very unhealthy white bread with a quarter of corned beef between them and half a bottle of ketchup dripping down the sides. He was fine. His wife was going to be fine, and his son was a good lad. Or he might get a bag of chips. Chips and corned beef – he was going to heaven. Above all, he wanted to get his mitts on that visiting order. The process of finding the true perpetrator would begin very soon.

*

Eagleton had been turned into a circus. Clowns took several forms, some carrying boom mikes, others hiding behind cameras, while the precious few stood in front of the cameras, make-up exaggerated, clothes perfect, script scrolling up electronic idiot boards. Chas was of the Princess Anne school of thought when it came to journalists, so he told a few to bog off while he went inside his own house and begged permission to take a shower. Fortunately, the sergeant in attendance was Peter Haywood. 'We'll be out of your hair any minute,' he said. 'And we've lost Lily and Babs.'

'I know,' replied Chas. 'And I know why as well.'

'Yes.' The policeman took Chas to one side while white-covered SOCOs left the house for the final time. 'I think we've got the men who did this. They're from your neck of the woods.'

'Yes.'

'He's in Walton.'

Chas pretended to be ignorant. 'Who is?'

'Lily's husband.'

That was good news. Chas prayed that the authorities would not move him on just yet. 'Really?'

'Really. We all know who's to blame for this, you know.'

Chas could say nothing to Babs's Pete. Cops were not the enemy, but they were to be avoided when it came to certain aspects of life. 'I'll grab a shower,' he said. 'Is our Derek still here?'

Pete shook his head. 'No. He collected his mother's things, then went back through the graveyard. He was meeting a taxi on the top road, because he wanted to avoid that lot outside.'

'What do they want, all them flaming paparazzi?'

'The dog. It's a hero. Look, have your shower, then I'll take you back to the hospital. That way, you can avoid the crowd outside.'

While Pete waited, Chas took his much-needed shower in Eve's almost completed en suite. According to the lady, a house was nothing until the master bedroom had its own facilities. She knew it was a cottage, was aware that plumbing was primitive at the time it was built, but she was going incongruous. Never mind, because this was a very powerful shower, and Chas was glad of it.

He dried himself in the bedroom. The police were aware, then. They probably knew that Lily's ex had ordered the hit, that he had found a way to pay the hired assassins, that Chalmers was the real culprit. 'Keep him where he is,' Chas begged the air as he dressed. 'Keep him in Walton.' For now, the danger was over. Eagleton was a hot-spot. No one would try again for a while, and Lily was safely out of the way.

When Chas went downstairs, he was surprised to find Derek and a taxi driver waiting with Pete. 'I thought you were avoiding that lot outside,' Chas told his son.

Derek pointed to the driver. 'Tell them,' he said.

Thus Chas and Pete learned that Lily and Babs had probably gone to Blackpool. 'I'm Eric Johnson,' said the man. 'The woman told her little daughter she'd like Blackpool, and then they got in another woman's car. This was the second time I'd been to that phone box today, you see, once to drop off, once to pick up, and I just mentioned it to this young chap here. It was a red-haired woman I drove, the one who talked about Blackpool.'

'Aye, it would be her,' commented Pete. 'She's a right blabbermouth.'

'Wise enough move, Blackpool,' said Chas. 'Busy place, especially at this time of year. Half of Glasgow'll be there for a start.' He thanked the taxi driver and asked him to take himself and Derek back to the hospital. 'Save you a trip,' he told Pete. 'And see if you can locate Lily and Babs. Just to be on the safe side, like.'

The three men had to push their way through a gaggle of reporters with microphones. Derek and Chas climbed into the rear seat while their driver fought to get behind the wheel. 'Nosy buggers,' he yelled at the intruders. 'Leave them alone. They have to get to the hospital.' The car edged its way forward inch by inch until it cleared the crowd.

Chas exhaled loudly. 'Tell you what, Derek. If that's our fifteen minutes of fame, I could have done without it.'

Derek agreed. 'I hope I've got all my mam's stuff,' he said anxiously. 'I don't want her kicking off again. For somebody who's just had brain surgery, she looks like a very good candidate for the Olympics.'

'Naw,' replied Chas. 'They don't do mithering. If they did, she'd take gold. There'd be no contest.'

Stupid bleeding bastards. I've been questioned by police. Pleaded ignorance, of course, but the chances of them believing me aren't good.

They got the wrong woman. I'm sure my face would have changed when the cops told me that. Wrong house, wrong target, wrong everything. And there's something going on in here. Took a punch to my right kidney this morning, can't go to the gym any more. No real loss, because the gym's full of gorillas on steroids – don't know how they get them, but they do.

Even the screws are looking at me funny. When I was hit, one of the two lags holding me still said the blow was a gift from a man called Boswell. The other told me the screws will turn a blind eye, because Boswell helped a few repeat offenders on their way to the straight and narrow.

I should have used my own people. Messages can be sent just about anywhere; all it takes is careful planning. Bloody Scousers. They might be quick and funny, but they don't know their arses from their patio doors. Have to keep my wits about me now, because I could be in real danger. Boswell's wife's in hospital – I wish I was.

They were supposed to have cased the joint. I described her well enough, but now I wonder whether she's changed her appearance. She's got enough bloody money, I know that. The fact is that Leanne's a tart. Some of the letters she got from men who watched her on TV were filthy, and she just laughed at them.

'Beautiful and feisty' was one of the descriptions of her in the gutter papers. She loves being looked at, likes the thought of men panting after her, never gave a shit for the one that married her. What are my chances of getting her done in now? Will I be charged again? Will the Scouse canaries sing so loudly that I'll have no chance? I hope they move me. I hope they move me soon . . .

Eleven

Blackpool had developed a rather pleasing split personality. Neither Lily nor Babs had seen it before, but they had read about the most popular resort in England, how it had burgeoned, how people had flocked there during the first half of the twentieth century. Now it embraced bistros and taco bars, upmarket restaurants and some extremely grand hotels. Nevertheless, in spite of all the renovations and spectacular improvements, the soul of the town remained untouched. Although it probably had its fair share of crime, it was a place to which a family might come to feel safe and embraced, because it was friendly, welcoming and lacking in pomposity.

Fortunately, it did not yet boast the huge casino with which it had been threatened, so the town was not overrun by dedicated gamblers and nervy females addicted to one-armed bandits. It was a lively place, though, and Babs took to it immediately. Lily, aware of Babs's good-time-girl past, rented a flat well away from the centre. It wasn't that she wanted to extinguish completely her friend's fire; the fact was that she preferred to keep Babs where she could see her. 'We are supposedly in hiding,' Lily repeated at least twice a day. 'So stay in during the evenings and shut up.' For the most part,

Babs did as she was advised, though she still insisted on talking to strangers, since she was a self-described collector of folk.

Lily too rather liked Blackpool. Alongside all the recent developments, stalwarts upheld tradition by clinging to the glorious past like limpets to a ship. Seven glorious miles of pure golden sand ran alongside housing estates and newer commercial premises. But in the centre, the Golden Mile was still punctuated by all the old stalls selling candyfloss, kiss-me-quick hats and the inevitable Blackpool rock and naughty postcards. Here and there, fortunes were told by large ladies in flowing skirts and red headscarves, while fish and chip shops thrived among elegant and newer feeding troughs. All these factors proved to Lily that the past mattered, and that the real Blackpool lived on.

Cassie loved it. Armed with bucket and spade, she copied the actions of older children and concentrated hard on giving birth to her first intact sandcastle. Several abortive efforts were accompanied by unhappy weeping, but she finally mastered the art, leaving Mummy and Auntie Lee to bask in sunshine while they could. Like the rest of Lancashire, Blackpool occupied space west of the Pennines, so it enjoyed a better climate than Yorkshire, but wetter weather. Avoiding the showers was a skill that the two women were learning fast. Rules were simple. No matter what the temperature or how blue the sky, always carry collapsible umbrellas, raincoats and proper shoes. Wrap picnics properly unless you don't mind sandwiches turned to soup, and take a towel with you. Once the law was formulated and complied with, life in Blackpool was easy.

'I could stay here for always,' sighed Babs. She was

coated in cream of a factor so high that the sun needed to apply in triplicate for permission to kiss her skin. Like many redheads, Babs could not take too much ultraviolet.

'Could you?' breathed Lily sleepily. 'Without Pete? Could you really live anywhere without the love of your life?'

Babs shrugged. 'He may be the love of my life, or perhaps he isn't.'

'Fickle.' Lily laughed.

'He could get a transfer.' Babs stuck out her tongue, but Lily, whose eyes were closed, did not see the action. 'I'm going to phone him, Lily,' Babs went on. 'I can't bear the thought of him worrying.'

'So he is the love of your life, then?'

'Probably. But I'm not allowed to phone him, am I?'

Lily sat up and looked at her friend. 'He'll tell the police where we are, just as we had to when we first moved to Eagleton. The top brass will be asking about us already, but there are bent cops, Babs. Pete could tell the wrong chap, and we'd be found when that wrong chap sold the information. Do you want me dead?' She felt mean after Babs's last question, because she had been phoning Paul Smith without mentioning it to Babs.

'So we stay here incognito for the rest of our lives? Shall I put my daughter's name down for a Blackpool school? This has to end sometime, Lily. We've already run almost the length of England – do we try Wales or Scotland next?'

'No. We wait. According to the newspapers, three men are being questioned. If they sing – isn't that the word criminals use for confessing? – the authorities will be on to Clive. Hopefully, he'll be stopped.'

Babs threw the remains of a sandwich at her friend. A

brave gull swooped and snatched it away before Lily could wrap it for disposal. 'He'll be stopped,' Lily repeated.

But Babs, a lover of lurid fiction, had other ideas. 'There's a whole network, you know. Anyone in prison can find someone to do their dirty work. He can try again as soon as he likes.'

'There you go, then,' said Lily. 'All the more reason to stay here for now. Hoist by your own petard, Babs.'

'What?'

'Never mind. Be quiet and eat your choc ice.'

Babs groaned. The trouble with Lily was that she had rather too much common sense. For someone with an enormous gift for artistry and decoration, she displayed a total lack of imagination when it came to other areas of life. Babs liked to take chances, but Lily always weighed the odds. When it came to the prospect of being murdered, Babs had to admit that only Lily could act as maker of decisions. Nevertheless, she felt trapped and contained, her natural energy forced into a straitjacket of Clive Chalmers's making.

'I'd like to visit the Lakes,' was Lily's next statement.

'Not yet,' groaned Babs. 'Just a few more days in Blackpool, please. Cassie loves the sand and the sea.'

Lily smiled. Babs had played the trump card. Where Cassie was concerned, Lily was a walkover. 'All right,' she said. 'But your ice cream's dripped all over your T-shirt.'

Babs mopped her front with a baby wipe. 'Anyway, you,' she said, her tone engineered to sound cross. 'You always ask the questions like a teacher, while I have to be the good girl and produce the right answers. So it's my turn now. I get to ask a question. OK?'

'Goody,' said Lily. 'I can scarcely wait.'

Babs took a deep breath. 'You and Mike,' she said quickly, as if spitting out medicine that tasted bad. As soon as she had said the words, she wanted to take them back, because they were even nastier out than they had been inside. 'Sorry. But there's something, isn't there?' She half dreaded the answer, since Lily's love life had been spectacularly awful thus far, and the poor girl needed more trouble like she needed a hole in her head.

Lily nodded. 'There's something, but God knows what.'

'What do you mean?'

'What I mean is I don't know what I mean.' But she did know . . .

A breeze, made cooler by the sea over which it had passed, made both women shiver. They packed their bags, placed Cassie in her pushchair and began the difficult walk through sand back to the car. Halfway, Babs stopped, released the child and folded the chair – it was easier to carry than to push. 'Lily?'

'What?'

'It won't be long now, will it? Until we can go home, I mean.'

Lily frowned and concentrated. 'I shouldn't think so, but I'm not sure. If those three men crack, they'll still go down for the attack, but Clive will be charged as having instigated it. He'll be in court, and perhaps that will teach him a lesson.' She didn't believe the words she had just framed and expelled. She knew him. Once he got the knife in, he twisted it. Sometimes, she believed that the sexual jealousy that was the cause of all the trouble had literally sent him mad.

'Will we be safe after that?'

Lily was certain about nothing. 'Like you said, Babs – anyone can find anyone if they're determined. But, you know, I do rather like living in Eagleton. Once this particular issue is resolved, we'll think about what to do next.'

'I really do miss Pete.'

'I know.'

Babs piled bags and pushchair into the back of the estate car. 'And you miss Mike.'

'Yes.'

'Bloody hell, Lee. We are a pair of idiots, aren't we? Falling in love within five minutes of relocating, hearts on our sleeves, forever teenagers.'

Both women stood on the pavement and laughed helplessly. Neither was completely sure why she was amused, but glee took over and rendered them useless. Cassie joined in. She giggled until she got the hiccups, and the hysteria started all over again.

Once settled in the car, Lily mopped her eyes. 'He loves me, Babs.'

'Right.'

'And he's amazing.'

'Right.'

'Stop saying right.'

'OK. Wrong, then. He's a priest, my lovely. They have to be – what's it called? Celibate. They can't have a wife or a mistress.'

'But they do. It's quite common.'

'Common as in cheap and nasty?' Babs turned and looked at her daughter, who had already fallen asleep. 'Is he any good in bed?' she asked in a stage whisper.

Lily closed her eyes, opened them, looked up to heaven. 'Don't go all vulgar on me, Babs.'

'Is he?'

'Is Pete?'

'Yes.'

'Good. I'm very pleased for you.' Lily started the car. She pulled into the traffic and aimed the car in the direction of their rented holiday flat. Babs's question hung large in the air like a balloon that hadn't lost all its helium. The subject would be raised again later, of that Lily was certain. So she bit the bullet. 'He's very good. End of.'

Babs giggled. 'Well, you certainly take the whole Ryvita, don't you? Nothing as ordinary as a custard cream, because you're too keen on your figure – but Lily, how can a Catholic priest be part of your daily diet?'

'He isn't. It happened just once. And if it doesn't happen again, I'll be very sad, but I dare say I'll survive. Don't tell anyone – not even Pete. Mike has issues with his faith, and I'm not a part of that. If he leaves the Church, it won't be for me. It'll be for himself.'

Babs was suddenly sober. 'If he leaves the Church, the village will blame you. They love him. Even the non-Catholics think he's an asset. Look at what he does – arranging for the elderly to be fed and helped, going out of his way for the panto – they'll say it's your fault, kid.'

'Perhaps. Just don't ask your horse to jump before you reach the gate, Barbara Cookson. Now shut up and let me concentrate. There's a tram behind us and a horse and cart in front.' She edged out to overtake, trying hard to avoid startling the placid animal, although its stolid plodding seemed to indicate that it had long come to terms with the nuisance of the internal combustion engine.

They drove the rest of the way in silence, and Lily was relieved. Back at the flat, she made supper while Babs bathed her daughter. It was an undeniable fact that they couldn't stay here for ever. Apart from anything else, Babs had started to work again and was enjoying it, while Lily had been forced to pass a couple of weddings to another florist. The business had to be dependable, or it would fail.

Then there was Mike. Yes. Father Michael Walsh, who wanted to quit the priesthood and spend his life with a woman he scarcely knew. This should be the time during which they could become better acquainted ... A smile played on her lips and she stood still, a fork in one hand, a plate in the other. The wondrous thing was that neither she nor Mike needed to know more about each other, because it was already there. Whatever 'it' was ... Hadn't Prince Charles used something like that line when trying to define the term 'in love'? But whatever existed between Lily and Mike was overpowering, and it had to be love. Real love. She placed the cutlery on the table and crossed her fingers. 'This time, let it be real, God,' she whispered.

'Are you setting that table or dreaming about bedtime with Mike?'

'Shut up, Babs. Did she eat her banana?'

'Yes.'

'Have you cleaned her teeth?'

'Yes. Honestly, Lee, anyone would think she was yours— Sorry, love. You know I didn't mean—'

'It's all right. It's always been all right.' It would never be all right, yet it had to be.

Babs sat down and awaited the arrival of the gourmet meal – fish fingers and baked beans followed by fruit salad from a tin. 'Sometimes, I could cut out my tongue. After all you've done for me, after what I did to you, I should know better.'

'Stop it, Babs. You did nothing to me. You're my best friend, so be quiet or I'll hit you with this serving spoon.'

They spent the rest of the meal fighting about which bit of the town they might visit tomorrow. Babs wanted to go to the top of the tower, which was, as she reminded her friend yet again, a grade one listed building and a piece of history. 'It's a half-scale version of the Eiffel,' she said.

'And I go dizzy on a thick carpet, so you can go on your own.' Lily longed to visit the Grundy Art Gallery, but she realized that both Babs and Cassie would be bored, so a compromise was reached. They would go to Blackpool Sea Life Centre and watch all the weird creatures that lived there. She had already half promised Cassie, anyway, so that was an end to the argument. The Grundy would be a solo trip, and— Lily glanced through the window to the opposite side of the rather broad avenue on which the flats stood. 'Babs?'

'Yes, ma'am?'

'That car. It's come back again – it was there last night.'

Babs peered out. 'Yes. And there's a man sitting in it.'

Lily swallowed a mouthful of fear. Not yet, surely? Weren't people being charged, wasn't Eve only just out of hospital, hadn't Clive been interviewed by police? And no one knew about Blackpool – no one except Paul. Even after the trick he had played on Mo's wife, Lily believed in him. Paul knew what it was to be hurt and disappointed; Paul would never tell a soul where she was. 'Did you tell anyone?' she asked.

'No.' Babs was cross. If Lily didn't trust her now, she never would. 'I haven't even phoned Pete. I promise you, Lee, I—'

'All right. You pack, I'll watch.'

'But where are we going?'

Lily turned and looked at her best friend. 'No bloody idea. But I have our passports, took yours with me by mistake when I moved across the road, because they were both in one envelope.'

'No, Lee.'

'It may be the only way.'

'No. I'm not going abroad. My daughter is English and she'll remain English.'

'Who said anything about emigration?'

Babs had taken enough. She raised her voice and both hands in order to emphasize her words. 'It's inevitable. Blackpool for a week, not far enough. We can't go back to Somerset, so where do we go? When will we be safe – in five years, ten? Might as well go the whole hog and shift to Canada, because at this rate you're going to be running for the rest of your life.' She stilled her arms by folding them. 'Sorry. You're on your own, sweetie. I'm taking Cassie back to Eagleton. There are two of me, you see.'

'Yes.' Lily blinked away some tears.

'I know that hurts, but I still need to emphasize it, love.'

'I understand.'

'She needs a proper and predictable life. I'm not dragging that poor child from pillar to post. I want her settled. I want her to have friends, school, college, university.' She caught her breath. 'And I need Pete. I think he's the one, Lee.'

Lily sat down, her eyes fixed on the car outside. She asked Babs to turn off the lights before coming to sit nearby, and, in near-darkness, they ate a little of the fruit salad Lily had served. Everything Babs had said made sense, but it didn't eliminate the fear. Clive was crazy enough to try almost anything, because he had no fear of a longer sentence, didn't care about anything beyond his ideas for revenge. She reached out a hand and touched Babs. 'Do what you have to do,' she said.

'You know I can't leave you on your own. You know I won't abandon you.'

Lily stared at a wall and looked into the past. She opened a door in her mind, plus a door in the house she had shared with Clive Chalmers. At the other side stood an angry, russet-haired woman. The uninvited guest asked to see Clive . . .

'Lee?'

'What?'

'Don't go there. Don't think about that.'

This was how well Babs knew her now. Their first contact had been made at that front door, and it had involved a slap from Lily that had left the slighter woman reeling and in tears. These days, Babs knew what Lily was thinking about, understood her better than anyone. Lily blinked. She could hear the screams now behind the door she had slammed. 'I'm pregnant,' the little woman had yelled. Down the years those words echoed, as clear now as they had been on the evening of their birth.

'Stop thinking about it, Lee,' repeated Babs softly.

Lily stabbed a bit of pineapple and forced herself to eat. She needed energy, because she had to do this thing, and she had to do it right away. It was time to stop running, and perhaps Babs was right. Returning to Eagleton had to be an inevitability.

'Where are you going?' Tired of eating in the dark, Babs switched on a lamp and closed the curtains. The man in the car was still sitting there. 'Lee? What the devil are you up to now? Good God – Eve was nearly killed! What if he's come from Liverpool like the first lot did? Lee!'

Lily draped a cardigan across her shoulders. 'I'm going to ask him why he's there. If I can't get a straight answer, I'll tell the police to shift him. There are houses everywhere, and it isn't completely dark yet. It's time I faced my demons. He's loitering with intent.'

Babs stood by the window and peeped past the edge of a green curtain. Lily didn't often lose her rag, but when she did it was as well to be in residence somewhere at a distance. Like Jupiter or Saturn. Babs bit her lip, flinched when the downstairs front door slammed, watched round-eyed as Lily approached the parked vehicle.

She marched across the road and hammered on the windscreen of the silver-grey Vauxhall. She walked round to the pavement, standing with her arms folded until he opened the passenger door. 'You're being watched from many windows,' she warned. 'So don't do anything stupid. Who the hell are you, why are you here, and when do you plan to bog off into the bloody sunset? Because I am sick of the sight of your damned car, mister.'

The man left the vehicle and came to stand next to her. 'Miss Latimer?'

Shivering slightly, she stood her ground. 'Who wants to know?'

'I do.'

That wasn't good enough, and she told him so. If he had come on behalf of Clive Chalmers, guest of Her Majesty the Queen, he could bugger off and tell said Clive Chalmers that she wasn't afraid any more. Furthermore, loitering in a decent neighbourhood was never a bright idea, and the neighbours were all up in arms, especially those who were permanent residents of Blackpool. 'I can die only once,' she added. 'So get it over with, because I don't mind missing *Coronation Street* this time.'

He shook his head. 'No wonder that priest's going out of his mind,' he said. 'Have you any idea of the trouble you caused by buggering off without a word? People miss you.'

'What?'

'And Pete Haywood's fretting like mad about your mate.'

'What?' she repeated stupidly. 'Look,' she said, drawing herself to her full height. 'Lock that flaming car and come into the flat.' She looked him up and down. 'You look about as dangerous as a fish supper without vinegar. Get inside and I'll put the kettle on.'

The man stood for a few moments before doing as he had been ordered. His cover was blown, just as Pete had predicted, so what was the point in worrying? After securing his vehicle, he followed Lily up to the flat. Like a man being led to the gallows, he hung his head, because he had some idea of what was coming to him.

Babs was waiting, rolling pin at the ready. 'Unless you've come over all domesticated, put that away,' ordered Lily. 'He's harmless. You can tell just by looking at him that he couldn't crush a grape.'

The man edged in and sat at the uncleared dining table.

'Who sent you?' Babs asked. 'I suppose it's us you're watching.'

'Yes – sorry.' He went on to explain that he was a retired police sergeant, that Pete Haywood had tracked the pair of them to Blackpool and that he was here for their own good. 'My name's Alan Burke,' he informed them. 'I'm in charge of you.'

'God help us,' uttered Babs.

'How did they know we were in Blackpool?' Lily asked.

'Something Miss Cookson said to the child when they were in the taxi. I think she said she hoped it would be Blackpool.'

'Sorry,' Babs mouthed to her friend.

He continued. 'It was just a matter of Pete getting some young PC to phone all the letting agents and find out where you were staying. I'm a private eye now. Pete and that priest are paying my fees. So I've been doing my job, no more than that.'

Lily sat opposite the detective. 'We've been reading the papers. Is there anything we don't know?'

He nodded. 'Chalmers will be charged. All three sang like thrushes once they got going. It's attempted murder for them, and Chalmers will get done for arranging the attack. Incidentally, I've met Mrs Boswell – she's home, and she wants to see the pair of you. She needs her friends after what she went through.'

Lily asked after Eve's health and was told that the steel plate in her head allowed her to pick up Radio Four as long as she stood at the top of the stairs, that she could change channels on satellite TV by wiggling her ears, and that her magnetic personality was interfering with reception on her mobile phone.

'That's Eve,' said the two women in unison before laughing out loud.

He read out a list of all who missed them, reminding them that their presence at the wedding of Dave and Philly was compulsory and that Mo and Paul wanted Babs back. 'They say it's too much without you and there's nothing to laugh at,' he concluded.

Lily went to make the promised tea.

Babs asked about Pete and was told he was well, though unhappy. She shot a quick look over her shoulder. 'What about Father Walsh?' she murmured.

Alan too made sure that Lily was not within earshot. 'He's going to marry Dave and Philly, then he'll tell the congregation on the following Sunday that he's opting out. He wants her back. If you could see the state of him – he worships the ground she stands on.'

'Oh, bugger,' whispered Babs.

'She's not the reason,' he said. 'I was asked to stress that if you accosted me. It's all tied up with human rights and contraception and other stuff. But he's resigning whether she'll have him or not.'

Lily came in with the tea. 'You can sleep on the sofa tonight,' she told him. 'And we can't come straight home, because I promised Cassie she could see the funny fishes at some stage. We'll leave tomorrow afternoon.'

Alan Burke stirred his tea. 'Is Cassie Clive Chalmers's child?' he asked.

'Yes,' snapped Babs. 'Charming Chalmers fooled me into believing he was a single man. Then I met Lily, and she marked my card for me. We've been close ever since he . . . ever since what happened to her.'

Alan Burke looked at Lily and wondered at her calm facade. After all that had happened, he would not have been surprised if she'd finished up in a psychiatric unit. 'It's good that you have each other, and better still that I don't have to sleep in that car. Thank you, ladies.'

They put him right on that one, because they weren't ladies, they were women. He was invited to eat anything he could find that didn't smell strange, and then Lily and Babs went off to bed. It was early, but tomorrow would be busy.

Lily was settled with a book when Babs came in. She listened while Babs told her about Mike's intentions, about how he needed Lily by his side. 'He's doing it whatever you say,' Babs concluded.

'I know. Good night, then.'

Alone, Lily turned to the wall and waited for sleep to come. 'I know,' she had said so glibly, so easily. But was he sure? Or was Lily a part of the mix that had finally made him decide to give up, to stop looking after Catholics in three or four parishes?

The real worry about what the villagers might say was compounded by the fact that she was an incomer, a stranger from a part of England many of them had never seen. It might all be blamed on her, and she would need to be strong.

'Am I recovered enough for that?' she asked the darkening room. She didn't know the answer, wasn't even sure of the question, because the kind of decision he was making might well stretch her beyond anything she had experienced so far. He was a good priest … Itwould take a very special kind of strength, but she would find it. Wouldn't she?

Whatever, Babs was right. Two women and a child

could not run for ever. Cassie needed stability, while her mother should be working in order to gain a degree of independence. And the flower shop was important; perhaps, given time, the business could become part of a wedding-planning consortium. There was even a chance that Leanne Chalmers might return to her old job, the career she had really loved. Could *Makeover Madness* ride again? Could Clive be contained in a unit so solitary that he would never meet another soul?

Lily gave up after an hour and crept into the kitchen. To her surprise, she met Alan Burke, who was making cocoa. 'Want some?' he asked.

'Yes, please.'

They sat on the sofa that had become his makeshift bed. 'Lily?'

'What?'

'Eve Boswell needs you.'

'Oh?'

He nodded sadly. 'She's all right, and she begged me not to tell you, but I think I should. She had a fit the day she came home. Because she pleaded and cried when it was over, Chas let her stay at home, though he spoke to the doctor when she was asleep. The doc said it could be a one-off. But then the second one happened. Eve has epilepsy. Chas is selling the off-licence and hanging over her all the time. She wants you to take him in hand.'

'Right. Bit of a mess, isn't it?'

Alan sighed. 'Yes, but better to go home and face the music.'

Eve was sick to the back teeth, and she made sure that everyone in her household was aware of it. She got her new wigs, was indulged completely by her doting husband, was forced to have daily help in the house, and was generally treated like a total invalid. The tablets were great. As long as she remembered to take them, she was perfectly all right except for the odd headache and slightly blurred vision. But she was fed up with Chas, and was tired of telling him to go away and leave a bit of oxygen just for herself. 'I can't breathe,' she told him accusingly. 'You keep panicking. If you panic, I panic, and we all know what might happen if I end up in bits. So go away, buzz off, make yourself scarce, because you are ruining my nerves and I can't take any more!'

Chas stood his ground. He was getting rid of the off-licence, and that was the end of it. She could mither till the cows, goats, hens and geese came home, but her working life was over, as was his. 'Do as you're told,' he said.

She folded her arms and straightened her spine. 'I'm not in my dotage yet, Chas, and if you think I'm—'

'Don't get worked up. The doc says you haven't to get worked up.'

Her foot tapped the floor. 'Not get worked up? With you hanging round me twenty-four hours a day? Impossible. If I sneeze wrong, you're like an old mother hen hovering over me, do I feel all right, should you get a cushion, do I need the doctor? I can't be me any more! Now bugger off and take that shop off the market before I do us both some damage.' The foot tapped again. 'I mean it, Chas. This is the closest I've come to wishing I could be single again. You've got our Derek daft as well – he keeps looking at me to make sure my head's not fallen off. The bloody village grinds to a halt every time I step out. I was thinking of getting some squirty cream and putting it round my mouth so they can all say they saw me in a fit and get it over with. After all, I'm the cabaret and we don't want to disappoint our neighbours, do we?'

Chas ran a hand through already tousled hair. 'I'm trying to be sensible.'

'Well, there's a novel idea if ever I heard one. Charles Boswell and sense? That's a new partnership. Please, please don't go all sensible on me. I'm alive. Yes, there's a bit of brain damage, a loose wire or something, but these pills will stop it, Chas. Once they've found the right dosage, I'll be fine. Go to the shop. Don't sell it. If I don't have a fit for two years, they might even let me drive again. The best way to put me back on my feet is to bugger off and let me be.' She nodded angrily. 'Sell the shop, and I'll leave you. I'll go and live with our Vera.'

'You can't stand your Vera since she moved to Crosby and started putting her aitches in the wrong places.'

'Blundellsands,' said Eve. 'I have to correct you there, because our Vera's living on the bit where the posh Vikings landed, the ones who took off their horned helmets before raping and pillaging. It's nice up there. Like the seaside.'

'It's the River bloody Mersey.'

'I like the bloody Mersey – it runs in my veins. Lovely bungalow on Mariners Road, stand at the front gate when the tall ships come and go – did I tell you the river's visible from our Vera's gate?'

'Only about three hundred times, yes.'

'And the kiddies come past to go to the swimming baths or play on the beach – it's great. Hi shall heven put my haitches where they hought to be. Just because hit's Blundellsands, like.'

307

Chas left the room. It was difficult to know what to do for the best, as he could never tell when she was serious. They'd been engaged three times because she'd kept saying she was joking. Now, she was having epileptic fits, and he was flummoxed. He loved his shop. Even these days, when he was turning down cheap booze and other ill-gotten goods, he made a fair living. And he would miss it, since he enjoyed the comings and goings, looked forward to meeting people and forging friendships across the counter.

She didn't like having a home help, didn't like not being allowed to drive, was fed up with being watched and cared for. The trouble with females these days was that they didn't know how to lean on a bloke, had no idea of how to make him feel needed.

As he perched on the end of the marital bed, he admitted to himself that he probably needed her more than she needed him. Epilepsy could cause added damage with each episode, and therefore the fits had to be stopped, because he couldn't face the concept of life without her. The tablets could go some way towards achieving that goal, but Eve needed to be calm. She wasn't calm with him around. It had never been a peaceful marriage, because it had been filled with laughter, rows, practical jokes and some hard work. He and Eve ignited each other even now, after all these years of wedlock. Chas grinned. Would he swap her? Would he hell as like.

Compromise. That was a big word. Eve needed to be forced to accept help in the house, yet had to be allowed to continue planning and decorating the place. He had to watch over her, but he must keep the shop in case the selling of it upset her too much. 'I've heard of folk going to some lengths to get their own way,' he told the wall, 'but she's in a class of her own.'

He would give in to her yet again. It was the easiest course, as it involved little or no decision making and no effort whatsoever. If she had a lot of fits, he would set his foot in concrete and there'd be no discussion about the matter. Yes. If she carried on having bad attacks, he would ... Would what? He was kidding himself all over again. Unless she went completely doolally, Eve was always going to win. That had been the unspoken arrangement from the very start.

He stood up and took a deep breath. Northern women were a tough breed. If fielded in the arena of battle, they would be tanks with huge guns in their turrets. Yorkshire and Lancashire had produced a legion of war mares that were supposed to have died out a century ago, but no. They were here, they were well and they were cunning. As for the females from Liverpool – they defied description. And he had married one.

Downstairs, Eve was experiencing a similar period of introspection. She was scared, but she daren't let him see it. The loss of control had terrified her, and she didn't like the idea of waking repeatedly after a fit with no idea of what had happened to her, no concept of what those around her had seen. The doc had been positive enough. Epilepsy like hers, which had happened after trauma to the brain, was potentially manageable. He had ordered her to rest, just as she had already been told by the hospital, and to give her grey matter time to settle. 'It could all stop of its own accord,' he had said. 'But, to be on the safe side, I'll write a prescription . . .'

She had the pills. She had her son, and she had her

wonderful husband. But Chas was useless when in the vicinity of illness. He fussed too much, worried himself halfway to death, couldn't control his fear. Chas needed to go back to work, while she wanted to tackle her situation in her own way. Her own way. She would have it, or he would suffer . . .

Like many other villages, Eagleton was in possession of a process whereby gossip travelled silently, because no one would ever admit to starting the process. When Lily and Babs had been gone just a few days, a form of osmosis took over, and messages were passed chemically, almost of their own accord.

Father Walsh was giving up the priesthood. Father Walsh loved Lily Latimer. Father Walsh had already been struggling with his conscience long before Lily had moved to the village. He believed in contraception and the right of individuals to make decisions regarding their own bodily functions. He had absolved people of sin when he should not have done so; his relationship with God was too personal to be affected by the dictates of Rome. So he disagreed with the Pope, and he had to leave. He would remain Catholic, as the faith was closest to his basic beliefs, but he would no longer be a member of the clergy. It seemed fair enough, and all but a few rigidly bigoted people remained on his side.

Pour Les Dames had metamorphosed into a whispering gallery. Paul, who was lighter of foot since meeting a new man at Sisters, wanted to scream and tell them to mind their own business, but he managed, just about, to keep his counsel. People should be left alone to get on with life, and he longed to yell that message until he learned, from the little he overheard, that most folk were supportive of the prospective changes.

Today, the gossip was audible, since Mo had announced to a fascinated audience that a new client would be arriving at any moment.

Valda almost dropped her cup. She couldn't wait to rush back and tell her mother-in-law what was happening. Things were much better now that she and Mary had made their peace. Mary watched the kids while Valda had a break, and today's break was special, because everyone was getting hair styled for the forthcoming wedding of Philly and Dave. 'Never,' said Valda after saving her coffee. 'Can Sally do my nails in here, Mo?' She didn't want to miss anything.

'Sorry,' replied Mo. 'Standing room only in the salon, and you're nearly done. But you can leave the door open if you like when you go through for your manicure.'

The congregation stilled itself when the door was thrown inward. 'Well?' shouted the newcomer. 'Are you going to help me in or not?'

Paul rushed to handle the unwieldy contraption. He wheeled in Enid Barker and helped her across to one of the sinks. She leaned heavily, and he was almost gasping for air when he deposited her in position. 'I'll ... I'll get you a gown,' he said.

Enid looked at all the silent people while Mo pushed her wheelchair out of the way. 'What's up with you lot?' she asked. 'Never seen the mother of the groom coming to get her hair done? Paul would have done it at home, but I fancied a trip out.' She knew what they thought of her, but they were just a little bit wrong this time, because she was trying her best to be decent. Ever since poor Eve Boswell's tragedy, Enid had kept her mouth shut. Well, nearly shut. She still went on a bit when her son was around, but that was an old habit that would take some murdering.

'I want a bit of colour,' she told Paul. 'And cut it. It's neither one thing nor the other at this length.' She looked at all the starers. 'You can put your eyes back in your heads, because I only talk behind your backs, not to your faces.' She winked at Paul. 'Oh, there is one thing, though. Lily and her friend are on their way back. I found that out this morning when I trolleyed over to see Eve. She won't let him get rid of the business, by the way. Now, if you don't mind, I'm getting my hair done.'

The room buzzed once more and, for the first time, most people were glad that Enid was among them. Because of melegs, she missed nothing, and everyone listened carefully when she told them about the night of the attack. 'Two of them were big bruisers,' she said. The fact was that Eve's attackers grew several inches with each telling of the tale. 'But it was a little fellow that was watching. He wasn't what you might call a dwarf, because he was all in proportion, just shorter than any man I've seen. He smoked a lot. Happen that stunted his growth.'

'That's a clever dog,' said Valda as she made her way towards the rear room. 'Skippy – she's bright.'

'My Dave's clever and all,' answered Enid. 'I know he does himself down, but he reads a lot, doesn't need a fancy degree and letters at the back of his name. He'll have that dog trained to deliver the newspapers soon.'

There followed a short silence while the audience digested that, as Enid was known for giving her son a hard time.

'What's Philly wearing?' enquired Paul.

Enid laughed. 'Don't ask, because I'm sworn to secrecy. There was near blue murder before I came, because he came into my flat without knocking and she had to dive behind the sofa so's he wouldn't see her suit. Still, never mind. It'll all be over tomorrow.'

Paul went out to the back in order to pick up some products for Enid's hair. Sally was doubled over behind the door when he and Valda went in. 'Bloody hell,' said Mo's wife. 'Who's been cheering her up?'

Paul put a finger to his lips. 'Sally, miracles happen,' he whispered. 'Shut up, or we might frighten her away.'

But Enid was clearly in her element. She was speaking to a small crowd. People were listening to her at last.

Philly was what Dave termed 'in a tizz', because getting married had proved to be slightly more complicated than she had at first expected. Dave, who was of the opinion that new suits and two witnesses were enough, had been forced to give in to Philly's wishes, and the whole thing had escalated beyond even her expectations.

Everyone wanted to come. Both bride and groom were well respected, and people from Eagleton and several of the smaller satellite villages had promised to come to the church, many protesting that they didn't expect to be fed. 'We just want to be there for you,' was the statement made by most. 'What you and Dave have done for us all – that Reading Room – is brilliant. It's somewhere to go for a cuppa, and it's nice for the old folk since our libraries got closed. Oh, we'll be there.'

Philly had been cooking and baking for days. Every freezer in Eagleton was full, because she was parking her food wherever she could, and lists were getting out of hand. As the school was closed for the summer holidays, Father Walsh and a few other men had turned the hall into a reception area with full-sized tables and chairs. Philly had hired glassware, cutlery and crockery, but the guest lists were in such a muddle that the seating plan had to be scrapped. Now, she had a huge hall with tables against walls, and the whole thing was a confused sort of buffet with a dance floor in the centre.

Philly and Dave stood in the middle of chaos. 'Where's the cake going?' he asked. Philly had made her own wedding cake. It had two layers and no chance of feeding all the guests unless some didn't mind just a few crumbs and a bit of icing. 'And people have to sit somewhere,' he added. So they pulled out the tables and began the task of lining the walls with chairs. 'They'll be stuck behind the tables now,' he protested.

Philly awarded him a withering glance. 'They can please themselves,' she said rather sharply. 'I don't know what's happened, Dave. The whole thing ran away with me. I never wanted all this.'

'Yes, you did. Right at the start you carried on about feeding folk. I told you we didn't need all this business.' He grasped both her hands. 'They just want to see you happy, Phil. If they only get a pie and a pint, they'll be happy.'

She burst into tears.

'Right,' he said, 'that's it. Enough is enough, Mrs Nearly-Barker. Hairdresser, then home. Leave all this to me.'

'But I—'

'Go.' He pointed to the door. 'Get out before one of us bursts a blood vessel. Think of the baby.' He kissed her forehead and gave her a gentle push in the direction of the exit.

When she had gone, he looked at his watch. Surely they would be here soon? It was all very eleventh hour, but he would give his lovely bride the party she deserved even if it killed him. He walked outside and began his vigil. When Lily's estate car finally hove into view, it was four o'clock. Lily was a miracle worker; Lily would sort it out.

She didn't even get the chance to visit poor Eve, because Dave was on her like a ton of bricks the minute she stepped out of the car. 'Lily,' he pleaded. 'She's my princess and my saviour. I want her to have the best. The wedding's at three, and I'll keep her away from the hall. Women all over the place have the food, and they'll bring it across tonight and in the morning, because it needs time to thaw. All that cloth you have, all those lights and silk flowers and ... oh, I don't know. Make it fit for a princess.'

'Is it all right if I breathe first? Babs, go and see Eve – take Cassie with you – you can phone Pete from Eve's house. Tell Eve that Dave's on my case, it's his fault, and I'll see her as soon as possible.' Lily paused and leaned against the car for a moment. 'Listen, you,' she said to Dave. 'Dig up every man you can find – get them out of their graves if needs be. I've an attic full of wedding bling and tat, but I'm doing no carrying.' She looked closely at Dave. 'Are the arrangements a mess?'

He nodded wordlessly.

'Leave it to me. I do the impossible every day of the week, but this miracle is going to take all night.'

'She's worth it,' he said.

'Of course she is. Right. Find me six men, then buzz off for a pint. I don't want you there, and Philly is banned.'

'Thanks, Lily.'

She smiled. She was home.

Mike wrapped his arms round Lily and lifted her up in the air as soon as she entered her house. 'Thank God,' he repeated several times.

After a long kiss, she cried, 'No time, no time. Unhand me, varlet, and get up those stairs immediately.'

He grinned. 'I thought you'd never ask.'

But she wasn't asking, she was commanding. 'Attic. Boxes marked wedding. Fetch. Don't ask me to fill in the missing words—' The door shot inward, and Dave marched in with Valda's husband Tom, Chas, Derek, Tim Mellor and a couple of men whose names Lily didn't know. She sent them off upstairs in pursuit of Mike before going to change into overalls and an old shirt. Weddings usually looked beautiful, but those who planned and furnished such occasions were invariably reduced to wreckage.

When Dave had been sent to the pub, Lily sat for several minutes in the centre of the school hall, which she considered to be a disaster zone. Mike, complete with silly grin, kept his eyes on her. If he thought said silly grin would get him out of helping, he could think again, since this was a matter of dire urgency. In less than twenty-four hours, the mess had to become beautiful for Philly, who deserved only the best. So the best had to be made of an appalling job. 'Should I be getting jetlag after travelling from Blackpool?' she asked of no one in particular.

The school hall was not the perfect venue for a reception. It had huge windows, plasterboard walls and harsh lighting. But Lily refused to be daunted. Yard after yard of cream muslin was pinned by helpers to walls and windows while Lily worked on a gigantic chandelier made from wire, crystals and large fairy lights. Silk roses were pinned here and there to break the muslin monotony, and every wall was lit by tiny fairy lights just strong enough to show through the sheer drapery.

'It's like fairyland,' Mike declared when the room was almost finished.

'I'm glad you're so easy to please,' said Lily. 'Now, open the curtains on the stage and put a small table up there – I've brought some Irish linen cloths. Tim – you cover these terrible buffet tables and the smaller one for the stage. They can cut their cake up there. I'll do napkins and decorate the stage tomorrow.' She waited until her orders had been obeyed.

'Right – sit,' she said.

The men were fed up. 'We need a drink,' Chas complained. 'I've a sick wife at home, and–'

'Oh, shut up,' snapped the woman in charge. 'Favours.'

'I'm doing no more favours for anyone,' said Chas.

Lily threw a pile of net circles on a table. 'Fifty should be enough, as they're just for women. So do a few each.' She demonstrated with a handful of sugared almonds, one of the net circles and a piece of satin ribbon. 'Chas,' she said, 'you are excused. Go to your shop and take beer to my house. You and the rest of these reprobates can get your reward there. I'll pay you later.'

'No need,' said Chas gratefully. He was glad to escape the making of favours, and he needed to check the shop anyway, as it was still unattended and closed.

The vet looked at Lily. 'I can sew up a cat and I can probably neuter an elephant at a push, but when it comes to sugared almonds—'

'And I'm OK with baptisms and weddings—'

Lily glared at the man she adored. 'Get on with it. Anybody with less than ten out of ten stays in after school and does extra arithmetic.'

She smiled as she watched large fingers trying to do the work usually apportioned to women. After a few minutes, she sat with them and helped, because they were remarkably slow learners. Just after eleven o'clock, Lily declared herself satisfied with their labours. 'Take this lot of favour-makers to my house,' she told Chas, who had reappeared sometime before. 'I'll go and see if Eve's still up.'

While the men made their way to the ex-presbytery, Lily walked past the church and into Rose Cottage. Cassie was asleep on a sofa, while her mother dozed in a chair. 'Don't get up,' whispered Lily to Eve. 'I am absolutely exhausted. How are you?'

Eve smiled. 'Good to see you, girl. He's not getting rid of the business, so that's a start. And I've decided not to have epilepsy, because it brings him out in a rash, and we can't have that.'

Lily sank into an armchair. 'I am so, so sorry. It was meant for me. I believe Clive's being charged with something or other, and they've got the men who did the crime for him. I shouldn't have run away. What sort of friend runs when she's needed most?'

'A frightened one with a child to save. Stop it, Lily. What happened saved me from paralysis or some such thing – they didn't know what that cyst thing might have done to me. I could have ended up talking broken biscuits and walking like a ruptured duck. Look on the bright side.'

Lily exhaled slowly. 'I am so tired. But we've got the hall almost ready, and all the men are at my house chilling out with beer. I suppose I'd better go and supervise before they wreck the place.' She stood up and planted a kiss on Eve's forehead. 'Send Babs home when she wakes,' she whispered. 'See you at the wedding.'

Lily walked slowly past the church that had owned Mike for many years. He was about to turn his back on many parishioners in the cluster of villages, and she would be seen as one of his reasons. It always came back to this, she told herself silently; it always reached the point where she worried about herself and what folk would think of her. It wasn't about her at all. Mike was the one who was going to suffer most.

Her house was as silent as the graveyard next door. Standing at the French windows, she saw a few glimmers of light in the orchard, and deduced that her favour-makers and curtain-hangers were enjoying their reward al fresco and were using her storm lamps as illumination.

'Lily?'

She shivered when his hands crept round her waist.

'Thanks for telling Paul to let me know you were all right.'

She turned to receive his kiss before clinging to him as if she might never let go. 'I was so afraid,' she said. 'Terrified, in fact. There was Cassie, there was Babs, there was me. I had to make sure we were safe.'

'It was reaction,' he said. 'Is Cassie his?'

Lily nodded mutely. After a short silence, she continued. 'Babs came to our house because she was angry and afraid of being a lone parent. He had seduced her and she was a couple of months into the pregnancy.' She paused. 'That was when everything started to go completely haywire.'

He stroked her hair as if comforting a child. 'You're exhausted.'

'And you're sober.'

He laughed. 'Two pints is my limit. If I have any more, I either defy the law of gravity or succumb to it completely. I had an uncle the same. He fell asleep in Liverpool and woke next morning on the Isle of Man.'

'No!'

'Yes. The trouble was, he was getting married that day.'

'Good Lord. What happened?'

Mike shrugged. 'She married a Protestant, I think, decided he was the safer bet.'

'And Uncle?'

'The crew liked him so well that he joined them and spent the rest of his days ferrying folk from dock to dock.'

'Liar.'

'Yes. Go on. You're too tired for my anecdotes.'

She nodded. 'I need a bath. A couple of hours in a car followed by the school hall frenzy is just too much. I am forbidden to get tired. Doctor's orders. Are you staying tonight?'

'Yes. Go and have your bath while I get rid of the fairies at the bottom of your garden. It's a big day tomorrow.' He turned to leave the house. 'By the way, I love you.'

'And I love you.'

It was as simple as that. He was just a man, albeit a rather wonderful specimen. He was an adult who was about to change the course of his life, and she would be there to comfort him when the Church showed its impatience with him. The love between Lily and Mike had come suddenly and unbidden, but that was the nature of love. It homed in and focused on the bull's eye and to hell with all the outer rings on the target. Love was not controllable. She went to have her bath.

They lay together that night in a bed that was far too small, and apart from a few kisses, there was no love-making. Tomorrow would be Mike's last wedding, and they shared the unspoken knowledge that he had to be at his best in the morning. Lily turned to the wall, and he fitted himself behind her like a spoon against its twin. They slept for ten hours, and when she woke, Lily knew that she had definitely arrived home. She would hang her hat in Eagleton. As would he.

Sudden silences, then mutterings when they think I'm out of earshot. Those who spoke to me before now ignore me completely. I should have used someone who knew her, or somebody with the sense to find out properly before wading in.

The name Boswell has come up a few times. From the little I've heard, he's been good to cons on the outside. He's well thought of. There's something going on, and I've asked for a move. Even the screws won't look at me. They tell me I'll be moved when the governor's ready, and not before.

Whisperings again this morning. Not content with seeing me dragged out of prison and into court, they want more from me. This is frightening. The worst was last night just after lights out. When the screws had checked after lockdown, the lags whispered in unison. It hissed along the landing till it reached my cell at the end. The word sounded like 'Chazzer', but I'm not sure.

Escape from here's impossible. This morning, I told a screw about the whispering. He said nobody heard a thing. Well, I heard it...

Twelve

The day started well. Some runt called Walter spat in my breakfast, so had to do without. Threw the plate in his face and got marched out by screws. If some old con tells you he got beaten up by prison staff, don't assume he's lying. Some of these officers are psychos. Others are so ugly, they're probably sexually frustrated, so they hit us instead of clobbering their women. If they have women, that is.

No breakfast? No problem. The food in here is in breach of the Trade Descriptions Act, because there'd probably be more nourishment in the crockery. Even the water tastes bad, as if the purification works is leaving in half the sewage and most of the bog roll. I'm told I'm too picky and that some prisoners even enjoy the food. Well, they must have been living out of dustbins before they got here, then. Seems some folk will eat anything.

I'm on laundry. It's exciting work if you like other people's pyjamas and underpants. Got punched in the gut. Hard. Two held me behind a skip while the third waded in. 'That's from Chazzer,' they said. It's this chap Boswell. Walter the Spitter's brother got helped out by this Chazzer, runs a stall now on some market or other. Chazzer is the good egg who gets reformed crooks stalls on markets and I am the bad bastard. There's an ill wind blowing in my direction and it's coming not just from the inmates. Even the decent screws don't talk to me any more. As long as they don't put me back on 43 . . .

Lunch. Gravy like congealed blood floating a raft of fat, mutton dressed as lamb with watery mint sauce, spuds lumpy with that greenish taste they get when they're seriously diseased and unfit for human consumption. Losing weight now. Talk, talk, talk. Jabber, jabber, mutter. It was Chazzer's wife who got the bang on the head. Yeah, yeah, I knew that. Daren't say anything. Daren't say it was bone-headed Scousers who got it wrong. It wasn't me. I was curled up with Len Deighton when the job went down. Went wrong.

They're building up to something and I'm the target. Bleeders know I've been in court, know I sent the loonies to do the job even if I did plead not guilty. Need eyes in the back of my head, but no money would buy them. So I'm stuck here waiting to be crippled while they go on about Chas/Chazzer Boswell, sainted man who helps old lags to walk the narrow when they get out of the big house. I suppose I am scared. Acting laid back is one thing, but feeling it is impossible.

More news. Seems Chazzer's coming in to visit Walter the Spitter. He visits him a couple of times a year, according to the whispers and mutters. Chas has done well for himself, owns a row of shops and an off-licence. Leanne got away and Chazzer's missus copped it and she's gone epileptic or some such tragic thing. Anyway, I'm in everybody's bad books, so things have taken a turn for the even worse.

Thinking of a half-attempt at suicide, make sure they find me and move me to a hospital. Or I could just act

crazy and start spitting in food, I suppose. But they
wouldn't notice. See, what most people fail to understand
is that the screws can be as bad as the cons.

It's all wrong. The system's gone to pot and I'm going to
get done over while the screws go deaf and blind. Still. As
long as they leave me alive, I'll get out of this bloody dump.
Survived the day. Another day in paradise. Get my head
down, try not to think about tomorrow.

The rain was torrential. Philly jumped out of bed and ran
to the window, hoping against hope that the lashing
sound had happened in a dream, but the noise didn't
stop. Today was the day of her wedding, and the heavens
had opened. She shivered and hugged herself – was this
a bad omen? Was God punishing her for getting pregnant before being married? She prayed inwardly for it to
stop, but it showed no signs of abating.

'Shut up,' she said aloud. 'Anyone would think you'd
considered becoming a nun, all this praying and penance.' She almost smiled when she remembered the shy,
silly girl who had gone as a postulant to the Poor Clares.
St Clare, a favourite with many impressionable teenage
girls, had given up a privileged lifestyle to live in prayer
and contemplation, and had been a contemporary of St
Francis of Assisi. 'And I thought I could exist like a
Franciscan,' murmured Philly. The sisters made altar
breads for distribution throughout Britain, and their days
were spent in communion with Christ. 'Not for me,' she
concluded. She enjoyed the good things in life; loved
cooking, reading, theatre and concerts. 'I wasn't holy
enough,' she said gratefully as she took her wedding
outfit from the wardrobe. And it was still raining malevo-
lently. 'Please, God, help me to be good enough for Dave

and for my child. Oh, and I'd be delighted if You'd stop raining on us.' Would He listen? Should she stop begging and act normal? Rain was rain, and life went on even when dripping wet.

There was a French saying that translated roughly into 'rainy wedding means a happy marriage'. All well and good, but rain as heavy as this also made for straggly hair, damaged clothes and ruined shoes. Women were already arriving at the school hall with food for the reception, and Philly watched them for a few minutes before going to draw a bath. They were scuttering about with bags and umbrellas, and every one of them had probably paid for a decent hairdo. Dave wasn't here. He had spent the night at Eve's house, as Chas was to be his best man. He hadn't to see his bride before church, but Philly wished he could be here. He was such a comfort, such a gentle, caring man. Skippy whimpered a little, because she missed her master. A bone quietened her while the bride gathered her thoughts and tried to look on the bright side. Better a wet wedding to Dave than a sunny one to someone who didn't care for her . . .

Lily had been up to something, but the bride had been ordered to stay away. There had been activity in the hall last night, and it meant that she probably didn't need to worry about the reception, because Lily was a genius with weddings. Everyone had been so kind. Instead of wedding gifts, Dave had asked for DIY vouchers, as he intended to put a new kitchen and a new bathroom in Philly's house. Up to now, they had received enough for everything except flooring, so they were lucky people.

'I'm fortunate,' she said. 'I've got a really good man.'

Lying in the bath, Philly thought about poverty, chastity and obedience lived in a world that was completely

326

enclosed, a place where the laughter of children would never be heard. At the time, it had seemed to be the right thing, and her Irish family had been thrilled, as there were no boys to become priests. But Philly had failed them. Now they were all dead, or still in Ireland. She had invited none of the Mayo clan, because a mixed marriage would not be good news for them. Better to tell them after the event than to listen now to the moans and pleas of aunts and uncles who still stuck to the old mores of Catholicism. His mother had relented and would be at the church. That, in itself, was miracle enough.

It was going to be Father Walsh's last wedding. The Church was losing a valuable man, yet Philly understood him. Her one experience of the physical aspect of love had proved surprisingly pleasurable, and it was only normal for such a handsome man to fall for a beautiful woman like Lily. It was rumoured that his real reason for quitting went deeper than that, but Philly was sure that he would soon be married, and that finding a true soulmate had given him the courage to depart. Newer gossip divulged his intention to lecture in psychology – he was supposed to have had a successful interview. Or was it philosophy? It didn't matter. As long as he was happy, Philly and Dave would be pleased, as would most of his congregation.

Having gone overboard with perfumed bath oil, she decided to finish with a shower, because she had never been a fan of strong scents. Her hair, held in a net under a shower cap, was protected from the ablutions. Paul had done it yesterday, and had refused payment. Everyone was so good. She was marrying the loveliest man and would continue to live in Lancashire's best ever village. After drying herself, she went down to make coffee. Her stomach was all over the place, so she decided to postpone breakfast for a while.

The phone rang. It was Lily. 'Oh, I am so glad you came back. How are you? How are Cassie and Babs?'

'Tell you when I get there.'

'Get where?'

'I'm coming to do your make-up. And, before you start, you won't look like something that's patrolled the streets of Soho for five years. Tell me the colour of your outfit.'

Philly described her suit. She wanted to ask whether Mike had stayed the night at the presbytery, longed to discover the truth about the relationship, but she did not own Dave's mother's cheek. Instead, she thanked Lily for volunteering, then drank her coffee. Several hours stood between now and the wedding. It was going to be a very long day.

Then the rain stopped. Philly ran through to the kitchen and looked at the sky. There was a brilliant rainbow with a paler echo in the distance. God was smiling after all, and blackbirds were singing His anthems.

Just lying with him was simply wonderful. He touched her face a lot, tracing cheekbones with tender fingers, stroking her hair and neck, planting small kisses on her flesh. There had been no sexual contact. Lily knew he was holding back because he wanted to give all of himself to today's service. It was probable that they would not make love again until after he had left the priesthood, but it didn't matter. Just having him near her was almost, but not quite, enough. He was kind, he was fun and he was clever. And she loved him with all her being.

Lily pushed a few curls from his forehead.

'I didn't get a proper haircut,' he said.

'Yes, I can see it's still highly improper. And you're breathing in my ear.'

'But I did build an ironing board.'

It was on such ridiculously misplaced remarks that their relationship had been founded. The rabbit, the foxes, the ironing board – these were all part of something she had never known before. Her marriage, built on a highly volatile foundation of physical desire, jealousy, anger and cruelty, had allowed no space for the smaller and more important signals of love like ironing boards, cups of tea and cold beans on burnt toast. 'What's wrong with the old one?' she asked.

'Erm ... Well.' He cleared his throat. 'One of your programmes – I think it was in Plymouth or some such foreign-sounding place—'

'You know who I am?'

'Of course I do. I've bought the DVDs of series one. You were giving grief to some poor kitchen fitter who was stuck under the sink with cramp in an arm. You shouldn't have laughed at him, sweetheart. Anyway, they had this fancy contraption that fell out of the wall and became an ironing board.'

'How long have you known?'

'Eh?'

'How long?'

'About four and a half feet with a heat-resistant bit for the iron. It's sheets, you see. Ironing boards need to be longer for the sheets. Especially when we get a bigger bed. I must have got it a bit wrong, though, because—'

'Mike?'

'Shut up, woman. Just don't use it. I nearly got

329

concussion in my hip bone. Can one have concussion in a hip? Anyway, it hurt like hell, so don't use the board till I find some hydraulic system – oh, and it brought down a bit of the wall, just some plaster, five tiles and a couple of loose bricks. Also, you should stop bleaching your hair, because I have photographs now. You are even prettier as a brunette.'

Lily got out of bed and put the phone back on its charger. She had to finish the hall, help Philly prepare for the big day, get herself showered and changed, summon some other willing company because the bride was too nervy to be left to her own devices, and he knew she was Leanne Chalmers. 'Secrets in this village don't survive long, do they?'

'It's in the old scullery that you're making into a utility room. It'll be a good idea when I get it right.'

He was impossible. The recipe from which he had been made was unworkable, yet it did work – perfectly. He was near-genius wed to silliness, generosity with an added pinch of common sense, naughtiness bonded with a respect for a God in whom he placed his full trust. 'You're a madman,' she said. 'A lunatic. Why can't you leave things alone?'

He winked. 'I am deliberately leaving some things alone, madam, and most of those things are fastened to you. The puritan in me tells me to be chaste, so I use up my energy on ironing boards. You were the one who buggered off to Blackpool. I had to do something. My boss was cross with me, and my woman had gone missing.'

'Bishop not pleased?'

He shook his head and wiped away an imaginary tear.

'Wanted me to go on retreat for a couple of months to think about things. He made me feel thoroughly guilty, said that many priests have to answer to their consciences when it comes to certain sins like contraception – he didn't listen, and I listened with just half an ear. It was a draw. Or he may have won on points.'

'I'm sorry.'

'Well, I can't have it both ways. Do you have an electric drill?'

Lily clouted him with a pillow. 'Shall we ever have a sensible conversation?'

'I hope not,' he replied. 'There's concrete in that pillow. And I see we are to have paper napkins.'

'Listen, Nancy Mitford. For a wedding, I would normally hire linen. The tables are covered with my own emergency stuff, but I don't happen to have a hundred napkins, so yes, paper will have to do. You can come and help me fold them.'

'Bugger that – I have to put my best frock on. It was sewn by nuns and there's real gold in it. But I don't know whether to go for the peep-toe sandals or those sequined Indian mules. I shan't wear heels this time – they throw me off balance. Bad enough falling over at a wedding. Christenings can be a minefield in my Jimmy Choos.'

Lily lowered her head and refused to look at him. She wouldn't laugh. If she started to giggle, there'd be no napkins and no make-up for the bride. He knew who she was. He knew she'd buried a pair of sewing scissors in her husband's side after he'd . . . She mustn't think about after or before, not today. She thanked God that Clive had lost his temper in court, because he had tried to make the jury believe that she had stabbed him first. That day in court had been the one time when she'd been glad about his short fuse—

'Stop it, Lily.'

Like Babs, he could get into her head. 'Who told you?'

'Chas. After Eve was injured. Not the full story at first, but I wheedled the rest out of him when you were in Blackpool, then I went to the library.' He jumped out of bed. 'May I borrow your heated rollers?'

'No.'

He flounced out of the room like an injured Paul Smith, arms akimbo, nose in the air. Lily heard him as he stumbled over something on the landing. The words he uttered when responding to pain should never come from the mouth of a man of God. Seated on the bed, Lily tried to compose herself. A wedding planner cum interior decorator cum florist cum Jill-of-all-trades needed her wits about her. She pulled on some ragged clothes and went to find napkins. Philly would like swags and bows, so she rooted out a few for the cake table before going to find Mike.

He came in from the garden and sat at the dining table. 'By the way,' he said, his tone casual. 'Will you marry me?'

Lily pretended to think about it. 'Only this once,' she said eventually. 'I don't want to start making a habit of it.' She saw the tears in his eyes. This clever man needed her. 'I love you,' she said. 'But stop the home improvements, yes? Remember, I'm the *Makeover Madness* girl.'

He bit his lip. 'Ah. So you don't want me to triple-glaze the windows?'

'Er . . . no. The windows here are precious.'

'Draughty.'

'No, Mike.' It wasn't going to be easy. He had a little devil in him, some sweet, childlike imp that allowed him to continue being a young offender. His nickname should be Asbo. She knew he would never touch the windows. She also knew that she would never find him predictable. 'I'm going,' she said. 'See you in church.' Yes, he would carry on being predictably unpredictable. He was wonderful.

Dave was thrilled to bits. The rain had stopped, he was getting married, Philly was delighted, and he had lost even more weight, because he could get his fingers down the waistband of his new suit, and it had been completed according to measurements taken just three weeks ago. He wasn't fat any more and he was happy at last.

Eve walked round him in a slow circle. 'Shoulders back,' she commanded. 'You're the groom, not some little altar boy who doesn't want to be noticed. Don't twitch.'

He felt as if he was back at school with the headmistress giving him gyp. 'You'll be asking have I done my homework next,' he grumbled.

'Oh, you've done your homework all right.' Eve grinned at him. 'She's pregnant, so eleven out of ten for that. And get that pocket hanky straight— Chas? I hope you're ready. And I hope you're not going to show me up by pushing your finger down the collar of that shirt all the time.' She cast an eye over the groom. 'My husband is allergic to suits,' she said. 'Chas?' The tone was firm.

'What?' came the reply from the hall.

Eve found her husband fiddling with his mobile

phone. 'Right. What's going on? Did you say something about going over to Liverpool on Monday?'

He cleared his throat. 'I thought I'd go and see our Jack. Their Tracey's got herself up the duff by some loonie druggie from Kirkby, and our Jack wants me to talk some sense into her.' It was nearly the truth. It was the truth, though it wasn't the whole truth, not the absolute version of—

'You're clearing your throat and holding your head to one side. How long have I known you, eh? And what are you hiding from me? You always tilt your head when you're hiding something or other.' She tapped a foot. 'Out with it.'

'It's nothing.'

Eve opened a small bureau and took an envelope from one of the internal drawers. 'A visiting order from Wally Willie.'

'I've not seen Walter Wilson in a while, and he's due out soon. I thought I'd call in, because our Jack's house isn't far from Walton.'

Eve sighed and folded her arms. She was supposed to be going across to sit with a nervous bride. She'd just promised Lily on the phone that she'd go and keep Philly company. 'Why now?' she asked.

'Why not?'

'You always tell me what's going on, Chas. But first you get a manager in the shop without mentioning a dicky bird to me, and now you're gallivanting off to Liverpool – which I'd never have known except for our Derek.'

'I just want you to rest,' he said.

'I could rest at our Vera's. It's nice in Crosby this time of year.'

'Blundellsands,' he corrected her, his accent very clipped.

Eve nodded. She was using her special cleverness. She had discovered over the years that when she tackled him head-on, the result was more satisfactory if she distracted him for a few seconds in the middle of the attack. Vera had served her purpose, as had Crosby and Blundellsands, and it was now time to move in with the big guns. 'Is he still in Walton?'

'Walter Wilson? Course he is – he got a three stretch and he's served nearly all of it for causing bother. Always kicking off, is Wally. No time off for good behaviour, so I don't know how I'll help him when he gets out. But Mrs Wilson was good to us, so I feel as if I should—'

'Clive Chalmers, I mean.'

Chas stopped in his tracks. 'Eh? Who?'

'Don't make me repeat myself, lad. You know what I'm on about. Wedding or no wedding, I'll clobber you if I think you're up to something. Then you can have a black eye while you make your best man's speech.'

Chas took the letter from her and folded it carefully before placing it in an inside pocket. He straightened his spine. 'Eve, leave it.' There was a steely edge to his tone.

She looked hard at him. His head was erect, and there was no more throat-clearing. Two or three times during the marriage, he had put his foot down so hard that it would have taken a JCB to shift him. He met her gaze, did not flinch when she continued to stare. There was no need for words, because she knew full well that nothing she could say would alter the course of imminent events. 'You've feelers out, I take it?' she asked.

'I'm not walking blind, girl.'

The joking, teasing and threatening would not work,

because her Chas had made up his mind. He was a clown and a mischief, but he was also a man. 'Are you safe?'

He nodded.

'Is Walton Wally Willie safe?'

'Yes. Well, as safe as any daft sod can be in that dump.'

Eve blinked back some saline. There was to be a wedding, and she must not weep. 'But Lily isn't safe.'

He made no reply.

'And Cassie isn't. Because Cassie's his daughter, right?'

'Yes.'

She clung to him. 'Promise me you'll be careful. If you went inside, I'd die. You know I can't live without you.'

He clenched his fists. 'Same here, kid. Don't worry. I've picked a good team. The score'll be one-nil and there'll be no comeback. Now, stop this, or the pills won't work.'

Eve nodded. 'I'm taking the medicine and I feel ... different. As if something's clicked back in place. In my head, I mean. I really believe I've had my last fit, but I'll take no chances.'

'Good.'

'And I don't want you taking chances, either. So mind what I said.'

'I won't take any chances. Nobody will connect any-thing to me. Just stop your mithering, woman.'

'I'll do my best. But if you do to him what he did to me – by proxy – you'll be as bad as he is.'

'Will I?' He inhaled deeply. 'Whatever I've done in my life has been for us, Evie. For you, Derek and me. But

I've never killed a child. Nobody I know would stoop that far. Now, you know you're not going to get round me on this one, so go over to Philly's and make sure she's still in one piece. Tell her everything in the school hall's lovely.'

'Is it lovely?'

He almost growled, then laughed. 'It was all right last night, but Lily's in charge today and we're all banned. Tell Philly it's all absolutely beautiful, or she'll be in pieces.'

'All right.' She kissed him, wished Dave all the best, then left the house.

Chas stood for a while watching her crossing the road. He could not help nursing the terrible fear that she would collapse outside and get run over. Whenever Eve was out of his reach, he felt terrified, since he lost control every time she went out. He had some idea of how to deal with a fit, but not everyone could cope. It should never have happened to her, should never happen to anyone. With luck and a following wind, it would not happen again.

She went into Philly's house, and Chas returned to the groom. As best man, he had a duty to perform. Monday must not overshadow today, because Dave and Philly deserved the best from everybody. Monday was just another fly that would land in the ointment named life. And flies should be exterminated . . .

Philly and Valda were weeping with laughter. Dressed only in their best underwear, they could not quite manage to pull themselves together.

Lily, who was wearing old jeans, a T-shirt and one of her more determined expressions, stood over the pair and tutted. 'What's got into you now?' she asked. 'Aren't you supposed to be having a civilized game of whist while we wait for the main event?'

Valda could not speak, while the bride simply bowed down and placed her forehead on the table among a tumble of playing cards. If she laughed any more, she wouldn't be able to walk.

'Some kind of wedding this is going to be,' said Lily despairingly. 'There was nothing else for it, Valda. I couldn't have you sitting here in your new frock till three o'clock. As for Philly – think of her amazing suit. It would have been wrinkled past saving by now.'

Eve entered after leaving her new clothes upstairs. She was wearing a bathrobe, and she threw a couple of dressing gowns at the other two women. 'It's playing whist in their knickers that got them reduced to melted butter,' she told Lily. 'Come on, put these on and let Lily do our faces.'

Lily began with Eve, who was the least hysterical of the trio. Napkins and cake table were done, but Lily needed to make up the women before going home to prepare herself. She was proud of the bride, because Philly had been so incredibly brave with her wedding suit. A nice, sensible blue-grey three-piece had been returned to the shop, because Philly had made a decision.

The decision was oyster satin, the skirt full length but with a kick at the back. This item was paired with a long-sleeved blouse buttoned high to the throat, and an Edwardian style hat with an open-weave veil. Because she wasn't tall, Philly had opted for heeled shoes, and she was going to look spectacular. The village would be taken aback when they saw that the butterfly had emerged from its chrysalis. She had surprised even Lily, who had not expected such self-confidence from the quiet little woman. And she was decidedly sleek, since she seemed to have lost most of her extra weight. 'There won't be a dry eye in the church,' she promised. 'You are going to look stunning. The Edwardian look is so right for you. We're all proud of you, lovely.'

When Eve's make-up had been perfected, Lily started on Valda. Valda was more up to date than the other two, so the job was easy except for mascara that had run during the whist-in-knickers session.

Then it was the important person's turn. She had amazing skin that had suffered no contact with heavy make-up, and Lily stuck to browns and beiges, finishing with a flourish of a lipstick named fourteen carat, because it had a sheen over a pink-brown base. The bride was ready. 'You're done and dusted,' Lily announced. 'I'll leave you the lipstick, but no cups of tea, no eating, and none of you is to get dressed before half past two. All right?'

'Yes, miss,' Eve replied, the other two echoing her words. 'You'd better do something about yourself,' Eve continued. 'Unless you're coming as the lucky chimney sweep. You look like you've stepped out of a pigsty.'

Lily ignored her friend. 'No make-up on clothes. Try not to pull anything over your head while dressing.' She looked at the three of them, told them they looked well prepared but gormless, then went home. Was gormless a Lancashire word? Oh well, she thought as she opened her gate, perhaps if she hung round for thirty years, she might be accepted as a Lancastrian . . .

He was in the front drawing room, and he looked so beautiful, so right. Lily stood in the doorway and gasped, because he was almost as pretty as the bride. 'Hello,' she whispered.

He turned, and was suddenly a prince dressed in splendour so magnificent that he was clearly prepared to pay homage to a king. 'Hello,' he replied. 'This is my best frock. I had to come back from the vestry, because I'd forgotten my grandmother's missal. Even though it's in Latin, I always carry it during a sacrament.'

'They should have kept the Latin,' said Lily. 'It was a universal language that worked no matter which country you were in.'

'True.'

'And your shoes?' she asked.

'Alas, black and sensible.'

Lily sat in an armchair. 'Tell me about the clothes.' He would lose the ability to dress in splendour, to baptize and marry people, to administer the last rites, to bury the dead.

'Well, there's the alb, the white undergarment that goes from neck to feet. It symbolizes innocence. The maniple – here on my left forearm – is a sign of endurance. My matching stole is supposed to mean patience, while the gorgeous chasuble represents charity. Pretty, eh? And very, very hot in this weather.'

She smiled. 'Mike, you must have regrets.'

'Of course. Don't you?'

'Yes.'

He sat opposite her. 'Don't be impressed by the vestments – there's just a man underneath all this cloth and embroidery. It's a man who is sure he wants to leave the priesthood because it isn't right for him any more. Your arrival on the scene is not significant.'

'Thanks.'

340

'You know what I mean.'

She had known from the start what he meant, had recognized a traveller whose company she might enjoy on the journey through life. Friendship had turned to love and need in so short a time that it had taken her breath away. 'And tomorrow, you leave the Church.'

'Right. I shall announce it, but they know already. They probably knew before I did. I stayed because of Philly. Even she has accepted my decision, and she was as old-fashioned as they come. Some of the elderly people are taken aback, but we soldier on, you and I.'

Lily voiced a worry that had sat with her for some time. 'And we can't be married in your church, since I am divorced.'

He turned and looked through the window. 'Lily, I can give you a list of wealthy people who have been granted annulment even after they have had a full marriage – including children.'

'So Rome is purchasable?'

'Yes,' he breathed so softly that he was scarcely audible. 'Everything has a price.' He looked at her again. 'My God will marry us out there in the orchard, at the top of Rivington Pike, or on the number thirty-two bus from Moor Lane. My God forgives, and He doesn't need money.'

He had decided. She'd already known that, but seeing him in his uniform had made her wonder yet again.

'Are you going to a wedding like that?' he asked.

She looked down at her wrecked clothes. 'Would your God mind?'

'He wouldn't even get off His horse to look at you. But I think Philly might have something to say about jeans full of holes and a shirt that looks like a dishrag.'

341

'OK, I'll get changed.' She went upstairs, stood on the landing and listened while he left the house. A quick shower was followed by a rush to get dressed, and she applied a bit of make-up just before leaving for the church. She closed her gate and stepped onto the pavement. After a very wet start, the day had become promising, and the sun was trying to shine through a layer of white cloud.

'Lily?'

She turned. It was Mrs Barker in her wheelchair, and she had clearly taken care with her appearance. At long last, she had made an effort for the son she had never valued before. 'You look great,' Lily said.

'I waited for you, because I didn't want to be a pest. Everybody thinks I'm a pest, but you don't know me, so I thought you'd do. A few offered to come for me, but they're all up to their eyes in flans and vols-au-vent and God knows what else, so I told them I'd made my own arrangements. You push me. And take me to the front, because I'm his mam.'

'Yes, you are.'

They began the short journey. 'When is he leaving?' Enid asked. 'The priest, I mean.'

'Tomorrow.'

'Well, he's a nice enough man, I suppose. Just be careful – you haven't known him for more than five minutes. Don't be rushing into anything, because you can't keep changing your mind and getting divorced, can you?'

'No.' Lily pushed Enid to the front and left her in the first pew on the right. She didn't look at Mike – didn't dare. If he winked or grinned, the whole thing could turn into a fiasco.

But it didn't. The service was short, as there was no nuptial mass because it was a mixed marriage, and Philly had not asked for a dispensation in the matter. Dave's mother had been anti-Catholic for a very long time, so the ceremony was simple.

Philly almost wept when she saw the decorations in the school hall, but she managed to remain dignified. Lily watched bride and groom and knew that Dave had played a part in the strengthening of his wife. The expected child, too, would be a factor in Philly's improvement.

Mike, after changing into a suit, arrived when an hour had passed. He took Lily to one side and informed her that he had spoken again to the bishop and would be released from Holy Orders in just over twenty-four hours. 'I'm still doing all the other stuff,' he said. 'Including the pantom—' The sentence was curtailed when a very tall and well-muscled black man picked him up with no apparent effort.

'What's going on?' Mike asked helplessly when his captor flung him into the fireman's lift position.

'Nothing, really,' replied the assailant pleasantly. 'Just kidnap, that's all.'

They left. Lily found herself standing open-mouthed until she noticed that Maurice and Paul had also disappeared. The stranger was probably Paul's new partner, and they were definitely up to something. She went to the door and looked across the road. Five men were entering Pour Les Dames, and Sally was ushering them inside as quickly as she could. They were gone for over an hour, and Lily could scarcely wait to see what they had managed to dream up. There was definitely a plot on, but she kept it to herself.

It was a rare treat. The tall black man, Maurice, Paul, Mike and a man in his eighties were all in female attire, and they sang 'Sisters', a piece they had been practising for the pantomime. There wasn't a dry eye in the hall, as everyone found the act ridiculous to the point of tears. The rendition might have offended Irving Berlin and a host of stars from some ancient movie, but it was hilarious.

Lily held a tissue to her face. Then she stopped laughing, because a thought had popped into her mind. It was all just clothes. A couple of hours earlier, Mike had been the celebrant at a wedding; now, he was an extremely ugly woman in fishnet stockings and a basque that did nothing to enhance his masculine shape. Blacked-out teeth contributed to his comic appearance, and he was clearly enjoying himself.

The song neared its conclusion with a well-staged fight that had obviously been rehearsed for *The Ugly Sisters*, as the pantomime was now called, and the old man, complete with Zimmer frame, was appointed referee of the fracas. It was the perfect mad celebration of a wonderful day, and Philly was doubled over with laughter. Dave climbed onto the stage and thanked the participants, giving each of the 'women' a peck on the cheek. He raised a hand and waited for quiet. 'Thank you all for coming, and thanks to Philly for marrying me and saving me from becoming a hopeless case.' He cleared his throat. 'A very special thank you to my mother, who made us a wedding gift of her share in the Reading Room. We both promise to take care of it.' He looked directly at Enid. 'Thanks, Mam,' he said.

The silence in the room was heavy at this point. Everyone knew Enid Barker; almost all had been vilified by her at some point in their lives. Had she made a grand gesture just in order to be forgiven by a village whose memory was notoriously long? Or had her conscience finally surfaced from beneath layers of acid bitterness and acrimony? Only time would tell, many thought as the whispering started.

'Carry on eating, drinking and enjoying yourselves,' commanded the groom before stepping down.

Before the guests had time to obey Dave's orders, the vet stepped out of the wings. He raised a hand and asked for silence. 'Right, you lot,' he said. 'You've seen two of today's stars, but what about the really important one? She runs my surgery waiting room and is becoming an excellent secretary. She also helped save the life of someone special to us all. Skippy, come.'

The dog hopped her way onto the little stage, while Chas brought on a table, then a chair, then a large box.

Tim Mellor sat down and set the scene. When all was prepared, his mobile phone rang. Skippy picked it up and passed it to her boss. When the applause subsided, the more intricate trick practised by man and dog began. He set a bin and a wire basket on the floor before starting to open envelopes. Anything rejected was squashed and given to Skippy with the spoken word 'Bin', and she tossed the offending item into the rubbish. The command 'File' meant that she placed the page in the wire basket.

The vet screwed up many pages and threw them out of the dog's reach, and she fetched and binned the lot. But when given a ruined page and told to file, she froze until the order was corrected. Similarly, she refused to bin anything that remained flat. When the act speeded up, she made no mistakes, and the audience continued enraptured.

The finale involved the phone again, but this time Tim answered it and held it to the dog's ear. 'It's for you,' he said.

She woofed politely into the instrument, then followed her employer and took a bow.

Eve was trying not to weep. This Labrador bitch had persevered until her owners had followed her into the cottage. There were some terrible things in this world, and then there were animals. She vowed there and then to rescue an unwanted dog as a tribute to Skippy.

Lily and Enid were both watching Eve. She didn't stand up when most people started to dance. 'She was near tears while that dog did its tricks,' remarked Enid. 'She's still a long way from right.'

Lily knew that Eve wasn't right. None of it was right, because she shouldn't have suffered in Lily's place. Anger rose in Lily's chest until she thought it would choke her. If she'd changed the name of the house, if she'd never met Clive Chalmers, if pigs could fly . . .

Enid turned to Lily. 'They don't believe I can change,' she said.

Lily snapped out of her reverie. 'Mike does. He has a great deal of faith in you.'

'And in you as well. I'm sat up there at that window on my own a lot.'

'I know.'

'And I mouth off. I've always had a runaway gob. But I see people. And I see the way he smiles at you and teases you, and I wish some man had loved me like that. Look after him and make sure he does the same for you.' She sniffed, then stuffed a vol-au-vent in her mouth.

Lily grinned. Enid Barker didn't get emotional, so she would never weep, would she? 'That was a nice gesture – giving Dave and Philly your share in the business.'

The older woman swallowed. 'Not as daft as I look, see. They'll be grateful and they'll look after me.'

'And that was your only reason, of course.'

'Aye. And if anybody says different, refer them to me.'

Mike arrived. He had thrown someone's raincoat over his costume, so he looked slightly less drag artist, though still rather deficient in the dental department. 'That's a very smart suit, Enid,' he said.

'Bloody sight better than yours. And you'll get a few bob off the tooth fairy tonight.'

He rubbed at his teeth, but made little impression on the mess Sally had made. 'I'm going home,' he told Lily. 'Are you staying or coming?'

'I'll come.' She made her decision then, while everyone could see her. He was reaching out, so she placed a hand in his, and called goodbye to bride and groom before stepping out for the first time with her man. Let them all see, she thought. Let them know that he is loved, that he will be cared for. It had been a long day, and her back was aching. 'I have to get my tens,' she said as they entered the house. 'It helps with the pain.'

His eyes narrowed as he watched her climbing the stairs. He had read the old newspapers, had trawled through microfiche at the library, but he still wanted the story from her. Pain? She had never mentioned that before. He followed her up and watched as she manoeuvred pads and wires across her lower back.

'Sciatic nerve,' she said.

Mike sat on the bed. 'He did that?'

'I think so. I also lost my spleen and some of my intestine.'

'And the baby.'

'Yes.' She placed herself next to him and took his hand again. 'Sorry about the wires, but this is preferable to drugs.' She waited for a reply, but none was forthcoming. 'Mike?'

He sniffed and dragged the sleeve of someone else's coat across his face.

'Don't cry,' she begged.

'How could a man . . .'

'Please, love. We're both tired, and it's better to go through all that when we're in better shape. Just don't cry, or I'll start. Go and get that ridiculous stuff off your teeth, then come to bed.'

He left the room and went down to his own part of the ex-presbytery. Kneeling on his hassock, he poured out grief and anger to the man on the crucifix. Tomorrow, Mike would not say Mass, but he would act as server for his friend, the priest who would take over the parishes. The tears came not as goodbye to the Church, but as a greeting for the woman he hoped to make his wife. Her past had to be faced by him; she needed to go through it again as half of a couple, because he wanted to know her properly, and she must let go before taking on the future. 'Between us, let us conquer this, dear Lord. We will conquer it with Your help.'

He went down, locked doors and windows, looked for foxes but saw none. Bearing two cups of cocoa, he walked back up to Lily's bedroom and saw that she was fast asleep. Quietly, he placed the cups on a table and went to stand over her. She was wearing one of his T-shirts. In a loosely curled hand on her pillow, she held the plastic box enclosing batteries that would help with her pain. She bore it well, he decided. And he, too, must bear it all with fortitude.

Trying hard not to disturb her, he pushed a paper napkin under her pillow. It contained a piece of Philly's wedding cake, and folklore decreed that Lily would dream tonight of the man she would marry. 'Dream about me,' he whispered. She was not well. In spite of that, she worked hard and seldom complained. And this stabbing in his chest was hatred. He had never experienced it before, and it came as a great shock. At last, he understood Chas Boswell. The need for revenge was not a primary factor; Chas just wanted to make sure that it would never happen again.

Sleep proved elusive. Mike found his foxes, put down food for them, heard music emanating even now from the school hall. The sky had clouded over, so there was no star on which he might wish. So he did what he knew best and prayed to his Father, to the Son who had perished on the cross, to the Holy Ghost who mended souls and distributed gifts of charity, joy, peace and benignity. 'Help me, great Spirit,' he begged. 'Help me not to help Chas . . .'

Thirteen

TWO CONVERSATIONS . . .

Eve had been doing her best to ignore Chas when it
came down to her greatest worry. If she asked him about
his visit to Walton jail, he put his foot down hard and
refused to discuss the matter. She had to wait for him to
open up, but he didn't. So, when Sunday evening arrived,
she felt time slipping through her fingers like water from
a tap. She had to try again, because Chas might well end
up in more trouble than he was bargaining for.

She decided to tackle him after the evening meal,
when Derek had left to lend a hand in the shop. Patrons
liked to see a member of the family behind the counter,
though the temporary manager was a pleasant enough
man. But Eagleton wanted familiarity, and Chas would
have to get back to his work sooner rather than later.

Eve dabbed her lips with a napkin. She needed to go
softly, because she had only just got Chas to agree to
the purchase of a set of banisters with special knops that
had been hand-carved in the eighteenth century. By the
time it had been adapted to fit the staircase of Rose
Cottage, the item was going to cost a fair amount. Chas
had already complained rather loudly that it would leave
him with no legs to stand on, so he wouldn't be needing

stairs with or without fancy hand-carvings on the spindles. 'Chas,' she began. 'I just wondered whether—'

'No. Don't start, love. I'm telling you – don't go there.'

'I haven't started, have I? But I'm about to. Somebody has to do it.'

He grunted, but offered no intelligible reply.

'Wasn't yesterday lovely?' she breathed quietly. 'A perfect, perfect wedding.'

The response was another grunt, this time accompanied by a frown.

'The thing about epileptic fits,' she said in a tone designed to be neutral, 'is that you have to let your feelings out. If I don't let them out, I could have a bad turn. They told me that at the hospital.'

At last, he spoke. 'And they told me you hadn't to get upset.'

'I don't want a fit.' She paused for a few seconds. Wasn't yesterday lovely?' she asked again. 'See, we have to think about the Middlers.' The Middlers were those who lived in the centre of Eagleton, which had always housed a close community. 'Dave and Philly – so happy,' she said. 'As for Pete and Babs – I know they're not real Middlers, and I know they've been together only a couple of months, but they're like a pair of socks that got separated in the wash – they belong together. I reckon they've always belonged together, so fate made them meet.'

Chas raised a suspicious eyebrow. 'What's that to do with the price of fish on Bolton Market? What's your point, Evie?'

'Then Lily and Mike,' she continued seamlessly. 'They're happening people. They remind me of the flower power days when everybody buggered off to San Francisco with flowers in their hair.'

'And not just their hair – they had flowers painted on their passion wagons in psychedelic colours,' muttered Chas. 'Bloody vans with daisies on them and daisies inside them as well. I saw a programme about that rubbish. All drugs and no knickers.'

Eve was not going to be dragged into unnecessary discussion. She had tailored this conversation and was building up towards a big finish, and the Love Children of the sixties would not be allowed a starring role. 'Valda's getting on all right with her mother-in-law – even Enid Barker looks as if she might take a turn for the better. It's all nice and settled.'

'And?'

'And you're going to bugger it up by arranging to kill the man who saved my life.' There, she had said it. Well, she had said most of it. 'When Eagleton has a murderer in its midst, how are they all going to feel? And just when everything's getting nicely sorted out. Even Paul's OK now he's stopped hankering after Mo.'

Chas jumped to his feet. 'Clive Chalmers didn't have you clobbered to save your life, Evie. He had you nearly murdered instead of Lily Latimer. What happens to your happening people when she happens to get killed, eh? What about when he rings the bell for round two and sends some other bruisers to kill Lily? How will you feel at her funeral? Who'll do the flowers? Because she'll be in no fit state for making floral tributes and pretty wreaths.'

Eve shook her head. 'He won't do it again,' she said.

'Oh, well, I'm glad you did your doctorate in psychology. He's focused on Lily, obsessed with her. One of the psychiatrists at the trial said he should be in a secure facility for the insane – he's not right in the bloody head, girl. The chances are that he'll keep trying till he's dead, or till he runs out of cash. He wants her dead, Evie. He's got money somewhere, and there's plenty of folk about that would do anything for a bit of brass.'

A weighty silence followed. 'So you'll not stop at home tomorrow and look after me?'

Chas laughed, though there was no humour in the sound. 'You've lost your place in the hymn book, Eve. Usually, you tell me to bugger off and let you get on with it, but now that I'm doing something you don't want me to do, you decide to be ill enough to need watching. Look. What happened to you is headline news in Walton – and not just there. Every prisoner in Britain knows what was done to you. It's already started. The grapevine's spread beyond my reach. It's already too late, love. But I can try to make sure Wally Willie stays safe.'

'How?' she asked.

'I don't bloody know till I bloody get there, do I?' Chas left the room. He prayed that she wouldn't start crying. If she wept, he would go back to her and promise her the earth, but Eve was not manipulative. She wouldn't cry for effect, or to get her own way. Eve was a good woman. She was the best. Anyway, Valda was coming round soon, so Evie would hold herself together.

Eve fiddled with her napkin. Since the incident, she seemed to have changed. She saw things differently, more clearly. It was as if a thin veil had moved away, and her inner vision had improved as a result.

But. The world was going mad, and most of the madness was man-made. There were bad females, but it was the male who never grew up, who wanted to be

353

cock of the walk, who needed to be the one who could piss highest up the wall, get the best woman, drive the fastest car, start and win every war. 'I am sick and fed up,' she told her reclaimed fireplace. It had been a good buy, thanks to Lily.

Lily. Could Eve really live with the knowledge that her new best friend's life would be on the line for ever? Would Mike on his own be strong enough, wily enough, to stop the next invasion of Eagleton? 'I don't know, do I?' she whispered. 'It's out of my hands.'

Then the doorbell sounded.

They sat in the Man and Scythe, Chas with a pint, Mike with a St Clement's. He was driving, so he was the one who had to remain sober. He needed to have a clear head anyway, because Lily was in pain and he was learning how to massage her lower spine. He couldn't leave her for too long, yet he wanted to speak to Chas. 'Sorry to drag you all the way to town,' he said.

Chas shook his head. 'No. I was glad to hear that doorbell. My Evie was coming to the boil.'

Mike grinned ruefully. 'If we'd gone to a pub in Eagleton, I'd have been plagued, because they'd all have been asking about the new priest and my plans as a layman. So. You go tomorrow, then?'

'Yes.'

'To see Walter?'

'That's right.'

Mike could see that his friend had taken an ear-bashing already, and the ear-basher was probably Eve. 'Is she giving you a hard time?'

Chas nodded. 'I've left her waiting for Valda. Valda's expecting her umpteenth child, so that should give them

354

enough to talk about. Evie will be wielding her crochet hooks and patterns – it'll keep her occupied for an hour or two.'

'Right. What are you going to say to Walter?'

'I don't know, do I? I mean, the jail network knows everything as we speak, so it's past the stage where I can call a halt. I admit I was angry at first and I put pressure on for a visiting order. Yes, I regret that. But prisoners have their own way of dealing with this kind of crap, and they would have found out eventually.'

'Especially now the men have pleaded guilty and dropped Chalmers in the soup.'

'Exactly.'

Mike looked round the pub. He had never been here before, though he had read about Ye Olde Man and Scythe, first mentioned in 1251 in a market charter, and the oldest premises in the town. 'This place was partially rebuilt in the seventeenth century,' he told his companion, 'though the vault is original.'

Chas offered no comment.

'And over there's the famous chair where the Earl of Derby sat before the Roundheads chopped his head off. We're in one of the ten oldest pubs in Britain.'

At last Chas broke his reverie. 'The poor bugger who lost his head owned the pub,' he said. 'But Bolton was famous for wanting royalty dead, buried and disinherited.' He took a long draught of ale. 'I hate Chalmers,' he announced.

'So do I. And neither of us has met him. But Eve's right, Chas.'

'I can't stop it now. It'd be like trying to stop this lot beheading the Earl. Prison's a machine with its own engine. Once it starts running, nobody can stop it – they seem to have built the bugger without brakes. All I can do now is see what's what.'

'You've helped a few ex-cons, haven't you?'

Chas nodded.

'Then surely you can pass some sense down the line?'

'Depends what you mean by sense. You should listen to our Derek and his Old Testament stuff – he reckons folk were violent as hell before Jesus came along. The wrath of God, he calls it. Mike, I don't know what they intend to do, but they won't stop Chalmers this side of death. In his mind, Lily belongs to him. If he can't have her, nobody can, so he sounds very Old Testament to me.'

Both men stared into their drinks for a few minutes. Chas could hear Eve going on about how peaceful the village was, about the vet having transferred his affections from Lily to a glamorous new veterinary nurse, about how even their Derek had started courting an office temp, about everything in the village being lovely except ... except for the fact that Lily's life was still in danger. 'He could kill her yet, Mike.'

'I know.'

'And you can live with that?'

Mike raised his arms. 'I don't know. We could move.'

'There's no hiding place. Unless you want to emigrate.'

'I don't. This country might be in a bloody mess, but it's our bloody mess.'

The conversation circled for a few more minutes before dying of natural causes. They finished their drinks and left the pub.

On the way home, they continued to talk, though nothing changed. Mike's lecture on revenge fell on deaf ears, while Chas simply sat in the passenger seat and offered the same arguments as before. It was too late. The machinery was in gear, and nothing short of a miracle would close it down.

Fourteen

Although Chas had paid many visits over the years to Her Majesty's Prison, Liverpool, the sight of the building never failed to upset him. The sheer size of the fort from which no man could escape was overwhelming, as were the perimeter walls that seemed to reach higher towards the heavens each year. Most places seemed to grow smaller when a person reached adulthood, but this was the exception.

There were worse prisons, he supposed, jails with tiny rooms into which two or three men were sandwiched for twenty-three hours out of the twenty-four, but Walton was a forbidding and evil-looking place that seemed to bleed all residual hope from the soul of any newly arrived observer. But he had to go in. Soon, his brother might be an inmate, and Chas shivered when that thought hit the front of his mind.

He parked his car and glanced at nearby council houses, ordinary homes containing ordinary families. The people who lived cheek by jowl with Walton probably scarcely noticed it after a while. It was here the way St George's Hall was in town, the way the Liver Birds sat on the shore watching out for returning sailors, the way the pub was down the road and the church was round the corner. But Chas saw it sporadically, so he feared it. Yes, his brother might be here soon, but that problem was not to be on today's agenda. This was the day on which Chas might learn what was about to happen to the man who had tried, albeit by proxy, to kill a woman. Eve. It should not have been Eve, yet it had been Eve. A shiver travelled the length of his spine, causing him to grind to a halt near the gate through which visitors were beginning to walk.

He could hear her, could hear Mike asking him not to cause any more trouble, but what could he do but go on? He couldn't change anything. If Walton had decided on the fate of Lily's ex-husband, nothing would stop the march of the contained. In prison, everything was magnified, because life was small, restricted and edgy. An imagined slight could result in a broken arm, while even a dirty look could begin a war between landings. Old lags remembered the Boswell family. Their mother had been kind, while Chas's brothers had earned the respect of many who lived on that delicate cusp between lawfulness and criminality. Chas had helped some who had been determined to reform, so the Boswells were a kind of royalty. Eve, a Boswell by marriage, had to be defended at all costs by the folk behind these walls.

Chas didn't know what to hope for. Wally Willie was known by friends and enemies alike as a mad bastard, but he wasn't a killer. Wally knew killers; killers knew and respected Wally, because he kept the jail alive and amused through long, grey stretches of time filled with little beyond model-making and banter. God. Chas neared the gate and swallowed. He would never get used to this dump. Those inside made delicate boxes out of matchsticks, sewed together tobacco pouches for friends

359

at home, used any method available to plod their way through days that seemed endless.

While queuing, he concentrated on what he had read in Charlie Bronson's *Good Prison Guide*. Charlie had awarded Walton five stars out of ten, because Scousers had made him laugh, while his destruction of the roof had cost the government over a quarter of a million pounds. Guards had allegedly beaten Bronson senseless after the event, but who would listen to a crim with a bad habit of kidnapping people and refusing to be subdued? It took up to ten screws to shift Bronson when he didn't want shifting, so they had punished him for making them look inadequate.

There was a new rumour about inmates getting together to prepare suits against guards, civil actions to be mounted after release, but it would be a waste of time, Chas believed. Anyway, most of the warders here were OK. But the few bad men who concentrated on torturing those with long sentences made a mockery of the whole system by becoming criminals themselves. So. He tapped a nervous foot. His wandering thoughts had passed several minutes while he got inside, and he handed over his visiting order. Yes, he was inside, and that knowledge made him shiver anew.

'Chas?' said the guard.

'Oh – hiya, Mr Martin. How are you doing?'

'Seen better days, lad. I'm getting past it now. Come to see old Wally again?'

'That's right. How's he getting on?'

Mr Martin laughed. 'He's more trouble than a pimp at a Methodist Sunday school picnic – he'll never learn. Still causing bother. Some don't improve with age.' He leaned forward and lowered his tone. 'There's been a bit of trouble. Go careful, lad.' Immediately, he drew back and reverted to normal. 'Enjoy your visit. Wally's in fine form. There's a rumour he's caught a mouse and started to train it, God help us.' He moved on to the next in line.

Chas placed his coat in a locker before sitting in the visitors' lounge. A bit of trouble? Martin was a man who could be trusted, a screw who had always been more than fair. He had a reputation for kindness, since he often carried sweets for prisoners and, when he found time, would even listen to their grievances and worries. A bit of trouble. Chas went though the search, walked past a couple of sniffer dogs, stood by while his personal belongings went through a scanner. When he had retrieved his money and bits of jewellery, he stood among the rest and waited for the automatic doors to open.

Immediately, he sensed the atmosphere. Guards who usually stood around the walls were dotted about among prisoners' tables, while those behind glass at mezzanine level stood to attention, eyes scanning the room below. Inmates sat very still and quiet, though a low buzz of conversation began when relatives greeted loved ones. This was a tough prison and it allowed for no nonsense. Rumours abounded about the availability of drugs, but, at this moment, Chas could not imagine any quarter being given by the currently rigid, sour-faced staff. They appeared to be in shock; something of moment had happened, and it had happened today. They were on red alert, and it would be better not to breathe too deeply just now . . .

Wally Wilson was at the far end. His bib sported the number nineteen, and Chas hastened to greet the old reprobate. Guards hovered. They seemed to be steering themselves away from families and towards those who had just one male visitor. As Wally and Chas fell into the latter category, they were plagued. After the exchange of pleasantries, Chas went to buy drinks and biscuits from machines. Following the prison code, he left the lid on Wally's drink before handing it over. A removed lid could mean drugs concealed in the cup, so it remained sealed.

They discussed prison food, the length of time Wally still had to serve, football, the Iraq war. Wally eyed the hovering guard. 'If you come any closer, we'll have to get married,' he snapped. Then he turned and nodded almost imperceptibly in the direction of a group at another table.

Pandemonium erupted, though it seemed to be a harmless enough chaos. While prisoners banged on their tables, everyone in the room sang Happy Birthday to someone or other. Under the weight of this noise, Wally finally managed to convey a message. 'It's happened,' he said. 'Over half an hour ago. Fazakerley Hospital.' He joined in the singing and banging. Whistles blew, guards brought the room to order, and Wally ordered Chas to stay where he was.

Chas understood. If he tried to leave too early, the guards would suspect that Wally might be connected to whatever had happened. Clive Chalmers was in hospital. Beyond that certainty, Chas knew nothing and would discover little while the wardens remained on red alert. They talked about Wally's brother, about Derek and his new girlfriend, about Liverpool's year as Capital of Culture. 'They should come in here if they want culture,' said Wally, his voice deliberately amplified. 'There's all

kinds growing in that shower block. Oh, and we're training our cockroaches to do the military two-step.' He
winked at his companion. 'Some of these screws are
talented, too.'

'Really?' asked Chas. 'What can they do?'

'They can make three years feel like ten.'

The man near their table stood and glared at Wally.
There'd been a reason for the sudden singing, and he
suspected that Wally might well be at the back of it, but
there was nothing he could do when it came to proof.
Chas looked up and winked at the guard. 'Turned out
nice again,' he said in the manner of George Formby.

'You're becoming a Woollyback,' pronounced Wally.

There were many things worse than Lancastrians,
Chas thought. Woollybacks were long-ago miners with
sheepskins stretched over their bodies as protection.
Underneath the slower-than-Scouse speech, they were
solid folk. The hour dragged, but he was finally liberated
and breathing air that was not fresh, but it was free.
Fazakerley. Bloody hell. He didn't know what to do
next . . .

Chas spent several hours not knowing what to do next.
He ordered a meal in a city centre bar, scarcely tasted it,
could not have described what he had eaten. After four
pints of beer, he shut himself in his car on the dock road
and waited to get sober. To that end, he consumed over
a litre of water and a full pack of biscuits rescued from
the glove compartment. The biscuits made him sick, and
he deposited the contents of his stomach as neatly as he
could in a roadside drain. There was no point in contact-
ing the hospital, because Chalmers would be under
guard and Fazakerley might well refuse to admit that he

was housed under their roof. He didn't phone Eve, didn't speak to anyone, since he had no idea what to say.

After sleeping himself sober, he woke to a darker Liverpool. A small idea popped into his head, and he drove to a newsagent to pick up the *Echo*. Nothing. He looked in the stop-press column, found no late report about the condition of a prisoner, decided that the authorities had actually managed to keep this juicy item from the press. The paper would be filled to the centre when Robbo and his cronies got sent down for receiving stolen goods, yet the murderer attracted no attention.

It hadn't been just Eve. His first murder attempt had been against Lily, and he would try again if Satan spared him. Was he alive? Was he crippled or dead? Chas tossed aside the newspaper. He sat on Crosby Road North and wondered about driving up to see Vera, but Eve's sister would be full of questions, and there were no answers. Going to see his brothers was not advisable, either, not if there was huge trouble afoot. He had better travel homeward. Eve could be worried sick by now. He sent her a text – *hope you get this babe bad reception round here see you later.* That should keep her quiet for a couple of hours. He really could not go home while his brain was in such turmoil . . .

Then his phone rang. 'Hello?'

'Chas?'

'Yes?'

'It's Bill Martin from Walton. Got your mobile number from Wally. I took your visiting order off you this morning – remember? I'm off duty now. Are you still in Liverpool?'

'I am.'

'Then meet me at the town end of Stanley Road, Bootle.'

'What's going on, Mr Martin?'

'Not on the phone, lad. See you in a few minutes.'

Chas drove to Stanley Road. Bill Martin, still in uniform, got into the car. 'Where've you been since one o'clock, Chas?'

'Pub, dock road, asleep in the car.'

'For over seven hours?'

Chas shrugged. 'Time flies when you're having fun. Anyway, what's going on?'

Bill Martin fastened his seat belt. 'Drive,' he said. 'Turn left at the bottom. I'll tell you as we go.'

It was just clothes. But beyond that was the clear fact that Michael Walsh didn't seem to give a fig about how he looked. He could be a priest in gilded vestments, a drag artist in a corset, or a tramp in torn jeans. Lily wasn't sure what he was supposed to be at the moment, though he definitely didn't care. How many men could sit at a kitchen table in Bolton Wanderers underpants and a pink silk dressing gown? His face sported shadow far denser than the famous five o'clock stuff, while his hair, which had grown wilder than ever, was a mess. And he was still beautiful. In the bedroom, he had been all soft words and tender touch, and Lily knew that he was in love with her. Yet in the kitchen he began to play the fool again, because that was his gift. This was when he loved her best, because he laid himself completely open, warts and all. There would be no lies, no cunning plans, no threats.

Now was the moment he had chosen to persuade her

to tell the truth. He didn't need to know what had happened, as he had discovered all that for himself, but he wanted to know how she felt today, how she had felt in the past, and whether he could help her move on.

'You look ridiculous,' she advised him. 'And I shall have a rash from your beard. Pink is not your colour.'

'It was the only thing to hand when we got out of your bed,' he replied smartly. 'Which item of furniture is still too small. If you will drag me off to have your wicked way with me when I am wearing only underpants, what am I supposed to do when I have ceased to be of use? Wander about naked? Shall I go and change?'

'No.'

'Then get on with it. I have an ironing board to invent.'

She sat opposite him and took a deep breath. 'You realize I've been through all this stuff with doctors and head-shrinks, most of whom were dafter than I was.'

'Yes.'

'And it's not easy.'

Mike smiled. 'Nothing's easy. Just thank God that you met someone wonderful who can help absorb your pain.' He stood up, lifted her hand to his lips and kissed it. 'Come on outside. I have put together our upholstered garden swing, and it was built for two.'

Lily prayed that he had done a better job with the swing than he had with his famous ironing board, but she followed him as bidden. They sat in the swing and held hands like a pair of teenagers, away from phones, from doorbell, from the rest of the world.

She told her story exactly as it had happened, beginning with her grandparents' farm, the move to Taunton, schooldays, college, meeting Clive. 'He was spectacular,' she said. 'So handsome and funny. Of course, I didn't notice at first that he couldn't laugh at himself, or that his car was rather better than it ought to have been – he was just a salesman for windows and conservatories. Then I allowed myself to be dragged into the conservatories – I did blinds, floors, furniture and so forth. I curtained the plastic windows he sold, tried to make them look decent. We were a team. He bought me a two-carat diamond, and we were suddenly engaged.'

Yes, it had been sudden. She supposed that the term 'swept off her feet' was applicable in her case, because she couldn't recall a proper courtship. Her gaze slid sideways to the man of the moment – had this been a proper courtship? She thought not, but he was the right one.

'Was he a criminal?' Mike asked.

'Yes. An entrepreneur was how he described himself latterly. Anyway, the owners of conservatories and plastic window frames liked my work, and I got commissioned to do whole rooms – sometimes, a whole house. So he married me.'

'Because?'

'He needed to own me. The penny didn't drop until the glossies began to follow me around. There'd be Linda Barker on one page, me on the next. But the straw that really broke his back was *Makeover Madness*. He thought I was having affairs with every craftsman from Dundee to Paignton. The programmes he recorded were played over and over while he decided which man had bedded me, which one was planning on bedding me – it was a nightmare. I was away from home for days at a time, so he gave up his legitimate work and began to travel with me. But he still had money. When we were at home, some less than savoury characters called at the house – I knew he was up to no good. He got phone calls at all hours of the day and night. Some of his conservatories fell off lorries, I think.'

'But not the glass?'

Lily grinned. No matter what, Mike managed to winkle out the ridiculous option. 'I worked out that he was acquiring materials and that the visitors to our house were building conservatories and fitting windows while Clive followed me all over the country. He had his cake and was eating it.'

'And he still wasn't content?'

'No – far from it. So he made me pregnant.' Lily stopped and shivered, though the evening was warm. 'I have a DVD of my baby – one of those special ones. It shows his face. He was a thumb-sucker and a mover.'

Mike gripped her hand tightly. 'You can stop for a while if you like.'

She sighed. It was now or never, so it had better be now. 'How did I feel? That was what you wanted to know. Trapped. Contained. If I didn't speak, I was sulking. If I spoke, I said the wrong thing.' She paused for a few seconds. 'Life picked up a bit when I became too big for work and he started to go out alone at night. He hated my appearance when I was heavily pregnant, but I didn't care. My face was prettier, he said, but he wasn't keen on my shape. I was happy on my own. I was nesting. Then, when I was nine months along, Babs arrived at the door. She had discovered where he lived, and wanted to talk to him about her pregnancy. She thought he was single. Everything negative went into the blow I gave her. I can still hear the scream she gave when my hand crashed into her cheek.'

'It's all right,' Mike whispered.

'It isn't. Well, it wasn't. I couldn't hit him, so I hit her. He came home, found her crying outside and threw her into the road.' Lily smiled sadly and shook her head. 'When I woke in hospital about twelve days later, she was sitting there reading a magazine. I'd been hearing her droning on about Leanne Chalmers and her interiors, but I hadn't been able to answer, because I was still semi-comatose. She looked at me, put down the magazine and told me that he'd almost thrown her under a Ford transit van. This had offended her sensibilities, because she would have preferred a Merc or a Rolls. "I have my standards," she said.'

'That's Babs,' Mike said.

Yes, that was definitely Babs. She had become almost a sister to Lily. Cassie would have been a sister to Daniel, but Daniel had never been born.

'Lily?'

'He killed my son. He deliberately put the knife through my abdomen and … and I felt …'

'You felt his death?'

She nodded. 'I lost a kidney, a piece of intestine, and pints and pints of blood. I almost lost my mind. But the biggest loss was, of course, Daniel.'

'Yes. Lily, look at me.'

She obeyed.

'I love you.'

'I know you do.'

They sat in silence for a while before she continued. 'He said I'd stabbed him first, but, when questioned in court, he lost his temper and the truth came out. I was making curtains. I buried my scissors deep in his side to stop him stabbing again. But I missed all the vital organs and, as far as I know, he was back on his feet in a week.' Lily turned and looked at her man. 'My womb was cut through. Even my spine was damaged. They stapled me together again as best they could. There's a chance that I cannot have children.'

'Yes.'

'You don't mind?'

He put his arm across her shoulders. 'I mind. I hate hating the man, and I know you wanted that baby. But for myself, I am happy to have just you. We'll be all right as long as I find my own dressing gown. You may cry now. I'm here, and I'll always be here.'

Lily didn't want to cry, didn't need to produce tears. She had handed herself over into the care of this wonderful man, and she had a future with him. He had been right all along, because she had needed to share the past with him. Being right all the time might become annoying, but—

'I can't help it,' he said.

'What?'

'Being right all the time.'

Lily shook her head before hitting him with a cushion. He was clearly a mind-reader, and he—

'Lily? Lily? Where the bloody hell are you?' Eve rushed along the side of the house and into the rear garden. 'I've been phoning and phoning and I've rung the doorbell—' Eve stopped and blinked. Even in the dim light of evening, she could tell that there was something wrong with Mike Walsh's clothes, but she didn't have time to work it out. 'You have to come,' she told him. 'Have you got satnav?'

'Yes, we have,' he replied.

'Hurry up,' urged Eve. 'Fazakerley Hospital near Aintree in Liverpool. I can find my way if I'm in Liverpool, but not if I'm here.'

Mike, who had grown used to the demands of parishioners, dashed into the house.

'You and all,' said Eve to Lily. 'You've got to come.'

'Me? Is Chas all right?'

Eve nodded frantically. 'It's a woman called Diane.' She placed herself next to Lily on the swing. 'She wants you to come. She says she can't do what needs doing until she's spoken to you.'

Lily swallowed hard. 'Diane Chalmers?'

'Yes.' Eve grabbed her friend's hand. 'She's your mother-in-law?'

'She was. She's in Somerset.'

'Not any more. The police brought her to Liverpool. It took hours for her to get there, and she's in a terrible state. Look at me, Lily. I know it's gone dark, but I want you to look at me.'

Lily looked. 'Yes?'

'Your husband – I mean, your ex – is in a critical condition. His mother's terrified and all on her own – she won't speak to anyone until she's seen you.'

Lily felt the blood draining away from her head. She didn't want to go anywhere near him, didn't want to be on the same planet, let alone—

'I'll be with you. Mike'll be with you. Chas is already there. Nothing can happen while the man's ill and you have friends around you. It's for Diane, love. My Chas says she's a lovely woman.'

She was a lovely woman. Too afraid to visit her daughter-in-law in hospital, she had made herself scarce since the attack. Clive had always been able to pull the wool over his mother's eyes, because she had adored him. An only child, he had been smothered by the love of his single parent. She had probably handed over money to pay Eve's attackers, though she would not have been aware of its purpose. Always, she had tried to believe the best when it came to her son. She was a mother first, last and always. 'All right,' said Lily. 'But Mike mustn't leave my side for an instant.'

Relieved, Eve exhaled and took Lily's arm. 'Come on, babe,' she said. 'Let's get it over and done with.'

For Lily, the journey was a blank. She didn't notice the motorway, the East Lancashire Road, the flattening of the landscape as the Pennine foothills petered out to make way for the Mersey plain. The first thing she recorded consciously was a sign for Aintree Racecourse, famous for its steeplechases, including the Grand National. She didn't like the jumps, because horses died or became winded for the rest of their lives. This was a killing place, and her killer was nearby.

Mike, who had attempted conversation at the beginning of the journey, gave up. He caught a glimpse of the florist who had arrived in Eagleton just a few months earlier, saw the pale, drawn face, the absence of life in features that had been so mobile just an hour ago. This was the woman whose negligee he had worn to make her laugh, whose body he had touched and loved, who had unburdened herself only for the nightmare to start all over again.

Eve, in a rear seat, had her own worries. Did Chas know what had happened in the prison, was he part of it, would the police come looking for him? When would life revert to normal? When would Lily be able to walk about free and happy? It wasn't fair. From the sound of things, a third woman was suffering untold agony at this very moment in Fazakerley Hospital. When would this business end?

The hospital was a huge, ugly place. Parking cost two pounds, payable on exit, and Eve wondered how poor people managed to visit relatives. If they had a car, their visits would be few; if they had no vehicle, bus fares cost more than a meal for a household. Perhaps they lived in their old bangers on the car park and paid just the once? Life had gone crazy.

Lost and mistaken, the three entered the main reception area of A and E, looked at the seated and wounded, read the board that pronounced a three-hour wait. Mike went and stood in a queue only to be told in the fullness of time that he was in the wrong building. 'I can see that,' he told the lacklustre receptionist. 'It should be condemned.'

Under direction from a sympathetic visitor, they followed various paths until they reached neurology. 'It's supposed to be the bee's knees for neurological stuff,' announced Eve. 'But you should go and look at the main building where the wards are, Mike. It's a ghetto. It should be called a stalag or something. It looks like one of those terrible blocks of flats they built in Russia.' She took Lily's arm. 'You'll be all right. I promise you.'

Would she be all right? At last, she asked the question. 'Is he hurt?'

'Yes,' Eve replied.

'Who did it?'

'Does it matter?' Eve held on to her friend. 'No idea, love. Now, it's Diane who needs you. After what he did to you – and to me – the details are what you might call irrelevant.'

The neurological centre was spick and span, carpeted, comfortable and so unlike the main body of the hospital that Eve felt she was entering the foyer of some five-star hotel. 'Is this still National Health?' she asked Chas after greeting him.

'Yes. It's Aintree Trust's special area of expertise, babe – they 'copter people in from all over the place.' He nodded towards Lily. 'Looks like she's not of this world, just like when she first came to the village.'

Lily stood as still as stone in front of the seated figure of her ex-mother-in-law. Diane Chalmers was small, round and grey-haired. Her clothes were creased, while a battered hat lay on the carpet at her feet. On the seat next to hers sat the statutory handbag and a photograph album. She looked as if she had got past tired ages ago – her face was devoid of emotion and drained of all colour. Lily recognized the shell, because she had lived in a similar cocoon for long enough before getting to know Mike and some of the other villagers. 'Hello, Mum,' she said softly. It was like looking into a mirror and seeing an older version of herself – sad, confused and in shock. But Lily was better now. As soon as she returned to Eagleton, she would be whole once more. 'Mum?'

At last, Diane reacted. 'Leanne?'

'Yes.' Lily squatted on her haunches.

'They've got a lot of lavatories,' said the older woman. 'Every one of them's big so they can get the wheelchairs in. See, this place is for those who can't get about properly.'

'I know.'

'And computers to play on while you wait, and a lovely cafeteria, and nice people ... Oh, Leanne, I'm sorry. It was opened by Princess Anne.'

'Right.'

'Centre of Excellence. I never went to see you, did I? Just left you there, I did. So ashamed of myself. I was scared of seeing you in that other hospital where they put you, because—'

'It's all right, Mum.'

'Because he killed my grandchild and he nearly killed you.' Coming to terms with the real character of a much-loved son had not been an easy process; the deepening lines in her face were proof enough of that.

There was nothing she could say, Lily thought. How might she comfort the mother of a killer? How could anything be done for Diane Chalmers now? The poor woman looked as if she belonged nowhere, and Lily knew exactly how that felt, too.

'I swear to God, Leanne, I didn't know what the money was for. That man – Chas – his wife got hurt.'

'Yes. Yes, she did.'

'And it's all my fault.'

'No.'

Diane jumped up. 'I raised him. I spilt him. I let him explain everything away and sometimes I knew he wasn't right, that he was up to no good—'

Lily stood up. 'You did your best. No one can do more than that.'

Diane picked up the album. Inside, treasured photographs of her little boy preceded pictures of his wedding, of the honeymoon, of high days and holidays enjoyed by Clive and her daughter-in-law before the world had ended. She had lived for and through her son, had bragged about his cleverness, had boasted to neighbours about his wife in the fancy magazines and on the television. The album was all she had left.

A doctor appeared. 'Mrs Chalmers?'

Both women turned to look at him. Old habits did die hard, decided Lily, because some part of her still responded to the old name. She noticed Chas, Eve and Mike in the corner with a uniformed man, possibly a prison guard. There was blue carpet on the floor. Leanne Chalmers would have chosen a different shade.

'Is it done, all that scanning?' the older Mrs Chalmers asked.

'Yes. I'm sorry, but there's no sign of improvement.'

Diane drew herself up to full height, achieving all of five feet and two inches when her spine was straightened. 'Then we do what needs doing. I waited for my daughter-in-law, you see.' She grasped Lily's hand. 'Come with me. Be with me when ... when ... They can't use any of his stuff. There was something wrong with him – he wouldn't have lived long anyway.'

The room moved. Lily remained completely still while the world shifted around her. Mike caught her just before she fell. But she hadn't been falling, had she? 'This is Diane,' she managed before being pushed into a padded chair. Seated, she regained her equilibrium. Where was the joy? He wasn't going to live, and all she felt was a terrible, cold sadness. Didn't it say somewhere that Mike's God suffered when a sparrow died? Clive had been a person – a terrible person, but ... Poor Diane.

Mike knelt in front of the woman he adored. 'Sweetheart,' he began. 'Clive's had several tests and scans, and he's not alive any more. Diane could have had the support turned off an hour ago, but she waited for you because she needs you to be here. Meanwhile she made them test again just to be sure there was no brain

376

activity. Can you help her? Can you do this one last thing for her?'

The doctor hovered and expressed concern, but Lily shook her head. 'It was just the shock,' she said quietly. 'I'm all right, no need to worry about me.' He was gone. Clive had left the world, had been dying before the incident at the prison. 'What was wrong with him?' she asked the doctor.

'He fell in jail,' came the reply. 'Probably because he had a heart condition that had somehow managed to remain undetected.'

'So he wasn't killed or pushed by another prisoner?'

'There's no evidence to suggest that he was. It was an accident, we believe.' The medic looked at the two women and sent Chas for cups of tea. The patient's mother was in shock, while the newly arrived ex-wife also seemed to be suffering. Clive Chalmers had given little to the world and had taken much out of it, including an unborn child. Even his organs were not usable, so he had died exactly as he had lived – without sympathy and without generosity. 'I'll be upstairs when you're ready,' he told Mike. 'Give these two the time they need.'

Diane managed to drink some tea before finding some words for the woman she knew as Leanne. Clive had fallen down some stairs, and his back had been broken in two places. The hospital staff had now declared him to be brain-dead, but Diane, as the only living relative, had to give permission for life support to be withdrawn. 'He looks like he's breathing, but he's not,' she said sadly. 'Such a good little boy, he was.'

'I know,' said Lily.

'Drew pictures for me, brought me breakfast in bed,

picked flowers and tried to help with jobs round the house.' She smiled wanly. 'Course, the flowers were probably stolen. What happened, Leanne? What went wrong?'

'I don't know.'

'All that hatred. All that nastiness – where did it come from?'

Lily offered no reply.

'Come with me,' Diane begged.

Lily looked at her love. 'You have to come, too,' she told him. 'He's a priest,' she advised Diane Chalmers. 'He can say a prayer.'

They went up in a lift and walked along corridors that led to wards. Mike held Lily firmly, while she clung to Diane's hand. Music was playing somewhere. It was soft, gentle music that reminded Lily of birdsong travelling on a summer breeze. The walls were cream. Machinery bleeped and stuttered. He was in a white bed. The nurse who had accompanied the group in the lift melted away into the background.

Lily looked at the man she had feared, and he was still beautiful. With no lines on his face, no hard eyes fixed on her, he was just an ordinary man with extraordinary good looks.

Diane pulled herself away from Lily and went to straighten her son's hair. She placed on the bed a photograph of a small boy before nodding to the doctor. A switch was pushed, and the machinery grumbled until the classic flat line appeared on a screen. Mike walked to the bed and placed a hand on Clive's forehead. He prayed for a man who had murdered a baby, who had almost killed the child's mother, who had ordered the attack on Eve.

Diane turned to Lily. 'I have to take him home.'

Lily brushed away a tear and hugged the little woman. 'Not tonight,' she said gently. 'And not on your own. Mike and I will go with you to Taunton.'

The ex-priest followed the pair out of the room towards the lift that would return them to the ground floor. He knew why he loved Lily. She had a generosity of soul that was far more valuable than her obvious assets. Lily, or Leanne as she might now choose to be called, was a real woman, a good person who would always try to do the right thing.

As they drove back to Eagleton, he listened to the two women in the rear seat. Lily was telling Diane that she could stay with her in Eagleton, perhaps for a holiday, perhaps for ever. 'Don't decide now,' she said. 'But Lancashire worked for me.'

It occurred to Mike that there was irony in today's situation, a grim sense of fairness about what had occurred. Clive had killed his son; Clive's mother had turned off machines that had kept the man alive in the technical sense. The difference was, of course, that Diane's actions had been born of kindness, whereas— He didn't want to complete the thought. Sometimes, thinking was not a good idea.

Fifteen

She still sat upstairs for most of the day, though she had moved slightly to the right and was occupying a different window. Enid had a lodger, and there had been a re-boot on the bedroom front, but she was just one of the people who had endured change. In Eagleton, 2008 became known as the Year of the Shuffle, because people moved around like men on a chessboard, hither and yon, a few pauses for calculation, some stalemates and the knocking down of several walls.

But Enid remained *in situ*, as did the village stocks and a couple of Ice Age boulders around which fences had been erected. However, Enid's place of residence was now above the re-named and re-located Lily's Bloomers, and the Reading Room occupied two units, one of which had ceased to sell flowers, while the other no longer operated as Pour Les Dames. Fullers Walk currently housed the off-licence, a veterinary practice and a florist, while the extended Reading Room took up the last pair of shops.

Maurice and Paul, having reached the final of a national talent show, were currently working in Las Vegas, though Sally, mother of a newborn, had stayed in the village. She was happy, her marriage remained solid, and she waited patiently for her husband to return from cruises and tours all over the world. Blessed with a temperament that was placid and accepting, she carried on her life away from the glitz and noise that surrounded her talented partner. Wealth neither worried nor excited her, because she lived for her son and for the day when her man would come home from his latest tour.

The invasion of Eagleton had begun in the autumn of the previous year. Like Holmfirth in Yorkshire, the village became famous, though for different reasons. No Compo or Foggy had wandered its streets, yet hundreds had come, in the wake of Clive Chalmers's exit from the world, to catch a glimpse of the Leanne they remembered from TV and magazines, the poor woman who had suffered greatly at the hands of a terrible husband.

She gave few interviews, wrote no book, accepted no payment from editors who wanted to hear 'her side of the story'. Her ex-mother-in-law took over the flower shop, and she, too, developed a way of coping with intrusion – she simply closed the shop until questioners gave up and went home.

Diane Chalmers had been absorbed into Eagleton and was fast becoming one of its fixtures. There were two chairs at Enid's bedroom window, and the pair of old women often looked down to watch the world and his wife (and his children) on the green below. Enid was frail, and she preferred to eat in her room. Diane coaxed her out as frequently as she could, but resistance was sometimes tiring, and the immigrant from Taunton was no spring chicken.

However, they got on like the proverbial burning house. They sat now side by side, cups of tea on small tables, biscuits spread on a plate, each leaning forward to study the Mothers' Union as it assembled on the grass. Valda was there with her youngest son. She had named him Patrick, and he had a shock of red curls inherited – or so it was said – from a great-grandmother. Valda's husband had been heard joking about the milkman or the window cleaner, but all remained well in the Turnbull house.

'There's your Philly,' cried Diane.

Philly looked up and waved, turning the pram so that Dave's mother could see Simon.

'He's a little belter.' Enid smiled. 'Pity I never loved his dad like I love him. I was a selfish, good-for-nothing, cruel young woman, Di.'

Diane patted her companion's arm. 'We were both useless, my lovely. You can love a child too much. You can love him too blindly. My son did more damage than yours ever would or could. They never did find out for sure whether his death was an accident. It doesn't matter. What sort of mother can say that? It should matter.'

'Oh, you're all right, you are. Take my word for it – I know all about bad, because I was no better than a bloody prostitute.' Enid shook her head sadly. 'Till I got past it and became a Methodist instead.'

Unfortunately, Diane's mouth was full of tea, and she almost choked on it when she heard that. Enid didn't know how amusing she was; she took life too seriously and blamed herself for everyone's ills these days. 'God, I wish you wouldn't do that, Enid.'

'What?'

'Make me laugh when I'm eating or drinking.'

Enid sniffed. 'Come forth with that stargazey pie thing

again, and there'll be no more eating in this house. I don't care about your Cornish mam and her recipes – I'll never look another sardine in the eye as long as I live. Bloody heads poking out of the pie crust – whatever were you thinking of?'

'Home.'

'Do you miss it?'

'No. I'm all right here, thanks all the same.'

'Then shut up and fettle with yon teapot. See – there's young Sally arrived now with little Jonathan. All boys, eh? Not a one of them with a little lass to dress up nice and pretty. Still. As long as they're happy, eh?'

'They'll be happier still this afternoon, Enid.'

'They will. And so will you, pet.' In a rare gesture of true affection, Enid grasped her lodger's hand. 'Aye, by tonight, it'll all be great. And if anyone deserves great, you do.' The wetness in her eyes was because she had a cold, Enid told herself. Because she never wept . . .

People had flocked to see Lily/Leanne, but they continued to come in droves long after her tale melted into history, and Dave was due some of the credit for that. His double unit served several purposes, and he used both levels to maximum advantage. After long discussion with Health and Safety – most particularly with the fire service – he and his staff manned a ground-floor restaurant with permission for corkage and a menu that stretched as far as Philly's imagination would allow. As mother of a tiny child, she functioned in a supervisory capacity only, working on recipes and doling out orders from her modest home.

Dave got the glory. The whole village felt that he deserved it, because he had worked like a dog since time immemorial. Then there was the actual dog. The eccentricities of Skippy, along with several other factors, meant that people continued to think of Eagleton as a place to be enjoyed. Bed and breakfasts sprang up out of nowhere and, in spite of financial recession, visitors continued to come. The scenery was magnificent, the village friendly and pleasant, so outsiders arrived all year round, and there was even talk of a Christmas meal in the Reading Room.

Dave's cleverness meant that his Reading Room was always busy. Those who used the place as an Internet café grew younger, while those of the clientele who liked to eat out brought their own wine in the evening and enjoyed a decent meal, live music at weekends and good service at all times.

Until the dog got in. With the passage of time, Skippy developed skills that might have been admirable in a foreign diplomat, because she granted herself full immunity and nowhere was verboten. She went where she damn well pleased, was happily disobedient and extremely well fed. Her proper job was with Tim Mellor, and she was very serious about her chosen career in the area of veterinary science. But once the surgery was closed, Skippy entered a twilight zone created by and for herself, a dimension in which rules were no longer applicable. She could get through the smallest of holes, was not averse to creating and improving such apertures, and, as a result, attracted dog lovers from miles away. When she entered the restaurant, applause was sometimes deafening, and staff who had once chased the three-legged Labrador learned not to try, because Skippy's public needed her.

The bookshop thrived. Even now, in a period of recession, folk wanted to buy *The Story of Skippy*, a hardback coffee-table book without which no home could be considered complete. The large, slender publication was filled with photographs, and each copy of the book was signed by the author, David Barker, and by the subject. Her signature was smudged, usually in purple, and no issue of the work could be regarded as complete without that paw mark. This was a dog whose life had been saved, who had gone on to save a human life before leading detectives to damning forensic evidence. She had been national news, and her fame continued to be impressive.

At the beginning of summer 2008, Skippy adopted a paper boy. His name was Mark, and he had a tendency to fall off his bike, so the bitch took him under her wing and went with him each morning to take papers from bike to houses. As a result, Mark's round was extended, since people seemed extra pleased when Skippy hopped her way to their doors with a *Guardian* or a *Mail* between her teeth.

But Dave's true genius lay in his love for and his treatment of good literature. Twice a month, a book club met in the ground-floor shop. Authors came to read and sell their work, and when no writer was available Dave would do the reading. On alternate weeks, amateur critics gathered in the same place to discuss their homework, a book they had all read, or pieces they had written. Dave was over the moon. Anything that encouraged people to read and compose in an age filled by easier entertainments was worthwhile. His clientele grew, with people driving in from Manchester, Cheshire and even from Yorkshire. The Wars of the Roses were put to bed while reds and whites came together to read, criticize and write. It was a triumph.

Dave Barker stood with his dog in the doorway of his and Philly's little empire. Philly was on the green with two other new mothers; visitors were walking up and down, some in footwear heavy enough to proclaim their intention to do some serious tramping over moorland. Life was almost perfect; by this afternoon, the picture would be complete. He nodded to himself. This was the day on which the jigsaw could be finished.

Diane nudged her companion. 'Wake up,' she admonished. 'I think we're under starter's orders.'

After a small snore, Enid opened her eyes and sat up. 'Look at the state of him,' she said, pointing a finger at Mike Walsh. He was dashing from the church in his altar-boy uniform, hair all over the place, legs going nineteen to the dozen. 'To think he used to be the priest,' she said, her head shaking. 'He favours a man what nobody owns.'

'He's looked after Leanne,' whispered Diane.

'I know, love. I know he has.'

The man stumbled, righted himself against the grave-yard wall, slipped off a shoe and emptied from it some foreign object.

'He is funny,' Diane admitted.

Enid nodded. 'You should see him in a corset.'

A streak of humanity shot onto the green. When it ground to a halt, it was seen to own auburn curls and a small girl. 'Babs and Cassie,' remarked Diane unnecessarily. 'Is Pete at work?'

'I suppose so. Look at her.' Babs left Cassie with Valda, Philly and Sally, ran towards Hope House, came back with a colouring book, ran again, stopped, returned with Cassie's juice. Enid sighed. 'It'll be a rum do with her,

Eve and Chas in charge. They couldn't organize a riot in Strangeways. Where's he gone?'

'Mike?' Diane shrugged. 'He's in the house. I suppose I'd better get ready.'

'A cardy will do,' Enid called to her disappearing friend. 'Too hot for a coat. And don't start skriking.' She paused. 'That's Lancashire for crying.'

Diane presented herself for inspection. 'Will I do?'

Enid nodded. 'Aye, you'll pass muster. Go on. Get gone with you. I'll still be here when you get back.'

The door closed behind Diane, and Enid wiped her face. She wasn't weeping. It was sweat, wasn't it? She watched while her lodger crossed the road and entered Hope House. After a few moments Diane and Mike emerged, got into Mike's car and drove off in the direction of Bolton.

Then it all began. Sally was left to mind three babies in prams and one small girl who was trying to colour the village green red. Wax crayons made little impression, so there was no danger of too much change in that area. But the rest of Eagleton was a flurry of poorly coordinated activity.

Chas, Eve, Babs, Philly, Valda and Dave struggled with bunting, strings of coloured lights and home-made signs. Chas had to do all the climbing up ladders, and he made a poor fist of fastening items to street lights and telegraph poles, but it was fun to watch. Enid's laugh made its way up rusty pipes before bursting out of her body and into the room. She hadn't howled like this in years; the scene below was funnier than anything ever produced by Buster Keaton or the Keystone Cops.

They had to be quick, because the people for whom

the surprise was being arranged were no more than five miles away. On a whim, Enid picked up her phone. She nursed not the smallest hope of preparations being completed satisfactorily, so she stepped in. 'Listen, love, you keep them there for as long as you can,' she begged. 'Because they're making a right pig's breakfast here.' She paused. 'Well, I don't know what you must do, do I? Just ... oh ... give them some advice, some lists about how to do stuff...' Chas Boswell was wrapped in flex and light bulbs. 'Look, there's a bloke here going to be electrified if we don't shape. Right. Right. That's the ticket. Thanks.'

She put down the instrument and leaned through the open window. 'Oi!' she yelled. 'You've an extra ten minutes, so buck up. It's like watching a bloody Charlie Chaplin film. And that sign's not straight.'

She leaned back and closed her eyes. If she didn't stare at them, they might do better. And the above-mentioned pig might fly to its breakfast ...

As soon as Diane Chalmers entered the room, Leanne passed Matthew to her. 'There you go, Grandma,' she said softly. 'He won't break.'

'So tiny,' remarked Diane. A tear ploughed a lonely furrow down a careworn cheek.

'Tiny?' Leanne pretended to frown. 'He was a bag and a half of sugar when he was born. He's huge now. Aren't you, Matthew?'

Mike lingered in the doorway and surveyed the scene. Only his beloved wife could hand her child over to a woman whose son had killed this baby's half-brother. Only Leanne seemed blessed with sufficient generosity of heart to blame no one for anything. He swallowed hard and walked to the window.

It had been hell. Leanne had spent months in the unit, monitors and drips attached, blood pressure gauge always *in situ*, people forbidding her to worry, sometimes not allowing her to walk, always watching, taking blood, testing, scanning, listening to her belly. Had he heard the word placenta one more time, he would have screamed.

They had delivered Matthew by section at thirty-three weeks. Leanne had refused to leave him, and had remained with the Augustinian sisters until this very day. She was brave, strong, wonderful and adorable. As for his son – well – he was definitely a fighter. Right from the start, the baby had gripped his father's finger every time it had made its way into the incubator.

'Mike?'

He turned to look at her. 'Yes?'

'Will you carry my bags, please?'

A nun rushed in. She stared hard at her little upside-down watch and began to gabble in a thick Irish brogue. 'Now, you know not to overfeed, don't you?'

Leanne nodded.

'And,' continued Sister Bridget seamlessly, 'we've written down a few bits and bobs and found some interesting items that say about development and suchlike and so forth.' She looked at the watch once more. 'Now, you're to treat him just like any other baby, but a few weeks younger than he actually is when it comes to the picking and choosing of clothing and what have you, and he may wean a bit later than usual. Now, I had a thought, and—'

Leanne wondered whether Bridget was going to start every sentence with the word 'now'.

'—don't be wrapping him up too tight, for he's better upholstered in himself than most prems at this stage.'

Mike raised an eyebrow and Leanne fought a giggle. Had their son just been compared to part of a three-piece suite?

'Out of the sun, of course,' the nun continued. 'And ... er ...' She glanced at the watch once more. 'I wonder would Mrs Chalmers bring him to the office so we can all say goodbye? He's been such a blessing and a treasure, and we'll miss him sorely, so we will ...' The voice faded into the corridor as nun and adoptive grandmother left the room.

Mike sank into a chair while Leanne stretched out on her bed. She would be glad to leave behind all this clinical whiteness, found herself longing for colour, sound and texture out there in the real world.

'You all right, darling?' he asked.

'Fine. I just want to get the hell out of here.'

Mike smiled. He knew what they were all up to back in Eagleton. Chas had been flustered for two days, bunting had disappeared from beneath the school hall stage, and there wasn't a coloured bulb to be found in the whole village. Would Leanne want a fuss? He looked at her. She wouldn't mind as long as she got a decent cup of tea. Her gifts were many, yet her needs were few and simple. The nun was in on the surprise; she was stalling them because someone had phoned to request it.

At last, they made their escape. When the baby was in his safety harness and the grandmother had settled next to him, the new mother and father got into the front of the car. Leanne found herself almost overwhelmed by the outside – so many shades of green along the road to Eagleton, so many different colours of cars, doors, flowers in gardens. Everything was bright and beautiful, but Matthew would soon be hungry.

WELCOME HOME signs stretched across shop fronts, while almost every resident had crowded onto the green to welcome home the youngest member of their community. As soon as the car came round the corner, applause rang out. Skippy, with a blue bow on her collar, waited at the gate of Hope House.

It had all been leaked, of course. A news crew approached Leanne as soon as she stepped out of the car. Diane took the baby indoors while Mike remained on hand if his wife should need him.

'How are you?' asked a journalist. 'How's the baby?'

'Fine,' she answered, looking not at them but at Enid in her wheelchair, her son and daughter-in-law by her side. She smiled at Eve and Chas, at Babs, at the vet and at a very happy Labrador. 'It's good to be home,' she said into the mike.

'And Mr Walsh?' came the next question.

Leanne sighed. 'As well as can be expected. Now that the baby's born, we have the full grid for noughts and crosses.' She tried not to smile when the man looked puzzled. 'But I have to tell you this,' she said. With the air of one looking for interlopers, she glanced over her shoulder. 'There is no such thing as a perfect man. He is absolutely hopeless with ironing boards.' With that, Mrs Leanne Walsh turned on her heel and walked into the house.

Mike followed her. 'You shouldn't have said that,' he told her.

'Why?'

'Because I fixed it.'

She stared very hard at the man she adored. '*You* fixed it?'

'Yes. Well, sort of. There was a bit of plastering, so I had to get an expert in after the brickie had mended the wall. Then the tiler did his bit. Oh, a painter made good, and . . .'

'And?'

He shrugged. 'Well, I bought you a new ironing board.'

She hit him with her handbag and pushed him into the kitchen.

Acknowledgements

I thank Gill Currie, who keeps my household ticking over – she has the common sense with which I was never endowed.

Also cheers to a certain young man who spent some weeks at Her Majesty's pleasure in Walton, our local prison, where the guards are nowhere near as cruel as they are painted herein.

Thanks to Billy Guy, Cassie, Tilly, Fudge and Treacle. Billy is not a Labrador, but the rest are.

Special gratitude to Avril, my captive audience, who listens to every plot-line and absorbs every developing character. She would escape, but MS keeps her contained.

Readers – thanks yet again.

extracts reading groups
competitions books new
discounts extracts events
competitions extracts
books new reading groups
events books extracts discounts
new books reading groups
extracts new titles reading groups
interviews
books events extracts events
discounts events new
new books events interviews books
events new extracts

www.panmacmillan.com

extracts events reading groups
competitions books extracts new